Also by

AMBER BENSON and CHRISTOPHER GOLDEN

Ghosts of Albion: Accursed

WITCHERY

WITCHERY

a GHOSTS OF ALBION novel

AMBER BENSON

AND

CHRISTOPHER GOLDEN

BALLANTINE BOOKS · NEW YORK

A Del Rey Trade Paperback Original

Published in the United States by Del Rey Books,
an imprint of The Random House Publishing Group, a division of Random House,
Inc., New York.

DEL REY is a registered trademark and the Del Rey colophon is a trademark of
Random House, Inc.

Library of Congress Cataloging-in-Publication Data
Benson, Amber.
Witchery: a Ghosts of Albion novel / Amber Benson and Christopher Golden.
p. cm.
Sequel to: Ghosts of Albion.
ISBN-13: 978-0-345-47131-4
ISBN-10: 0-345-47131-8
1. Supernatural—Fiction. 2. London (England)—Fiction.
I. Golden, Christopher. II. Title.

PS3602.E685W58 2006
813'.6—dc22
2006045495

Printed in the United States of America

www.delreybooks.com

2 4 6 8 9 7 5 3 1

Book design by Mary A. Wirth

For my dad, who always wants to know "Why?"
And to Beverly, Adam, Diane, and Danielle—my family.
—A.B.

For my daughter, Lily Grace. Always.
—C.G.

ACKNOWLEDGMENTS

The authors would like to thank Tim Mak and Steve Saffel, the editors who have shepherded the Ghosts of Albion novels, and the entire team at Del Rey for their tireless work. Thanks, also, to Peter Donaldson, Adam Rosen, Bill Schaefer, Timothy Brannan, and Rob Francis, for their support and assistance, and to all of you who've helped spread the word about GoA from the very start. Chris would also like to thank Connie and the crazy kids, without whom life would be boringly sane.

WITCHERY

Cloaked in shadows, Aine skulked through the orderly corridors of Stronghold and slipped past the guards, out into the wild wood in search of love and magic.

Oh, there was magic aplenty within the walls of that gleaming citadel, and in the spire that thrust upward from the heart of the forest, but it was a pale shade of the passionate magic she dreamed of, and knew existed. All she had to do was take that first step, beyond this world, into Faerie, the land of her birth.

The sisters of Stronghold still held to the old ways, but the ordinary world had begun to influence them so that this outpost between the worlds had become tame.

Aine yearned for wild magic, for unfettered love. She withered from the taint of the humdrum.

No longer.

Tonight she would embrace the wild of the wood and the chaos that true magic was meant to unleash. If she could not cross back over into Faerie, then she would find that magic here. The moment she passed through the door and moved into the trees beyond the walls of Stronghold she began to run, laughing softly, her heart exulting in this freedom. Her long, royal blue cape was clasped firmly, with the hood pulled low over her head, to obscure her face and disguise her from anyone she might pass. The color was deep enough to hide her as she moved through the shadows. The night was cloudy, so shadows were plentiful.

Aine had left her bedchamber dark, with two large pillows forming a soft outline under the thick bedclothes. She knew the ruse wouldn't fool anyone who came too close, but there was no reason for anyone to seek her out this evening. Unless the winds of fate blew ill and by some coincidence one of her sisters or cousins sought her companionship, all would be well.

There was a chill in the air that touched her face with cold breath and tried to slide its icy fingers inside the folds of her cape. The garment had been a gift from her aunt Giselle, a member of the council that ruled Stronghold. She wrapped the woolen drape more tightly around her shoulders, grateful for its warmth, as well as its cover.

Now she came to a small clearing and paused in the dim moonlight. She slid her fingers along the cape's hem, until she found the hidden pocket that lay within, and produced a tiny whistle. Aine put the whistle to her lips, tasting it, but did not blow. She was only supposed to use the instrument when she reached the safety of the sacred circle of rowan trees, in the woods south of Stronghold. There she would play the haunting melody that the sprite Serena had taught her.

A mischievous grin touched her lips as she thought of Serena. Though fairies and sprites were kin, Aine had been taught all her life to avoid her people's tiny, capricious cousins. Sprites visited Stronghold from time to time on one bit of business or another, but rarely were they welcomed within the outpost's halls. Aunt Giselle had tried to discourage Aine's friendship with little Serena, but the sprite had become her dearest friend. She was pure emotion, and entirely honest, and Aine loved her for it.

"Sprites may be kin, but they are better allies than neighbors," Giselle had often said.

Aine always nodded gravely, long having realized there was no point in arguing against this prejudice. And if her friendship with Serena had made her more mischievous herself, in truth she cherished that part of her heart.

Magic was meant to be wild.

Like love. Love, which had driven her out into the forest tonight. The melody she would produce with her whistle was a powerful Calling. It would create a phantom manifestation of her true, destined love, no matter where he might be. Aine so longed for love that she was determined to discover what the future held for her, what man would hold her, and take her, and want her forever.

So she walked on, continuing southward.

It was strange to think that she didn't know his name or even what he looked like. She imagined that his hands would be strong and warm, burning his touch into the soft skin of her shoulders as he pulled her ever so gently toward him, their lips brushing in that first magnificent kiss. It was all childish fantasy, of course, and she knew that it was only his image she would summon, not the flesh and blood man.

The crunch of dirt underfoot yielded to the soft hush of dew-touched grass, and soon Aine found herself surrounded by the majestic ring of ancient trees. Their beauty took her breath away. The others in Stronghold rarely ventured this far south. There was many a tale told of human girls—and fairies, as well—being captured by the ghostly Wild Edric and ravished by his retinue of huntsmen, undead creatures that roamed the woods, embroiled in an eternal hunt.

Aine paid no heed to these tall tales. There was no creature, human or magical, that could frighten her away from her destiny. She wouldn't allow it.

Something shifted in the woods nearby; a tree branch cracked, and the leaves rustled in the rowans. She squeaked, startled, and turned her head toward the sound, but saw nothing. Aine listened intently, but after a few moments of silence, she shook her head, assuming that her fright had been prompted by the prowling of some nocturnal beast.

I am not afraid.

She had work to do, and she wasn't going to let some woodland creature chase her away. She slipped off her cloak, setting it carefully in the grass, and went to stand in the middle of the grove. She took a piece of bloodred ribbon from her dress pocket and pulled her straight, chestnut hair into a loose knot at the nape of her neck. At her shoulder blades she could feel the tickle of magic, the place where—if she wished it—gossamer wings might emerge.

But that was for another night.

Aine knew that most considered her pretty. Of course, humans could not be trusted to view the creatures of Faerie objectively. Magic clouded their vision, so that they could only see great beauty or abject terror when looking at fairies and sprites and their like. But all of her friends at Stronghold assured her she was beautiful. In a mirror, Aine might admire her own face. Her eyes were soft and brown, ringed by a fringe of dark lashes, and her lips were pink and fetching, forming a perfect bow. When she smiled, her eyes crinkled up at the corners, and the sprite Serena had once said that her laughter was like the sound of a thousand tiny silver bells, all being rung at once.

Yet Aine never *felt* beautiful. At sixteen, her gangly body often seemed beyond her control. In her mind, she moved with the awkwardness of a newly born colt. Her body felt cumbersome, causing her to continue to see herself as a child, rather than the young woman she had become.

The wind picked up, and Aine wished she had not taken off her cape so quickly. She ran her hands briskly over her exposed forearms, trying to warm her chilly body, but only managed to bring out more gooseflesh.

She looked up, her eyes scanning the cloudy heavens. A patch of open night appeared as a large cloud was shifted south by the whim of the wind, revealing the full moon that the sky chart had promised her.

If she did not complete the Calling before midnight, she would be forced to wait another *month* before she could try it again. That would be an eternity. No, tonight had to be the night.

Another loud *crack* filled the air, echoing around the sacred circle. The sound came from somewhere behind the trees. She felt the tiny hairs on the back of her neck stand up, and a cold shiver spread down her spine and into her back. She turned, her eyes wide with fear—and saw . . .

Nothing.

Aine slowly released the breath she had not known she was holding, her eyes refusing to believe what they saw. She could sense something large watching her from behind the thicket. Yet, the fact that she saw nothing actually frightened her.

She began to understand why people told ghost stories about this place. She took a deep, calming breath and felt her heart skipping double-time inside her chest. The moon disappeared behind another cloud, throwing the little grove of trees into darkness.

Aine almost screamed as she heard a low rustling to her right. Peering into the shadows, she saw a large, flowering shrub begin to shake.

"Who's . . . who's there . . . ?"

Her voice was shrill, even to her own ears.

Something erupted from inside the bush, bulleting toward her. Aine did scream this time, the sound ripping from her throat as terror seized her.

She spun and began to run, but immediately lost her footing on an exposed root and fell hard onto her hip. She cried out, pain shooting down her side, and squeezed her eyes shut against the on-coming tears.

Frantically she pushed up onto her hands and knees. She bit her lip against the hurt, and began to crawl as fast as she could away from her attacker.

Aine put the tiny silver whistle to her lips and blew furiously on it. She was no longer focused upon her original purpose, instead merely hoping that someone would hear, and come to her aid.

The entire grove was overtaken by the sound. It filled the air, suffusing the forest with the tintinnabulation of a thousand ordinary whistles. The sound was accompanied by the scent of crushed rose petals.

As she drew in a shaking breath, the whistle fell from her lips, and she sank to the ground. She looked up and stared at the beast that had frightened her so, feeling more than a little ridiculous.

The fawn stood, trembling, in the middle of the grove, its liquid brown eyes locked on the terrified girl who lay sprawled in the grass. It shook itself, and bits of shrub still attached to its tail fell softly to the ground.

Aine began to gulp air, and that became a giggle, shock causing a mild hysteria to overcome her. She pulled herself up into a crouch, careful of her injured hip, her heart drumming loudly in her ears. She reached out with a tentative hand.

The fawn took off like a shot, the scent of fairy magic frightening it into action.

Something *behind* the fawn caught her attention and her heart seized in her chest. Then she remembered the whistle, and the magic she had set out to perform this evening, the purpose of that Calling.

Apparently, it had been successful.

"Hello, there," she whispered, the words still etched with a trace of giddiness.

The young man blinked, his silvery face contorted in confusion, as he stood before her in a pair of loose-fitting britches and a longish nightshirt.

Aine moved closer, letting her hand touch the translucent outline of the young man's figure. It was cold and clammy, and she immediately pulled her fingers away from him.

"You're so cold," she said, but the young man did not reply. His gaze was far away.

Aine sat back on her heels, wincing at the sharp pain that shot across her side, and took a better look at the man she had called.

She felt a pang when she realized he was really more of a boy than a man, with longish dark hair that curled in hanging coils, framing his face. She couldn't tell if his eyes were dark or light, but there was a kindness that emitted from them that warmed her heart, and chased away her fleeting disappointment.

He had a nice face, his aquiline nose holding court over a smallish mouth and high, patrician cheekbones. He sneezed, and his thin shoulders shook, making Aine laugh.

I wish you could hear me, she thought. *Or, at least, tell me your name.*

Slowly, the apparition began to fade away.

"Please, don't go!" Aine called, but it was no use. After a few moments, the vision of the young man disappeared entirely.

More saddened by the experience than comforted, Aine used the trunk of one of the rowan trees for support as she pulled herself to her feet. She reached for her cape, draped it over her shoulders, locked the clasp, and was immediately enveloped in its warmth.

Her hip hurt when she put her weight on it, but it was sturdy enough to hold her up. Her eyes on the ground in front of her, she took a step forward, then stopped, as a long shadow crossed her line of vision.

She looked up, expecting to see the fawn again, or perhaps the phantom young man. Instead, she found herself face to face with a stranger.

"Oh," she stammered, and she froze.

The figure wore a heavy brown cloak, its hood pulled low enough to hide its entire face. It stood less than three feet away from her, but made no move to close the gap between them.

"What do you want?" she demanded, emboldened by the fact that it made no advance.

The creature offered no reply. Instead, with startling speed, it reached out a gnarled hand and grabbed her by the throat, cutting off any cry for help.

Aine fought desperately against the creature's hold, raking her long nails across the heavy fabric of its cloak, trying to claw at the flesh beneath. The thick garment protected it, but still she lashed out, again and again, trying to hurt it, to break its hold on her.

The world began to swim around her as its grip on her throat choked off her air. She struck out with her fist, knocking its hood back, revealing its long, twisted face, and eyes that gleamed in the pale glow of moonlight.

Aine raised her hand to strike again. The creature gave a shrill cry, mouth cruelly contorted, and with its free hand it grabbed her arm, stopping the blow before it fell.

With a quick twist, it shattered the bones in her right forearm.

Its grip on her throat tightened, closing off her scream. Glaring into her eyes, it intoned a spell in an ancient, barbaric tongue. If only she could breathe, she thought she could have made out the words, understood that old, dead language.

The flesh of her face rippled with magic. Needles of agony shot through her mouth, and then she understood. But Aine could do nothing as tight little stitches threaded through her lips, suturing her mouth closed.

Blackness pooled in her peripheral vision as the last of her strength began to leave her, only the pain in her shattered arm keeping her from losing consciousness.

Now that she was unable to scream, the creature released its grip on her throat. She breathed desperately through her nose, the threat of suffocation receding with the blackness around her vision.

Wildly she searched her mind for some magic that would not require words or the gestures of both hands. She could think of nothing.

A single spark of hope remained.

With a thought, she summoned her wings. Diaphanous and glittering with vivid color, they unfurled instantly from her back.

Aine reached deep within herself for a single, last drop of

strength. With her good hand she hammered at the creature's grip even as she raised her legs, propped her feet against its torso, and pushed.

She broke its grasp. Hope blossomed and she spun desperately in the air, wings beating, driving her skyward. She could see the moon and the stars through the opening in the trees above, and flew toward the dark, velvet sky.

A hand caught her by the wing and pulled her back down. The creature got a fist tangled in her hair and held her fast. With the other, it ripped her left wing from her back.

The agony was such that Aine shrieked, tearing the stitches in her lips, spilling her blood down her chin.

The creature struck her in the side of the head and she went down on the ground, barely able to stay on her knees. Once more it gripped her hair. It lifted her up and dragged her toward an old, thick rowan tree.

There came a terrible ripping sound, and the trunk of the rowan began to split apart. It opened wide, a queer darkness yawning inside. Broken and bleeding, she hadn't the strength to make any protest as the creature thrust her through that opening in the rowan.

It tucked her limbs inside the tree and then raised its hand to cast another spell.

The rowan began to close around her. Aine thrust her unbroken arm forward to try to stop the tree from sealing her within.

Ignoring her struggle, the creature finished its spell and watched as the tree closed around its thrashing prey. Satisfied that its job was complete, the thing vanished into the night. The only sign of a struggle left in its wake was a twisted protrusion that jutted oddly from the thickened truck of a rowan tree, in the shape of a young girl's arm.

The moon reappeared from behind a cloud, bathing the empty grove in a soft, glowing light. The only sound, there in the dark of night, was a soft keening that might have been the sad whistle of the wind through the trees, or the quiet weeping of a shattered, hopeless young fairy.

One

On a late spring day in Highgate, north of London, the warm air was heavy with the promise of rain. William Swift sat in a room on the third floor of Ludlow House and gazed with determined hatred at his father, who peered back at him with a demon's eyes and a madman's smile.

Evening was still hours away, but in that chamber darkness had already fallen. It was no ordinary darkness, no mundane arrival of night. It was a living, churning shadow that had swallowed the room and blotted out every bit of natural daylight, so that the windows were black as pitch and a fog of darkness pulsed and breathed, filling the space between the two living beings who sat facing each other on hard wooden chairs.

The only light came from thin white candles that had been placed every six inches in a rough circle around the center of the room, a circle that included both William and his father, Henry, within its boundaries. The candles had been made by virgin hands and cooled in holy water, and an unnatural blue tint engulfed each wick. The color was beautiful and calming and strong. The shifting shadows that swirled about could not touch that uncanny blue light.

The room had once been a nursery. Both William and his younger sister, Tamara, had slept here in their infancy. He was determined that once the demon was gone, and his father was restored, no one would ever use the nursery again. With his own hands he would board it up, nail it shut, and remove the knob. They were, each member of the Swift family, forever stained by their contact with the evil and the damned, and their home was equally tainted.

This infestation in particular, though, could not be allowed to remain. At the same moment as he and Tamara had inherited the abilities and duties of the Protectors of Albion—novices though they were in a perilous and eternal war—their father had been possessed by this demon Oblis. As they studied and practiced and honed their knowledge and their skills, each new triumph convinced them that now they would have the fortitude needed to exorcise the creature from Henry Swift.

Yet each time they tried, they failed.

William had been growing more and more restless. The knowledge that his father was trapped within his own body, enslaved to the demon that was housed therein, haunted the young man, awake and asleep. His work as manager of the family bank, Swift's of London, had suffered. Too often he wandered around, little more than a ghost himself, dark circles under his eyes. At times he nodded off, waking to find himself in the midst of a conversation, or having walked into a room without remembering why he'd gone there or what he'd been seeking.

But now the moment had come. He would not rest until the demon had been extracted from his father's flesh.

The creature sat across from him, grinning in the shadows that danced with the blue light of those blessed candles. The eyes that opposed him were not those of Henry Swift, but of Oblis. The demon often attempted to manipulate the members of the household by speaking in Henry's voice, exhibiting the gentle kindness of a father. And from time to time, William thought that perhaps it really *was* his father, wrestling the demon down or slipping through when Oblis was distracted.

But he could never be sure, could never know if he spoke to the man or the beast.

All of that was going to end.

The darkness was cold. A rime of ice frosted the windows and the floors, the walls and the chairs. William and the demon stared at each other, both breathing evenly. Oblis's expression was strangely curious.

In the center of the room, precisely midway between them, stood an elegant, handmade perfume bottle swirled with pink and red and blue glass and stoppered with a handmade glass butterfly.

"Well, now, this is lovely, isn't it?" the demon said in Henry's voice. "Just the two of us, and a pretty bauble."

William glared at him. "We're not alone."

Oblis sat back in the chair, comfortable in spite of the chains that bound him to it. They were, after all, only physical bonds to prevent him from causing harm to Henry's body, or attacking anyone who entered the room. Once the chains themselves had held many spells, binding magic. But he had managed to escape more than once, and William and Tamara had become very, very careful. The numerous spells that kept him prisoner were in the walls themselves; they would not allow him to leave the room while his demonic essence was within the flesh of Henry Swift. The young Protectors made no attempt to shackle his spirit alone—they wanted the demon to depart their father's flesh, more than anything, and their spells would not prevent that—but Oblis was not quite through tormenting them yet.

"No, we're *not* alone, are we?" the demon whispered, in his own voice now, a kind of serpentine rasp that seemed spoken just beside William's ear. "Your father's here with us, isn't he? Though he's a bit tongue-tied at the moment." He chuckled at his own wit.

William remained impassive. He had learned not to rise to the demon's bait.

Another voice flowed from the darkness. "This is a bad idea," it said. "I wish to make certain that, later, you'll remember that I warned you."

The demon arched an eyebrow.

"When I said we weren't alone," William told him, "I wasn't referring merely to my father."

"Oh, I'm well aware of the presence of the ghost," Oblis replied, not bothering to glance into the shadows from which the voice had come. "I simply take no notice. I don't like to encourage this impression they have, that they are of some consequence."

A low chiming sound filtered into the shadows of the room, and a figure began to manifest in the corner, beside a blackened window. The specter had one arm and was dressed in the garb of the Royal Navy, but the navy of years past, not the present day. Lord Admiral Horatio Nelson was one of many ghosts who functioned as allies for the Protectors of Albion, attempting to aid them in defending the mystical soul of England against sinister forces that would corrupt or destroy it.

"I'm also not sure what you hoped to gain from the phantom's participation," Oblis went on. "He cannot harm me. Not while I occupy the form of your dear, dear father."

William opened his hands. "True enough. Oh, Horatio could hurt you a great deal, but he wouldn't, as long as you possess my father. But we'll soon have you out of there. And then you'll find the fury of a ghost of far greater consequence than you've ever imagined. We've each a reason to make you suffer, but I suspect Bodicea's vengeance upon you will last an eternity."

The demon only scowled, but William saw a flicker of doubt in Oblis's eyes that pleased him. The ritual ought to work, but if it went poorly and Oblis tried to escape, Horatio ought to be able to hold onto the vapor demon long enough to imprison him. He might even be able to destroy the demon once it had left its human host.

One way or another, they would cage him. And if they could cage him, they could destroy him.

But the ghost of that brave, if slightly pompous and effete, admiral had not been enlisted to take part in this ritual as a combatant. William had simply wanted someone there to watch over him, to warn him if he seemed to be falling under the demon's influence, and to sound an alarm if the worst happened.

"William . . ." the ghost cautioned.

"I'll remember, Horatio," the young man replied.

"You don't know if it will work."

William stared at his father, his gaze locked again upon the eyes of the demon within. "No, I don't. But I've run out of patience."

Oblis smirked with Henry's lips. "This should be interesting, then."

Though there was a tremor in his heart, William kept his hands steady as he raised them, revealing the straight razor clasped in his

hand. He flicked it open with a flourish, the gleaming steel
ng out of the ivory handle.

Before he could begin to doubt, he drew the blade across his left
wrist, hissing through his teeth with the sting. A line of blood
welled up instantly and began to trickle across his palm. Several
drops fell to the floor.

And then the blood began to pulse from the cut, the flow increasing.

When he spoke, the words were in halting German, memorized
from a handwritten journal produced by a demonologist whose
work William had discovered in the course of his research.

"With the blood of his blood, I summon you," he said. "With
the blood of his blood, I draw you out."

Several drops that had begun to fall were abruptly arrested
in mid-air, quivering there a moment. Then they began to flow
across the room, sliding through the air slowly, like mercury rising.
Before long, the string of blood stretched toward the center of the
room, until it reached a point just above the perfume bottle—the
receptacle—he had placed there.

For the first time, the demon looked concerned. Henry's brow
furrowed deeply.

"What do you think you've discovered, boy?"

William ignored him, massaging his left arm, running his hand
down from the elbow to the wrist so that the blood flowed from
the slit. More and more ran out and into the air, and the stream of
blood that led from him to the center of the room thickened.

From that point above the perfume bottle, the blood began to
streak outward in multiple strings, tracing the air in straight lines
that led toward the white candles that circled them.

The demon stared at William from beneath heavily lidded eyes.

William's arm ached and the cut stung, and when the flow began to diminish, he reached up without hesitation and sliced more deeply.

Blood raced through the room now. Like spokes on a wheel it extended from the center to a place three feet above the flickering blue flame of each of those candles, and then from candle to candle, quickly tracing a circle around them. Indeed, it *was* a wheel now.

A wheel of blood.

Thin though the lines were, William knew he'd lost a lot of that fluid. If he succeeded, it would be worth it. And if he did not, he might well lose *all* of it.

Suddenly the wheel was complete, and a final spoke began to thrust from the center point, creeping through the air toward the body of Henry Swift and its demonic occupant.

William bent over, elbows on his knees, struggling to keep his head upright. The combination of blood loss and exertion was beginning to take its toll.

"William, you should stop this," Horatio said softly. Again, the ghostly voice sounded as though it originated just at his ear. "You'll be too weak to—"

But it was too late. The flow of blood had reached its terminus, directly opposite William. A straight line of his blood ran from his wrist, across the room through the center axis of the wheel, and then touched his father's chest, between the chains that bound him there. Henry's shirt was immediately drenched in red.

The blood of his blood.

The blood of his son.

The ritual would draw the demon out of his body, and force Oblis into the bottle, leaving him trapped there like a genie.

ιe moment the blood touched him, the demon screamed.
ς let loose with a guttural roar of anguish, and threw back his
ι. When he leveled his gaze again, and glared at William, his
yes were utterly black.

He screamed, opened his mouth again, and this time there were *voices* there. Not just the two William would have expected—Oblis and Henry—but a dozen more at least. They were cursing and shouting in a jumble of different languages, yet Henry's lips were not moving. It was as though he were a horn, and those voices were merely the sounds that came from it.

Then suddenly he slumped down in the chair, sagging against his chains.

Slowly he stirred, and his eyelids fluttered open. The expression on that face—his father's face—was pitiful.

"William?" Henry said. "Oh, my boy . . . have you finally done it?"

William held his breath. He dared not respond, fearing to be made a fool of yet again. How many times had Oblis convinced him, or Tamara, that they were speaking to Father, only to have them discover that they were being manipulated?

But that voice, the weariness in it . . . could it be?

"You have no idea what it's like down there, William," his father said, anguished. "The things I've seen. And there's no rest, oh, no. None at all."

Still William said nothing. The fingers of his right hand tightened on the ivory handle of the straight razor. The blood had begun to coagulate in the slice across his wrist—that was the very reason he had cut horizontally, and not lengthwise. But there was enough blood now for the ritual.

Then the demon grew impatient.

Henry's face contorted into a hideous visage, far closer to the true features of Oblis, William thought. Horns thrust up under the skin of his temples and his forehead rippled with ridged plates, as though Henry's skull was being transformed.

And he screamed again, furious and ugly, thrashing against his bonds.

William hated the way the spark of hope extinguished in his heart.

The wheel remained. Again he repeated the spell, beginning haltingly, but his voice growing stronger. *"Mit dem blut seines bluts, rufe ich sie. Mit dem blut seines bluts, entleere ich sie heraus."* He repeated it several times and the blood pulsed as it flowed around the room in that circle, and along the spokes of that wheel. Where it touched Henry's chest, the blood grew darker, turning a purplish black instead of red.

Oblis shook Henry's head.

"You're still a novice, William. No matter how you and Tamara study, no matter how you practice, it doesn't matter. You may have the power of the Protectors of Albion, but you haven't the skill.

"Vapors are not of this ordinary, touchable world. While I control your father's body, I exist both on this plane and in the inferno of my birth. I may be trapped here, but I am always aware of the other plane, able to touch the demon world . . . And there are others who come to visit me, for whom I am a tether to this place."

William didn't like the sound of this.

The edges of his vision were darkening from loss of blood, and his head felt heavy and dull. He frowned, his mind becoming sluggish.

"Others?" he said.

Oblis smiled at that.

He opened Henry's lips. In the blue light of those blessed candles and the swirling darkness and ice of that room, William saw something shifting in the recesses of his father's mouth.

With a chorus of wails like the suffering of the damned, the vapors came streaming out. The ritual had not drawn Oblis out, but had instead summoned forth the other demons with whom he communed. They were still intangible and had no hold upon the flesh of Henry Swift, so they could not withstand the magic of the ritual. But Oblis remained, holding fast to the body he had commandeered.

Drawn out by the ritual, the furious vapors attacked.

William shouted in alarm and stood, knocking over his chair. He swayed on his feet, razor held stupidly out before him, as though a simple steel blade could cut the fabric of hell itself. His wits were slack, but a kind of despair came over him, even as he raised both hands and muttered the words of a spell that burst from his fingertips with such force it seared them.

The vapors were thrown back, as though an ethereal gale had swept them away.

But it was only a moment of disorientation, and then they were upon him. William's own malaise was not so fleeting. He tried to summon more magic, but could manage only a meager mystical shield. He knew they would tear through it in moments, these hideous, gape-mouthed spirit demons with their slashing claws.

Horatio was there, then, bellowing a war cry as he began to hack at the vapors with his spectral sword. One of the demons slashed at him with talons of mist and tore at the very fabric of his soul.

Horatio cried out, but pressed his attack even more ferociously. The phantom blade sliced through two of the demons in an instant and they dissipated. Several of the others turned on him, and William tried to see how many there were. Dozens, at least.

The admiral continued his battle against the ethereal creatures, but there were too many. Across the room, still chained, Oblis laughed heartily in the voice of Henry Swift, enjoying the show.

At the center of the room, the perfume bottle meant to imprison him shattered in a shower of beautiful glass.

∼

On that gray June afternoon, Tamara Swift gazed out the window of her carriage as it rambled along Hampstead Lane past the Dufferin Lodge. The Fitzroy farms spread out behind the lodge, and over the hills she could see the steeple of a distant church.

It can't be St. Ann's, she thought. *Not at this distance.*

"You haven't said what you think of the design."

Tamara turned in her seat. Beside her sat her brother's intended bride, Sophia Winchell. The girl was gazing at her expectantly, and not a little bit anxiously, as well.

It felt odd to Tamara. She and Sophia had been at each other's throats—nearly mortal enemies—just months ago. For William's sake they had entered into an unspoken truce, and since then, Tamara had found that she didn't hate Sophia as much as she had thought. Yet neither did she enjoy the other girl's company. Aside from the fact that both of them had lost their mothers at a tender age, they had nothing in common save love for William.

That was enough for Tamara to make an effort to get along with Sophia; enough, even, that she offered to help with plans for the wedding and to help prepare Sophia's trousseau. Sophia had no family of her own to ask for help, after all, and it had seemed the polite thing to do at the time.

Now, though, Tamara found within herself a monumental lack of interest in all things related to the impending celebration.

"It's beautiful, of course," Tamara told her, putting a hand to her chest and hoping to communicate the sense that the fact ought to have gone without saying. Sophia needed frequent reassurance, and Tamara was trying to break her of the habit. "The seamstress is going to do a lovely job of it."

She was being truthful. The dress would be made of blue silk and white lace, with a fitted bodice and a small waist over a full skirt that would accentuate Sophia's figure. The veil would be of sheer white lace to match the pattern of the dress.

Beautiful.

But Tamara had never been the type of girl to be preoccupied by a dress, wedding or no. Her own bridesmaid gown was pretty enough, if simple, but her complexion did not favor white, and so she doubted she would wear it again after the wedding.

"Have you chosen a date yet?" she asked, touching upon one of the few details that did interest her.

Sophia smiled appreciatively. "Not yet. Do you have a suggestion?"

"You know the date is the bride's prerogative," Tamara replied.

Her future sister-in-law leaned in conspiratorially. "You know what they say: marry in May and rue the day."

Tamara nodded. "Marry in September's shine, your living will be rich and fine."

Sophia gave her a grateful look. She could be a terrible shrew when the mood took her, but she did seem genuinely pleased that Tamara appeared to have taken such an interest in the proceedings. In fact, Sophia was at Ludlow House nearly every day with her ladies' maid, Elvira, just as often to visit with Tamara as to see William.

It made Tamara feel guilty that she cared so little, but she did her best to play along.

Once upon a time, she had been a little girl who dreamed about the perfect wedding to the perfect gentleman. The flowers and the diamonds and the gown, all had been in her fantasy. But she had learned that men in general did not appreciate a girl who had interests *other* than marriage, and that had soured the yearning a bit.

When she had discovered that, along with William, she shared the power and responsibility of the Protector of Albion, such girlish musings had been banished almost completely.

Yet there *was* a man. John Haversham. A bit of a rogue, a novice magician, an artist, and a thief, he was a cousin to Sophia. Tamara knew he wasn't the sort of man she ought to consider, yet she could never seem to entirely erase him from her thoughts.

"So it's September, then?" she asked.

Sophia nodded. "Middle of the month, I think. William says the bank will be quiet then. A Wednesday, I believe. The best day of all, the old rhyme says."

Tamara arched an eyebrow. "I didn't realize you were so superstitious," she said wryly.

Sophia's expression shifted subtly, indicating a switch to more serious matters than dresses and wedding dates.

"When I learned the truth about magic and the supernatural world, when I lost my father to it, and witnessed the dangers you and William face . . . well, let us just say that I've learned not to take any superstition lightly."

The carriage slowed. She heard Farris, the stout fellow who served the Swifts as both butler and driver, coo to the horses. And then they were turning north up High Street.

"That's probably wise," Tamara admitted.

Once again, she felt the sympathy for Sophia that had driven her to offer her help with the wedding plans. Aside from Haversham and a few cousins so far away they might as well have been myths, the girl had no family at all. William was always happy to offer suggestions, but he had been quite busy at the bank, where there had been trouble of late, and had taken to spending all of his free time researching a spell to exorcise the demon from their father. Tamara searched as well, but William had become utterly consumed by the effort, attempting anything that seemed even remotely possible.

As disenchanted as she was with the idea of marriage, Tamara would help Sophia, for William's sake, if for nothing else.

Shortly, Farris turned the horses down Peacock Lane toward Ludlow House. The sky had begun to clear a bit, and in places patches of blue peeked through the gray, and splashes of sun touched the summer fields.

"What has William chosen to wear?" Tamara asked.

A cloud passed over Sophia's features.

"He . . . hasn't had a chance to choose as yet. I've recommended a mulberry frock coat and white waistcoat."

"I'm certain he's just having trouble making up his mind," Tamara assured her, though she was certain of no such thing. It was yet another example of how distracted her brother had been of late.

"What do you think about the flowers?" Sophia asked. "Orange blossoms are traditional for the bride. Would you advise roses for the bridesmaid?"

Tamara looked at her and wanted to laugh. She resisted the urge, knowing Sophia would take it poorly. But, really, did the girl think she was some sort of expert on marriage—she who had lost all interest in the subject many months ago?

"I think that would be perfect," she said brightly. "I've always thought the orange blossoms were a lovely touch. Did you know the custom originated in China, and only came west during the Crusades?"

"I hadn't been aware of that," Sophia replied, a bit archly. "But leave it to you, Tamara. It's just the sort of thing you always seem to know."

Tamara had written about a wedding in one of the penny dreadfuls she authored under the pseudonym T. L. Fleet, and had found it necessary to do research on the subject of orange blossoms. That bit of lore had intrigued her. She could have chosen to take offense at Sophia's indulgent tone, but she chose to take it as a compliment instead.

"I cherish such minutiae whenever I encounter it," she said.

Moments later, Farris reined in the horses, and the carriage rolled to a stop in front of Ludlow House. Tamara waited for Farris to climb down and open the door before she stepped out, taking his hand to steady herself. Sophia exited next, and the two women stood together outside the house a moment as Farris got back up on the driver's seat and started the horses moving again.

"You'll stay for tea?" Tamara asked.

Sophia nodded. "If you'll have me."

"I think William would horsewhip me if I let you go home before he'd seen you."

As if I could drive you away, Tamara thought. Sophia and William saw each other at least every other day.

"Excellent. There were some details concerning the ceremony and reception I'd hoped to discuss with both of you," Sophia said.

Tamara nodded, and gestured for Sophia to lead the way to the door. The two young women went together up the walk.

A shudder went through Tamara then, accompanied by a chill that had nothing to do with the weather. She had no precognition, no clairvoyant ability. That wasn't an area in which the Protectors were naturally gifted. But still, she felt certain that something was out of place.

From above their heads came the explosive sound of glass shattering, joined by a cry of panic.

Tamara looked up to see William crashing out through the window of the third-floor nursery, wreathed in tendrils of shadow and the screeching, clawing forms of half a dozen demonic vapors. Even as he twisted in the air, plummeting toward the ground, the wan daylight weakened both shadow and ethereal, and they slid off of him, dissipating in what little sunlight sifted through the cloud cover above.

He flailed as he fell.

Beside her, Sophia screamed.

"William! Translocate!" Tamara shouted, reaching up with both hands as though she could catch her brother.

Arms still pinwheeling in the air, William closed his eyes. Tamara saw his fingers contorting in the beginnings of the spell. It was one of the earliest they had learned, and was so ingrained in them that the words were now barely needed. That familiarity saved William's life.

"Under the same sky—" he shouted, and disappeared.

Only to reappear a moment later, lying on the ground, shaking and trying desperately to catch his breath.

Shouts came from above, and again Tamara looked up.

The ghost of Admiral Nelson passed through the wall of the nursery, pursued by more vapors. Both the ghost and the demons were little more than ripples in the air when seen in daylight, but to Tamara, Horatio was unmistakable. He was her friend, and one of their staunchest allies.

As he flew out through wood and glass he slashed his phantom sword through the air, bisecting two vapors at once, and the demons faded into nothingness.

William managed to climb to his knees.

Sophia called his name and ran to his side. She knelt there, taking his hand in hers. Tamara joined them, taking stock of her brother's condition. His left wrist had been badly cut and he was bleeding, yet there was no blood at all on his clothing. Beyond that, he bore several scratches and scrapes from the attack. Ghosts couldn't touch humans, but, though they seemed equally insubstantial, ethereal demons suffered no such limitation. Without a host body they weren't solid enough to do significant damage, but she thought at the moment William would have argued with her about the definition of *significant*.

"William, what's happened?" Tamara asked.

Disoriented as he was, her brother had trouble focusing on her. "Well, *that* didn't turn out quite the way I'd hoped," he said.

But she was not amused, nor was she in any mood to be misdirected. He'd obviously tried to exorcise their father on his own.

"What of Oblis? Did you drive him out?"

Her brother shook his head. "No, I don't think so."

But Tamara had to be certain. Even as Horatio joined them, she spread her arms.

"Under the same sky, under the same moon," she whispered, beginning her own spell of translocation.

The magic felt like a hook set into her chest, and she was pulled forward and upward. For just a moment the world became insubstantial, appearing only as a warped blur.

Then the sensation ended abruptly, and she found herself in the nursery at the top floor of Ludlow House. Despite her ladylike attire, Tamara stood ready for battle, fingers poised to cast a spell, knees bent and ready for a physical attack if one was forthcoming.

Yet there was her father, chained to his chair, just as he'd been when she'd left. There was a circle painted on the floor in spattered blood, and thirty or forty white candles, all half melted and extinguished. In the center of the room were the shattered bits of a perfume bottle that had once belonged to her grandmother.

"Father?" she ventured, though she had only a faint hope that William had succeeded.

Oblis did not even attempt to deceive her. He only smiled and gazed at her with demon's eyes.

"How sad, my dear, that you've missed all the fun."

~

THE NIGHT SKY WAS OBSCURED by thin clouds that allowed only glimpses of the stars, like a veil across the face of some demure Eastern princess. The wind came from the west, and Holly Newcomb could taste the tang of salt upon her lips, smell the ocean six miles distant. The village of Camelford was a border of sorts between the rugged coast of northern Cornwall and the great moors that stretched further inland, and it shared the culture of both regions.

Camelford had beauty, in its way. She had never doubted that. The wide main street was lined with stone buildings; some were homes and others were shops. The church steeple was a beacon of faith that was visible from any point in the village. The jail was an old, unpleasant structure whose appearance reflected the character of its purpose, but it had held French prisoners during the Napoleonic wars, and a certain glory radiated from that.

The lands around the village were lush and green, with trees and ancient stone walls—likely built by Romans—lining the Camel River. Holly lived with her mother in a cottage on the northern edge of the Camelford. Her father had dropped dead on the eve of his thirty-ninth birthday, and they'd been alone together ever since.

Her mother worked as a chambermaid at the Mason's Arms, and Holly had done the same until she'd turned fourteen, when she'd prettied herself up to look as mature as she could and convinced the owner, Mr. Price, to give her a job as a barmaid. There was considerably more money in that than in changing sheets and dumping chamber pots.

And as a barmaid, she got a better look at the foreign gentlemen passing through Camelford, and they at her, as well.

Mr. Price had let her out early tonight. It was just gone ten P.M., but the pub was quiet. The inn itself was hardly half full—the only new arrivals this evening had been a Scottish gentleman who seemed little interested in the pub, but overly concerned with the welfare of the horses that pulled his coach.

Normally her mother would have come back to walk home with her, concerned for her daughter's virtue, though Holly was sixteen and secretly wished some gent would take an interest in robbing her of that very treasure. Often when she got off earlier than expected, she'd have an escort in Frank Turner, the farrier, a gray-haired, bearded gent with a fatherly smile and a protective air about him. Holly thought Frank had his eye on her mother, and the thought pleased her. The life of a widow didn't suit Mum.

But since the Scots gentleman was so concerned about his horses, Frank had been unable to leave with her. He'd been concerned, but Holly had brushed off his suggestion that she wait for him. It was Camelford, after all. No harm would come to her, or to her reputation. It wasn't as if she was a young lady of privilege, who needed a chaperon.

So she'd laughed, though gazing at him fondly, and waved as she'd gone out, wondering just how much of Frank's concern was due to his desire to see her mother.

In truth, kind as Frank was, she relished the opportunity to wander Camelford after dark. The night and the stars and the cast of the moonlight that sifted through the thin clouds above made it almost possible for her to dream that she was in another place— another country, far away.

Holly hadn't gone far. The Mason's Arms stood on the bank of the river, beside a stone bridge that spanned the gently rolling water. She paused, halfway across the bridge, to breathe in the summer night and listen to the currents flowing by. From here she could see the outline of the town against the night. The Bridge House loomed on one side, and the inn on the other. Beyond those there were other buildings, including the church and the village hall, up on Chapel Street, with its odd weather vane.

Foolish travelers had, over time, convinced the far more foolish locals that the desert pack animal, the camel, ought to be associated with the town, and so the image of the beast adorned several of the structures, and a camel-shaped weather vane topped the village hall.

Mr. Price didn't hold with such nonsense, though. His family had lived in the village for centuries, and he was well aware of the fact that the name came from the Cornish name "Camalanford." *Cam* meant crooked, *alan* beautiful, and *ford* referred to the river. Roger imparted this knowledge to travelers and locals alike, and it never failed to sour his mood when he spotted the image of a camel in town.

As Holly glanced up at the silhouette of the village hall, the darkness a cloak around her there on the bridge, the sight of the camel had an entirely different effect, creating within her a profound longing. Her mind raced with images of vast deserts, of pyramids and tombs, of exotic marketplaces filled with the smell of spices.

Holly Newcomb dreamed of seeing the world. In the quiet moments just before bed and just after waking she fancied that one day an exotic foreign gentleman would pass through Camelford, take a single glance at her, and be so consumed by love that he would have no choice but to sweep her off her feet and take her along on his travels round the globe.

At sixteen, she was old enough to be aware that her dreams weren't very original for a girl from Camelford. The village had been a stopping point along a trade route as far back as medieval times, and likely before. No doubt centuries of young girls had spied foreign gents along the road or stopping by an inn, and wondered if they might somehow go along when those gentlemen departed.

Still, Holly figured that by working as a barmaid at the inn, she made certain her odds were better than most. And she fancied that her yearning was more powerful than that of other girls. It *had* to be. One day, she would meet such a gentleman. And not some Scotsman or American, either, but a Spaniard, or Italian, or Egyptian.

One day, he'll come for me, she thought. A smile lifted the corners of her mouth.

She took a deep breath, loving the sounds that came out of the summer darkness, the songs of night birds and the splash of something below in the river.

But she had given over enough time to her dreams tonight. Her mother would be angry if she discovered how early Mr. Price had sent Holly home, and realized how long she had tarried at the bridge.

With a sigh, she turned her back on the inn and started toward the opposite side of the bridge. The breeze brought her the scent of the ocean again and she breathed deeply. The church bell rang once, tolling the half hour. *Another night passing by, and me still in Camelford.*

As she walked she gazed longingly up at the weather vane atop the village hall, and thought of Egypt.

But then she realized there was something else in the sky. A dark silhouette flitted through the night above the buildings. Holly's step faltered, and she narrowed her gaze. The dark shape moved swiftly, passing from near-total darkness into splashes of moon and starlight that filtered through the thin clouds. It took her a moment to realize there were two of them.

At first she thought they were birds of some sort, large night hunters, and she was mesmerized. She tried to follow their progress across the sky as they slipped in and out of cloud shadows. Even when the moonlight reached them, they seemed darker than dark, as though the celestial illumination could not touch them, and instead revealed their presence only by avoiding those patches of blackness as they slid through the air.

One of them darted upriver and Holly watched it for a long moment until she lost it against the night sky. For a moment she was distracted from the other one, and now she turned to see that it had gone downriver a short way.

In a stray shaft of moonlight, it hovered for a moment, and she saw that it was no bird. The black-sheathed figure was human in shape, most like a woman, with long hair as black as raven's wings. Holly's breath caught in her throat. Yet even now it was with wonder that she gazed into the night sky.

Until the moment when the figure darted toward her, slipping into darkness but unquestionably descending. She lost it in the darkness, and her legs were frozen as though turned to stone, while her eyes frantically searched the sky. When the shadow-woman passed through another patch of moonlight she was close.

Much too close.

Holly wanted to scream but her voice failed her.

Finally her feet obeyed her and she turned to flee, heels striking the stone bridge as she raced for the other side and the buildings that beckoned beyond. Camelford wasn't London, and many of its people would be already asleep, or preparing to retire for the night. But if only she could scream, she might summon aid.

Her skirts flew around her as she ran. Terror raced through her veins like fire. The scream welled up in her chest. She opened her mouth to set it free.

But she had forgotten the other raven shadow, and even as she saw the movement to her left, out of the corner of her eye, slender yet powerful hands reached down from the dark night and grabbed hold of her, lifting her up and up and up into the clouds and the shadows and the patches of moonlight and starshine.

The other took hold of her as well, and then they were hurtling through the night at such speed that when at last she did loose the scream that had built up within her, it was lost on the wind.

Two

The sun broke through the swath of cloud that covered the sky, giving the town of Camelford the first hint of golden daylight it had seen in a fortnight. For days on end, the small Cornish village had been plagued by the sickly gray of a sunless existence. Now, delicious rays flooded down upon the small hamlet and its outlying environs, warming the hearts of the townsfolk, and of their hidden neighbors: the fairies and sprites.

Under normal circumstances, Serena would have enjoyed the return of the sun, but today her usual good spirits were severely dampened by a cold chill that had entered her heart earlier in the morning, and refused to go away. At the moment, the nasty feeling was lodged in her throat, and the little sprite was sure that if anyone had spoken to her, she would have started sobbing, no matter how mundane the question.

Serena had always had a propensity for mischief. It wasn't that she craved trouble—quite the opposite—but somehow she always found herself in the thick of some harebrained plot or looming fiasco.

This occasion was no different.

The disaster had started with a silly, stupid dare; one that she, Serena, had leveled at her dearest friend in the whole world. She had dared Aine to go to the sacred rowan circle south of Stronghold, and Call out her true love. She hadn't really thought the silly girl would be so insane as to actually leave the safety of the fairy outpost in the dark of night, and head off into the woods by herself. But Aine had taken the challenge, and now, because of it, Serena was responsible for whatever horrors had befallen her friend.

She had waited for Aine to come back the night she had given her the melody to perform the Calling. When dawn arrived with Aine still not returned, she had become desperately worried.

Serena had flown out to the grove, hoping against hope that she would find Aine curled up in a ball, sound asleep against the base of one of the old trees. Finding the sacred circle empty had only intensified the cold, hard knot of fear in her stomach that had dogged her ever since she had visited her friend's bedchamber that morning and found only pillows under the blanket.

Now something at the edge of the grove caught Serena's eye and she felt all the remaining warmth drain from her. The sprite alighted on the ground beside a shiny metal object, her eyes marveling at its delicate, miniature beauty.

The silver whistle lay on its side, half-hidden behind a thickly twisted tree root. Surely it had been lost in haste, or during a struggle, because Serena knew that Aine would not part with it willingly.

Weighted with guilt and regret and grief, Serena realized she would have to tell the Council of Stronghold, so that they could begin searching for the missing girl as soon as possible. Something terrible had happened in this grove. Serena could feel it in her bones, hollow though they might be.

She could also sense that her own fate loomed in the balance. Fairies were noted for their rash, vindictive nature, and they would never forgive her for her part in Aine's disappearance. They disliked sprites enough to begin with. The feeling was mutual. Though the two races were kin and both hailed from Faerie, when the tiny sprites came through to the human world they set up their tribal homes far from the outposts of the fairies. Serena's tribe lived the nearest to Stronghold, and that was more than fifty miles from here, in the forest outside of Blackbriar.

Serena had never been like her brothers and sisters. She had never disliked fairies, in spite of their usual arrogance, with the same passion as other sprites, and she had even begun to appreciate humans of late. Also unusual among her tribe, she made a pilgrimage back to Faerie at least once a year to visit the homelands and the pure, untouched skeins of magic that wound through them. She visited family who thought her by turns brave and foolish to have taken up residence in the human world.

The simplest way to journey back to Faerie was through Stronghold, which as an outpost between worlds existed on both planes; there traveling to the homelands was as easy as stepping through a door.

On one of these pilgrimages, Serena had met Aine and, in her, found a kindred spirit. Aine had never understood the prejudice that fairies had toward sprites. "What?" she'd said once. "Just 'cause we're nearly as large as the humans and our wings only appear when we summon them, that makes us somehow better? That's foolish. We're all cousins, all Fey, all of Faerie."

They had become fast friends. Serena's presence around Stronghold had, at best, been tolerated. Sprites were not banned from the outpost, of course. They traveled through from time to time. But it was always made clear that this was an indulgence, a courtesy.

Serena knew that would change by the end of the day. She would find herself banished from Stronghold. Bad enough, but since her own tribe had spurned her because of her friendships with fairies and humans, she would be a true outcast. And if she couldn't enter Stronghold, it would make it that much harder for her to visit Faerie.

The very thought made the tears she had held back all morning start to gather at the corners of her eyes.

Yes, she still had human friends, but it was not the same. If something had happened to Aine—and she felt sure, in her heart, that it had—then she had lost not only her best friend, but all connection to her heritage and kind. It was unthinkable. There had to be *something* she could do.

With a flit of her wings, she darted off into the trees, pirouetting through branches as she flew toward Stronghold, searching the forest with her eyes. Serena moved with a grace and speed even fairies envied, her shimmering form no more than a flicker in the air.

She didn't stop to speak to any of the forest creatures as she flew past the trees and across part of the yawning moorlands, too caught up in her own thoughts to pay them any mind. No, she had decided upon a course of action, and she was moving as quickly as she could to carry it out. First, she would return to Stronghold and reveal to the council her part in Aine's disappearance.

Then she would begin the second, and trickier, phase of her plan.

Stronghold came into view ahead of her, the first sight of it causing her breath to catch in her throat as it always did. The fairy outpost was majestic. From its tall, intricately carved battlements to the silvery spire at its center, the place was like a dream come to life—a dream that was about to end for her.

The fairies had created this place so long ago that there was no one still living who could tell tale of its construction. Some said that Stronghold had been built as a wedding gift for a long forgotten human king and his fairy wife, providing a bridge between the magical realm and the ordinary world, given as a sign of goodwill in the days before humanity ceased to believe in magic—and by extension, all the world's magical beings.

Whether or not this was true, Serena could not say, but it made a pretty story.

Bypassing the front gates and the sentries that stood silent as carved idols beside them, Serena flew over the stones that encircled Stronghold. The magical wards and protections would not delay her. This place recognized her as a friend.

She knew a shortcut to the Great Hall, a secret way she and Aine had found when they were amusing themselves in the seldom-used hallways of the outpost.

Serena flew in through an open window in the armory, then buzzed through a series of empty rooms before slipping inside the sewing room.

That room was empty, so Serena was able to fly over to the giant armoire that was pushed up against the farthest wall without anyone stopping her to ask questions. Grasping the small metal pull on the front of the cabinet, she opened the door a few inches so that she could fly inside.

At the back of the armoire was a small hole, perfectly sized for a sprite. Serena flew into the hole, and found herself speeding down a long tunnel that seemed to span the length of the keep at Stronghold's center. She pressed forward in the darkness until she came to a section that was illuminated by a dazzling yellow light. The tunnel veered off sharply to the left, but Serena followed the glow of the light out into a long corridor that led up to the anteroom of the Great Hall.

There were a few fairies milling about, waiting their turn for an audience with the council. Serena ignored them, flying so low to the ground that most of them didn't even know she was there. She slipped under the crack between the door and the floor, moving as silently as she could.

The council was already in session when Serena arrived. She quickly darted behind an antique tapestry, the thick woven material practically a bas-relief depicting the coronation of the last queen of Faerie. It was stuffy, hovering behind the fabric; dust that had collected for more than two hundred years found its way onto Serena's wings, making them heavy and hard to control.

Her nose began to twitch, but she pinched her nostrils together, stopping the sneeze. She didn't want to be detected just yet.

"We have no cause to blame the humans, but then again—" the voice began, the cadence quick and whiny.

That can only be Zacharias, Serena thought to herself, darkly. *His voice is as prissy as the rest of him.*

Zacharias was one of the eldest members of the council, and one of the few males. Indeed, males were scarce at Stronghold. Female fairies seemed to have a much easier time adjusting to the human world, so most of the males remained behind in their own realm, never wishing to cross over.

"Enough, Zacharias!" said a commanding voice that could only have belonged to Giselle, Aine's aunt. "We do not know who is behind these horrors, or why, but we must not distract ourselves from discovering the truth by engaging in wild and unfounded suppositions."

From her vantage point, Serena couldn't see the wise fairy warrior, but in her mind's eye she called up an image of Giselle, her long silver hair braided in a thick rope down her back, silver-blue eyes that seemed to see into the dark recesses of your soul. This was a woman who preferred the bloody battlefield to a verbal duel of words.

Regardless, she was fair, and listened to all sides before passing judgment. Stronghold was lucky to have her on the council, helping to make their laws and mete out justice. It was her wisdom and compassion, along with a view shared by other true voices on the council, that kept the more conniving members in check.

"Mellyn is dead, murdered in the forest. Were you not listening?" Giselle went on. "Her body lay tangled in the upper limbs of a towering oak. What human could do such a thing? This horror is all the more troubling in light of the news that no one has seen Tamsyn in days. I'd thought her off on some flight of fancy, but now I fear the worst."

Giselle's words jarred Serena and she could not breathe.

Dead, murdered in the forest.

"The shadow grows longer, Giselle Ravenswood," old Zacharias wheezed. "My granddaughter, Wenna, has long loved to watch the sun set over the Celtic Sea. Last night, she did not return."

Silence reigned in the council chamber. The council knew nothing of Aine's disappearance, but with her also gone that made three fairy girls vanished, and Mellyn murdered.

A cold chill of fear and dread went up Serena's spine, and she tried to tell herself that Mellyn's death did not mean that the other girls had met the same fate. But even if she was right, something terrible was afoot in the woods, something that stole away young girls and did not return them. And now her truest friend was at this thing's mercy.

Serena realized then that there was no more time to spare. Nervously, she slid out from behind the tapestry, and began to fly across the large hall.

Giselle noticed her immediately. Wise and beautiful though the silver-haired fairy might be, she was also known for her wrath.

"Sprite!" she thundered, and every head in the council chamber turned.

Serena darted into the center of the chamber and alighted upon the floor, an eighth the height of the smallest among them. Still, as she knelt before Giselle, she kept her chin up, held on to her dignity.

"Wise Giselle—" she began.

"What do you mean by this intrusion?" Giselle demanded. "No one is allowed within the chamber while the council is meeting. You dare much, little fool!"

Zacharias sniffed in disgust, and the bent, crooked old fairy glared down at her. "A sprite? Outrageous!"

In that moment, Serena wanted to scream and to fly. Every time she came to Stronghold she tried to pretend that the disdain of the fairies did not hurt her heart. She could pretend no longer. In that moment, she felt small not in size but in worth, and she hated them for it.

But she loved Aine, and so she met Giselle's angry gaze with one of her own.

"We comes with awful news, we does," the little sprite said, her wings buzzing behind her in punctuation to her words. "Our greatest friend, Aine, were out in the forest last night. To Call her true love, she went, just to see, to see his face, ye ken."

Her lips trembled and a hot tear streaked down her cheek.

"She doesn't come back," Serena whispered. "Aine doesn't come back last night."

Voices erupted in thunderous debate, her transgression momentarily forgotten. Serena glanced around at the members of the council as they argued about what was to be done regarding the missing girls, and whether or not they were still alive.

The sprite leaped into the air, tiny wings beating rapidly, and hovered three feet from Giselle's face. She spun around in a circle, crying out to the others.

"Listen. Listen, ye must!" Serena said. "We knows what to do! We knows who will help!"

Giselle clapped her hands and all fell silent. The silver-haired woman stared at Serena.

"The council will continue its discussion of these matters momentarily. First, however, we must attend to this sprite, and her intrusion. She has violated these chambers and thus broken our law and our trust, and for that there must be punishment."

Serena stared at her. "Ye're mad, woman. Listens to us! Send us to the Swifts. The Protectors of Albion, they helps find Aine and t'others, before they be as dead as Mellyn!"

Zacharias snorted in derision. "Ah, so she was eavesdropping as well. Furtive, nasty little bug."

"Hush, now, Serena, before you condemn yourself further," Giselle said, eyes flashing darkly. "You'll accept your punishment. As for the Protectors, we have no need of human help. Stronghold can look after its own."

Serena glared at her. "Aye, ye've done so well thus far."

Giselle glared a moment longer, then looked toward the doors. "Summon the guard to take her."

"Fools, all've ye!" Serena cried in anguish and fury.

She darted away, flitting across the room toward the tiny hole through which she'd entered. One of the council members, an elegant, gauzy young thing, sprang into the air, pretty gossamer wings appearing at her back, and tried to intercept her.

Serena was quicker. She slipped through the hole and out of the council chamber. Thanks to her friendship with Aine, she knew every secret and tiny path in all of Stronghold. They would never catch up to her before she could leave.

In moments, she was out, flying among the trees and then above them, soaring toward the southeast, toward London. It would be an arduous journey at such speed, but she would not stop to rest. She must get to Farris as quickly as possible, and hope that he would intercede on her behalf with the Protectors.

Our Farris, she thought, *so brave.* He would help. He must.

Aine's fate hung in the balance.

∼

At that very moment, Serena's only hope was asleep on a wrought-iron bench in the gardens of Ludlow House, his pale face turning salmon pink in the sun.

Farris let out a snore, the sound so loud and grotesque that it startled him awake. He looked around sheepishly, his eyes still blurry from his catnap, hoping that no one had caught him. Out of the corner of his eye, he caught Tamara Swift trying to stifle a giggle, and she was trying very poorly indeed.

Her honey-blond hair was caught up in a loose chignon, accentuating her high cheekbones, and her face was flushed with exertion. The dark gray muslin dress she wore clung to her womanly frame in all the right places, enhancing her burgeoning sexuality.

It made Farris worry more every day.

He knew that she was naïve when it came to the opposite sex, but sensed that this was a lack she wanted to remedy. The very idea that some rogue might take advantage of her innocence made his blood turn to ice. He thought of Tamara as his personal charge, and looked after her fiercely. He would sooner die than let anything happen to her.

Normally he felt confident that he was quite adept at performing all of the various services he provided for the Swifts—butler, footman, valet—yet he had absolutely no idea how to be a successful chaperon for a girl who did not desire one.

～

IT TOOK ALL OF TAMARA'S CONTROL not to laugh at poor Farris's discomfort. Since she didn't want to embarrass him any further, she looked down to the end of the garden where the archery target stood.

As she watched, John Haversham pulled the last arrow from the covered hay bale they had been loosing their weapons upon all afternoon. He waved at her, half a dozen feathered arrows in his hand, and began to jog back to where she stood, staring at him curiously.

She turned back to Farris, and saw that he had an odd look on his face as he watched John trot back toward her. She wondered—not for the first time—if Farris disliked John Haversham as much as her brother did.

William despised Sophia's cavalier cousin, and made every effort to dissuade Tamara from spending time with him. Had her brother any idea of her true feelings for John, he would never have allowed his sister to leave the house in the man's company—not even with Farris as chaperon.

The rakishly handsome young fellow strode toward her across the grassy slope, his head erect, a mischievous gleam in his eyes.

His dark hair was a bit wild, always appearing to be windblown, even indoors. He possessed sharp gray eyes and a wide, sensual mouth. Just being near him made Tamara's heart race, and she was tempted to swoon so that he would catch her, so that physical contact would be instigated "against her will."

And it *was* against her will. Intellectually, she didn't *want* to be in love with John Haversham. In fact, she felt small and stupid in his company, knowing that he could easily make use of her vulnerability, her need to be close to him. It bothered her terribly that she couldn't control her emotions, as he clearly could.

They had shared a few intimate moments, but John had made it more than plain that while he found her attractive, that didn't mean he wished to court her. Which led them to afternoons like this: Tamara pining away for him under the guise of helping him hone his magical skills, and John accepting her assistance without recognizing her discomfort.

"What do you think?" John called out to her. "Shall we have another go? Or have I worn you out already this afternoon, milady?"

She was certain his little innuendo was engineered to annoy her, but she let it pass. He cocked an eyebrow, waiting for a nasty dig in response, but when none was forthcoming, he began to smile.

"Has someone gotten up on the wrong side of the bed this morning?" John's smile widened. "Why, you've been as calculating as a cobra these past few hours, biding your time, waiting to strike the death blow, I suspect."

"John, you really are—"

He began to laugh, pleased to have riled her. The rich baritone of his speaking voice translated perfectly into laughter. She loved this sound, especially, and would have done anything—under different circumstances—to make it appear more often. She also liked that he had a sense of humor and wasn't afraid to show it.

"Come, Tamara, you can only remain stoic for so long. I shall continue to tease you until you crumble under the onslaught and spar with me properly . . . or at least unlock your sweet smile."

Tamara said nothing, only clenched her jaw harder to keep from opening her mouth.

This only made John laugh harder.

"Tamara Swift, I know you better than you think. It's impossible for you to keep that lovely mouth of yours shut for very long. Your brain will burst with all of the poisonous barbs and tart ripostes you're holding back, if you don't just *speak*."

Her eyes flared at that. As much as she hated it, when John called her mouth *lovely*, her heart had skipped a beat—perhaps even two or three.

But she shook her head, and took a deep, calming breath.

"I have no idea what you mean, John. I have nothing but kind words to impart, each and every day." She smiled sweetly.

John snorted.

"You'll have to do better than that, milady," he countered, the corners of his mouth still curled in the last vestiges of a smirk.

Tamara ignored him now, her expression turning serious, and reached out and plucked one of the arrows from his hand. She put the long, thin shaft against her bow, and drew her hand back, releasing the arrow high into the sky. It sailed upward in a long arc, gaining momentum as it flew. She watched it, waiting, and it began to curve back down again, directly on target.

At the last moment, Tamara called out *"ignate,"* and the arrow burst into flame just as it hit the target, a perfect bull's eye. With a wave of her hand, the arrow ceased its burning, leaving no charred or even singed bits in its wake.

"Amazing, as usual," John said, as he deposited the rest of the arrows into a wide leather quiver that rested on a small wrought-iron table.

"Thank you," she answered, offering him a prim smile and half a curtsy.

John rested his weight against his longbow, and he leaned there, watching her.

"You know, as much as I've enjoyed this afternoon of silence, I do prefer the old Tamara Swift. What have you done with that clever beauty I first met at the Wintertons' dinner party, all those long months ago?"

Tamara blushed, silently enjoying his compliment. She decided to use the light moment to broach a subject that had been on her mind for some time.

"John, may I ask you something?"

Sensing her hesitation, he nodded, encouraging her to go on.

"I know that you're not an innocent, that you've dabbled in the dark side of nature, seen things that have . . ." She paused.

"Terrified me?" he finished.

She nodded.

The smirk was gone from his face now. He regarded her with utter sincerity.

"Go on," he said. "There's no question you could ask me, Tamara, that I wouldn't answer."

She sighed.

"Demons. What do you know of them?"

John narrowed his eyes, but let her continue.

"And what do you know of how can they be cast out of someone they've possessed?"

"Your father?"

She nodded, relieved to be talking to someone other than

William about this. As a member of the Algernon Club—the exclusive gentlemen's club that catered to stage magicians, and whose inner circle were well acquainted with real magic, not just stagecraft—John had at one time been assigned to spy on her. The club's directors had wanted to know who had become Protector of Albion in the wake of Sir Ludlow's death. Those true magicians had dedicated themselves to combating the forces of darkness. Ludlow had been one of them, and they wished to have the new Protector join their club, as well, if only they could determine who it was.

John Haversham had been the club's spy, and in other instances, their thief. And though their relationship had begun under false pretenses, Tamara had forgiven John that deceit when, once it had ended, it became obvious to her that his affection was genuine.

It was clear he had true feelings for her, but still he kept his distance and refused to court her, which frustrated her no end.

I know you want to love me, she thought. *Why* can't *you then?*

Tamara believed it still had something to do with his obligation to the Algernon Club. She and William sat upon the board of directors now, much as it made them all fidget endlessly to endure the presence of a woman in the boardroom. But she felt sure that Lord Blackheath must still require John to make regular reports of his activities as they related to the Protectors. Therefore, she surmised, if John courted her, he would end up betraying either her trust or his duties to the club.

It was an untenable position.

At the moment, however, Tamara was acting upon the belief that the Algernon Club's members knew more than they ought to know. Surely they were aware of her father's circumstances, though she and William had always avoided the subject as much as possible. It was safe to assume, then, that John was well aware of Henry

Swift's condition. But he was too much of a gentleman to let on what he had discovered. He kept things close to his heart, which was one of the reasons Tamara had decided to ask him for help.

"The demon that possesses Father's body," she began. "William and I have tried everything to expel him, but to no avail."

"Do you know its name?" John asked.

She nodded. "He calls himself Oblis. Does that name mean anything to you?"

John shook his head. "No, I'm sorry, Tamara. I wish that I was better equipped to help you, but my knowledge of the demon world is sparse at best."

It had been a long shot, she had known that. But at least she felt better talking about it to—dare she say it—a friend.

"You will keep this to yourself?" Tamara said, realizing that any knowledge she imparted to John Haversham still might be funneled directly back to the Algernon Club.

"I will speak to no one concerning what you have told me," John said, interrupting her thoughts. "You have my word on that."

He had such a look of complete earnestness on his face that Tamara felt as if she had no reason *not* to believe him.

At least she hoped so.

～

SERENA'S WINGS WERE ON FIRE—they felt as if they were actually burning from overexertion.

She had traveled with a speed she did not know she could achieve, pushing her tiny body to its utmost limits. Now she could see the peaks of Ludlow House, only a few miles away, but that didn't allow her to slacken her pace. She *refused* to slow down, driving herself even harder.

Serena hoped she would find her Farris at Ludlow House with

his masters, but even if she didn't, she would continue on, seeking them wherever they might be. She had spent a fair amount of time with the Swifts the previous year, after they had come to Blackbriar to investigate a group of mysterious changeling births in the area.

Serena had given them her help, and in the process become enchanted by their trusted butler and footman. How she admired his great heart, and was amused by his gruff exterior.

Ah, Farris.

She did somersaults of happiness whenever he was around, such was her fascination with him. Farris was not young, or tall, or thin, or beautiful. In every way he was the opposite of the sort of men so often obsessed over by her sprite sisters and the fairy girls she'd known. Yet Farris was a stalwart friend, courageous to a fault, though he had no magic to protect himself in battle. He had saved her from a tragic end, once upon a time. But in truth it was his heart that made her yearn to be near him, made her flit and giggle in his presence.

Farris had the kindest, truest, gentlest heart of any male she had ever met, whether human or fairy or sprite. Serena *trusted* him, and that meant the world to her.

Only her desire to make a pilgrimage to Faerie had drawn her back to Cornwall, first to Blackbriar to visit the rest of her tribe, and then to Stronghold and on through to Faerie. But afterward she had been unable to resist the temptation to spend time with her great friend, Aine.

And now . . .

A shudder of horror went through her.

As Ludlow House drew nearer, she again wondered why human beings and most fairies wanted to live indoors. Sprites spent most of their time in the woods, sleeping in the nests they built on the higher branches of oak or rowan trees, but sometimes they appropriated the odd abandoned rabbit- or foxhole, burrowing deep underground.

If you were going to have a house, however, she would have been forced to admit that Ludlow House was quite stunning. Three stories of Gothic architecture at its most haunting, with tall windows that looked more like shuttered eyes, and a long wrought-iron fence that surrounded the whole property like a row of sharpened teeth.

In the moonlight, the place had an eerie, haunted air it did not possess in the daytime. She had spent many a night following Farris around as he patrolled the property, but had never noticed how unsettling the place could be.

Serena followed the fence to the back of the grounds where the carriage house stood. She saw the flicker of a candle through the window and flew straight toward it, almost knocking herself out on the glass before realizing that the window was closed.

In all her life she had never been so exhausted. Her whole body tingled with an odd numbness and all she wanted to do was lie down and drop off to sleep.

But she saw Farris inside, checking on the horses, and mustered her resolve. She began to bang on the glass with her tiny fists. He looked up, surprised, and stepped over to the window, pushing it open so that Serena could come inside.

She touched down on the whitewashed windowsill, and immediately crumpled into a heap. Farris picked up the tiny sprite in his hand, cradling her limp body carefully in his palm.

"Serena?" Farris said, his voice full of worry.

"Farris—" she began, but she could not finish the sentence. She had no strength left with which to speak. Finally, unconsciousness took her.

～

FARRIS SMOOTHED SERENA'S bristle-spiked hair with the tip of his index finger, marveling at the beauty of her sparkling blue skin and flame-red hair. He was always so frightened of hurting her. She was small and delicate, like a little bird.

Unsure of how to proceed, Farris carried her through the carriage house and across the lawn to the main house. He pulled out his keys to open the door to the kitchen, and went inside, blowing out his candlewick before setting the taper down on the butcher block.

The kitchen was large and spacious, and there was a separate larder—reachable by a set of stairs that led down into the cellar—that was almost the same size. In the past, Ludlow House had been used for entertaining on an almost weekly basis, but since Sir Ludlow's untimely death and the possession of Henry Swift by the demon, the house had been open to very few guests.

"Serena?" Farris repeated, whispering still. She opened her eyes, but could only blink miserably at him, her little chest heaving from all the exertion she had endured during her flight.

Farris picked up a set of cloth napkins that the housekeeper, Martha, or one of the new maids had left on the counter, and created a soft nest to set Serena into. When she was settled in her little napkin bed, Farris moved to the cupboard and pulled a bottle of whiskey from its back shelf. He set the whiskey on the counter top near Serena, then left the room, only to return a moment later carrying a small, porcelain thimble. He poured a few drops of whiskey into the thimble, and brought it to Serena. He propped her into a sitting position with his left hand, feeding her the thimbleful of whiskey with his right.

She pulled back abruptly, then coughed and spluttered, but the whiskey seemed to revive her.

"Is that better, little one?" Farris asked.

Serena nodded, though she was clearly still disoriented, now from both exhaustion and the alcohol. She blinked several times, becoming more alert, the whiskey warming her.

Then she tried to speak, desperate to tell her story, but Farris wouldn't let her. When she opened her mouth, he shushed her, using his index finger to once again stroke her hair.

"All in good time, poor thing. Got to get your strength back up."

She settled back into the napkins, relaxing her body and wings until she began to doze slightly. For perhaps twenty minutes she lay that way and Farris watched over her, the gentle rise and fall of her chest, the flutter of her wings. Much of the time her frantic attentions perturbed him and so he was often gruff with her. Yet her reckless nature had made him protective of her as well.

Serena was valiant and fierce but so small that he could not help fearing for her.

After what seemed like an eternity, Serena sighed, and the sound had a musical quality that let him know she was feeling better. She sat up, wings fluttering, casting off sparkling gold dust. Then her wings settled like soft down against her shoulders and back.

"Farris, 'tis yer help we needs," Serena began. "Your help, and that of your young masters."

"What is it, Serena? What's wrong?"

She shook her head. "It's terrible things happening, it is, at the Stronghold. Something attacks the fairy girls, Farris. Three is missing, and pretty Mellyn is dead!" Serena waited for him to take in her words before continuing. "We comes to ye for help, my brave

Farris. Whatever hunts in the woods, mayhap it takes more girls even now, even tonight!"

Farris pulled a hand through his thick, graying hair, and sighed. "I'll go and wake Mistress Tamara and Master William."

He had no idea why he was feeling so generous toward the little sprite—usually she annoyed him terribly—but the sight of her at the window, half-dead, pitifully knocking against the glass, had frightened him dreadfully. Perhaps he had grown used to having Serena around, even fond of her. Seeing her like this, he realized for the first time how shattered he would be if anything were to happen to her.

He nodded, giving her one last pat on the head before heading off into the hall, and upstairs to the Swifts' chambers.

∼

SERENA SIGHED, settling back into the softness of the napkins, the cool cloth like a balm against her aching wings. She wanted to close her eyes for just a moment, but knew that if she did, she would be asleep in a heartbeat.

No, she needed to impart her story and acquire the Swifts' help as quickly as possible. Time was of the essence, if she wanted to help find Aine. She thought of Mellyn, dead, her body tangled in the highest limbs of ancient oak.

Oh, Mab, let Aine be all right, Serena prayed to the queen of Faerie, the words running like a mantra in her head.

Let her be alive.

Three

A knock on the door roused William from his slumber. He sat up in bed, rubbing his eyes, and glanced at Sophia where she lay asleep beside him. She was so beautiful in the moonlight, her long dark hair loose on the pillow around her like a halo of shadow. As though sensing his regard, she sighed happily and turned away.

"Sophia, wake up," he whispered, more loudly than he'd intended in the silence of the room. She turned back to him, opening a sleepy eye.

"William . . . ?"

She propped herself up on her elbows, the sheet slipping down to reveal one perfect breast. When she realized what had happened, she covered herself again. Her porcelain skin shone in the moonlight, and desire rose in William. He wished he could shout at whomever had knocked, drive them away so he could ravish Sophia again that very instant.

"There's someone at the door, love," he said in low tones.

Sophia sat up, now fully awake, wrapping the sheets more tightly around her slender frame.

"What do we do?" she asked in a whisper. Her eyes were wide and she shivered, though from a chill or the threat of discovery, he knew not.

William made a show of confidence he did not feel.

"I'll put on my dressing gown, and find out who's there. Be very quiet, and don't move an inch."

He slid from the warm bed, and the floorboards were cold under his feet. He grabbed his nightshirt, slipping it over his head, then retrieved his robe from the armchair by the vanity and went to open the door. He was careful to swing it only wide enough for him to peer out, but not allow the intruder to look in.

"Yes?"

Farris stood on the threshold, anxiously tugging on the hem of his coat. The butler stepped back, and William took the opportunity to slide out of the room, making sure to close the door firmly behind him.

"What troubles you, Farris? Is it Tamara?" William glanced down the long hallway to his sister's closed door.

Farris shook his head. "No, sir. It's got nothing to do with the young miss. It's Serena, Master William. The poor little thing's back, come all the way from Cornwall. And she's awfully upset. 'Pears there's something terrible afoot there."

William frowned. In the past the sprite had proven herself prone to hysteria, of a sort. But that was her nature—the nature of her people. And hysterical or not, her mad behavior had never come without some sort of prompting. If Serena had rushed all the way to London to bring them some dark news, there would be a ring of truth to it.

"Where is she?"

"The kitchen, sir. Shall I fetch Mistress Tamara?" His brow creased and his jaw tightened as he spoke.

"Yes, please do," William said, studying him. "Is there something more, Farris?"

The older man nodded once.

"It's only that she don't look so well. Serena, that is. I think she may need a doctor, sir."

William arched an eyebrow. A doctor for a sprite? *This inheritance of ours brings new surprises every day,* he thought. *I only wish some of them were pleasant.*

∾

WHEN TAMARA ENTERED THE KITCHEN, Farris close on her heels, she had no real idea what to expect. Farris had seemed extremely worried, his dark eyes haunted by his inability to help the tiny creature who was so taken with him. From his tone and pallor, she had assumed that Serena would be on death's door, but, instead, she found the little sprite sitting up on her nest of napkins, chattering away with William.

"Is everything all right?" Tamara asked.

William leaned against the wooden cutting table, his black hair wild, brows knit in dark attention as he listened to the sprite's high, musical voice. Upon Tamara's arrival, he turned and gave Farris a quizzical look.

"I thought you said she needed a doctor, Farris?"

Farris seemed startled by the change in his miniature charge.

The way he had described her, when Serena had arrived she had been near death. Now she sat up with no apparent effort, her ruby-colored eyes bright with interest.

"Sir, I—" the butler started, but he had no words to finish the sentence.

"Did you give her anything, Farris?" Tamara asked, noticing the thimble and bottle of whiskey sitting on the counter. "Anything at all?"

Farris looked sheepish. "A touch of whiskey. That's what my own father gave us when we were ill."

Tamara smiled.

"Very smart, Farris. It appears to have been just the thing. I think she's in *very* good spirits now."

"You mean to say she's *inebriated*?" William said incredulously. "Here in our home? You're not serious." He turned an accusing stare upon the butler.

Tamara could only sigh in response to her brother's vigilant propriety. It rarely abandoned him, even in the most dire of circumstances.

Sometimes it was difficult for her to believe she and William were related, let alone brother and sister. Her impatience with his priggishness had only grown with each day of his courtship of Sophia. Hypocrisy appalled her, yet it also dogged her. Everyone in the household knew that they shared a bed, even though they were only betrothed. At first it had infuriated her, but then Tamara realized that was her own hypocrisy speaking. After all, William was the proper one. Had it not been for his attitude, she would have found no objection to his behavior.

Yet she knew that if the situation were reversed, and she had been the one taking a lover to bed—fiancé or no—he would have been apoplectic. She comforted herself with the knowledge that in some strange way, this reasonable approach was a triumph.

William would never understand.

Now she quieted him with a withering glance.

"Serena's come a long way to see us, Will. Don't you think that rather than admonish Farris, we ought to be encouraging her to speak?"

Serena stood up then, and spread her tiny wings, producing a musical trill and a sparkle of light. *Like stardust,* Tamara thought. She loved the sprite's iridescent wings, which were shaped like a dragonfly's. Serena fluttered them, testing them out before lifting up into the air. She darted toward Farris and alighted on his shoulder, snuggling against his neck.

"Our Farris," she cooed. "He'll protect us now, won't he? Farris with his strong, rough hands."

William raised an eyebrow.

Tamara tried not to giggle at the discomfort that played across Farris's face, tightening his wide jaw, and putting a dark mote in his eye. Despite his awkwardness, she found the whole scene rather sweet.

"Serena, Farris mentioned something about trouble," William prodded impatiently. "You weren't meant to return to London for quite some time. What's happened in Cornwall? What troubles you?"

The sprite busied herself, tickling the white flesh just below Farris's ear with the tip of her wing, making him blush.

"Serena?" Tamara prompted loudly.

When Serena met her gaze, the sprite's ruby eyes flickered, and her smile faded.

" 'Tis Aine, our friend, our very best friend," she said. "Gone, you see, vanished in the wood. They takes her away, and more. Not only Aine, but other fairy girls from Stronghold as well. Takes them away. And . . . poor Mellyn, they finds her dead. We wonders, oh we wonders . . . We fears the worst!"

The sprite shook her head, as if to clear it of the alcohol's effects, and then faltered. Had her perch been more precarious, she would have tumbled drunkenly from Farris's shoulder. The tiniest belch escaped her, and her eyes went wide as she slapped a hand over her mouth in response.

"Go on then," Farris urged. Tamara had never heard him sound so gentle.

Serena sat down in a woeful heap on his shoulder, and put her head in her hands. When she looked up, there was anguish in her expression.

"We doesn't know any more. They takes the girls, the fairies, sisters and cousins, takes them off into the woods in the dark. We doesn't know who takes them, only that they be gone. We needs you, friends. The sisters of the Stronghold, they *needs* the Protectors of Albion.

" 'Tisn't right. Not at all. Ye must come, friends. Come and find them, before all the fairy girls is gone from the wood, forever."

The little sprite shook her head. "Our dearest friend in the whole, wide world, and they takes her. Just takes her." A single tear traced its way down the sparkling blue skin of her cheek. "Our bestest friend, Aine."

Serena hiccupped, then wiped away another tear. This was followed almost immediately by another belch. With every moment, she seemed groggier, less giddy with drink.

"You've been a friend and ally to us, Serena. Even if we weren't the Protectors of Albion, we'd be duty bound to aid you in whatever way we can," Tamara assured her.

"Hear, hear," Farris added.

William remained dreadfully quiet.

Tamara frowned and pinned him with a dark look.

"I'm sorry," William said. "I can't travel to Cornwall now, not on a sprite's whim. We've no way of knowing what's really happening up there, while here at home I have work—and, of course, the wedding—to think of. Besides which, Horatio and I are very close indeed to finding a cure for Father. I am sorry, all of you, but I am thus bound."

Tamara glared at him, fighting the urge to slap him. "William, Serena has almost killed herself to come and enlist our aid."

He regarded her with icy distance. "Perhaps I wasn't clear."

"Oh, you were quite clear, I'd say. But perhaps someone ought to make it clear to you that if you do not stop *acting* the part of an ass, you will very soon *become* one."

William stared, his mouth hanging open in particularly piscine fashion. As he began to utter some protest, Tamara cut him off, addressing the air around them, calling for the ghosts in the ether.

"Horatio! Byron! Show yourselves!"

After the merest pause, the two ghosts materialized in the middle of the kitchen, a familiar discordant jangle accompanying their manifestation. Horatio was in the midst of complaining about being dragged away from the pub, where no doubt he had been in the midst of recounting some glorious tale to some of his spectral comrades. He did so enjoy reliving his greatest battles as a navy man.

On the other hand, the ghost of George Gordon, Lord Byron, beloved and debauched poet, seemed nothing but pleased to be pulled away from his nightly duty. He had been guarding Oblis, regaling him with odes dedicated to love, which he composed solely for the purpose of tormenting the demon. Some of Byron's greatest works had been posthumous.

And, Tamara thought, *some of his filthiest, as well.*

Along with the specter of Britain's warrior queen, Bodicea, these two had been their staunchest allies in the greatest war of all, carrying the light against the darkness. Just before their grandfather died, he had imparted to William and Tamara his great secret, that he had been the magical Protector of Albion, mystic defender of the soul of England. The Protector had many allies in this struggle, not least of which was a host of phantoms, ghosts who loved the Empire and served her eternally.

Since his death, the ghosts had helped them to learn the duties and the tribulations of the Protectorship, and to begin to master their control over the magic that had been passed to them when Sir Ludlow Swift had been murdered by monsters in service to the darkness.

As the two spirits took shape, a snore ripped through the room, and they all turned to find Serena curled up in a tiny ball on Farris's shoulder, fast asleep, her wings wrapped tightly around her small body like a blanket. Tamara smiled at the sight and even William seemed touched.

Horatio, ever the military man, comported himself with great dignity. His miasmic form took on greater solidity and he went rigid as though at attention.

"You summoned us, Miss Swift," he said, glancing from one sibling to the other, and then back at the sheepish Farris.

Tamara nodded. "Trouble brews in Cornwall. We must travel there at once in search of fairy girls who've either vanished or been taken. At least one has already been murdered. Dark forces are at work."

Byron rolled his eyes and gave a dramatic sigh. "What, Cornwall *again*? I feel as if we were just there. I hope there are no babies involved this time."

William smiled tiredly. Tamara ignored him, piqued by his intractable nature.

"We ought to leave as soon as possible," she said. "Perhaps it's not quite as dire as it sounds, but it's best to make certain. And it couldn't hurt to improve our relationship with the fairies. We ought to be allies, but thus far they have looked upon us doubtfully."

"Fairies?" Horatio repeated. "Not that lot."

"Indeed," William agreed dryly. "The missing girls are of that magical persuasion."

"Which does nothing to lessen their plight, Will!" Tamara said curtly. She hated the disdainful way he spoke of the missing fairies, as if they were of less importance than humans. "One girl has already been murdered, or have you ignored that bit?"

Her brother shook his head with a sigh. "Tam, sprites are capricious at best. If a fairy girl has died, I grieve for those who loved her. But we can't know what transpires there."

"No, we can't . . . unless we go and find out for ourselves," she chided him.

"Lord, help me," William sighed. He turned on his heel. Tamara watched as he left the room, closing the door with a slam behind him.

Byron turned to Tamara.

"What in the world was *that* all about?"

Tamara shrugged helplessly before turning and following her brother out of the kitchen. Her irritation grew as she was forced to pursue him, calling after him as he stalked down the hall toward the wide stairway that led up to the second floor.

When she was nearly upon him, William turned around, and his face was bright red.

"Yes?" he said.

Tamara clenched her jaw, breathing slowly to get hold of herself. How often had they fought? *Often enough,* she thought, *that I have learned a bit about dealing with my brother.*

She pulled her robe tightly around her shoulders, since the hallway was particularly cold. "Much as I am disappointed with your decision, I thought I ought to apologize for calling you an ass."

He glared at her.

"Now? Now, you apologize. Of course. You think it's perfectly all right to embarrass me in front of Farris and his . . . friend, not to mention Byron and Horatio, and then you think a simple 'I'm sorry' will absolve you?"

"Sometimes it seems as if you think I exist only to provide you with a dramatic foil, Tamara. That you can speak to me however you like, no matter that I *am* your older brother, and as such the head of this household. That I am about to be married, even—"

Tamara snorted. "Just because you and your precious Sophia gad about this house like a pair of lovesick rabbits—"

She cut her own words off, and her face flushed warmly. She hated fighting with him. More and more these days, they had been at odds. She supposed it had as much to do with their burgeoning social lives as it did with the overwhelming responsibility of their role as the Protectors of Albion. Still, she missed the closeness they had once shared, before Sophia Winchell had invaded their lives.

I intended to apologize, she thought miserably. *And now I've succeeded in adding insult to injury.*

"Sophia is my betrothed, Tamara, and as such, should be afforded the utmost respect—"

Tamara squeezed her hands into fists, trying desperately to control herself. Her fingernails dug into her palms. She had been born with a quick temper but this verged on the ridiculous. As her magical ability grew, so did her volatility. Only of late had she noticed the connection, but as time passed she found herself less and less able to rein in her emotions.

Still, she had to try.

"I meant her no disrespect, William. I was only trying to apologize. Please—"

William seemed on the edge of accepting her apology, and he remained silent, his lips pursed. But then he shook his head, apparently determined to pay her back in kind.

"You had John Haversham to the house again, didn't you?"

Tamara blinked in surprise, but did not answer, unsure where the question was leading. William only smiled smugly, nostrils flaring as though speaking John's name was repugnant to him, even though the two had formed a begrudging friendship.

Yet she was well aware that any truce between the two was jeopardized by the time she spent with Haversham. William could not trust him. Tamara knew she ought not to do so, either, but she could not stop her heart. William had grown ever more wary of her infatuation with the man, no matter that Haversham showed damnably little romantic inclination toward her.

"What business is that of yours?" she countered.

"What . . . what *business*?" he sputtered furiously. "The business of Ludlow House, of course, of the Swift family, and of the honor of your good name, sister, all of which are my responsibility for as long as Father is unable to bear that burden. I'm certain you wish his release from the demon's influence just as much as I do, but until then, it is *all* my business. And I don't think it's appropriate to include John Haversham in that business. I would appreciate it if you would not invite him to Ludlow House in the future."

Tamara glared at him. "How *dare* you? If I wish to have him as my guest, whether in courtship or in friendship, I will certainly do so. This is my home, too."

Her brother sighed and shook his head. "I know you think that because he has helped us in the past, and because he is a member of the Algernon Club, he is our friend. But he spied upon us on behalf of the club, Tam. Regardless of the intentions he voices, you must not forget that. And you have no right to include him in matters relating to the Protectorship of Albion. He is only after one thing from you, Tamara. I refuse to believe you cannot see that."

"One thing? And what might that be?" Tamara asked through gritted teeth. "You're a bloody fool, Will. John's had ample opportunity to seduce me, if that was his intention. If he spends his time with me under false pretenses, I assure you it is as an observer for the dabbling magicians of the Algernon Club. And if that is the case, then so be it. I enjoy his company. Certainly I prefer it to yours. And as you are so free with your tongue this evening, brother, I'll joust with you, if that's your wish. Truth for truth. Perception for perception.

"You may be my elder, and society may demand that I defer to your *supposed* wisdom and judgment, but your taste in companions is no better than mine. We all know what a slatternly creature Sophia Winchell is, and how she has seduced your mind, *as well as your body.*"

William flushed pink, then deep red again, and fumed in silence. Tamara had never seen him so livid. Even the tips of his ears were burning with anger and embarrassment. For her to announce—to *denounce*—his dalliance with Sophia was the worst kind of slap to his sense of propriety.

Tamara had gone too far, she knew it, but there was no way to take back the words. The truth was not so clear. Sophia had never been quite as terrible as Tamara so often painted her.

William glared at her, anger like a mask on his face. She could see him trying to control it, tamp it down so that it did not overwhelm him.

"Haversham is a rogue," he said, his lips tight, his voice flat. "When it suits him, he will take you to his bed, as long as he has use for you. You are a font of knowledge, Tam, about us, about the ghosts. He will use you and think nothing of it.

"You are *nothing* to him, Tamara," he added.

The words stung, even more so because she could not be completely certain that William was wrong. Yes, John was a scoundrel, but she could not believe that he meant her ill. He had been nothing but kind, a true gentleman, in her presence. But always there seemed a distance between them, and there could be no doubt that he had done questionable things in service to the Algernon Club.

If only she could see into his heart and know what he truly felt.

"Sophia has a good heart," William went on. "She may not be exactly what you would like for me, but I love her, Tam, and she loves me. She doesn't trust John—her own cousin—and worries for you whenever you're in his company. Does that not mean something to you?"

Tamara wanted to stop, wanted to make peace with the brother she dearly loved, but found that she could not. If William had merely continued to express his own concern, the fire in her might have died and they could have spoken calmly, as brother and sister should. But now she had to worry what Sophia thought, as though the girl was some sort of new stepmother? The very idea repulsed her.

Tamara could not keep silent. Her sharp tongue would not allow it.

"This world is not measured by the moral compass of Sophia Winchell, William, and I thank God for that. If she disapproves of

John's behavior, she does so only when it's convenient. Honesty is not *her* strong suit either, Will."

William flinched.

"You are callous and cruel and sometimes very stupid, Tamara," he replied. "Let's allow silence to reign for a time within these walls, shall we? Conversation with you brings only pain and sadness."

William did not stay for her reply. He turned and took the wide, wooden steps two at a time. She watched him go, but this time she did not follow. When he hit the first-floor landing, Tamara heard him stomping across the wooden hallway, all the way back to his bedroom.

Upstairs, the bedroom door slammed, and she heard no more.

With a sigh, Tamara sat on the bottom step and buried her face in her hands. For the very first time in her life, she realized that she was alone. Philosophically, she had known this was the case for quite some time, but it wasn't until now that it had become real in her own mind. Without William, she had nothing but her own wits to guide and protect her.

No, her brother did not belong to her anymore. It stung, this revelation, but in her heart she knew that it was the way things were meant to be. They could not remain best friends forever. They both had to grow up someday, to find out what the world held for them, to fall in love and raise families. William was the elder, and a man, so it only made sense that it all would happen to him first.

Yet she wondered if such a life would ever find her, or if she would haunt these halls eternally, as much a ghost in Ludlow House as Horatio or Byron, though she still lived.

Her relationship with William was changing, and Tamara pondered now where those changes would lead them as siblings and as the Protectors of Albion.

She found that she had no answer.

～

Sᴏᴘʜɪᴀ sᴛᴏᴏᴅ ʙʏ ᴛʜᴇ ᴛᴏᴘ of the steps, her face wet with tears. She had moved back into the shadows, hiding herself as William stormed up the stairs and back into his room.

She had heard every word that Tamara had said. *Every nasty, mean, hateful thing.* She had thought they were becoming friends, sisters even. But now she knew that was not true. Tamara was not her friend.

She hates me.

Sophia wiped away the last of her tears, and stepped back into the shadows.

There's only one person I can speak with. Only one person who will understand.

Four

The wood spoke to him.

Richard Kirk's father had been a mason, and he had wanted his son to take up that craft. But the thin, quiet young man was ill suited to masonry. He admired the ability to build with stone, to construct a hearth or an arch, a wall or an entire home. Yet he felt nothing when he touched stone. It was cold and hard and did not retain the passion of humanity the way so many other objects did. Certainly it had no personality of its own.

His father would have argued, if Richard had ever spoken his heart. So he did not. Instead he quietly asserted his preference and endured the old man's indignation. It was Richard's good fortune that his uncle Norman was a furniture maker—considered by many to be the finest in all of Cornwall—and had offered to take him on as an apprentice.

The furniture shop was on the outskirts of Camelford, near enough to the river that when he paused to rest in his work, Richard could hear the ripple of the water passing by. He preferred a solitary life and so the distance from the center of town suited him. Too many people around meant that he was sure to touch something filled with emotion, and then it would happen . . . those emotions would enter him and he would have a window into the secret heart of the owner of that object.

It had happened first when he was only a boy and a touch of his mother's brooch had shown him images of the generations of women who had owned it before her. Yet the brooch had often been worn with a silver ring, and that had long been lost. Until Richard *felt* it, and told his mother where she might find the heirloom.

Even just a brush of his fingers often enabled him to "read" an object, know things about it. He had found Mrs. Wade's dog, Pansy, one autumn, simply by touching the chair upon which she often slept. Pansy had gone wandering and come across something wild. Badly wounded, she had lain by the river, bleeding, unable to come home.

Until Richard found her.

He had been nine years old at the time. His mother had called it a gift. His father had pretended it existed not at all, and afterward did his best to pretend Richard did not exist, either.

Uncle Norman never said a judgmental word to his brother, but Richard was content to see the disapproval that registered in the man's eyes. At times his grim expression flared with utter contempt for his brother, but otherwise he was kind and gentle, in deed and in word. From the moment, nearly two years before, that he had agreed to take on Richard as his apprentice, Uncle Norman had proclaimed him a natural woodworker, joyfully guiding the boy in his education.

And from that first day, the wood had spoken to Richard. Sometimes, it even sang. All this afternoon he had been in the workshop, toiling on a cradle for Walter and Lucille Broward, who had a baby due later in the month. If the Browards had known that a mere apprentice had done the lion's share of the work on the cradle—for which they were paying handsomely—they probably would have been furious. But Uncle Norman was aware that there were certain types of furniture for which Richard had a special affinity. Cradles, headboards and footboards for marriage beds, and dining tables in particular. Whenever he worked on such things, the finished product was superior even to what Uncle Norman could have made.

His uncle never pressed him to explain, and Richard was glad.

How would he have explained the way the wood spoke to him?

All through the afternoon and into the early evening he worked steadily. Uncle Norman had been crafting a cabinet for another customer, but at some point he had set his tools aside and told Richard he was closing up shop for the night and going up to the house. He urged the young man to go home, but Richard was communing with the wood and could not tear himself away. There was an image in his mind of what the final piece of the cradle—the headboard—would look like, and he dared not let it fade before carving it into the wood.

So he was alone now. The deep rush of the river and the whisper of the wind were his only company, save for the occasional noise of a rider on horseback going by, or a carriage rattling toward town.

He touched the wood, ran his fingers along the smooth planes on top of the headboard. With his eyes closed, he pictured a mother looking down into the cradle as she rocked her baby girl to sleep, humming a lullaby. It wasn't merely his imagination, he was sure of that. His younger sister, Sally, had suggested to him that he had a bit of fairy blood, but he lent no credence to the idea. Richard had never seen a fairy, nor a sprite, nor any of the magical creatures that were supposed to live in the forest, and he was not at all sure they existed.

But one glance in a looking glass told him all he needed to know of his bloodline. To his regret, he was an awkward, nearly homely boy, with only his mother's soft eyes to counter the otherwise precise re-creation of his father's unpleasant countenance.

Fairies, real or not, were meant to be beautiful.

No, he was all too ordinary. Or he would have been, if not for the touch he had, and for the whisper of the wood in his heart.

Richard opened his eyes and studied his handiwork. In the light of a lantern that hung from a hook above his workbench, the finer detail he had carved into the headboard was blurred by shadow, yet with his fingers touching the wood he did not need more light.

A smile touched his lips. The Browards' baby girl—*Constance,* he thought, *they'll name her Constance*—was going to be happy in this cradle. The wood was warm and soft and the flowers he had carved into it would make the baby smile.

He could almost see her face.

A noise reached him. Richard blinked and glanced around, wondering what had caused the disturbance. Then he heard it again. A voice, calling his name, tense and alarmed.

He stood away from the workbench, breaking contact with the wood. Regret flooded him instantly and he looked back at the unfinished cradle, at the headboard that remained incomplete.

Would he have so clear an idea of what it ought to look like tomorrow? Surely not. The wood still would resonate with the shape it was destined to take, but some of the intricate details might be lost.

Richard sighed. He would do his best, as always.

Again he heard his name, and this time it was shouted. He became alarmed, and stepped quickly to the heavy oaken door, but it swung open before he reached it, and Uncle Norman stood on the threshold, staring at him, urgency and sorrow etched upon his face as though carved in hard wood.

"Richard!"

"What is it, uncle?"

"Your sister, lad. Sally's gone missing."

～

THE WORD PASSED SWIFTLY. Within half an hour, dozens of men had taken to the fields around the Kirk house and begun to spread into the forest, searching for Sally with lanterns held high. Peter David brought hunting dogs along, and their baying could be heard echoing amid the trees. The night was clear, the moon was bright, and though an undercurrent of fear ran through all of Camelford, it was laced with hope. After all, the girl had been gone two hours, no more.

Any other time, Sally Kirk's disappearance would have been attributed to a tryst, or even elopement. She was fifteen, after all, and such things happened. But the Newcomb girl had disappeared only two nights earlier. There had been those—her employer in particular—who believed Holly Newcomb had run off with a traveler passing through Camelford. But surely two girls in three nights was more than coincidence.

When Richard and his uncle Norman arrived at the house, several men were standing at the edge of the property, near the woods. Voices called from within the trees, and lights flickered and bobbed in the darkness of the forest as the search went on.

Richard ran to the door, Uncle Norman hurrying as best he could to keep up.

"Mother!" he shouted, rushing in. "Mother, where are you?"

She appeared from the kitchen, hands twisted nervously in her apron. With the turn the night had taken, she had never had a moment to remove it. Her face was wan and thin, her eyes haunted.

"Richard," she said. And her mouth pursed as though she'd eaten something sour. "Our Sally . . . we were baking scones and the horses began to neigh. You know Sally and those horses. They might be good for nothing save pulling a cart, but they were the joy of her heart. She . . . she went out to see to them, try to calm them a bit.

"I heard a terrible noise then, a shriek, but it wasn't Sally, son. It was the horses. Never heard an animal scream like that before. I sent your father out to see to them and look after Sally, but she'd . . . she'd *gone.*"

His mother bit her lip and a single tear streaked her left cheek. She wiped it swiftly away, as though ashamed.

"Give me her hairbrush," he said.

His mother frowned. "What are you on about? She's gone, Richard. Sally, out there somewhere, on her own. Some ruffian's got his hands on her, mark me. Your father's out in the woods now, trying to find the trail. You've got to go help him. Try to—"

"Ellie, stop," Uncle Norman said, and there was such taut confidence in his voice that she went silent immediately.

"Norman?" she asked a moment later, as though she'd lost her way.

"Richard's touch, Ellie. He may be your best chance of find-ing her."

Ellie Kirk blinked as though she had just awoken. "Oh, I'm such a fool. Yes, of course." With a new kindness, a sweet relief, she gazed at Richard. "Let me just get her brush, then, as you say."

They waited in the parlor. Richard could not seem to focus his vision. His breath came too quickly and he felt his pulse throbbing in his temples. Despite his father's contempt, he had never hated living in this house, thanks to his mother's sweet patience and Sally's good humor. His sister adored him, and Richard knew it well.

A strong hand clutched his shoulder. "We'll find her, Richard."

He turned toward his uncle, reassured, as always, by the sheer goodness of the man. How his uncle and father could be brothers was beyond his capacity to understand, but he was forever grateful for the one, and took the other as his penance for whatever sins he might have committed.

"If anything were to happen . . ."

"We'll find her," Uncle Norman repeated, blue eyes clear and cool, soothing. "The night the Newcomb girl went missing, her ab-sence wasn't noted till morning. Sally can't have gotten far."

Richard nodded, holding on to that reassurance as tightly as he could. A moment later his mother returned and he could see hope and fear and curiosity all at war upon her features.

"Here you are, love," she said, handing over Sally's hairbrush.

No mention was made of what she expected him to do with it. In all the years since that first time, she'd only ever referenced what she called his gift in a vague fashion, and had never directly asked him to use it. If she had lost something, she might tell him, and idly wonder aloud how she would ever find it again, but she had never outright asked for his help.

On this night, though she had lost what was most precious in the world to her, she still could not bring herself to speak of it plainly, as though it made her afraid.

Richard did not need to be asked.

He took the brush eagerly and clutched it in his hands. It felt warm to him and his mind was filled immediately with images of Sally, humming to herself as she sat before her mirror, brushing her hair. He saw ribbons and bows and felt the soft comfort of her bed. Heard her laughter. Knew, suddenly, that she had kept her eye on Johnny Miller, the merchant's son, for some time.

Barely aware he was doing it, he walked toward the door. His mother and Uncle Norman followed in silence. She had her hands up beside him, as though afraid he might fall and damage himself, her porcelain, brittle young man.

Outside, he started first toward the small outbuilding where the horses were stabled and the cart was maintained. A terrible loneliness touched him as he felt Sally's presence through her hairbrush. His fingers plucked at the bristles and came away with several strands of her hair.

He felt her.

Here.

Richard shuddered, weak with relief. "She's alive."

"Oh, thank the Lord," his mother said, and she began to sob. From the corner of his eye he saw her cling to Uncle Norman, weeping on his shoulder.

"Can you find her?" his uncle asked. His voice was husky.

Richard thought he could, but dared not say so. Instead he wandered about, trying to get a sense of where her presence could be felt most strongly. His touch took him to the edge of the woods.

Richard stepped into the trees and his stomach lurched, bile burning up the back of his throat. He doubled over. Fear unlike anything he had ever known surged through him, an ancient, primal thing that hurt his bones and clutched at his heart. Something dreadful, some devil out of the earth and the wood, slid into his skin like a thousand needles, and panic seized him. Richard shook uncontrollably for a moment, and then he froze.

His mouth opened in a silent scream but he could not make a sound. He felt that if he could only let the terror out, could only give voice to the horror that clawed at him, it would be all right. But he could not. His fingers gripped the brush with such force that its handle snapped.

And he wept. Silently.

With a spasm, the fear slipped from him and he collapsed to the ground, knobby roots bruising his knees beneath him. The tears that coursed down his face were strangely cold.

What he'd touched, what he'd felt, had been his sister's fear.

"Oh, Sally," he whispered.

"What is it?" Uncle Norman asked, striding toward him, grabbing him by the arm and lifting him up.

"Richard?" his mother said. "What's happened?"

He was bereft. What was he to tell her now? That he had touched Sally, that her daughter was out there somewhere, but he could not reach her? No, Richard could not inflict the truth upon her. The moment he had entered the forest he had been overwhelmed by her fear and now he could not sense her at all.

But Sally was still alive. He would join the others, catch up with his father and the other men and search for her, or for some trace of her, some *sense* of her that he could follow. The wood had always spoken to him, and he thought that perhaps, if he listened hard enough, the trees themselves might whisper the answers he sought.

"She was frightened," he admitted, only half turning to his mother, hiding his tears. "I'll find her, Mother. I will."

Then he moved deeper into the woods, brushing low branches out of his way, snapping twigs underfoot. Uncle Norman muttered some assurance to Ellie, and then followed.

That silent scream was still trapped in Richard's throat, but he would not release it yet. It was Sally's terror he had touched, and if his holding on to it meant he could somehow share it, could lessen her fear, then he would gladly hold it within him forever.

~

𝐓HE NIGHT AIR WAS FILLED WITH STARDUST, swirling on the eddies and currents of the wind. Rhosynn danced with it, pirouetting on feet that barely touched the forest floor.

Moonbeams filtered through the branches of the trees and the stardust drifted with each gust. She laughed softly and spun, weightless, into a small clearing. Once, ages and ages past, there had been magic here. She could feel it. The fabric of the curtain that hung between the human world and Faerie was so thin that she shuddered with pleasure.

"Rhosynn, *please*," Lorelle said anxiously, following her into the clearing.

With a sigh and a fond smile, Rhosynn regarded her sister. Lorelle was glorious, simply radiating joy. Or she was on other nights. This evening she was so subdued that she seemed almost human. The pale green gown she wore was sheer, and her lithe form was visible beneath as she passed through a splash of moonlight, but there wasn't a trace of sparkle around her. She walked with her hands clasped like an anxious mother, gaze darting about in search of some threat, and her step broke twigs under her weight.

The lightness of heart that was the gift of Faerie, even here in the human world, had left her.

"*Please* yourself," Rhosynn said. "Our family's lived in Cornwall for centuries. If trouble comes, I shan't run from it. And until it does, I want to laugh and dance and make mischief. Can you not understand that?"

Lorelle fixed her with a grim stare. "*If?* If trouble comes? It has already arrived, Rhos. Mellyn is dead. Tamsyn, Wenna, Aine, all missing, with no trace or trail to follow. Evil has befallen us, and—"

"And what?" Rhosynn snapped, her joyous mood crumbling. "Would you have us all abandon Stronghold?"

Lorelle came hesitantly to the center of the clearing. Skittish as a fawn, she twitched her head every few seconds, shifting her gaze to a different part of the forest around them as though a threat lurked behind every tree.

"Not all. Only we two. Something is hunting us in our own home, in our own wood. If you would go with me, I would fly from here on the morrow."

Rhosynn crossed her arms over her tiny breasts, the midnight blue of her gossamer gown dark as a starless evening sky. "You shame me, sister, and yourself. Whatever enemies lurk in the darkness, we cannot run from them or they have won before the war has even begun. No, I shall not leave the wood. You'll have to choose which you fear more: going without me or remaining here."

With an angry twist of her lips, Lorelle spun away and marched halfway across the clearing, back the way they'd come. Then she paused, hesitated a moment, and turned to cast a pleading glance back at Rhosynn.

"All right, we stay," she surrendered. "But must we be so foolhardy? Something stalks this forest, yet you wander the wood and delight in the stardust as though no threat exists. I know your heart, Rhos. I know that it is anger and defiance that drive you now, but it is arrogant and foolish to tempt fate so."

A breeze rustled the leaves and swirled stardust through the clearing. Rhosynn shook her head, laughing softly, and started back into the thick of the woods. Lorelle followed quickly, afraid to lose sight of her.

"It isn't funny," she insisted.

Rhosynn sighed and slowed her pace. She reached back and took her sister's hand, their fingers twining. Side by side they went through the trees and at last some of the weight seemed to lift from Lorelle, for her footfalls made no sound, nor did they leave any trace upon the ground.

"I agree," Rhosynn said softly. "There is nothing at all funny about what has happened. But still I will not hide. If we have secret enemies in the forest, I *dare* them to come for me. I shall fight them with tooth and claw if I must. The others at the Stronghold court have been seeking our missing for days, with no sign. I grow angry and frustrated. I want to see these enemies, to wrap my hands round their throats.

"Let them come, Lorelle. And until they do, I will take my joy from the wood as I always have, and secret enemies be damned."

Rhosynn paused, troubled by the grim conversation, and turned to Lorelle. Gently she reached up to touch her sister's face, and stardust shimmered from her fingertips, illuminating Lorelle's elegant beauty.

"Smile, dear one."

Lorelle nodded slowly, and a smile blossomed upon her face. It was nevertheless a troubled smile.

Rhosynn laughed giddily and took her hand again, and the two of them began to run through the woods, dancing and darting around trees. Night birds sang in the branches above them and soon their bare, delicate feet no longer touched the ground at all and they were capering several feet above the forest floor. Rhosynn gazed lovingly into her sister's eyes and decided, in that moment, that if Lorelle truly wanted to leave Cornwall for a time, she would go along. To France or Prussia, or through the worlds to Faerie, though she thought perhaps they would feel far more like outsiders there than in some other human nation.

Soon they heard the quiet babble of the river.

The night was filled with the scent of flowers and freshwater, but there was something else as well: the aroma of passion.

"Hush," she whispered, still giddy but trying to compose herself.

Rhosynn tittered once, and then she and Lorelle were both silent. They crept through the trees and peered around the trunk of a magnificent oak. Not far away was Slaughterbridge, the very place where Arthur had slain his son, Mordred, and been slain by him in return. The earth in that place was dark with power, resonating with hate and sorrow and the blood of legend. Arthur had been human, but was still a legend nevertheless, even to those of fairy blood.

A couple was crossing the bridge, a boy and girl from Camelford, no longer children but not quite fully grown. Rhosynn held her breath watching them. Though they had not the grace of the creatures of the forest, she loved to watch humans move, to watch the way they spoke together and touched one another. A newborn colt was awkward on its feet, and humans never seemed to lose that gawkiness. Rhosynn guessed it was the weight of them, the solidity of their contact with the earth. They were tethered to it from the moment of birth, as if their flesh was aware that it would someday mix with the soil.

She loved them.

The boy took the girl by the hand and led her away from Slaughterbridge, farther from the town, to a place where the river curved and an enormous old split-trunk tree spread its boughs out across the riverbank. There in the shelter of the tree, hidden from the other side of the river, where a carriage might go by, the boy sat on the ground and the girl lay down beside him.

Rhosynn's heart quickened and she smiled at Lorelle. The sisters moved silently at the edge of the forest, their passage rustling the leaves as though they were the wind itself, a sprinkle of stardust the only evidence of their wake. When they were near enough, they arranged themselves so that they had a perfect view of the couple in the hollow beside the tree.

The girl's bodice had been undone and even now the boy slid it down her arms so that her upper body was entirely bare. Her breasts were pale and beautiful in the moonlight, nipples dark and taut. The boy kissed and caressed them, and the girl giggled shyly. Rhosynn could feel the heat of his desire deep within her and that passion made her catch her breath. Excited, she glanced at Lorelle, and she could see that her sister was flushed. Her eyes were locked upon the sight of the young lovers, as though entranced.

Rhosynn had long known that human desire had its own sort of enchantment. She was charmed by the pair, and aroused as well.

Their kisses were deeper and longer and soon the girl began to moan softly and squirm beneath the inexpert ministrations of her lover. The boy slid his hand along her bare calf and farther up beneath her dress. A small squeak of halfhearted protest escaped the girl's lips and she began to push his hand away.

No, Rhosynn thought. *The passion is risen in you, as well. You mustn't cage it.*

But the boy withdrew his hand, a disappointed look passing across his face for a moment before he smiled and began to stroke her hair and bent to kiss her again.

"This is no fun," Rhosynn whispered to Lorelle.

There was caution in her sister's eyes, but Rhosynn only smiled and raised her arms. She took a deep breath, felt herself rising from the ground, and then she spread her fingers and allowed a shower of shimmering green to sprinkle down around her.

Then she rose farther, riding the wind, and she beat her wings and flew out of the forest in the form of a nighthawk. She soared in an arc through the night sky and then glided down to the enormous split-trunk tree beneath which the lovers sprawled.

Again the boy ran his hand along the girl's bare thigh. She laughed and squeezed her legs together.

On a tree limb just above them, the nighthawk had a breathtaking view of the girl's lovely nakedness. She could smell the boy's arousal, could feel his frustration and his urgent need for release. The girl's desire was even stronger, and yet she fought against it.

Rhosynn hated to see beauty and passion denied.

The nighthawk spread her wings and stardust fell from them, swirling on the gentle breeze, eddying downward until it dusted the young lovers.

With a sigh, the girl opened her legs. The boy moaned with hunger and surprise as he was allowed, at last, to touch her. The girl arched her back and her right hand caressed the boy's chest and then moved down to clutch at the thickening pressure at the crotch of his trousers. Hurriedly, he reached down and replaced her hand with his own, pushing his garment down so that she could reach her goal.

Burning with her own passion, the nighthawk took flight again. The leaves rustled with her passing but the lovers noticed nothing, caught up as they were in their desire and the magic of a sprinkle of stardust.

When the hawk alighted upon the forest floor, only inches from the place she had stood previously, she was Rhosynn of Stronghold once again. Her heart beat wildly with mischief and lust and she looked for Lorelle, knowing her sister would share her fascination with the humans' lovemaking.

Rhosynn frowned.

Lorelle had gone.

At first she was hurt, and becoming angry. She began to search the trees for some sign of her sister's departure, thinking Lorelle had allowed herself to grow anxious again and fled back to Stronghold.

But there was no sign of Lorelle at all, as though she had never been there to begin with. Rhosynn was confused and for the first time her heart fluttered with concern.

Then she caught the scent of her sister's fear, and she knew that Lorelle had not fled at all. Panic rose within her.

The enemy had taken her.

With the sounds of human passion whispering through the trees, Rhosynn sank to her knees in the forest and wept, her bravado scattered in the whispering wind.

∼

Silence had reigned all the long day at Ludlow House, and now that night had fallen, it deepened.

Tamara sat at the writing desk in the room she would always think of as her grandfather's study, no matter how much time passed since his demise. There was fresh paper before her, but the ink was drying on the tip of her pen. She had spent much of the day laying plans for her departure to Cornwall, and then had retreated to the study late in the afternoon. In the hours since, she had written two and a half pages of "The Poison Parchment," a new penny dreadful she had begun nearly a month past and upon which she had made little progress, even before today.

Two and a half halting, frustrating pages.

Pitiful.

Tamara consoled herself with the knowledge that there were other things on her mind, that she ought to forgive herself a certain amount of distraction. But her writing was meant to be an escape from such things, and her frustration stemmed from disappointment that she had been unable to settle her nerves enough to become lost in the story.

She took a deep breath, sat up straighter in her chair, looped a stray lock of hair behind her ear, and dipped the pen into her ink bottle again, freshening it. The hero of her story, Thomas St. James, had just discovered an ancient parchment among the belongings of a man who had died most mysteriously. Her intention had been that the moment St. James touched the parchment, some supernatural guardian would appear and attack him, attempting to destroy him before he could gain possession of the document. But though she wracked her brain, she was unable to determine what sort of creature she wished to set against her hero. Something subtle, if possible, so as not to alienate readers entirely.

Subtlety be damned, she thought now. Tamara had encountered enough horrors in the flesh that she ought to be able to describe them well enough. *Rakshasa. Oh, yes, they'll do just fine.* And the memory was fresh.

The moment she set pen to paper there came a rap at the door and her hand jumped, scrawling a smear of fresh ink upon the page. Tamara closed her eyes, gritted her teeth, and then set the pen aside.

"Come."

The door swung open, but William stood on the threshold, appearing reluctant to enter. He wore a look of practiced indifference.

"Good evening, Tamara."

"William." She let the irritation that lingered after their fight enter her voice.

He ignored her tone. "Have all of the preparations been completed for your journey to Cornwall?"

"I'm quite sure Farris has everything in order by now. Of course, Bodicea and Serena will accompany me, but they require no preparation. As for Farris, I expect you'll manage to get by without him during our absence."

William shrugged, as if distracted. "It can't be helped, can it?"

"No. No, it can't."

He nodded slowly, his tension evident in even the smallest of motions. "I truly regret that I am unable to accompany you. But with the wedding coming on so soon, I am more determined than ever to find a way to exorcise the demon from Father's soul."

A look of concern passed across his face. "So many times, I have thought we had found the answer. The other day, Horatio and I ran across a promising passage in *The Lesser Key of Solomon* unlike any other spell our research has uncovered. It took minutes before I realized it was a spell not for exorcising a demon, but for driving out a human soul! Can you imagine if we'd attempted that spell haphazardly, out of desperation, driven out Father's soul and left the demon in residence?"

"My God," Tamara whispered. "Father would be gone forever."

William ran his hands through his hair in frustration and then turned to her. "I cannot imagine my wedding without him, Tam."

Tamara held her breath. All day she had nurtured her fury at

William, and she could not deny feeling a certain relish in that spiteful simmering. Now a wave of guilt went through her.

"I know, Will. And I do understand. From what you've said, and what Horatio has told me, I believe you're close to finally driving Oblis out and returning Father to us. I dare not allow myself to hope, but it would be wonderful to have him back with us again, to have him as master of this house. No, you're doing precisely the right thing. Farris will look out for me in Cornwall."

William thrust his hands into his pockets. He strode into the room, but walked away from her toward a window in the far wall.

"I have no doubt. And if trouble arises, you have only to translocate back to London and fetch me, and I shall join you in the north immediately."

He stared out at the night as though searching for something, but whatever it was, William did not seem to find it.

"I'm certain we'll be fine," Tamara said. "Though it would be much simpler if translocation magic allowed us to transport others along with us. On the other hand, I daresay that Farris, stalwart as he is, might be undone by the experience."

William did not respond. Tamara rose from her chair, studying him closely.

"Is something else troubling you?"

The answer seemed obvious. Brother and sister both were troubled by the fight they'd had earlier in the day, but Tamara did not want to be the one to reopen the wound. She was not yet sufficiently calmed to return to their debate without the risk of immediately becoming angry.

William, though . . .

From his manner, she thought his trouble might be something else entirely.

"Father's condition is not the only reason I must remain behind. And, to be honest, my disapproval of Mr. Haversham was not the only thing that had me on edge before."

Tamara rested her hand upon the back of her chair. She wished to comfort him, but was still too stung by their earlier exchange to make any such overture.

"Of course," she said, keeping her tone neutral. "With the wedding approaching, Sophia has every right to want you here in London. Already she is put out that you have not been more involved with the planning. Were you to accompany me—"

William turned and regarded her grimly. "There is that, yes. But something more, as well. You know that of late I have been spending more time than usual at Threadneedle Street."

"Swift's of London is your responsibility, William. You have a great many duties, and they have been heaped upon you just recently. You do your best to attend to them all. I'm certain Sophia will come to realize that."

"It isn't just the business of the bank that has kept me long away from the house. Or it is, but not ordinary business, to be sure. I have kept this entirely secret. Of the staff, only Harold and Victoria are aware. Along with the police, of course."

Tamara touched a hand to her lips.

"The police? Why? What's happened?"

"There's a thief, Tam. For weeks we have suffered small losses. Yet the total has begun to accumulate to a tidy sum. We have tried a dozen ways to secure the place and to lay a trap for the perpetrator, and yet this bold thief continues to thwart us, stealing gold and jewels from the vault. With all of the precautions I have taken, I am beginning to think that there might be only one possible answer."

"Yes, of course," Tamara said, brows knitted in thought. "Magic."

"Exactly. I could be wrong, but I cannot discover another explanation. I thought it only the business of the bank until now. But if there is indeed magic involved, then we may have to take a more direct approach to solving this mystery."

"I can see why it troubles you so," she said, nodding. "And, of course, that you have no choice but to remain in London for the moment. If it has not been resolved by the time I return from Cornwall, we'll work together on it then."

William let out a breath of air, perhaps a fraction of his tension alleviated. "I appreciate your understanding. Our lives have become quite complex of late."

"Indeed they have."

"Still, I will worry about you, Tam. Bodicea is formidable, of course, but Farris—stout as he is—is only a man. We have no idea what you will encounter in Cornwall. I wish I could accompany you."

"You cannot be in two places at once," Tamara said. "And, truly, I will be fine. But if you really are concerned, and Nigel is unavailable, perhaps I ought to ask . . ."

She paused, letting the words trail off. Tamara had been about to suggest she invite John Haversham along, but given the row she and William had had, she thought better of it.

Too late, however.

William glared at her. "You amaze me, Tam. Truly, you do. Don't think I don't know what you were about to suggest. How could you even consider it? Are we to engage in this duel endlessly? Lord, how tired I am of hearing the name John Haversham."

Her fingernails scratched the back of the chair as she gripped it.

"Hold your tongue, William, before you say something more that you'll regret. You lashed out at me for my feelings about Sophia, insisting that she was the woman you loved, that you would marry. Well, perhaps John and I have not quite reached that point as yet, but if I'm to give you the freedom to love as you will, you must do the same for me."

He let out a sigh of frustration and spun on his heel, turning back to the window. When he spoke again, he did not look at her.

"Be that as it may, you know how disgustingly inappropriate it would be for Haversham to travel with you to Cornwall. This is a conversation we should not even be having."

The worst part of it all for Tamara was that he was right. For her to travel together with John Haversham to some country village in Cornwall would be scandalous indeed. As independent as she fancied herself, Tamara would not wish to bring such shame upon her family, or to her name.

Still it rankled her, and she would not allow William the satisfaction.

"Why do you hate him so?"

William turned, and his voice had softened. "I don't hate him, Tam. I simply do not trust him."

"But why?" she demanded.

"For many reasons, not least of which is that—as we both know—he is an accomplished thief."

Tamara narrowed her eyes, nostrils flaring. Her skin prickled and a sphere of blue energy began to crackle around her free hand. The way William held her gaze, she did not have to ask him to clarify further.

"You suspect him as the thief who is plaguing the bank."

"The thought has crossed my mind."

She raised her hand, magical energy roiling around her fingers. "You would do well to leave me now, William. By the time I return from Cornwall, perhaps the urge to hurt you will have passed."

He stared at her for a moment, his grave expression revealing nothing. Then he strode from the room, leaving the door hanging open behind him. For a time she stared into the corridor after him, wondering if he would return and knowing that if he did, it would not be to apologize.

Tamara wished she were leaving for Cornwall this very minute, instead of tomorrow. In all her life she had never been more eager to leave Ludlow House.

Tonight, she would rather have been anywhere else in the world.

～

BETSY PICKED HER WAY through a tangle of tree roots, her thick hide boots keeping her feet safe and unharmed. She had spent many an afternoon amid the trees, and was familiar enough with her surroundings to know how to keep to the path.

Today, she was out in the woods on an errand for her mother, her job to gather the plants and herbs needed for mother's home-made remedies. Folk from all over came to their door to receive her homespun cures. Her mother's amazing curative abilities were something Betsy was very proud of. There wasn't another midwife in the county who was half as talented as Sarah Harper.

Betsy was always more than happy to be sent upon such er-rands because it meant an entire day free from housework. She would much rather spend that time rambling the woods that sur-rounded Camelford.

Betsy was no dainty flower. She was as fierce a fighter as any of her five brothers, and had spent as much of her childhood in the woods running and playing with the boys as she had indoors. Even now, almost a young woman, she hated being cooped up inside. Neither was she any good at the sort of tasks as might be assigned to her around the house. She burned her fingers on the lye they used to make soap, and just the other day had cut her thumb as she chopped onions and potatoes for the family's meager stew.

During her outdoor wanderings, Betsy lost many an hour discovering sweet hidden springs and hollowed-out trees in which to curl up and daydream. On these excursions, she found herself surrounded by curious wildlife, small creatures that watched her every move to determine if she was friend or foe.

Deep in the woods, it was cooler than Betsy had expected. She stopped for a moment by an upturned tree stump to find the woolen cape she had brought along. She had shoved it to the bottom of the coarse burlap bag her mother had given her in which to gather herbs. The cape hadn't seemed necessary that morning, but she had brought it anyway, just in case. Now she was glad for its warmth as she slipped it over her broad shoulders.

Intent on fastening the cape, she didn't notice anything amiss until a powerful hand gripped her shoulder and pulled her backward, dragging her away from the stump and her bag.

With a cry of fright and anger, Betsy reached back, trying to get a hold of her assailant, but her hand was batted away. Bones cracked in her shoulder and her left arm fell to her side, useless. Never had she felt such pain. Her vision swam black before her eyes.

Betsy gritted her teeth, refusing to allow unconsciousness to claim her. She fought the blackness and the wave of nausea that came over her.

"No!" she screamed, the word a war cry. She dug her heels in, making it hard for her attacker to continue dragging her backward. She turned her head to the right and sank her teeth into the only exposed bit of flesh she could find: the attacker's hand. Her assailant shrieked, and stopped midstride, nearly yanking Betsy off her feet.

Betsy used her good arm to elbow her attacker in the gut, and suddenly she was free. Stumbling forward, she tripped on an exposed tree root. She fell forward onto her useless left arm, her forehead slamming into the ground with a sickening thud.

Dazed, she opened her eyes, but all she could see was her attacker, a hideous shape wrapped in a black cloak, its face set in a grotesque rictus.

A demon, she thought, risen from Hell to steal her soul.

"You will not have me!" Betsy cried, having found her voice once again. Using her right arm, she began to drag herself over to the stump.

She grabbed the bag and spilled its contents onto the dirt, grasping for the one thing she knew would save her. Even as the demon came upon her again, standing over her, glaring down with cruel hatred, Betsy thrust the monkshood flowers into her mouth. The little leaves on the stem tasted earthy and bitter, and little bits of dirt still clung to the herb, making it hard for Betsy to force herself to swallow.

It took only a moment for the demon to realize what she had done. It let out a terrific howl of anger and snatched her up by a fistful of her clothing.

The demon took flight, carrying her high above the trees, soaring across the night sky. Perhaps it thought to still take her soul, but Betsy smiled to herself as the dizziness of flight enveloped her.

It was too late. The poison had begun its work, and its effects were irreversible. The demon would be denied.

Her throat began to swell and her breathing grew labored. As Betsy's vision blurred, she blinked back tears of terror and pain. Her body grew numb, each breath bringing her closer to death. The creature howled in disappointment. She gazed blankly down at the village below, at the woods and the craggy tors atop the hills, at the moors in the distance.

She wondered if she could have seen the ocean from here.

As she breathed her last, she felt the demon let her go.

Betsy felt as though her soul were flying as the ground rushed up toward her.

Five

On the morning of her journey, Tamara rose before the sun had even begun its trajectory across the sky. She breakfasted before either William or Sophia had lifted an eyelid, and packed her valise and trunk within half an hour of that. Tamara hated fighting with William, but she did not think she would be willing to concede anything to him this morning, not while she still felt so angry.

Now she stood in the front hall surveying her handiwork. Normally her lady's maid, Martha, would have seen to the packing of her things for the journey, but Tamara had not asked for her assistance. As alone as she felt, it seemed only right and a kind of melancholy comfort to attend to the task herself. It had also afforded her the opportunity to practice a bit of magic. It required no great supernatural strength to cause her clothing, even the heavy dresses, to fly from the wardrobe to her bed.

But to fold them neatly and arrange them in her trunk . . . that required meticulous attention, great skill, and tremendous effort. Many lesser magicians—those not gifted with the vast power available to the Protectors of Albion—were wont to think that great magic must be brutal or at the very least ostentatious. But Tamara had begun to realize that in truth, sometimes the greatest magic came with nuance and subtlety.

This was excellent practice.

She actually had giggled as she worked, directing the toiletries and fancy lace-and-cotton undergarments through the air like little inanimate birds. She felt a bit like a symphony conductor, waving her arms around in time to some unheard musical score while she directed the flow of floating traffic.

"Mistress Tamara . . . ?"

She turned in time to see Farris coming through the sitting room door, carrying a small valise under each arm. He looked tired, his eyes rimmed in the coal of a sleepless night.

"Yes, Farris?"

"I wondered, miss, if this would be sufficient?" He lifted the valises a bit to display them. "It's only that I wasn't sure how long we'll be gone."

Tamara shook her head.

"Nor am I, Farris, but I think we can find a laundress wherever we venture, so long as we stay within the realms of humanity. I'm not sure how fairies launder *their* clothing, though."

This seemed to satisfy the butler, who had taken on so many roles for the Swift household. Tamara did not know what they would do without the stout and stalwart man if he ever decided to leave them. Farris seemed ever unfazed by the horrors they encountered. He acted as much like a defender of Albion as the ghosts or the Protectors themselves.

Tamara smiled at him and he gave her a polite nod, then went out the front door and toward the carriage house where the stable boy was already preparing the horses for their long journey.

She sighed and walked over to her own valise. Hoisting the bag with both hands, she managed to half carry, half drag the heavy case across the threshold and outside. It would have been proper for her to wait for one of the servants to take her bag, but more than ever Tamara wished to thwart propriety with her every action, large or small.

Once she stepped into the sunlight, she felt better. She didn't understand the magic, or the science, that made a beautiful day such a balm on a wounded soul, but it was. She stopped, setting the valise down on the marble steps, and soaked up as much sunlight as her fair skin could bear.

She wished that her mind could be as untroubled as her body, which was quite happy to remain motionless in the middle of the front drive. But her thoughts would not give her a moment's peace.

Could John Haversham really be the thief?

She knew that he had no qualms about stealing something in the name of the Algernon Club. Yet she couldn't bring herself to believe that John was some kind of petty burglar who stole just for monetary gain. It went against everything she had ascertained about the man's character. John was charming, intelligent, and compassionate, and not a little proud.

A smile came unbidden to her lips. It wasn't just the sun that warmed her. Thinking about John, no matter how well she policed the thoughts, brought a wet, warm, delicious feeling to the place between her legs. It embarrassed her to realize how entirely un-hinged she became at the mere thought of him, but the wantonness he inspired could not be denied.

"Penny for your thoughts," a voice said, startling her from her reverie. "And should you *really* be carrying such a heavy burden by yourself, Miss Swift?"

She looked up to find John Haversham standing beside her, pointing at the large valise that sat at her feet.

Heat rose and she felt her cheeks flush. He'd appeared as though summoned by her imaginings, and for a moment her fantasies seemed to merge with reality. But he was no fantasy, no illusion. Tamara took a deep breath, and hoped he could not read the emotions she knew her eyes must reveal.

"My goodness, was I really so distracted that I missed your arrival, John?"

He smiled, and her heart leaped. She liked the way his teeth sat crookedly in his wide-lipped mouth. It was enough to prove to her that he wasn't nearly as perfect as he first appeared.

"You were quite easy to startle, Tamara. You were in another world altogether."

She liked it when he was gentle with her, when he kept his ribbing at a minimum and his sharp tongue blunted. She didn't really *mind* the verbal sparring they usually engaged in, but the lovelorn woman inside of her yearned desperately to hear his honeyed adorations and passionate proclamations of love.

"And I think you're in danger of going there again," John added with a grin.

She put her girlish musings away then, and laughed.

"I suppose I had, hadn't I?" She let her words fall, then smiled up at him.

He picked up the heavy valise, and easily swung it over his shoulder.

"Where does this monster go?"

She pointed to the carriage house, then followed him as he began the short walk to the small, stone building.

"What brings you to Ludlow House so early in the day?" she asked, as she tried to keep pace with him, and failed miserably.

He slowed his gait and she quickly caught up to him. When he glanced at her she saw regret in his eyes.

"Business, I'm sorry to say. For the club."

She was surprised that anyone from the Algernon Club had business with her. She found the majority of the members to be misogynists who would rather stare at her bosom than engage her brain.

"Indeed? And the nature of this business?"

They reached the carriage house, where he set the valise down beside the open stable door and turned to appraise her.

"It has come to our attention—" he began.

She raised an eyebrow, and interrupted him.

"Don't you find it loathsome, delivering messages for that lot of effete codgers?"

He ignored her subtle jibe at his middling status in the Algernon Club, and continued.

"As I was saying, Tamara, it has come to our attention that you are harboring a wanted fugitive—"

"Excuse me? A fugitive . . . at Ludlow House? You must be joking. Where ever would I hide someone without my entire household staff, let alone William and the ghosts, discovering the person's whereabouts?" Tamara demanded.

She would not allow anyone—not even John—to accuse her in her own home.

"As you like, Tamara," John replied, returning her cold tone. "But I came today as much as friend to you as *messenger*. Lord Blackheath has been approached by a member from the north, with an appeal from the ruling council of Stronghold. They demand that the sprite Serena appear before them, and have asked our assistance. We know you have the sprite somewhere on your property—"

He paused as Farris came through the stable door, his shirt-sleeves rolled up to his elbows, his hat askew.

"Pardon me, miss," Farris said. "But I think Master William will be wanting a word with you before we go."

She groaned under her breath, and nodded.

"I'll be up to the house in a moment, Farris. Please tell William that I was just seeing a guest *out.*"

She took John's arm, guiding him away from the carriage house—and the empty stable—that at that very moment housed his missing fugitive. Serena had told them all the tale of her encounter with Giselle Ravenswood and the rest of the ruling council of Stronghold. The way the fairies treated sprites was horrid, but that did not worry Tamara overmuch. What concerned her was that they had forbidden Serena to seek aid from herself and William and now were using influence to try to retrieve Serena instead of simply coming down to London and attempting to capture her themselves.

Most fairies, as Tamara understood it, enjoyed contact with humans, and sometimes became fascinated and even enamored with them. But they preferred to encounter humans in the wild and avoided cities whenever possible.

Still, if the Council of Stronghold considered Serena a fugitive and were angry that she'd dared come to the Protectors of Albion for help, Tamara knew she could expect a very chilly reception when she arrived in Cornwall.

"John, there's a message I would like you to carry back to Lord Blackheath. Remind him that William and I are the Protectors of

Albion, and that the Algernon Club's directors have vowed to aid us in our duties. We do not now, nor shall we ever, answer to any but England herself."

"Tamara," John said reasonably, "a little bit of cooperation—"

"Shush."

He smiled. "I don't know if you've got the sprite here or not. But I told Lord Blackheath that you would never surrender her if she were."

She led him toward the end of the drive, careful to keep a steady hand on his arm. Tamara could feel the taut muscles moving under the thin fabric of his frock coat as they walked.

"Let us say only that if she were in my care, I would return her to Stronghold personally, and stand with her against those who condemned her unjustly."

John raised an eyebrow and glanced back at the carriage, laden with bags and prepared for travel.

"I see."

"I'm taking a trip to Cornwall this afternoon, John, and am unsure of when I will return. Bodicea will accompany me, and of course Farris, but I would be thrilled if you would decide to come along, as well."

Blinking in surprise, he pulled himself away from her grasp, letting her know the answer to the question even before he spoke.

"You already know my stance on the nature of our relationship, Tamara. I don't think *anyone* would find it appropriate if I were to travel with you," he said, almost primly. There was a hint of amusement behind his words, though, when he added, "*Especially* not your brother."

"My brother doesn't like you now, John, and I've no doubt he would *hate* you after that," Tamara said quietly.

John regarded her curiously, but did not immediately reply.

"Your brother has more than that reason to despise me."

There was a faraway look in his eyes. The chill in his voice shocked Tamara to the core. It was as if she were looking at another man entirely.

Someone cold and empty.

Then, as though a cloud had passed from across his features, his eyes lit up again and he smiled. "Well, then, I'd best be going. I don't think I'll get any further cooperation here today." The usual flirtatious baritone of his voice had returned.

Tamara watched him walk briskly down the drive to where his own carriage awaited.

There was something strange about him today.

∾

Swift's of London was housed in an imposing stone building. As a small child, William had been frightened of the place anytime he went to visit his father there. Its huge Doric columns supported giant marble lions that roared down at passersby from the roof's uppermost reaches. Such was London's atmosphere that the building's once pale gray exterior had become coated with so much dirt and coal smoke residue that it was almost black.

No longer a child, William found the building's stern façade more charming than frightening, and was proud that his family's bank had such a prestigious address on Threadneedle Street. He relished his position in society and found that he wanted nothing more than to settle down into matrimony with Sophia and grow old.

It was simply not to be.

William ascended the high marble stairs that led to the door, taking them one at a time. Savoring the pleasant warmth of the day, he paused for a moment. Once inside, he made his way quickly through the bank, waving a bright good morning to his employees but not stopping to pass the time with them.

Reaching the door to his office he turned to survey the bank once more, enjoying the industrious chatter and bustle of the workday. In this office, he was the center of that busy hive, and though he had not chosen this profession, he had come to appreciate elements of his responsibilities at Swift's.

William closed the door and crossed the room, taking a seat behind the heavy mahogany desk. The dark wood and thick glass, the marble and the brass, made the place a masculine stronghold. He was comfortable here. His true love and joy was architecture, a vocation he had been forced to surrender when Oblis had possessed his father. With Henry Swift unable to attend to the needs of the family business, William had stepped in. He found it challenging work, but it was not his passion.

A knock came on the door.

"Enter," William called.

The door swung inward to admit his assistant, Harold Ramsey. They had attended university together, but Ramsey had almost cherubic features and a ready smile that gave him the appearance of being several years younger than William.

"Good morning, William."

"And to you."

Harold stood in the doorway, a sheaf of papers in his hand and a curious expression on his face.

"There's a Mr. Stephen Roberts to see you. Shall I send him in?"

"Please," William replied, standing up and brushing off his trousers. He had expected Roberts at eleven. The man was early. This was a positive sign. He liked those in his employ to be punctual.

Harold closed the door behind him, giving William a few moments to collect himself. He looked around the room to make sure everything was in its place, and nodded, satisfied that all was as it should be.

When another knock came on the door, William called once more for Ramsey to enter. Harold ushered into the room a tall man with imposing features and an intelligent light in his eyes.

"Mr. Roberts, I presume," William said, stepping out from behind the desk to greet his visitor. "Do come in."

He shook hands with the stranger, then glanced at his assistant. "Thank you, Ramsey." The words were a dismissal and Harold took them as such, nodding once before turning to head back to his own desk.

"Mr. Swift," Roberts said, "a pleasure to make your acquaintance, sir." His voice was low and melodious, yet strangely unaccented. He followed William into the center of the room, taking the tall-backed leather chair that stood in front of the desk.

"I appreciate your making yourself available on such short notice, Mr. Roberts."

They sat across from each other, each man appraising the other. William once again noted how imposing were Roberts's features, the cool gray eyes punctuated by a long scar that snaked from beside his left ear down into the collar of his white shirt. He wondered how Roberts had acquired that particular beauty. It looked nasty, and extremely painful.

Catching William's gaze, the man smiled.

"A knife fight on Shadwell Street, a long time ago, when I had more ego than sense."

How odd, William thought. *There truly is no trace of an accent.*

"Are you English, Mr. Roberts?"

The man shook his head. "I was born in the Mongolian province of Darhan-Uul, but spent the majority of my childhood in Philadelphia."

"Mongolia? However did your family find itself there?"

"My father works for the American government."

Roberts did not elaborate. In fact, his stare dared William to press the subject further. It might have been best to let the matter lie, but something about the vagueness of the answer intrigued him.

"Was your father a diplomat?"

Roberts shrugged. "You could say that. Or you could say that he was a close friend of Thomas Jefferson's, and did whatever the president asked of him."

William had never met anyone who knew a president of the United States. He leaned forward in his seat, elbows on his desk.

"That's quite extraordinary."

Roberts smiled. "If you say so." He sat back in his seat, his eyes intent on William's face.

"Now that we've gone through the pleasantries, let's get down to business. I was told you had need of someone to carry out a discreet investigation into a matter of theft. Is that correct?"

William nodded. "During the past few weeks, I have noticed that things—small pieces of jewelry and the like—have begun mysteriously disappearing from our vaults. Most recently, the bank was relieved of a case full of rare gold coins. I have no idea who the culprit is, nor how he is carrying out the burglaries. Truly, it is a mystery."

"No suspects at all, then?"

"None."

"If I'm to help you, I'd like your permission to make a few discreet inquiries here at the bank."

"Of course," William said, nodding.

"I think that's all, then," Roberts said, standing. He extended his hand.

They shook rather formally. *What a curious fellow,* William thought as Roberts left the room. William had gotten the man's name from Ezekiel Ruscht, an old associate of his father's, who was also a member of the Algernon Club. Roberts had been a peeler before retiring to indulge in more exciting pursuits.

Ezekiel had called Roberts a "jolly fellow with a keen eye and an intriguing mind."

William had a hard time associating the man he had just met with the word *jolly*.

~

SOPHIA'S TROUSSEAU HAD GROWN by leaps and bounds, so that it now took up two wardrobes and an enormous trunk. She had hoped for such bounty, but with no immediate family to help and encourage her, she'd been uncertain whether she'd be able to acquire all the things she needed for married life.

What a surprise it had been when Tamara had offered to help her, taking time from her charitable works to accompany Sophia to several shops in London. Sophia had felt as though the two women were beginning to form a sisterly bond.

After last night, however, she harbored no such illusions. Tamara Swift would never like her, no matter what efforts Sophia made to ameliorate her relationship with her future sister-in-law.

This morning Sophia sat on the edge of the canopied bed in the room that was hers whenever she slept at Ludlow House, and stared into the yawning mouths of the two open wardrobes. Usually, she liked to touch everything inside, counting the assorted linens and bits of clothing and simply basking in the anticipation of her wedding, but she was too tired and depressed.

There were a great many things she was supposed to do today— she had even made a list—but she could not bring herself to do more than get dressed. She sighed, leaning back on the thick pillows that covered the top of the bed, and closed her eyes, wishing William was there to help her.

Sophia knew that he loved her and wanted to be with her, but lately he had been spending more and more time locked in his grandfather's library, looking up spells and doing research. He was obsessed with finding the spell that would finally free his father from the demon's power. She had been enthusiastic about the idea at first, encouraging him to continue his quest. She even sat with him in the library while he worked, quietly doing her needlepoint, listening to him as he mumbled foreign-sounding words under his breath.

But the whole business had taken on a sour taste after she had begun spending time with Henry. Tamara and William both insisted that he was completely under the influence of a demon called Oblis, but Sophia wasn't sure she believed he was possessed at all. To her, he just seemed like a sad old man who wasn't completely in his right mind.

Certainly there were moments when the supposed demonic influence revealed itself, but Sophia had seen people—particularly older people—afflicted by dementia in the past, and this seemed no different. She believed Henry needed and deserved the love and attention of his children instead of their pity and scorn. Yet she had said nothing of the sort to William. He and Tamara both would resent any interference on her part. Of that she was certain.

No, she would wait until all her beloved's efforts had been exhausted, and only then would she suggest that he and his sister consider whether perhaps they had been mistaken all along.

Meanwhile, she hoped to provide the mad old man as much comfort as she could.

It was entirely accidental that she had come to spend so much time in Henry Swift's presence. The ghosts all took their turns guarding the room where Henry was imprisoned, as did Nigel, Tamara, and William. Lord Byron's ghost seemed to spend more time on guard than the others, but he was also the specter most likely to abandon his post without a moment's hesitation, lured by his muses to work on some paean to love or lust, or by curiosity to spy invisibly upon the staff. Feeling guilty about his frequent vanishings, he had sought out Sophia and asked for her help to watch over Henry when he wanted a respite.

Upon her arrival at Ludlow House, Byron had been the only ghost who had seemed at all interested in befriending her. He said hello to her whenever they met, and one day in the hall had even struck up a rather long-winded conversation about ladies' undergarments. Her maid, Elvira, wanted nothing to do with the ghosts of Ludlow House, but Sophia found them fascinating. She cultivated her relationship with Byron every chance she could. If that included helping him keep watch over Henry without letting William and Tamara know that he was shirking his duties, well, she did not mind so much.

Byron, at least, seemed to feel for the old man.

Sometimes Sophia wondered if she was the only one in the household who genuinely cared about the elder Swift's welfare. She knew William loved his father, but she had recently begun to harbor the fear that his judgment might be clouded by Tamara's opinion.

Tamara was a powerful magician who also wielded great power over her brother and all of the other occupants of Ludlow House. If William's sister was foolish or misled or simply guided by an unconscious need to control him—threatened by the arrival of Sophia, the future mistress of Ludlow House—then their father might be doomed to nothing but a half-life, trapped in that horrible nursery forever.

The very thought made Sophia shudder.

Bored and miserable, Sophia stood and walked to the wardrobes containing her trousseau and quietly closed them, before turning and leaving the room. She left the door open in case Elvira came looking for her, though the chances of that were slim. Elvira *hated* Ludlow House, and spent most of her day locked in her quarters praying to be delivered from its evil. Sophia found the old woman's antics highly amusing, but she sometimes worried that one day she would wake up to find her lady's maid gone.

There was only so much a person could take, she supposed, and Elvira was very near her breaking point.

The older woman had not wanted Sophia to come to stay at Ludlow House at all. She had followed her charge grudgingly, making sure that Sophia understood the burden that had been placed upon her. Sophia suspected that Elvira knew about her comings and goings from William's room, but she never alluded to the fact.

Maybe she's storing up all her grievances so that she can leave me with a clear conscience, Sophia thought dryly.

She made her way down the hall, careful not to call too much attention to herself. She was not supposed to be in this part of the house, and Martha would shoo her away if she found her there alone. She quickly moved to the nursery door, and pushed it open without hesitation.

Byron floated by Henry's bed, a ghostly quill and parchment in his hands. He looked up from his work and gave Sophia a mischievous grin.

"My lovely lady," the ghostly poet said with a flourish, bowing from the waist. He floated toward her, his hand extended as if to take her own and raise it to his lips. Sophia appreciated the gesture, even though she knew his spectral hand would pass right through hers.

It hadn't taken very long for her to discover the limitations of contact between hosts and humans: the ghosts were ephemeral things, only able to touch human flesh or anything of the human world with great concentration, and even then only for the briefest moments.

Magical items were another thing entirely. Spirits could come into contact with anything that had a trace of magic. That was why the ghosts could fight demons and monsters without facing the same limitations they did with human beings. Sophia had often wondered just how much contact the specters might be capable of having with magicians . . . with the Protectors. Could Byron, for instance, have made love to Tamara if she would allow it?

The thought lingered in her at times, and whenever it did her face flushed with curiosity. And perhaps with other feelings as well.

Now, as the ghostly poet came toward her, pretending to walk although his feet could not touch the wooden floor, Sophia felt herself coloring.

"Hello, your lordship," she said, raising a hand to her flaring cheeks. She blew him a playful kiss.

Byron giggled happily, pretending to catch the kiss with his hand.

Beyond the ghost, Henry began to stir in bed. Sophia had been the one to suggest that he be moved from the chair to which he had previously been chained. Even if the siblings were correct, and their father *was* possessed, she had explained, if they did not properly care for his body, he would be physically damaged by the time they managed to exorcise the demon.

"Is that you, Sophia, dear?" Henry said weakly, narrowing his gaze and peering through Byron's shimmering, phantasmal form. The old man sat up in bed, beckoning to her. She crossed the room, coming to stand beside him.

"Get a chair, my dear. A chair . . ." Henry said, his voice quavering.

Sophia shook her head.

"Your bedside is a perfect seat." She perched on the edge, and took the old man's hands in her own.

Byron floated toward her, his face uncertain.

"You do not wish to tempt Oblis so, Sophia," Byron said. "Sitting so close, you'll only—"

Sophia waved away the ghost's concern.

"Byron, darling, are you truly frightened of such a kittenish creature as my father-in-law? He needs our love and care, not our cruel words and fear. You go on, then, my friend. I'll watch over him awhile."

Byron still looked unsure.

"You underestimate the danger here. Perhaps I ought not leave you."

"I don't mind," she assured him. "How many times have you left me with him? Has Father-in-Law ever troubled me? He sleeps, and sometimes I talk, just to hear myself speak. Come, Byron, do you mean to tell me you have nothing better to do? You, of all within these walls?"

Byron hesitated. "Well, there is a small matter to be addressed on the ghostly plane. An old publisher has need of a few sonnets that he says only I can provide."

Sophia nodded, Henry's hand gripping tightly.

"Go then, darling. I'll stay and guard the prisoner," she said, dryly.

"Are you sure? I can very easily put out a call to Horatio," Byron said.

"Quite sure. I shall be perfectly fine. You needn't trouble Horatio, just as I have never needed to trouble William or Tamara with *your* past pursuits."

"As you wish," Byron said, obviously pleased to be at liberty, but still reluctant to leave her.

"I'll be back, quick as I can," he said, and then he was gone.

Henry looked up at Sophia, his face old and disoriented.

"I'll look after you, Father-in-Law, I promise." Sophia leaned forward, pressing her soft lips against the cool, paper-thin skin of his forehead.

✑

WITH HER EYES CLOSED, Sophia did not see the malevolent grin that flashed across Henry's face, before his countenance once more slipped into the slack-jawed confusion of old age.

Six

Tamara stared out the window of the carriage, her mind awash with thoughts of John Haversham, oblivious to the picturesque scenery that surrounded her. This was beautiful countryside. Lush green hills sloped down into clear rivers. Expanses of jagged rock turned dramatically into sheer cliffs that fell away, exposing breathtaking views of the turbulent aquamarine sea.

She barely noticed, her mind's eye still fixated on the image of John as he looked down at her that last time, his gray eyes alight with frustration. Tamara realized he had come to Ludlow House to warn her that the magical community knew she and William were aiding and abetting Serena. This in itself was evidence that he cared for her.

It was his ambivalence—his unwillingness to acknowledge their mutual attraction—that made it utterly impossible for her own feelings to settle. Some days she thought she loved him with all her heart; others she hated him with all the passion she possessed.

The carriage wheels hit a bump in the dirt road, and Tamara was jostled out of her thoughts, her eyes truly focusing upon the scenery for the first time in hours. The geography had changed so the land was now flatter, and densely forested, making Tamara realize they were almost to Camelford.

In the close confines of the carriage, Bodicea's ghost floated beside her, the long spear she often carried resting against her thigh. She had died in the midst of casting a spell that had required nudity. Now as a ghost, she could have altered her appearance, but she chose to be seen as she was at the time of her death—naked but for her war paint. Bodicea claimed it distracted her enemies. Tamara had no doubt. Now the specter gave Tamara a grim nod but remained quiet. This close to her, the ghost's transparency unnerved Tamara more than usual. It was disturbing to be able to see the drapes pulled back from the window, to see the buttons on the seat cushions and the grain of wood in the carriage's enclosure, all through the gossamer veil of Bodicea's translucent presence.

The ghosts were staunch allies and had become her friends, but there were times when their presence still troubled her.

Tamara tilted her head down to check on Serena, who lay curled in a ball in her lap, snoring quietly. She still had not entirely recovered from the odyssey of her journey to London. *Best let her rest,* she thought as she pulled at the folds of her dress, letting the rich fabric cover the sprite's slender legs and shoulders.

With a yawn, Tamara let her eyes close and rolled her neck to loosen the taut muscles. Her eyes were so dry after the long trip that they stung a bit when she opened them again. She found she had been clenching her jaw so fiercely during the ride that the beginnings of a massive headache had begun to grip her forehead and temples.

She reached up and massaged her jaw as she watched the trees give way again to open spaces dominated by small homesteads, and a small stream that chased along the side of the carriage. The density of the cottages doubled and tripled until Tamara saw that they had reached the outskirts of the village.

What a quaint little place, Tamara thought as she took in the small wattle and daub cottages, their straw roofs glowing golden amber in the fading afternoon light.

The dusty dirt road they traveled merged with a larger path, and soon the road into Camelford became more defined, dirt giving way to large pavestones. At last she saw the Camel River to the left, its current strong and deep. After such a long ride she would have loved to wade into the river. The very thought of it was refreshing. But as a city girl traveling north, she knew she must hew to propriety even more than usual. *William would be so pleased.*

In the village proper, a stone wall ran alongside the wide main road as it climbed a gentle slope with a row of shops and homes on either side, their roofs and chimneys staggered in height going uphill, like steps for a giant. Wooden signs hung from posts above the doorways of the shops, and most of the dwellings above and beside them had windowboxes full of flowering plants, blossoming with bright spring colors.

They passed a dyer's and a blacksmith's and a basket maker whose wares hung from a string of hooks beside the door. A sternlooking woman pushed a pram and did not so much as glance up at their passing. Some of the buildings were whitewashed, but most had faces as stony as that grim mother's.

The road was cobblestone here, rough and dusty. Several men

in slouch caps stood on a cobbled sidewalk with a small girl in a pretty blue-and-white dress, and she turned as the carriage went by to smile and wave. One of the men clutched her hand and pulled her close, and all of them watched the unfamiliar carriage roll by with wary eyes.

Odd, Tamara thought. *Unless whatever danger troubles the fairies has imperiled the village as well.*

Over the tops of the buildings she could see tall trees, and beyond that to the east, the rocky tors and cliffs. Though she knew that the narrow side roads that branched off this central way must travel into the forest—some on the way to the sea, others across Bodmin moor, and still others due north along the coastal trade route—the center of Camelford was entirely civilized.

They entered the market square, empty now, and passed beneath the long shadow of a large, beautiful stone building. The roof of its clock tower was topped with a golden camel as a weather vane, which Tamara thought amusing, considering that the name of the place had nothing at all to do with camels, and instead had taken its name from the Cornish words for "winding river."

She sat up and stuck her head out the window of the carriage. Farris sat high upon the driver's seat and she called to him, her voice low and husky after hours of silence.

"We have rooms at the Mason's Arms Inn—"

Farris turned in his seat, and nodded.

"It's just up the way, miss, across from the Bridge House. Spotted it a moment ago," he answered, giving the reins a tug to slow the horses.

"Thank you, Farris," Tamara said, returning to her place back inside the carriage.

She was glad Farris and Bodicea had accompanied her to

Camelford. As pretty as any place might be, there seemed to be danger here as well. She would need all the help she could get.

It was reassuring not to be alone.

~

𝕿AMARA'S ROOM AT THE INN was smaller than she was used to, but it suited her perfectly: from the large bed with its goose-down comforter to the compact writing desk resting below a wide-paned window that revealed a picturesque view of the gurgling Camel River and the small stone bridge that spanned its width. *A taste of heaven's peace right in the middle of Cornwall,* Tamara thought as she began to unpack her things.

Shortly she paused to check on Serena, who was still asleep in the middle of a thick woolen horse blanket that Farris had set in a corner of the room. The sprite had wanted to go to the fairy Stronghold that very evening, but the little creature had been haggard and pale and Tamara had insisted that they put the visit off until the next morning so that Serena could rest.

From the visit John Haversham had paid her just before her departure for Cornwall, it was clear that the council that ruled Stronghold was less than pleased with the sprite's decision to seek outside help. Tamara knew that it likely was going to make her investigations far more difficult, but the council would have to adjust to the idea that they were not alone in this, just as they would have to accept that she would not allow them to punish Serena. The sprite was in her care. Somehow she had become just as much a part of the Swifts' magical family as Nigel and the ghosts.

At the moment, though, Tamara's only concern was that Serena rest and regain her strength before they made their way into the forest and confronted the fairies.

The sprite fluttered her wings in her sleep and then rolled over. There was a sweetness and beauty about Serena, but Tamara knew she had other, less admirable, traits. Yes, Serena had a kind heart, and she fairly sparkled with magic, but she had an infernal temper and could be vicious and deadly in battle. Tamara had seen as much in their dealings with Wild Edric in the forest outside Blackbriar the year before. Far better to be her ally than her enemy.

Tamara lifted a chemise from her trunk and placed it in the top drawer of the cherry wood dresser. While her mind wandered, she had nearly finished her unpacking. She didn't know where the time went these days. With William's impending nuptials, and all the extra work the Protectorship of Albion had placed upon her, Tamara was so busy that she barely had time for anything else. She knew her writing was suffering, along with her charitable work, but she still hadn't quite discovered how best to juggle all of her current endeavors.

Closing the lid of the trunk, she sat down heavily on the bed, and wondered how Farris was faring downstairs.

Upon their arrival, he had settled himself at one of the wide oak tables in the middle of the tavern, and happily accepted a pint from the hands of the lusty young barmaid. All the better to learn if the town had been plagued by troubles of late. Tamara had almost joined him there, but she was all too aware that propriety would not have allowed it. She didn't want people to gossip about her relationship with Farris. He was her employee, and such whispers would make it impossible for her to do her job here.

She wished the world were different, for she greatly enjoyed Farris's company.

Bodicea had made herself scarce upon arrival. True, Tamara had sent the ghostly queen off with instructions to see what information she could glean from the local spectral populace. But as her majesty had flitted off into the woods, it seemed to Tamara that the pale shade had fled the town quickly, eager to revel in her freedom after traveling in the carriage with Tamara and Serena for so many long hours.

It would have been a simple matter for the ghost to have gone ahead and met them here in Camelford, but Bodicea had not been willing to entertain the suggestion. Once Tamara had shared word of Haversham's visit and the potential threat to Serena, Bodicea would not be parted from them. The ghost watched over the sprite, and Tamara, and seemed on edge throughout the trip. Tamara had tried to pacify her, explaining that the fairy council was unlikely to attempt to retrieve the sprite since it was obvious they were bringing her back to Cornwall.

Even so, Bodicea remained vigilant.

Now that they had arrived, though, Tamara had given her a task, and Bodicea had pledged to fulfill it. Tamara assured the queen that she was more than capable of handling the Council of Stronghold on her own. She was the Protector of Albion, after all.

In retrospect, she wished she had not been so quick to send Bodicea away. There was no telling just how powerful the council might be. But she would not recall the ghost now. Not yet.

The fairies are vicious when aggrieved, Bodicea had said as they'd set out from Highgate, and Tamara agreed. Her last experience with the beautiful but temperamental creatures had left her quite wary.

Yet here she was, intending to stroll right into a heavily guarded fairy stronghold with only a single ghost, a fugitive sprite, and her butler to help her.

I must be insane.

∼

THE TAVERN AT THE MASON'S ARMS hummed with voices, some of them mere whispers and others braying with drunken laughter. Yet even the laughter seemed strained, weighted with some dark concern.

Farris tried to engage the pretty barmaid in conversation several times. She had smile marks around her mouth and eyes that implied she was no stranger to pleasant conversation, yet tonight she banged his drink onto the scarred oak table with scarcely a glance or a word.

Camelford might not have been a tiny hamlet, but its population could not have been vast. Given the number of men frequenting the tavern this evening, Farris gathered that most of the town's able gentlemen were out tonight, drinking and talking together in hushed tones. A palpable fear lay beneath their words, and Farris could not help adopting the same frayed, nervous edge. Normally a gregarious sort, tonight he hoped that no one would attempt to defuse their own tensions by initiating trouble with him. He wasn't in the mood to end a heated verbal exchange in a peaceable manner.

The town itself wasn't in the mood, really.

"I'm sure she's long gone and buried," Farris heard whispered at the table behind him.

The voice was cracked and gritty. Farris suspected its source to be the man with the scruffy gray beard and dark-rimmed eyes whom he'd seen as he'd taken his seat. A glance over his shoulder proved him right.

The man sat talking to his comrades, three older men with dirty, stained shirts, revealing a hard day's labor outside under the sun. They sat tightly bunched together at one table, quietly discussing the fate of a local girl who had recently gone missing.

"She might've run off, y'know. You've got to allow for the possibility. Happens all the time, these young girls eager to raise their skirts, or more often taking fright at the thought of raisin' 'em for someone here at home," one of the old men said.

Used to lecturing, whether his mates like it or not, Farris thought. The man was small, but taut as a bullwhip. Someone you'd definitely want on *your* side in a fight.

Farris knew that if something unpleasant plagued Camelford, beyond the magical matters that had drawn them here, Tamara would wish to be apprised of it. Whatever haunted the men gathered in the tavern tonight, it was more substantial than ghosts. Though he took pains not to be discovered, he continued to eavesdrop on the men as they argued about their various opinions regarding the fate of the missing girl.

"Lot of good our brave constables is doin' these girls and their families," one of them loudly announced.

The gray-bearded one he'd first seen, perhaps the eldest among them, scowled. "What, those two drunken louts? They're fine for breaking up a fight or settlin' a dispute, but they couldn't catch a fox in a henhouse. If there's a bit of mystery or danger involved, they're useless."

Farris grimaced. So much for any help from the local constabulary.

Evening had turned to full night outside and the coolness of the country air stole around the room, canceling the warm glow of the hearth almost completely. Farris finished his first pint and beckoned to the barmaid for another. She gave him a harassed look, but nodded.

Cheeky wench.

Two men entered the tavern and took the table to his right. They shivered with the coolness of the room and kept their cloaks on, their hoods, it seemed to him, deliberately pulled so their faces went unseen. At first Farris paid them little mind, his focus still on his eavesdropping and on the pint of bitters the barmaid brought him. As he took a long draught from his glass, however, he could not escape the sensation that they were staring at him. He turned to look, and found their attention pressed upon him as though they observed his every move in fine detail.

"Pardon me . . . ? Have you two got some sort of problem?" Farris asked loudly.

The two men, caught unawares, made no reply. They turned away, hiding their faces and behaving as though Farris was not glaring at them. At last Farris stood and took a step toward them. The four old men behind him quieted as they waited for the action to unfold.

"What I asked, in case the two of you are daft, or deaf, was if you've got some problem. The way you were staring, I'd wager the answer's yes. But if it's no, if it's only rudeness, then speak up now, or your real problems're only beginning," Farris said, the beginnings of real anger starting to stir inside him.

Still the two men made no move to answer.

The tavern's owner, a short, squat man with gold-red hair and bright pink cheeks, came out from behind the bar.

"I'll have no troubles here. Take your woes outside."

Farris nodded at the little barman, acknowledging that he'd heard him, and was more than willing to comply.

"That means the two of you as well, then," the owner said, stiffly, nodding to indicate the hooded men. A hush had fallen over the tavern and all eyes were upon the standoff.

But only for an instant.

The two men lunged, knocking over their chairs as they hurled themselves at Farris. He parried a blow that would have caved in half his skull, such was the strength of his attacker. In the same motion he struck back, staggering the fellow.

The other reached powerful hands out, grabbing for his throat, but in the same moment the four old men at the table behind him leaped to Farris's defense, clutching at the man's robe and helping Farris fend off the two hooded men with a rain of fists that belied their age.

Outnumbered, the hooded men turned and fled, but not before Farris grabbed the edge of the nearest attacker's hood and caught sight of what lay beneath.

This was not a man at all, but a *creature*, its features a patchwork of stone and earth.

～

THE PASSAGE OF YEARS had clouded his memory so much that Richard Kirk could not entirely recall when he had first sensed things that others could not. Simple truths, powerful emotions, the locations of objects lost and precious—he was attuned to all of these things. Sometimes it wearied him, and in those times, he always came to this place by the river.

Something about the place allowed him to forget his troubles, and to simply be at ease in a way he could not manage anywhere else. He thought it might have to do with the gentle rush and burble of the stream, the sound acting as some kind of buffer. It had also occurred to him that the running water might have some magical properties that helped to shield him from the influence of his strange sensitivity.

Whatever the reason, his supposed gift was dulled by proximity to the river, sometimes silenced entirely, and that suited him just fine. He felt saddled by his gift, and often wished he were free of it, regardless of the consequences.

This evening was an exception.

Tonight, he held his gift close as his only hope of ever again seeing his sister alive. And yet something was wrong. Often when he was visited by the intuitions of his gift, they came unbidden. But he had called upon them consciously more than once in the past. Thus, by clutching his sister's most precious belongings in his hands and focusing intently upon her, he ought to be able to touch her with his gift, to get an image in his head of her location, even feel whatever she was feeling at the time. And beyond his gift, he and Sally had always shared an emotional rapport.

Yet he had stood in her bedroom for hours, lain upon her bed, clutched to his chest the ragged doll that had been her companion and confidant from the cradle, and *still* Richard could not locate her. He could feel her—that much was true. And simply knowing that she was still alive gave him some comfort. But what he felt . . .

Fear. Pure terror.

And he could not discern his sister's whereabouts. Just a glimpse through her eyes had shown him a clearing in the forest, surrounded by thick trees. But nothing more. When he reached out to touch her, instead of images he was overwhelmed by emotion. He felt her terror, and was filled with the certainty that something hideous would soon befall her.

If only he could see where she was . . .

"Hello, over there!"

Richard blinked, his ruminations interrupted by a low, feminine voice. He turned to find a tall, slender woman with honey-blond hair standing on the far side of the small footbridge that arched over the Camel River.

She wore a light blue dress that cinched tightly around her

waist before flaring out into a wide skirt that just skimmed the ground. A thin periwinkle shawl draped comfortably over her shoulders. She offered a sweet, almost ironic smile as she crossed the footbridge.

"I hope I didn't frighten you," the woman said.

She had a lovely smile, her lips a natural ruby red. He could not discern the precise color of her large eyes in the semidarkness, but there was something warm and inviting in the way she looked at him. He felt immediately comfortable in her presence, quite unusual in his experience.

"Not at all," Richard said. "Only I was lost in thought a bit, and didn't notice you until you spoke."

The woman—more of a girl, really—hesitated a moment and reached up to tuck a stray lock of hair behind her ear. Now that she'd broken his reverie she seemed unsure what she wanted to say, and skittish enough that she might just run off and leave him there watching curiously after her.

Richard was pleased when she laughed softly at her own hesitation and forged on.

"I've taken a room at the Mason's Arms and I've a view of the river. I saw you here and, forgive me, but you looked so forlorn that I felt I must come down and say hello to you," she said. "Of course, it all seemed perfectly reasonable right up until the moment I actually put the plan into action. And now you must think me a fool, and horribly inappropriate."

Richard smiled, a bit dreamily. "Nothing of the sort." It wasn't often that beautiful London girls—for could this elegant creature be from anywhere else?—approached him as a salve for his loneliness.

"My name is Tamara. Tamara Swift," she continued. "I'm on

holiday, and shall be in Camelford for perhaps a week. The Cornish air is reputed to be wonderful for the spirit."

He arched an eyebrow at this curious claim. "Not that I've noticed." Then he inclined his head in a courteous little bow. "Richard Kirk, miss, at your service. I . . . live here. In town, that is."

The stupidity of his words made him blush, and for a moment, he felt like throwing himself into the river.

What a fool I am, he thought miserably. He was so caught in his own thoughts that it took the small voice in the back of his head a few moments to break through:

She's not being truthful.

The words echoed in his head, confusing him. She had said little, only that she was traveling. What could she have lied about, in so short a time? And yet the intuition was powerful. Camelford was too small a place to attract many tourists. Those who visited the town and stayed at the Mason's Arms were mainly passing through.

Suspicion crowded his mind, and he wondered if this newcomer might have something to do with Sally's disappearance. Almost immediately, he put the foolish thought from his head. His connection with his sister might be dimmed at the moment, but of one thing he was entirely certain: she had not been spirited away from Camelford by any ordinary man—or woman, for that matter.

"Are you not well?" Tamara asked, studying him closely.

"I . . . I'm fine, miss," he stammered, his heart thumping so loudly in his chest that he was sure she must have heard it.

All of his life Richard had been different. His gift had kept him apart from the other children in the town. Only his sister, Sally, had been unafraid of him. The other children weren't cruel, really. They didn't tease or assault him. They merely avoided him. And somehow, that was worse.

Now he felt his lack of social experience throwing up a barrier between himself and this woman. He thought perhaps if she had been unattractive he might have found the whole thing a bit easier, but her beauty dried up his mouth, and turned him into a stammering fool.

"You don't seem fine," she said, reaching for his hand. He pulled his arm away, terrified to touch her. Even though he was near the river, he knew there was something about this woman that made him think *anything* was possible.

"I'm sorry," she began, and she looked upset. "I didn't mean . . ."

He shook his head, stopping her. "I . . . just—I don't like to be touched," he murmured.

She nodded, mulling over his words. "Yes, I can understand how it might be a bit intrusive."

Richard sensed her sincerity, and it surprised him. Could she also have an intuitive gift? Did she know or somehow sense why he often avoided the touch of others?

"There are things in *my* life that are a bit awkward to explain, too, Richard," she said.

Her words set Richard's mind at ease. At the same time, he wondered what it was that this beautiful young woman could be keeping secret from the rest of the world.

They had made a connection. Richard felt that she had somehow shared a part of herself, and that he owed her some sort of explanation, some piece of him in return.

"It's my sister. She was . . ."

Tamara studied him, and he both relished and squirmed beneath her attentions. "What's happened to her?"

"You're only visiting, but you might already have heard that tragedy's befallen Camelford in recent days."

She shook her head. "No, I hadn't. Should I be afraid?"

Richard paused and studied her. This beautiful London girl did not seem afraid: not at all.

"Afraid? I'm not sure about that. But careful, yes. You should certainly be careful. Yesterday, a young girl was found dead right in the middle of Market Square, her body . . . shattered . . . almost as though she'd fallen from the sky."

He took a deep breath before continuing.

"Two other girls are missing, Holly Newcomb and my sister, Sally."

Tamara covered her mouth, brows knitted in horror and sympathy. "I'm so sorry. You must be frantic."

Richard nodded, then gestured toward the water. "I find the river quiets the feeling . . ."

"The feeling?"

"Yes, that something terrible is going to happen to her. Very soon." He let the words hang in the air.

On the longest day of the year . . .

He flinched as the words came unbidden into his mind.

"Richard?" Tamara said, her eyes full of worry now.

"On the longest day of the year, they will die . . . *All of them.*"

She took a step toward him, but Richard shook his head. He didn't want her pity, and that was all he could see in her eyes. Perhaps he had imagined this strange and sudden empathy between them.

"Richard, please. You must tell me what you mean by that. I don't understand."

Tamara reached out for his hand. To *touch* him.

"No!"

He shoved her away, sent her stumbling backward, and as she

recovered he turned and hurried off, back toward town. Only once did he glance back to see her watching after him anxiously.

Fool, to think a London girl might see something in you, he thought. *All you'll ever win from her is her pity.*

～

TAMARA HAD SEEN RICHARD from the window, staring at the river, and there had been something about his forlorn presence that drew her downstairs. Camelford had not been especially welcoming thus far. Certainly the townspeople had been friendly enough, but the whole village seemed steeped in the wariness she'd seen in the faces of those men on the street when they had first arrived.

Common sense had indicated a connection to the troubles at Stronghold, but she had wanted more information. The problem had been how to go about broaching the subject with the innkeeper or some other guest at the Mason's Arms.

She had just decided that her investigation would have to wait until morning when she saw the young man at the edge of the river. He seemed burdened by worry the same way so many in Camelford were, yet his solitary melancholy had drawn her to him. A lonely young man, even one who sought out a quiet place, might well be compelled to speak his heavy thoughts by the presence of a sympathetic ear . . . especially if that ear belonged to a pretty girl.

Tamara wished she could have been surprised by what she learned from Richard Kirk, but the dour spirit of the town had made her suspect the truth even before he had spoken.

It seemed obvious that the disappearance of young girls from Camelford must be related to the fairy girls whose vanishing had drawn her here. It was possible, of course, that there was no connection, but logic dictated otherwise. The idea that Mellyn, the fairy girl whose corpse had been found in the upper branches of a tree, had been dropped from the sky had not occurred to her. But now Richard's mention of the girl found dead and broken in Market Square made it seem so clear.

Whatever was taking these girls, fairy and human alike, was flying off with them somehow.

On the longest day of the year, they will die . . . All of them.

That was what he had said.

The longest day of the year would be the summer solstice, and that was only a week away.

A week to find out what in heaven's name is going on around here.

On the riverbank, she stood and stared at the place where Richard Kirk had been only moments before. Under normal circumstances it would have been only logical to suspect that he was involved with the murders and abductions, but he was only a man. The tiniest fairy could overpower a man with glamour or, if necessary, brutality, or escape him easily if she wished.

Richard did not seem to be an *ordinary* man. In her mind's eye there was an indelible image of his face with those sad blue eyes and an expression of true misery. He was haunted. She'd sensed something in him, seen it in his eyes, and his words had hinted as well at his possession of an intuitive gift. Such things could be natural, a part of the human psyche that no one quite understood yet, or they could be magical. Tamara wondered which was the source of Richard's gift.

Regardless, though he might not be ordinary, the gift of intuition was an intangible thing. He could not have stolen those fairy girls, or murdered Mellyn, and certainly he could not fly.

No, Richard Kirk was precisely what he appeared to be: a brother heartbroken by his sister's disappearance.

She wished that she could ease his troubles, but knew the best she could manage was to help the man find his sister. *And I have only a week in which to accomplish the task.*

There came a loud shout from across the river, and she spun to see two hooded men rushing from the inn and disappearing into the woods. A moment later the innkeeper burst out in pursuit, his face livid as he shouted after them.

Let that be a reminder to pay our bill in a timely fashion, Tamara thought lightly as she crossed back over the footbridge.

But even as she reached the other side of the river she saw Farris come out the door behind the innkeeper. Something about his stance stopped Tamara in her tracks. She changed course, making straight for the front of the inn.

"Farris?" she called out. "Is everything all right?"

He turned at the sound of her voice, and gave her a curt nod. The innkeeper paid her no mind, his attentions still fixed on the two men who had fled out into the night, as though at any moment they might reappear.

"A bit of trouble with some ruffians, Miss Swift," Farris replied, formal yet firm. "Nothing to concern yourself about."

Such were his words, but his expression conveyed a different message. There was a tale to be told, but he could not discuss it in front of the innkeeper, which meant that Tamara had to orchestrate an opportunity for them to have that conversation.

"All right, then. Have you checked on the horses?"

"Haven't had the opportunity yet, miss. I'll see to it right away."

"I suggest you do," Tamara said, allowing a bit of Bodicea's imperiousness to creep into her voice. Sometimes she enjoyed playing the role. Her voice was gruff enough that the innkeeper gave Farris a look of fraternal solidarity.

Farris gave her a nod and started around the building toward the stables. Tamara nodded stiffly to the innkeeper, who gave an obsequious little bow before opening the door for her. She gave him another nod of dismissal, and went inside.

Tamara knew the protocol one adhered to when one was wealthy, and could play the part of a haughty rich girl as well as any actress in London. Sometimes she found that it was easier to give people what they expected than to try and change their perception of her.

Not wanting to keep Farris waiting, she skirted the mostly male crowd in the tavern and went up the main stairs to the second floor. Making sure that no one saw her, she descended the rear steps—the servants' stairs—that led to the kitchen and the back rooms of the inn. Out a side door, she went quickly to the stables.

Inside, she found Farris standing by the Swifts' carriage. In the light of a lamp that hung by the door she noticed for the first time that his right eye was swollen and a bruise was forming.

"Your eye, Farris! What in the world happened to you?"

He shook his head.

"I have no idea, Miss Tamara. I was mindin' my own business, having a pint . . . overheard a couple of old fellows talk about local girls gone missing, I'm afraid. So it appears—"

"Yes," Tamara said quickly. "I've learned a bit about it myself. The trouble's in the village as well as the forest. But you've still not told me what happened to you."

He smiled, and winced as the expression hurt his bruised face.

"Getting to that, miss. Anyway, these two blokes come in and set down beside me. I didn't like the look of 'em, and I felt sure they were paying a bit too close attention to me. At first I paid 'em no mind, as I was in the midst of overhearing a conversation about missing girls hereabouts that I thought would be of interest to you.

But their eyes on me . . . it was unsettling, Miss Tamara. I asked them what they were thinking, if they wanted some trouble, like. Then it all went a bit mad, the fighting and such."

Tamara took out her handkerchief, and handed it to Farris, who dabbed at his bruised eye and glanced at the cloth for any sign of blood. Luckily, it was only swollen, not cut.

"Go on then," Tamara said.

Farris leaned against the wall, a bit unsteady on his feet.

"If it weren't for my fellow patrons, they'd have done some real damage, I'd say," Farris said. "But none of that's so important, really. See, their faces were hidden, like. Hooded. But just as they ran off, I caught a glimpse of one.

"They weren't men. Not as such. Sure they moved like men, and had the . . . the shape of men. But that face was nothing but dirt and stone. And, well, you'll forgive me, miss, but when that sort of thing happens I can't help thinking their interest in me was more of an interest in you, if you take my meaning."

Stunned as she was by this news, Tamara couldn't help smiling.

"I'm sure I do, Farris." Then her smile faded. "I've not run across them before, but from my research in Grandfather's library, it certainly sounds as though you ran afoul of a pair of homunculi."

Spurred by his mystified expression, she explained.

"They're just as you describe. Creatures made of earth, often stone and clay. Sometimes they're invested with human spirits, but mostly they're simply constructs that do the bidding of their creator. Dark sorcery, indeed."

"What do you suppose they wanted, miss?" Farris asked. "If they were sent after you and yours, who sent them, do you think?"

"I've no idea," Tamara replied. "But I'm sure we'll find out soon enough."

～

Bodicea moved through the ether, gliding effortlessly through the shadows of the spirit world. She well remembered the pain and pleasure of being a flesh and blood woman, and whenever she manifested her ghost in the tangible world it was both wonderful and terrible to know that she was no longer a part of it.

Even so, she disliked traveling the ether, moving through the spiritual realm among the lost souls and haunting spirits who lingered just beyond the veil of life on the earthly plane. The sadness and anger and regret there nearly overwhelmed her. Still, it was the quickest way for the dead to travel, merging with the ocean of souls and then slipping out of it into a new location.

Now she emerged from the ghostly realm into the thick of a dark forest. A light mist was moving low across the ground, caressing the trunks of trees. Night birds called and things shifted in the leaves above. Tamara had asked her to contact the phantoms that haunted the town and the wood, but Bodicea had found very few ghosts lingering around Camelford. Those who remained were withered, frayed specters with little surviving consciousness. They could tell her nothing.

This was a mystery unto itself.

A town like Camelford ought to have its share of wandering shades and lost souls, even mischievous spirits. So where had they gone? Had something driven them off? The thought intrigued her.

Here in the wood it seemed no different than in the town. There were only the sounds of a living forest, wind rustling through trees, animals skittering about foraging for food, the gurgle of a nearby stream.

Bodicea sighed, uncertain where to continue her search. There was little else she could do but lie in wait, listening to the night and the forest, and hope for some sign of ghostly manifestation.

She didn't have to wait long. Time passed for the dead with a fluidity that caused it to blur. Ghosts could focus and experience it in much the same way as the living, but otherwise time was relative, compressing or expanding at random.

Nearly an hour passed, but to Bodicea it seemed only a few moments before she heard the faint sound of distant hoofbeats. The spectral queen allowed her spiritual essence to fade so that she was nearly invisible to all but other ghosts. Even then, she hid herself amid the trees and kept her spear close as she spied between the trunks, awaiting the approaching riders.

Three men on horseback rode past, and for a moment she thought they were from the living, so grand were they. But the illusion passed and she saw that they were merely shades. A short way past her hiding place they slowed their mounts, hands tight upon the reins, and paused in a clearing, their bodies translucent in the moonlight.

She moved nearer for a better view, and saw that the phantom knights were wearing tunics over their armor and chain mail. They each carried a spectral shield engraved with a cross. Bodicea did not immediately recognize the coat of arms, but something about it seemed familiar.

The three knights sat astride their ghostly horses and conferred in hushed tones, unaware of her presence. Bodicea inched forward, spear clutched tightly at her side, straining to hear their conversation.

She could not make out more than a few words among their whispers, but it was clear they were troubled, and perhaps even a bit fearful.

A loud thrashing sound arose in the distance, and the ghostly knights started, then turned as one to stare in that direction. They spurred their spectral mounts and rode off deeper into the woods, presumably to discover the source of that strange sound.

Bodicea eased her grip upon her spear, relaxing out of her attack stance. She was sure that she had seen that coat of arms somewhere before.

But where?

Seven

John Haversham strode along the dirty cobblestones of Fleet Street and stopped in front of the Cherrywood Tavern, gazing up at the elegant façade of the building. It wasn't the sort of place he preferred. John had a predilection for houses of ill repute and other establishments where trouble was easily found. This afternoon, however, he navigated the streets of London on business not his own.

He pushed through the heavy oak doors and stopped, surveying the tavern's main room from the doorway. The walls and floor were hewn from a polished brown oak quite pleasing to the eye. Behind a long bar, a small man with distinctive gray muttonchops tended to his customers, pouring whiskey and pints of lager with confidence. Behind the bar, a broad, spotted mirror reflected back the whole of the room.

The polished tabletops caught the sunlight that streamed in

through the warped glass of the many-paned windows. To his right a door hung open. Beyond it was a small passageway that led to a second seating room where a staircase led upward. John suspected he would find his quarry there, lunching in one of the private dining rooms.

Turning back to the bar, John looked longingly at the pints already nestled in the hands of patrons unashamed to take a drink at midday. He would've enjoyed a drink himself, no matter the hour.

When he'd climbed to the second story, John noted the same rich, molasses-colored oak that he'd seen downstairs. If it was possible, the tables here were even more polished. The floor had been scrubbed with a deft hand, giving the space a clean feeling that John found rare in any culinary establishment.

Leave it to William Swift to find the cleanest alehouse in all of London.

Now he walked the length of the hall, peering into small, private dining rooms on either side. Within their confines, several highborn gentlemen grazed over roast rack of lamb, thick meaty steaks, plates of roast potatoes and root vegetables. The air was redolent with rich aromas, and he found that he was so busy admiring the victuals that he paid scant attention to the men who were consuming them.

Until the room where he found William Swift happily gnawing on a leg of lamb.

John leaned against the door frame. "Hello, Willy boy."

William looked up, a smear of grease staining his chin, and glared. Swallowing, William used his napkin to wipe the grease away, then said, "What do *you* want, Haversham?"

"I've come to speak to you about your recent houseguest," John replied, sliding out a chair and plopping himself down, much to William's clear annoyance.

"I'm referring to Serena, of course. Though it would have been in your best interest to release the creature to my custody, your sister refused to even acknowledge the sprite's presence at Ludlow House."

William studied him. Haversham wouldn't have credited him with the ability to keep his expression so entirely neutral. Perhaps William Swift was learning more than magic, now that he was one of the Protectors of Albion, and a member of the Algernon Club.

"Tamara has gone to Cornwall," William said. "I can't see that she has anything to do with whatever business you have with a sprite in London—"

"You're far too proper a gentleman to engage in such bald lies, William. I know the sprite came to you—the Council of Stronghold has made us aware that she flew to London. Where else would she go? She trusts you and Tamara implicitly.

"Now, why not stick with the truth. Deception doesn't suit you."

William's face turned a bright shade of pink, but he swallowed whatever insult he was set to hurl at John as a waiter appeared in the doorway, carrying a dish of sumptuous trifle. He nodded as he pushed the plate with the remnants of his lamb to the side. The waiter set the dessert before him and gathered up the dirty dishes before departing.

Haversham's stomach growled. He really shouldn't have neglected breakfast today. His man, Colin, always had a pot of steaming coffee and a plate of meat and eggs with toast waiting for him in the morning. The aroma, both rich and acidic at the same time, enveloped the apartments on Brook Street, mingling in a very pleasant way.

But he had awoken late this morning and had been forced to

forgo breakfast in order to arrive at the Algernon Club on time for his meeting with Lord Blackheath. The rest of the morning had run much the same way, always fifteen minutes or so behind schedule, making it impossible for him to catch up.

He watched with envy as William dug heartily into his trifle.

"I am trying to enjoy my lunch, Haversham," William said, a bit of pudding smudged across his chin. "Would you mind disappearing, as I have nothing whatsoever to say to you?"

"This is Algernon Club business, Willy boy—"

"Stop calling me that!" William said, glowering.

"All I ask is a bit of cooperation."

William glared at him, and put down his spoon. "What do you want, then?"

"A bit of your trifle for starters . . ." he began. William sputtered and John waved his protestations away. "Only joking, Swifty. Don't look so glum."

He stifled a laugh as he watched William's face color even more deeply.

"Go on, then; you're wasting my time."

John sighed and leaned back in his chair.

"Lord Blackheath was less than pleased that I returned from Ludlow House without the creature. Seems to think your sister's charms dissuaded me from pursuing the assignment to the best of my ability. Now he has insisted, rather emphatically, that I retrieve the sprite and see to it that she is promptly returned to the fairy council for questioning. We all know how *difficult* the fairies can be, and no one wants to incur their wrath."

William nodded impatiently. "Yes, yes. Well then, you've nothing to worry about. As you must suspect, Tamara has taken the sprite with her to Cornwall. I have no doubt she will approach the council soon after her arrival. If the belligerent butterflies at the Cornish stronghold have business with Serena, it will be sorted out quickly enough.

"It's no longer your concern, Haversham, or Lord Black-heath's."

John narrowed his gaze. "I did have that suspicion, but needed to hear it spoken aloud. As for Lord Blackheath, I rather think he will decide for himself what is and is not his business."

William Swift surprised him, then. The all too priggish young man had lacked confidence in his role as Protector of Albion from the start. Now, though, he lifted his chin and glared at John with surprising iron.

"Where our friends are concerned, Mr. Haversham, the Alger-non Club is not, and will not *ever* be in a position to instruct the Protectors of Albion as to our behavior. Serena has earned our trust and protection. Lord Blackheath interferes with that at his own peril."

For a long moment, John studied him. Then he nodded. "Well, the point is moot, isn't it? Now that you've confirmed that the sprite's gone home, we've nothing to quibble about."

They sat for a few moments, neither man speaking. Finally, the clanging of dishes from the next room broke the spell.

John stood to go.

"Wait, Haversham—"

He pivoted on his heel and regarded William, presuming he was about to be upbraided again for his . . . friendship with Tamara. But once again William surprised him.

"Look, *John* . . ."

The familiarity felt purposeful and forced, but it piqued his curiosity. "Yes?"

William looked down at his hands.

"I need your advice, actually."

John raised an eyebrow but said nothing.

"There have been some thefts at the bank," William said, when he realized no reply was forthcoming. "Swift's of London has always prided itself on its integrity and ability to protect the interests of its clients. And now . . ." He shrugged.

"You have no thoughts as to the culprit's identity?" John asked.

"None save that whoever is responsible is either very clever or . . . magically inclined."

Even more intrigued, John cocked his head and studied William. "Why do you say that?"

"Only four people, myself included, have access to the vault keys. I have placed wards upon the vault that ought to prevent magical intrusion, but—"

Haversham shrugged. "So it must be one of the other three."

William waved the suggestion away. "Impossible. I trust them all implicitly, or I would never have given them the combination to the safe where the keys are kept. It's got to be magic, don't you see? And someone clever enough to make their way past my wards, yet leave no trace. Someone skilled at both sorcery and thievery."

Slowly, John nodded. "Ah. I see. Of course the combination of the two is rare, and since you know only one man with experience in both pursuits, you've got one suspect already."

"Now, just a moment," William said, shifting awkwardly in his chair.

"Come now, Willy. Surely you're not the type to deny your suspicions. You think I'm your thief. Admit it," John prodded, grinning humorlessly. "Even *I* would suspect me, if I didn't know better."

The wealthy young banker tapped his fingers on the table and stared at Haversham, striving to regain his composure. He waited, as though he thought silence would force a confession.

John smiled.

"It isn't me, William. Which leads me to ask what you plan to do about discovering who *is* stealing from you."

"I've already hired someone to investigate at the bank, in the event that it is just a remarkably clever thief. If there's magic involved, though, I'd hoped you might have some suggestions as to how I might proceed."

"You've got wards up. Seems to me you've done what you can, other than sleeping in the vault yourself."

William averted his gaze. "Other responsibilities preclude me from taking such a direct hand in the matter, at least for the moment. Though it may come to that." He looked up. "Meanwhile, I'd be grateful if you'd keep your eyes and ears open at the Algernon Club. Perhaps you'll learn something an ordinary investigator— one who won't consider a magical source—could not."

John nodded. "If I come across any better suspects than myself, I shall be certain to inform you."

∾

WILLIAM MARCHED INTO THE FOYER of Ludlow House and slammed the heavy oak door behind him. It frustrated him no end that he had been forced to let Haversham get the upper hand in their conversation. He had never appreciated being taken lightly, and that was precisely what Haversham had done. The man was toying with him.

Or was he? *Is he really so innocent?*

The question was driving him mad.

Yet even that trouble paled in comparison to the issue that occupied nearly his every waking hour of late. William hurried up the stairs, taking them two at a time, impatient to return to his most vital task: exorcising the demon from his father's flesh.

~

ALL MORNING AND AFTERNOON the ghost of Lord Admiral Horatio Nelson had haunted the library of his old friend Ludlow Swift. Ostensibly he was doing research, but in truth he had spent much of the time reminiscing. He had begun searching through Ludlow's journals for any reference to possession that might help to exorcise Henry, and was slowly working his way through them from first to last.

Fortunately, magic lingered in all of Ludlow's possessions, making it easier for Nelson to manipulate them. With proper focus, ghosts could handle physical objects, but a residue of magical influence simplified the task.

Horatio had not realized how much he missed his old friend until he saw Ludlow's spidery scrawl stretched out across the page. They had shared many an adventure together, most of them chronicled in these very journals. With each flip of the page, he found himself reliving his own strange, ghostly past, one that had allowed him to continue his personal vendetta against evil long after death.

During his life, Horatio had assumed that he would be buried in the ground, or dropped down into the watery embrace of the sea, where his flesh would rot and he would cease to exist as if he had never lived at all. How astonished he had been to find himself still strangely conscious after he closed his eyes for what he'd thought was the final time.

During his fleshly existence, Horatio had been a tireless fighter in the battle to protect England from anyone who sought to destroy it. But it wasn't until after his death that he realized how many opponents he truly faced. There were far more perils facing Albion than he had ever known.

Byron and Bodicea had been a part of the battle for England's mystical spirit even before their deaths, had been involved in the war against the darkness during their lifetimes, but for Horatio it had all come after his death. Yet once he learned of it, how could he, of all people, fail to continue the battle? He would rather spend eternity locked in an unwinnable conflict than wander the spirit realm aimlessly, or worse yet, pass on to his final rest, never to enjoy contact with the human world again.

The door to the library flew open and William strode in, pulling Nelson abruptly from his reverie.

"Anything, Horatio?"

William dropped into one of the large, stuffed wingback chairs that sat beside the fireplace.

The ghost shook his head solemnly.

"We must find something!" William snapped. "The situation is becoming intolerable."

Horatio nodded. He felt exactly as William did, but he had the wisdom of time and experience that allowed him to see that no matter how frustrated they became, anger would not speed the process.

"You must have patience, William. Your anger will do nothing but hinder our progress."

William leaned back in his chair, his face set.

"We shall continue on with our research, and see what we can find," Horatio continued. He was sure that this day would not yield the fruit they sought, but they had to battle on regardless. In time, the solution would present itself. "We must persevere, my friend."

"As usual, you're right." William sighed, standing up and moping over to one of the bookcases.

Horatio smiled. He had come to think of William as more than just Ludlow's grandson; more like *his* grandson. Yet he found it difficult to express this fondness. It was . . . uncomfortable.

He had spent so many years in command of headstrong young men much like William that he could not seem to bridge the distance between them. As was common for him, he wished that the ghost of his Emma, the lovely Lady Hamilton, had lingered after her death. Oh, how he missed her good counsel. She would have known exactly how to lift William's dreary spirits.

Now William extracted a small tome from one of the lower shelves. It was a book that Horatio had never noticed before. This wasn't unusual, as there were hundreds of books arranged lovingly on these shelves. Silently, the two of them immersed themselves in their research. Horatio concentrated on a large volume he had left open on a nearby table.

"Horatio . . . ?" William called, his voice an octave higher than usual. He came toward the ghost, the book held almost reverently in his hands. "Were you aware that Roger Bacon wrote a grimoire that was lost in the late fifteenth century?"

"What do you want with a book by that blasphemer?" the specter asked.

"It says here," William replied, pointing to a page in the book he was reading, "that this grimoire contained a hex capable of compelling the spirit of a demon into an inanimate object, like a stone or statue."

Horatio shook his head. "That grimoire is a legend, as much of a myth as the idea of eternal life, or turning lead into gold—"

William began to pace excitedly, ignoring Horatio.

"No, it exists. It *must*. We must find it. It is of the utmost importance."

"But you said yourself it's been lost for four hundred years."

Now the young man smiled as he turned to face Horatio. "Lost to others, perhaps. But the magician who wrote this treatise claims to know its location. The last man purported to possess the grimoire was a Frenchman called Philippe Mandeville. We must go to Paris as soon as possible. It may be our last hope."

Horatio frowned, his spectral substance rippling with unease. "This Mandeville . . ."

"Yes?"

"I know of him. He is a very powerful sorcerer and alchemist, but he is also a collector of all things mystical. I have no doubt he would like nothing more than to possess one of the Protectors of Albion for his permanent collection," Horatio finished.

William raised an eyebrow.

"What do you mean? How would he collect a person?"

Horatio paused, choosing his words carefully.

"Mandeville was driven out of Paris many years ago. Whispers say he traveled to America—New Orleans, specifically—after an angry mob called for his neck on the guillotine."

William shook his head. "I don't understand. What was his crime?"

The ghost shuddered.

"His crime, William? The theft and trafficking of human souls."

∾

NEW ORLEANS. William had never been to America, and this seemed a less-than-auspicious occasion for his first journey there. But if there was a chance he could find Philippe Mandeville and through him, Bacon's grimoire, then nothing would keep him from making the trip.

He was in his chambers preparing for his journey when there came a knock upon the door.

"Come in."

The door opened slowly to reveal Sophia standing at the threshold. She wore a pale blue silk dress that set off the richness of her hazel eyes, and complemented the creamy smoothness of her skin. She looked like a china doll, her dark hair falling about her shoulders.

She waited for William to address her, but he was intent on packing his things. Finally, she cleared her throat. Realizing his discourtesy, he went to her and quickly placed a kiss upon the bridge of her nose before pivoting back to the wardrobe for his greatcoat.

"Nelson and I are off, my dear. We shall try and be as quick as possible, but with these things you simply never know."

~

Sophia listened, becoming truly aware for the first time how completely consumed he was with finding a cure for his father's illness. She realized with a start that she had somehow slipped to a secondary position in his priorities.

The realization chilled her.

Her whole life she had struggled with the idea of keeping separate what she *wanted* from what she *needed*. She had always reasoned that they were two different things, but now, too late, she saw that they were one and the same.

She had wanted William most of her life, desired him with greed and hunger, but when that *want* had turned to *need*, she could not have said. Now she knew for a fact that she couldn't live without him, that he was necessary in her life. Without him, hers would be only a half-life.

". . . and Byron will be here keeping watch over Father. If you have any difficulties, you can always rely upon Martha, and call upon Nigel if absolutely necessary. I shall make every arrangement to see that you are safe and comfortable here while I'm away," William continued, slipping on a pair of boots before picking up his valise and moving past her to the doorway.

"I shall be downstairs with Horatio, preparing. Come and say farewell and wish me luck before we go," he said, giving her another kiss, this time on the lips, and hurrying down the hall, leaving her alone in his empty room.

Sophia leaned back against the doorjamb, her head spinning. She realized she had not said one word to him during the entire encounter, and he had not even paused long enough from his preoccupation to ask her why.

She sighed and closed her eyes. The question she had come to ask him was a superfluous thing about the wedding dinner—something she was more than capable of deciding herself, but she had wanted his opinion nonetheless. Now she knew it might never be answered at all.

∾

"I'M A GHOST, MY PET," Byron said, his spectral form shimmering, almost lost in the dim corridor. "I've been privileged enough to see things I shouldn't have seen, so I know precisely the size of the member you've been impaling yourself upon."

His mischievous face floated only a few feet in front of her, and Sophia knew that even in the gloom of the hall he could see the effect his words had upon her. She found herself flushing a deep shade of crimson, but she tried not to let embarrassment overtake her.

They stood—though Byron, of course, actually floated—in the hallway by the second-floor landing. She had left William's room in a daze, uncertain of where she was going, only to run into Byron, who seemed to be waiting for her in the hall.

He had seen the look of misery on her face and proceeded to console her by trying to whisper sweetly in her ear. When she swatted him away, her fingers slipping through his ghostly substance, he had turned to lust and perversion in an obvious effort to lift her spirits.

"Byron, you're terrible—" she said, covering her mouth to stifle a laugh.

"Don't play coy with me, darling," he said, as he floated closer to her. "I wasn't born yesterday. For that matter, I didn't die yesterday either. I know everything—and I do mean *everything*—that goes on in this monstrosity of a house."

Sophia didn't doubt that he *thought* he knew everything that went on at Ludlow House, but she had worked very hard to keep her now almost daily visits to Henry well away from Byron's prying eyes.

"My physical encounters are really none of your business, Lord Byron."

He fluttered his fingers happily. "Oh, but that's where you're wrong, my dear. I am here to listen and assist. And usually not in that order: you know what a *hands-on* kind of a fellow I am at heart."

I know exactly where your hands would be if you thought they could do anything more than pass through my flesh. A hint of a smile crossed her lips.

Still, she found herself feeling a bit sorry for the ghosts. She could only imagine how much they must envy those who still had flesh to caress. Particularly a spirit as salacious as Byron.

"What are you thinking, Sophia, my sweet? You look a thousand miles away," Byron said.

"Only naughty things, my lord poet," Sophia shot back. Her tongue seemed to take on a life of its own whenever she was alone with Byron.

"That's my girl," he said, silently clapping his hands with glee.

"You know, there is one thing I can think of that *might* dispel my foul mood," Sophia said, the words sliding out of her mouth before she could stop them.

"And that is . . . ?"

"I would dearly love to be able to help William with his work," she said. She tried to keep her face still, hoping he wouldn't guess her true motives.

"At the bank, you mean?" Byron asked, his mouth turned down in distaste.

"No, I mean his work here."

"I see."

But obviously he does not.

"Byron, I know how much you detest research, but I wouldn't know where to begin in that stuffy old library. Do you think you could be a dear and select some volumes that I might search through? This way, if William's travels do not bear fruit, the work might continue in his absence."

"I do hate Ludlow's books. All about magic, and yet not a bit of it in the words themselves. No poetry, no lyricism. But if you'll be doing all of the actual reading and you only need a bit of guidance, I suppose I could . . ."

"Oh, thank you!" she squealed, starting as though to embrace him and then faltering when she remembered that her grasp would only pass through.

He chuckled, enjoying the attention. "Shall we reconvene here at a quarter past the hour, then? Or perhaps you'll just come to the library."

"Excellent!" Sophia proclaimed. "The library it shall be."

He blew Sophia a kiss before vanishing into the ether.

Sophia hiked the hem of her dress up so she wouldn't trip as she ran up to the third floor and down the hall to the nursery. She hadn't more than twenty minutes before she had to meet back with Byron, and she had news to share with Henry.

Good news.

He was sitting with his back against the cold, white wall of the nursery when Sophia eased the door open and stepped inside. She was dismayed to find that he had been moved back to the chair. Apparently his children thought him somehow more likely to escape captivity from his bed, and thus had changed their minds. Sophia scowled in disapproval.

When Henry looked up, his chains shifted against the wood of the floor. Sophia took a deep breath, pushing down the bit of nervousness she always felt in the first few moments she was alone with William's father.

"They've found the book you asked me to place in the library, Father-in-Law," she said quietly. "I know it because they're preparing to go to New Orleans, as we speak."

"That's excellent, my dear," Henry croaked, a wide smile alighting upon his wrinkled face.

"Most excellent, indeed."

Eight

The morning after her arrival in Camelford, Tamara set out along a little-used road that stretched northeast through thick forest and then to the misty moors. But she wasn't going so far as that. Not far at all, in fact.

Farris sat up on his seat and gently urged the horses on. Apparently the farrier at the inn was kind and skillful, for Farris had noted how well rested and content the animals seemed this morning. Tamara reminded herself to thank the man later, and perhaps set aside a few coins for him.

The road was rutted and dusty, and the morning had begun warm and was only growing hotter. Tamara took a sip of water from a small pouch she had asked one of the servants at the inn to fill for her before departing. The man had presumed that they were setting off for a lengthy journey, and Tamara did not disabuse him of that notion. In truth, though they did not have far to go, their destination was a world away.

Or nearly so.

Beneath a long jacket Tamara wore a dark blouse, and a pair of William's wool trousers. She felt faintly ridiculous with the trouser legs cuffed up and wearing the boots also borrowed from him, her feet wrapped in cloth to fill them out. But better to feel foolish than to *be* foolish, and it would have been absurd to endeavor upon such a hike in the elegant dress of a lady of London.

"Ho, me beauties," she heard Farris call to the horses.

Tamara smiled. He was never so comfortable in London as he was in the wilds. A gentleman's gentleman, to be sure, but there was a rough-and-tumble boy inside the man.

The horses whinnied and the carriage slowed.

After he'd stopped, Farris came around to open the door and helped her down. The sun was warm upon her skin and the back of her neck was damp with the heat. There wasn't so much as a salt breeze here to remind her that the ocean wasn't very far away. The road cut through the deep woods, and it was thick and wild on either side. Birdsong filled the air and the brush rustled with the wind, or the passage of the small creatures that made the forest their home.

"A most inhospitable wayside stop," Tamara observed.

"So it is," Farris agreed, glancing around at the deep woods on either side of the road, and the impenetrable darkness there. "But Serena says this is the nearest spot by road. You'll have to walk from here."

At the mention of her name, the sprite appeared from the front of the carriage as though summoned. A sprinkle of purple dust streaked the air in her wake as she flew to Farris and alighted upon his shoulder.

"Aye, good witch," the sprite said. Her wings folded behind her and she gazed at Tamara with a gravely serious expression on her beautiful face. " 'Tisn't far from here, we thinks. Feel it yourself, we're sure enough. Magic that strong, you must be able to feel it."

Tamara smiled kindly. "Serena, I've told you a hundred times, I'm not a witch. And it isn't precisely a compliment, is it? Could you please not call me that?"

Serena bowed with great sincerity.

"We apologizes, miss. It's only that your magic's too strong for an ordinary old sorceress, and you're no fairy, are you? No, we knows you're not. What else to call you, then?"

"I'm a Protector of Albion. Not a witch, as you well know. But perhaps you could simply call me Tamara, and be done with it."

Serena bowed again. "We's deeply honored, good lady Tamara."

With that, Tamara turned her attention to the forest. In fact, she *could* feel the magic resonating from within. The fairy stronghold was an outpost in the human world, and it marked the border between this realm and Faerie. From Stronghold, one could enter either world. An ordinary human would never find it. Walking through the woods, a man or woman would discover that they simply did not want to go in that direction, and their path would take them on a route around Stronghold. They would never realize that magic had influenced them.

But Tamara was no ordinary human.

"All right, let's be off, then."

As much as she wished that Bodicea were with her, it had seemed more important to have the ghostly queen search for the spirits of the wandering knights she had seen in the forest, to discover if they had any connection to the mystery in Camelford, or if they might have seen something that would be a clue.

And it would not do to leave the carriage on the roadside unattended, so Farris wouldn't be able to accompany her, either. Only Serena would join her. She had business with the fairy council of Stronghold as well.

But when Tamara began to walk toward the trees on the west side of the road, the sprite remained on Farris's shoulder.

"Aren't you coming, Serena?"

"Ye know we's not welcome," the little creature said, fluttering her wings, a shower of purple dust sparkling around her. "They means us ill, that's sure."

Tamara frowned and looked at her closely. "I could find it on my own from here, you're right about that. I *can* sense it. But I'd feel much better if I had you with me. And you may rely upon me, my friend. I'll not let any harm come to you."

For a moment, the little sprite lowered her head. Then she perked up, smiled, and beat her wings, flying up into the air with a mischievous twinkle in her eyes. "As ye say, Tamara. As ye say."

Serena darted toward Farris, kissed him on the cheek, then gave a musical little giggle as she flew toward the woods, calling to Tamara to keep up.

"You'll remain here?" Tamara asked.

Farris nodded. "For two hours, as instructed. If you haven't returned by then, I'm to go back to the inn and await you there. And if you have still not appeared by nightfall, I shall ask Bodicea to fetch Master William from London."

"Excellent," Tamara said. She smiled at him. "It sets me at ease, having you along, Farris."

"Thank you, miss. Can't say I'm at ease, however. What with you goin' off into the woods on your own."

"I'll be all right. Not to worry."

Farris nodded. "As you say."

"Back soon," Tamara promised, and she lifted a hand to wave as she turned and strode into the woods after Serena. She didn't worry that she would be observed, for there were no other travelers on the road this morning. Not *this* road.

The moment she stepped in among the trees she was embraced by the deep shadows of the forest, and a chill went through her. Tamara shuddered. The heat of the day was forgotten. She had expected it to be cooler, but the difference in temperature seemed greater than could have been accounted for by the shade alone.

A bead of sweat trickled down between her breasts, a remnant of the sun's heat, but it cooled and dried almost immediately.

"Serena?" she called into the darkness.

There came a slight whisper of a sound, the distant trill of a harp, and the sprite darted from the branches above her to flutter only inches from her face. Serena crossed her arms sternly.

"Got to keep up, lady fair. Can't keep coming back for ye, s'true."

Tamara nodded. "I'll do my best."

Serena hesitated a moment, as though something in the forest frightened her. Then she appeared to muster her courage, and she set off, darting through the trees and whirling around branches, barely rustling a leaf. The only thing that marked her passage was the trail of tiny sparkles that she left in the air. Here in the semidarkness, they glowed a faint lilac.

Tamara followed.

Though the forest was thick and the branches above intertwined in what looked to be an impassable tangle, the undergrowth grew thinner and thinner the farther she went from the road. Several times she lost sight of the sprite, but a light, musical trill in the air or a fine dust of sparkling light upon the air would lead her.

In truth, however, she discovered that she really did not need

Serena to lead her. For with each step she felt the magic of the fairies more acutely . . . and more unpleasantly. By the time an hour had passed, knots of pain had formed in her head and gut, and they increased the nearer she drew to the Fairy stronghold.

How much easier it would have been to walk another way, to turn from her current course. But that was their protective magic working on her. Anyone else would have bent to this manipulation without truly being aware of it. Tamara would not be turned away.

Her jaw was tight, teeth gritted together. Another quarter mile and her head was bent, eyes defiantly raised so that she could find her way through the trees. Despite the strangely cool air in the woods, a line of sweat slid down the back of her neck.

Then there was music in her ear and she glanced to the left to see Serena, fluttering about in a mist of magical light, the tiny, beautiful face crumpling with worry.

"You all right, lady fair?"

Tamara nodded once. "I shall be. Let's continue."

Serena shrugged. "Nowhere to continue to. We's here, isn't we?"

Three steps later, Tamara emerged into a clearing in the midst of the forest, and the weight of the fairy magic lifted from her. With a relief that weakened her legs and nearly caused her to fall over, she glanced around the large clearing. At first, there was nothing there beneath the sun.

And then she blinked.

The sight of Stronghold made her stagger backward a step. Though she was Protector of Albion, she and William had not held that title for very long and there were so many things they had yet to experience. The majesty of the fairy stronghold was one of those things, and it made her wonder if her heart could withstand the grandeur of Faerie itself, should she ever set foot into that other realm.

Stronghold was made of stone that had the gleam and grain of marble, but was as white as ivory. Where human structures clearly showed the cut of every stone, however, the fairy outpost looked as though it had been carved whole from a single block. It stood perhaps eighty feet high and four times that in width, rounded and tapered upward so that its peak was the pinnacle of half a dozen or more arches. The windows followed that design, as though the whole thing had been teased upward, or stretched like blown glass instead of stone.

She thought of her brother. William's first love was architecture. *You should have been here for this, Will.*

From her vantage point, perhaps thirty yards away, Tamara could not see the lower portions of Stronghold. The structure was at the center of the clearing, and all around, obscuring her view, there grew a line of trees so closely set as to be impassable. Their upper branches twined together, and the trees themselves bent in toward Stronghold, tops twisted one to the other to create a kind of defensive canopy.

Beside her, Serena whistled.

"Pretty magic, that," the sprite said in her high, singsong voice. "That's new to us, so it is."

New, Tamara thought. *Defenses they've only just erected. They're frightened, all right.*

Now that the pain in her head and stomach had abated, she lifted her chin and strode directly across the clearing. There was a gap between two trees that seemed almost wide enough to pass through. As she approached, she saw figures crouched behind the trees. Lithe, like wraiths, three of them slipped through the narrow gaps between tree trunks, their gossamer gowns all shades of green and blue, of forest and ocean.

An arrow struck the earth inches ahead of her. Tamara gasped, and stopped. She glanced up into the branches of the trees that shielded Stronghold and saw a tiny archer withdrawing behind a covering of leaves. *A brownie or some other mischief-maker,* she thought. The fairies of Stronghold must have enlisted strange allies in these treacherous days.

"You are not welcome," said the tallest of the fairies as she approached. She was a towering, thin creature whose every motion was like a dance. Her eyes were a staggeringly bright blue, gleaming with vibrant color in the sun.

All three of them were beautiful, of course, but there was a terrible cruelty in the beauty of fairies that those who fell under their enchantments never saw until it was too late. Tamara had encountered such creatures before, and had no illusions.

"I am Tamara Swift," she said regally, matching their haughtiness with her own. "I am the Protector of Albion. I have come to speak to the Council of Stronghold, who command this outpost, on matters most dire. And I would be admitted now."

The three fairies seemed almost to float toward one another. If they whispered together, shared their thoughts, Tamara could not hear them. Their mouths seemed to move, but did not form any words she understood. After a moment, the tallest one came forward again, halving the distance between them. She was a head and more taller than Tamara, and looked down upon her.

"We know who you are. Your arrival was expected, and your interference is unwelcome. You will go. First, however, you shall turn over the sprite Serena to us for punishment."

Tamara scoffed. "I'll do no such thing."

The fairy blinked as though Tamara had slapped her. "You had best watch your tone in our presence, girl."

An unnatural wind blew up suddenly and whipped at Tamara's hair. Anger and magic churned within her and she raised both hands, clenched into fists. Power crackled around them, a golden light that swirled with flashes of brighter silver.

"And you in mine," Tamara said evenly. "Albion is my realm, my responsibility. You and yours are guests here. Perhaps you ought not to forget that."

Uncertainty touched the face of the fairy for the first time. Then there came a flicker of a smile, though no amusement reached the creature's eyes. She inclined her head.

"We do not require your assistance, Protector," she said with derision. "We are more than capable of protecting ourselves. This is not the business of humans."

Tamara crossed her arms. "You haven't done the best job of protecting yourselves thus far, I'm afraid. And this business does involve humans. Girls from the village have been attacked and have vanished, quite like what's happened here."

The fairy frowned doubtfully. "The sprite is a fugitive. Serena must answer to the council for bringing you here, for speaking of Stronghold without permission, and she will be questioned about the disappearances themselves.

"It is thought that perhaps she has not told all that she knows."

Ever since the fairies had appeared, Serena had been nowhere in sight, but now she darted from the trees across the clearing and sped toward Tamara and the three sentries.

"A dirty lie, it is! Aine is our greatest friend. We *loves* her!"

Shadows seemed to gather around the three fairy sentries, but the darkness did not come from the trees above. The angle of the sun was wrong. It was just the grim cast of their hearts that brought this darkness. Tamara didn't think they were evil, but they were afraid and angry and suspicious because of the disappearances. And she knew there was a cruel streak in the nature of fairies to begin with.

The sprite alighted upon Tamara's shoulder.

"This is foolishness," Tamara told the sentries, lowering her hands, the magic dissipating around them. "Regardless of how I was summoned, I have come to offer my assistance in finding those you have lost and in punishing whoever is responsible. Surely you recognize the value—"

"For the last time, your assistance is not required. Go home, sorceress."

The words were cold. For the first time, she noticed that the fairies' teeth were sharp. No wonder their smiles could be so unsettling. She glanced past them, wondering what would happen if she attempted to force her way into Stronghold, if she fought them for the right to address the council.

"What could she have done that engenders such fury in you?" Tamara demanded. "What is it you think she can tell you?"

Still they said nothing.

"All right," Tamara went on, frustrated. "Know this. The sprite Serena is under my protection. Any attempt to harm or accost her or to interfere with her in any way will be considered an attack on Albion itself. My brother and I will respond accordingly.

"Now, then, as Protector of Albion, rightful defender of this land, to which you have no claim, I demand to speak with the Council of Stronghold!"

Tamara lifted her chin defiantly.

The fairy who had been speaking all along, whose eyes gleamed deepest blue, inclined her head in a gesture of modest respect.

"I am Sibille, of the Council of Stronghold, my lady Protector.

We are well met, but the council does not wish your assistance. You have no business here. See to the humans in the village, as is your true duty. Leave us to attend to our own ways and laws."

Tamara stared at her. So she had been speaking to a representative of the council all along, and hadn't realized it.

"I've just told you, Stronghold and Camelford face equal peril, and we must work together. I fear that time is wasting with our every word. I know one of your own has been murdered. At least one village girl has suffered the same awful fate. But those who have vanished are still alive, I'm certain of it.

"There is a young man, you see, whose sister is among the missing. They share a deep rapport, a bit of magic in them. He can feel her life waning with each passing day, and he is absolutely certain that whatever her condition now, she and all those who have been taken will be killed during the solstice, which is but days away."

Sibille bared her sharp teeth. There was nothing beautiful about her.

"That is as may be, but you are no more welcome here because of it."

The fairy councilor raised a hand and arched one finger. There came a grunt from behind the trees, and up in the branches half a dozen brownies appeared with arrows nocked in their bows. The two sentries on either side of Sibille began to gleam with a greenish light that spilled from their eyes like a kind of damp smoke.

"Begone, Protector of Albion. Fairy matters are not your concern."

Tamara let out a ragged breath of frustration and nodded once. "All right. Fools must be left to their own fate."

The fairies bristled, but did not attack.

The sprite gasped and hid herself in Tamara's hair, wrapping it around her like a curtain.

"But Serena comes with me. When you are willing to have me stand at her side while she hears the charges against her, then she will come to council. Until then, should you trouble her in any way, it will be war between us, and under the present circumstances, that is something neither of us can afford. But do what you will."

"Oh, lady fair, what are you doing?" Serena's tiny voice squeaked in her ear.

Tamara only stared at the fairies.

Sibille looked as though she wanted to eviscerate her on the spot. "You do realize that you would have no chance. Even if you were to kill some of us, our numbers are too great. You would not survive."

Tamara smiled, hoping her expression matched the fairy's in cruelty. "Perhaps. But I would most certainly kill you, Sibille, as well as the two with you, and several others. But which others?"

Again the Protector raised her fists, and once more they crackled with power. "So if it's to be war, have at it."

Sibille lowered her hand. The archers and the bogie withdrew, and so did the other two who had come out as sentries. After a few moments, Sibille herself slid between two of the trees and disappeared toward the fairy stronghold.

Tamara also backed away, slowly, not willing to turn her back on the place until she had reached the woods. When she was a comfortable distance away, she exhaled loudly and then began to hurry, moving through the trees as quickly as she was able.

The sprite took to the air, tiny wings making frantic music as she darted along beside Tamara.

"Thank you, thank you, thank you," she said. "But what now, lady fair? What do ye plan?"

Tamara did not respond. She could feel the time passing, the seconds ticking away toward the summer solstice. If Richard Kirk was correct, and his sister and the others who had been abducted were to die on that night, there was not a moment to spare. She had not expected the fairies to reject her help, and without their knowledge, Tamara would have to investigate the entire mystery on her own.

No, not on her own. She had Serena, and Farris, and Bodicea. And now she had Richard Kirk as well.

She would find the truth, and she would find those girls, before the solstice arrived. The fairies didn't want her help, but they were going to get it anyway.

~

THE BROOM LAY ON THE GROUND in front of the cottage, cast aside. Ellie Kirk sat on a wooden bench that her brother-in-law, Norman, had brought over just for this purpose. She had been sweeping out the cottage but the numbness and lethargy that had plagued her since Sally's disappearance had come upon her again, forcing her to rest.

Her little girl was gone.

The broom was forgotten now, and Ellie just sat on the bench and stared at the trees, hoping that her daughter would emerge as though she had never been away, and the whole family—the whole town—would laugh and be so relieved to have her home.

The summer sun was unforgiving today, yet Ellie did not move from the bench in search of shade. She only stared at the trees.

When she saw movement in the branches, her heart leaped. She tensed, ready to stand. Then a hound dog trotted out of the woods, followed by a second and third, all of them covered in brown and white fur, snuffling the ground like pigs in a sty. And last of all came Peter David, who offered his services to travelers who wished to hunt on the moors or in the woods, and trained the dogs himself.

Peter was a kind man, a friend, but Ellie's heart ached at the sight of him. She was crestfallen as he approached, his jaw set grimly and his eyes full of sympathy.

"Hope I didn't startle you, Mrs. Kirk," he said, stroking his graying beard. With a whistle, he called his dogs to heel and all three of them trotted to him and sat by his feet. "The boys need to eat and rest a bit, and then we'll go back out."

Ellie nodded. "It's kind of you, Peter, to spend so much of your time this way."

So many of the people of Camelford had volunteered their time to help search for Sally, and for the Newcomb girl, but none had been as good a friend to the Kirks as Peter, nor as useful. He had been out for hours each day with his dogs.

"We've all got daughters or sisters, Mrs. Kirk," he said solemnly. "I'll help as I can, and pray to get your Sally back safely. Your husband and his brother are still searching, along with Mr. Price from the inn and a few others. I'll rejoin them in an hour or two, once the dogs are fed."

They would have said goodbye, then, but their attention was drawn by the clattering of hooves and the rattle of a carriage that came round the corner and along the narrow road. Clouds of dirt rose behind it, and Ellie and Peter watched as the carriage came to a halt in front of the cottage.

The driver climbed down, a stout man, but powerful looking. He came round the side and lowered the steps, then opened the door and offered his hand to a most oddly dressed young lady. She wore a pretty blouse beneath a long coat, and a man's trousers cuffed over boots that must have been too large for her. Ellie had never seen the young lady before, but she was far stranger a sight than the typical traveler who passed through Camelford.

The driver stayed by the carriage, hands behind his back, all right and proper. The young lady—Ellie saw that she was little more than a girl, no older than twenty—came up the walk toward the cottage.

"Pardon the interruption, but might this be the home of Richard Kirk?"

Ellie frowned as she stood, Peter by her side. The hounds sniffed the ground in the direction of the new arrival and one of them whined softly as it watched the girl.

"It is," Ellie replied. "Richard's my son. I'm Eleanor Kirk. And this is Mr. David, our neighbor and friend."

The oddly dressed young woman stopped a few feet away and inclined her head. "I am Tamara Swift, Mrs. Kirk. My apologies for the intrusion. And I hope you will forgive my attire. I climbed to Roughtor this morning, and had not brought the proper clothing for such a hike."

Ellie smiled. An odd girl, trekking up to the tor herself. The thought made her smile fade. It was all too dangerous for a girl on her own in recent days.

"I know this must be a difficult time for you to greet visitors, so I shan't stay but a moment. I had hoped to speak with Richard, if he's at home."

Polite, at least, Ellie thought. *A Londoner, by her voice.*

"Our Richard's not here, I'm afraid. He's gone to town, I believe, to speak to folk about . . ." She paused and took a breath to calm herself. "About Holly Newcomb. You may have heard—"

"Yes," Miss Swift interrupted, saving her the pain of completing her thought. "I'm aware of what's befallen both Holly and your own daughter, ma'am. And the unfortunate girl found in Market

Square. I spoke to Richard yesterday afternoon, and as I'm going to be in Camelford at least a week, I thought I ought to offer what little assistance I may."

Ellie raised an eyebrow. The dark dread in her heart did not prevent her from feeling suspicion.

"I mean no offense, miss, but what sort of help could you provide? I don't imagine you'll be traipsing through the woods with a hound or two."

The girl smiled, and suddenly Ellie felt her suspicions dissipate. The kindness there was unmistakable. Also, in those clothes, and willing to climb Roughtor herself, the girl might in fact be willing to join the search party in the forest.

"My family owns a bank, Mrs. Kirk. Swift's of London. And I'm quite certain that my brother—at present the president of the bank—would happily provide a reward note to be posted in neighboring towns and villages for information leading to the safe return of the two missing girls."

Ellie felt like weeping; her hands trembled.

"That'd bring an army into the wood, searching for the girls," Peter said, crouching to rub one of the hounds behind a floppy ear.

The traveler gave him a look of earnest concern. "Is that going to be a problem for your hounds, Mr. David?"

Ellie looked down at Peter and saw regret in his eyes.

"I think not," the man admitted as he stood once more. "The pups found a trail on the first night, Sally's scent. Led us a merry chase, but then it ended, nothing left to follow. Might've been the river, I suppose. Peculiar thing, though, a scent so strong and then no trace at all. Almost like she flew away."

The words echoed in Ellie's ears and she closed her eyes a moment, hating to hear of it. It truly was as though Sally had just disappeared—as if she had been spirited away.

When she opened her eyes, she gazed at the girl before her. "Miss Swift, I don't know how to thank you."

"There's no need," the girl assured her. "I only hope it helps us find the two missing girls. When Richard has a spare moment, please ask him to call upon me at the Mason's Arms, and I shall make the arrangements with him. If I am not in, he might ask for my driver, Mr. Farris."

"Three," Peter said abruptly.

Ellie glanced at him, confused. "What's that, Peter?"

The man stroked his beard again. He was normally quiet and now as he looked at Tamara Swift, he seemed awkward. "Well, it's just the young miss keeps saying two girls, but we believe it's three now, don't we?"

"Three?" Miss Swift asked. "Who is the third?"

"No one's sure of it yet," Ellie noted. "The daughter of a farmer named Raynham turned up missing the night before Holly did, but her parents supposed she'd run off with a boy from the moors who'd taken a fancy to her. Now, though, with all that's happened, I've heard the Raynhams are wondering if their daughter didn't elope after all."

"I see," the girl said. Her expression was troubled. "That's dreadful news. I only hope we shall find them all still in good health, and soon. I'll take my leave, now, ma'am, Mr. David. I wouldn't like to take any more of your time."

"Thank you again, Miss Swift," Ellie said, a spark of hope igniting in her.

"Not at all," the traveler replied. She started back toward her carriage, but paused after a few feet. "Mr. David. Out of curiosity, the place where the trail disappeared . . . where the hounds lost the scent . . . where was that, exactly?"

The man frowned, and Ellie understood why. What good would

such information be to a wealthy girl from London? It wasn't as though she could do any tracking herself, or had hounds to do it for her.

"At Slaughterbridge, miss," Peter said finally. "The west side of the river, twenty paces or so from the bridge, at the edge of the wood."

Tamara Swift thanked them again, bid them farewell, and returned to her carriage. Ellie and her neighbor watched as the carriage rattled away and listened to the horses' hooves thumping the road. They were quiet for a full minute after the last sound had died away.

Even the hounds were silent.

∽

With richard kirk unaccounted for and Bodicea still exploring the spectral planes for further signs of the ghostly knights she had seen the previous day, Tamara decided that her best course for the moment was to return to the inn and hope that young master Kirk sought her out there. As loose and comfortable as her borrowed trousers were, it would be a relief to be dressed in a lady's clothes again.

The reward she had suggested to Richard's mother had been a last-minute bit of inspiration, invented on the spot to assure that the young man would seek her out, but despite its origins, she was very pleased with the idea. It was possible that the increased number of people searching the woods around Camelford would turn up some new clue.

At the very least, it would likely infuriate the fairy council, and Tamara did not mind that at all.

She hoped that Bodicea might provide some new information upon her return. Meanwhile, she knew that the only place to inquire about Holly Newcomb was right here at the inn where the girl had worked. The Mason's Arms was host to many well-to-do travelers passing through Cornwall, and Tamara had been pleased to discover that this had led the innkeeper, Roger Price, to open a makeshift tearoom in a small parlor off the dining room.

It was half past three when Tamara, in a lovely butter-yellow dress, ensconced herself in a chair in the tearoom. She sat by a window that gave her a view of the river that ran behind the inn, and the stone bridge that spanned it, leading out of town. Serena was flitting about somewhere, probably out in the stables, since Farris was seeing to the horses. Tamara had asked him to take the opportunity to speak to the farrier about the Newcomb girl. Farris had already discovered the man had been quite fond of her.

The only other people in the tearoom were a naturalist from Madrid and his wife, both of them on the threshold of old age. She passed a pleasant word with them, but otherwise kept her silence and enjoyed the view of the river as she sipped her tea and ate half a blueberry scone.

Guilt whispered in the back of her mind. To have this moment of peace, of pleasure, seemed somehow wrong when so many people in Camelford were even at that moment tormented by fear and anguish.

When the girl came to pour her a fresh cup of tea, Tamara smiled at her. With her reddish hair and the light spray of freckles across her nose, the bosomy thing drew a great deal of attention at the bar, which was her usual station. Tamara had noticed her the previous night as they went through the inn.

"Thank you," Tamara said.

"Not at all, miss," the barmaid said. Her smile was open and friendly. "Anything else you'd like? The scones are a bit dry, I'm afraid. There's a lemon tart that's—"

"No, no, I'm all right, thank you."

The girl nodded and turned to go.

"What's your name?" Tamara asked.

The barmaid paused and studied her. She seemed pleased to be asked. "Christine, ma'am. Christine Lindsay."

Tamara furrowed her brow and let gravity enter her voice. "You knew the girl who's missing, I take it? Holly."

The barmaid's smile winked out like a star at sunrise. "I don't like to think of it, ma'am. It's a terrible thing. Can't sleep at night, to be honest."

"I'm sorry. I shouldn't have mentioned it."

Christine's smile returned, though tinged with sadness. "No, no. It's all right. Just difficult, is all. I fear the worst. We all do."

Tamara reached out and touched her wrist. "Don't give up hope. She may be found yet, and the other girls as well."

Christine put a hand over her chest and gazed up at the heavens. "I pray you're right." She started toward the kitchen, but paused and turned back to Tamara. "Did you enjoy your ramble today, ma'am?"

"Indeed. It's lovely country."

"Truly, it is. But you'll be careful, won't you? You've got your driver with you, and that's a blessing. Still, have a care. I fear none of us is safe of late."

"I'll beware," Tamara said. "I still want to see more of the countryside, but I won't go anywhere alone."

A thought crossed her mind as she remembered the conversation she'd had with Ellie Kirk and her neighbor, the master of the hounds.

"Say, Christine, what do you know of Slaughterbridge? I'm told it's pretty by the river there."

The barmaid paused and a ripple of shadow seemed to pass

across her face. "It's pretty enough. Though not a place to linger. We pass back and forth across the bridge, from here to there, but it isn't the sort of place young men take their ladies for a stroll."

"No? Why is that?"

Christine gave her a sheepish look and a small laugh. "The legends, ma'am."

"What legends are those?" Tamara asked.

"Just stories, Miss Swift. Old legends. My grandfather used to tell me the stories when I was just a little thing. Tales of ghosts and goblins, bogies and fairies. Slaughterbridge is where they say Arthur was slain, you know. Murdered by his own son, Mordred. But round here, all the stories about Slaughterbridge are about the witches."

Tamara stared at her. "Witches?"

"They haunt the woods and the riverbank, searching for Arthur's true grave, for his bones," Christine said, and for a moment Tamara saw in her face the little girl she had been when her grandfather had told her those stories. "Half-human and half-demon, they are, or so the legends say. Beautiful and ugly both, full of dark magic."

"Witches," Tamara said again, and a shudder went through her.

Nine

Sophia's skirts swept the stairs as she descended in a fury, her pulse throbbing in her temples.

When she reached the foyer of Ludlow House she turned, listening for voices. Long shafts of afternoon sunlight reached deep into the house, but she knew there would be no sunlight in the room she was looking for.

She considered the dining room. Its curtains could be drawn easily. As she turned in that direction, two maids came bustling along the corridor from the rear of the house, chattering between themselves. One was Tamara's own lady's maid, to whom all of the household staff save Farris answered, and the other was a young, blond girl whose name Sophia had never bothered to learn.

"Oh, excuse us, Miss Winchell," Martha said, pausing in the hall and giving a small bow of her head. "We weren't aware anyone was about at the moment. Is there anything I can help you with?"

Sophia sniffed, trying her best not to take her anger out on these women, but she couldn't keep the edge from her voice.

"Indeed, you may tell me where I might find Mr. Swift at the moment."

"Why, in the parlor, I believe, miss. With Mr. Townsend."

"Of course," Sophia said, teeth gritted.

She left the maids to gossip about her demeanor and to guess at the strife that had erupted in the house. Servants would always whisper on the back stairs, she had learned that as a child. There was nothing to be done about it. As long as they kept their suspicions within the confines of the household, there was little reason to be troubled by it.

And yet she hated the idea of them talking about her behind her back.

Her heels clicked on the wooden floor as she strode toward the parlor door. It was open just a few inches, but she grasped the handle and pushed it wide, standing just on the threshold.

The curtains were drawn, just as she had expected. William stood with Nigel Townsend at the center of the room, and each had a snifter of brandy in his hand. Nigel had the glass to his lips, and was interrupted mid-sip by Sophia's abrupt entrance. Both men turned to regard her curiously.

"What is it, Sophia?" William asked. "Has something happened?"

Her mouth opened and closed. A small sound came out, but no words. She let out a breath and paused to collect her thoughts, then finally managed to find her voice.

"I have just been speaking with Byron," she began, casting a dark look at Nigel. "He informs me that while you and Lord Nelson are off on this adventure in New Orleans, *Mr. Townsend* is to oversee the household."

William blinked, his features etched with confusion. He cast a sheepish glance at Nigel, and then looked at Sophia again. "That is the case, yes. I've just finished discussing it with Nigel, and he's graciously agreed to look after things. As I told you, darling, I don't expect to be gone very long, but upon reflection I felt that in the event—"

"But . . . Nigel?" Sophia interrupted. She threw her hands up in exasperation and laughed a small, humorless laugh. "No offense meant, Mr. Townsend, but you and William are not exactly the best of friends."

Nigel raised his glass to her. "You have a gift for understatement, Miss Winchell."

William's face reddened and he attempted to affect a sternness that Sophia knew only covered his discomfort.

"Nigel has been a friend and ally of this family for decades, Sophia, as you are well aware. We may not always see eye to eye, but I do not doubt his dedication to Albion."

"*This* week," Sophia sniffed.

With a mischievous smile, Nigel winked at her and took a sip of his brandy. It only incensed her more that their conflict was a source of amusement to him.

"Surely, someone else—" she began. "*Anyone* else."

"Sophia," William said curtly, "I can't very well leave one of the ghosts to attend to the household. With Tamara and Farris both away, and given that there have at times been dangers associated with living at Ludlow House, it was vital that we have someone here who might have a chance to combat those perils, and still **be** able to deal with the day-to-day business of the household."

"But, he's a *vampire!*" Sophia cried.

William looked stricken, and glanced toward the corridor. Suddenly he rushed past her, brandy spilling from his snifter onto the carpet, and he shut the door, then turned on her.

"I would ask you to be somewhat more circumspect when you are here, darling," he said, tension clear in his voice.

Sophia crossed her arms without apology. "And what of me, William? If you must rush off on this fool's errand, with our wedding day growing closer by the minute, you might simply have left the overseeing of Ludlow House to me. It will be my duty one day soon, after all."

He stared at her, searching her eyes, and then he softened.

"Is that what this is all about? Sophia, as it is, we risk our reputations with each night you spend here before our marriage. When I considered it, I realized that if you were to present yourself to any visitors—couriers and such—as the lady of the house, the whispers would rise to a roar. For propriety's sake—"

"*Damn* propriety!" Sophia snapped.

"Oh, now I think I begin to understand what you see in her, William," Nigel said, taking another sip of his brandy.

Sophia turned away from them both and wiped at the tears that were beginning to gather in her eyes. She breathed evenly, forcing herself not to collapse into sobbing.

"I just can't believe you're disappearing on me again, William. You swore to me that you would plan this wedding with me, that you would be a part of it. It's a day that should be a glorious celebration of the love we share, and you've barely taken an interest."

He put one hand on the back of her neck, gentle yet firm, and the other slid around from behind to encircle her. "Sophia, please. I love you. You cannot doubt that. And I wish I could invest my every thought in the arrangements for our wedding, but every time

I think of it, I am unable to escape the shadow of my father's condition. I must have him well again, to bear witness. You don't understand what it means to me."

Sophia rounded on him and when he reached for her, she slapped his hand away.

"How dare you?" she said, tears beginning to stream down her face. "My father died horribly, William. You know that I would give anything to have him in attendance on the day I am to be married. I rejoice at even the faintest hope that you might find a way to cure your father.

"But you cannot slough off your responsibilities to me and to our future. You haven't even chosen the color of your waistcoat! You have a duty to your family, and to the bank, and most of all to Albion, but at some point, there must come a halt to this, and your duties to me must take precedence over all else. Just for a little while."

She hated how small her voice had become. The room had fallen silent. Sophia glanced up and saw that somehow, during the tension of the moment, the vampire had managed to slip away, soundlessly and unseen. She and William were alone now, and she could feel the way he struggled for the right words, for some sentiment that would comfort her.

With a soft, almost musical sound, the air in the parlor rippled and the ghost of Admiral Lord Nelson appeared.

"All is in readiness, William," Horatio said, his form transparent in the darkened room. "It is time to depart."

Sophia looked up and stared at William. He hesitated, still searching for some way to comfort her. She shook her head, turned on her heel, and left him to his distractions.

In her heart she made a vow: this was the last time she would forgive him. If he did not concentrate on the wedding when he returned from America, there would be no wedding at all.

~

AFTER SOPHIA'S DEPARTURE, it took William several minutes to calm himself. It was no small task to translocate across the breadth of the Atlantic Ocean, and even more of a challenge to do so when the chosen destination for the spell was a place he had only ever seen in paintings.

When he had sufficiently recovered himself, he glanced at the ghost of Lord Nelson, shimmering in the late afternoon light.

"The moment I arrive, I shall summon you, Horatio."

"Aye, aye, my young friend," the ghost said, giving a small salute with his only hand.

William reflected for a moment on how much more confident their exchange had sounded than he felt. But then he knew that the time for such hesitation was through. He had to concentrate on the translocation spell.

Swift's of London had recently made investments in the burgeoning city of New Orleans. One of their business partners was Clement Beauregard, with whom William had corresponded regularly since taking over the reins of the institution. Now he focused on the cordial letters he had received from Beauregard, who had mentioned many times his wife's love for the gardens behind their large Bourbon Street estate in the Vieux Carré of New Orleans.

He seized in his mind upon the bright purple of bougainvillea in full bloom, and upon the Bourbon Street address of the Beauregard family. And he spoke the words.

"Under the same sky, under the same moon, like a fallen leaf . . . ," he began.

Though he no longer needed to perform the incantation aloud

to achieve translocation, in this instance, with such great distance and so uncertain a destination, it seemed the best choice. Eyes closed, he repeated the words, breathing evenly, then he reached within himself, and let his heart touch the magic that had pulsed there every moment since he had inherited the power and duty of Protector of Albion.

The world shifted around him. Suddenly there was nothing solid under his feet. For just a moment it was as though he was hurtling through the air, and a chill touched his bones. Whatever limbo the magic brought him through, it was quite cold.

Then his feet were on the ground again and gravity took hold. Weakened by the effort, he went down on one knee as he opened his eyes to find himself surrounded by beautiful bougainvillea, redolent with heady scents.

"Well done," he whispered to himself as he stood, a bit shaky on his feet.

He was not normally disoriented from translocating, but then, usually he had Tamara with him. William told himself it was the distance and anxiety, rather than her absence, but he knew it was a combination of all three. Still, he recovered almost immediately.

The gardens behind the Beauregard home were indeed stunning, a sprawl of flowers and trees and plants, with elegant pathways that wound among them, perfect for a stroll. But the moment William stepped away from the bougainvillea he found himself in the sun for the first time, and the heat of the day touched him.

The time difference meant that the afternoon here was really just beginning, and it was going to be a long, arduous day. The heat was insufferable and the air humid. William had never been in a jungle, but exposed for only a minute to this weather, he felt certain he would have no desire to visit one.

The mansion loomed ahead. He did not see anyone at the rear

of the house, or through any of the visible windows, but still he wanted to be off the property quickly, before someone mistook him for a thief. That was one irony he hoped to avoid.

He slipped behind a large bush whose provenance he did not recognize, but which blocked him sufficiently from view.

"Lord Nelson, join me now!" he said as forcefully as he could without actually shouting. The words of the Protector were carried through the spectral realm when he performed a true summoning, as he did now.

For a moment, William was concerned that because he was not in Albion, Horatio would not hear him, but then the hot, sticky air shimmered and the ghost manifested before him.

Horatio executed a courtly bow. "At your service, good sir."

William smiled with relief. It surprised him how much better he felt to know that he had at least one stalwart ally with him on this journey.

"All right, then," he said to the phantom admiral. "Let's not waste a moment. I'd like to get back to Sophia as quickly as possible. I shall make inquiries in the Vieux Carré regarding Philippe Mandeville, while you consult the local spirits, and we will rendezvous in two hours on the steps of St. Louis Cathedral."

"Right. I'm off, then," Horatio replied. Then he narrowed his undamaged eye and studied William. "Have a care, young one. The Battle of New Orleans was not so very long ago. War leaves long memories. You may not be welcomed with open arms."

William nodded solemnly. This had been one of his greatest concerns. The British had laid siege to the city less than a quarter century before, and many remembered the final battle of the war quite well. "I will be wary."

With a light trilling sound, the ghost faded from the air, and

William was alone again. He stepped out onto the path that wound through the garden behind the Beauregard mansion and began to walk quickly. He attempted to adopt a carefree mien, as though he belonged in this place.

Good fortune was with him, for if anyone saw him that afternoon trespassing on the property of his New Orleans business partner, no one appeared at window or door to challenge his presence. In moments he was on Bourbon Street, beginning his first sojourn into the Vieux Carré.

Thanks to the heat, there were few people on the street at that time of day. Several carriages rattled past, and there were a handful of couples, well-dressed men and women who glanced at him curiously but quickly averted their eyes. Creole cottages and town houses were dotted among the shops and businesses. Beautifully intricate iron balconies hung above the streets.

The ladies carried parasols to shield them from the bright sun, and when he had turned up Rue Dumaine and then started along Dauphine, he heard voices rising from within shops and from the courtyards of private homes, all of them speaking French. It had been less than forty years since the French had sold Louisiana to the United States, and the Vieux Carré was still very much the *French* Quarter.

It occurred to William as he walked the street that he was not certain where to begin asking about Philippe Mandeville. Quickly, he realized that he knew so little about the man that there was no point in guessing. It would require luck to track him down. The only factor in his favor was that the Vieux Carré was relatively small, and that he would not have to stray beyond the French Quarter in search of Mandeville, who was obviously of French descent.

So he began to ask. At hotels and banks, at jewelers and cloth-
iers, at a cabinetmaker's and a bakery, he inquired after the mysterious Philippe Mandeville, describing him as an eccentric Creole
gentleman with a predilection for the strange and obscure, who
collected antiquated books and other artifacts. He went down
toward the river and stood captivated for a moment by the sight of
two majestic steamboats awaiting passengers.

Then William set his sights lower for Monsieur Mandeville, asking after him in bars, gambling houses, and theaters. From within
the latter, he heard the sound of music being rehearsed, and it was
vibrant and beautiful. As he passed restaurants that were open to
serve a midday meal, he smelled unfamiliar yet tantalizing spices.

From most of those he asked about Mandeville, William received blank looks. Some of the people of New Orleans were
openly hostile from the moment they heard his accent. There were
those who pretended not to understand English, and then, when
he spoke in French, made it clear they thought his French so atro-
cious that they still could not understand him.

Yet others did cooperate. Several thought that perhaps they'd
heard of Mandeville, and one helpful soul—a mulatto man William
met emerging from a tobacconist's—noted that he seemed to recall a Mandeville among the known associates of "the Widow
Paris." When William pushed for further information about this
woman—of whom the man spoke in a hushed, almost anxious
tone—the gentleman only smiled, shook his head, and turned
away.

It was nearly three o'clock when William arrived at the steps of
St. Louis Cathedral. That austere structure gazed balefully down
upon him, but it was as good a choice as any for a rendezvous
point. William was still an architect at heart—a vocation that his

father's "illness" had forced him to abandon at present—and he knew a great deal about the structure of churches. He also knew something about their nature. Other than those headed there for worship, very few people would look at the face of the church, and if they did, it would be to peer upward at the way the building reached for the heavens.

An odd young Englishman talking to himself wasn't going to draw very much attention there. No one would see the specter, only the man.

So when Horatio appeared at his side, barely a hint of the ghost visible in the afternoon light, William didn't worry about what anyone would think of their conversation.

"Any luck, Horatio?"

"Perhaps a scrap or two," the ghost replied, smoothing the jacket of his spectral uniform. "What of your own efforts?"

William grimaced. "Sadly, very little to show. Our Monsieur Mandeville seems next to unknown in the Vieux Carré. Though we might want to seek out a woman called the Widow Paris. Apparently, they are part of the same social circle . . . or may have been at some point."

A cloud passed across the sun and its shadow reached the front of the cathedral. William saw a look of deep concern, even dread, appear upon the ghost's face.

"What is it?" he asked.

"The woman you speak of, the so-called Widow Paris," Horatio began. "I was specifically warned against seeking her out. She is known by another name here, Marie Laveau, and the spirits of the dead who wander New Orleans are deeply frightened of her, even though they are no longer flesh and blood."

"She's evil, this Laveau woman?" William asked.

Horatio shook his head. "I cannot say. All I gathered was that she is powerful, and that they fear her. It was suggested that instead, we seek out another woman of Mandeville's acquaintance by the name of Antoinette Morton, in the Marigny district."

As William contemplated their next step he looked down at Jackson Square and saw an elderly woman walking past the front of the cathedral with another, not quite as old, who might have been her daughter. The heat was still oppressive and sweat dampened William's clothes, and he questioned the sanity of anyone who would be taking a stroll in such climes. But the locals, he knew, must be used to such horrid weather.

The women had paused to stare at him. He smiled at the elder of the two and turned to Horatio.

"We have few options, my friend."

FAUBOURG MARIGNY HAD ONCE BEEN a plantation belonging to a Creole family, but in the first decade of the nineteenth century it had been developed into quite a respectable neighborhood. Since it was just along the river from the Vieux Carré, William walked the distance, guided by Nelson, who remained unseen and unheard by any of the ordinary citizens of New Orleans.

William had his jacket over his shoulder and the top of his shirt unbuttoned. He had been sweating so much that he worried about dehydration, and knew he needed to stop for a glass of water, even if he had to summon a glass and use a spell to fill it. It would have been far simpler to translocate, but he was exhausted, and had no way of knowing how many witnesses would be there to see his arrival if he traveled by magic. Crossing the Atlantic had been necessary, a calculated risk. But this was only blocks.

No, he would walk.

At Esplanade Street he turned north. The road was busier now that the shadows had grown longer and the heat had diminished somewhat. William wished he could stroll back down to the river, to sit and watch it go by, perhaps have a glass of wine and taste the Creole cuisine. But that was not to be. Not today. One day, perhaps he would return to New Orleans on more pleasant business.

At Goodchildren Street, he turned right. A carriage stood in front of the third house he passed, and as he turned to examine it, he saw a man emerge from the house, a wealthy gentleman from the look of him. On the threshold stood a woman of color, her skin a gleaming caramel that suggested some white ancestry. The gentleman reached back for her and drew her to him in a passionate kiss. They laughed together and then the gentleman strode to his carriage.

In the doorway, a small child, no more than four, joined the woman, clinging to her skirts. The little boy was far lighter skinned than his mother, and it occurred to William that the man who now departed was his father—yet this was not the gentleman's household, to be sure. Or perhaps it was, but a second household.

The man saw William staring and glared at him a moment, as if affronted. William turned away and continued along Goodchildren Street, but his curiosity found him paying close attention to the houses he passed. If the behavior he had just witnessed was so commonplace as to be conducted out of doors, within sight of any passerby, how much a part of New Orleans society were such arrangements?

The moment lingered in his mind and he wondered at the strange layers of a culture in which Africans and the sons and daughters of Africans were still held as slaves, but white men took free women of color as their mistresses, gave them children, and set up households in which to keep them.

When they reached the address Horatio had obtained, William stood on the street for a moment, staring at the door. Something did not feel right about the place. The afternoon shadows gathered in strange patches in the upper corners of the windows, like spider-webs spun from darkness. An unpleasant ripple passed through him.

Warily, he went to the door and knocked. The sound resonated inside and something creaked on the other side of the door. Several seconds of silence passed, and then he heard a scratching against the wood.

There came the click of the lock being drawn back and William took a step away from the door. He glanced to his left and saw Horatio's ghost nearby, strangely substantial in the shadows at the front of the house.

The door opened.

The woman who stood within was breathtaking. Her skin was a rich coffee brown and there was a light in her almond-shaped eyes like nothing he had ever seen. Her hair was pulled back tightly and she wore white cotton that clung to her, a small breeze fluttering the material and tugging it against her, showing the outline of her body in fine detail.

William found himself speechless.

"Do I know you, mister?" she said, and her voice broke whatever spell he'd been under. It was sweet enough, but ordinary, and brought him back to the world.

"Are you Miss Antoinette Morton?" he asked.

She arched an eyebrow when she heard his accent. Her lips parted fetchingly as she was about to reply, but then she frowned and glanced into the shadows by the door, where Horatio stood, observing them.

"That ghost a friend of yours?" she asked.

William blinked.

At first he tried to find some other explanation for her words, but only an idiot would have denied the obvious. The woman was a sensitive of some kind, perhaps a medium or a magician, or both.

"In fact, he is," William replied.

She smiled, those almond eyes sparkling. "All right, then, I'll play along. Yes, I'm Antoinette Morton. And I'm unused to having strange Englishmen calling at my door."

Her breath smelled of cinnamon. William felt a powerful stirring and he forced himself to avert his gaze. Sophia was angry enough with him already. He could not allow himself to be captivated by this woman . . . and yet she was an alluring creature, no doubt.

Enchanting . . .

He frowned, wondering if she was, truly, enchanting him. He had sensed magic in this house from the moment of his arrival, and the shadows that gathered in the windows were not natural. A sorceress, perhaps?

"Miss Morton, I do hope you'll forgive the intrusion," he said. "My name is William Swift. I arrive upon your doorstep on a mission of some urgency, and—"

Cinnamon. The smell was almost overpowering.

"Your father, is it? Got a demon in him?"

William gawped at her. "How on earth could you—"

"Some people say I got voices in my head, Mr. Swift. I say they're spirits. You . . . you can call them whatever you like." Antoinette Morton smiled and stepped back, opening the door wide.

Within, William could see candles burning and small idols and paintings of men and women with their hands clasped in prayer like saints, or with the wounds and blood of martyrs, but they were unlike any saints or martyrs he had ever seen.

"Got some more whispering up here," she said, tapping the side of her head. "Why don't you come on in, and we'll talk a bit about your father, and magic, and then about the man you really came to N'awlins to find."

William paused on the threshold, new scents reaching him, incense burning within the house. "You know Philippe Mandeville, then?"

"Know him?" she asked, then gave a small laugh. "He's my daddy."

～

OLD PHILIPPE DOESN'T LIKE VISITORS, Antoinette had said. *No one out on the bayou is gonna bring you over to his place.*

She served him coffee and beignets in her parlor, and told him about the old sorcerer and alchemist who had fallen in love with her mother, once upon a time. Antoinette barely knew the man, but she was among the very few people in the world he would tolerate now. She was blood, according to Mandeville. That meant something to him.

So when Antoinette had suggested that the only way for William to see her father was if she took him out to Bayou Teche herself, he abandoned all thoughts of translocating there. Arriving upon the man's doorstep with his daughter ought to buy him at least an audience.

It had taken hours to arrange a carriage and then travel out of New Orleans on one of the levee roads that ran through Bayou Teche and the parishes surrounding the state capital. During that time, William confirmed what he had already begun to believe.

Antoinette Morton was indeed a sorceress, though she had another name for her magic. *Vodoun,* she called it. Apparently she was skilled in many mystical arts, thanks to her father, but had gravitated toward the beliefs of her mother's people, thanks to the guidance of the loa, the spirits she claimed spoke to her.

William did not waste a moment doubting her claim about those spirits. He might not be able to see them, but given that the ghost of Horatio Nelson sat with them in the open carriage as they rode out across the levee, the sun sinking into the bayou with a red gleam as the night swept over the water . . . he was in no position to question anyone's belief in spirits.

"You're certain we need to make this journey after dark?" William asked, disliking the idea immensely.

"No other way, chèr," she replied, a grim cast to her eyes. "The house you want—the Mandeville place—you'd never find it when the sun is shining."

"Some kind of spell?" Horatio asked.

She smiled at the ghost. "Powerful spell, that'd be, hmm? But it ain't invisible, that house. During the day, it isn't even there. Not there at all."

William grimaced and a small shiver ran through him. He liked this less with each passing minute. But he kept the purpose of this endeavor foremost in his mind. If they succeeded, at last his father would be free. For that, he would face the darkest of evils.

There was a cluster of ramshackle buildings on the edge of the bayou that might have been a town, and there Antoinette found a young man named James Leroi, who agreed to rent them a boat so they could get out to the small island in the bayou where Mandeville had his home.

The carriage driver had been paid handsomely to await their return up on the levee. Leroi watched uneasily as Antoinette showed William how to use the pole to propel the small boat through the water. A lantern hung from a post at the prow and cast a dim yellow glow ahead. Slowly, they made their way out of the inlet where Leroi and his family lived.

Once out of sight, William gave a sigh of relief.

There were oars, but he had no intention of using them.

"That's enough of that," he said, and he raised his hands. A kind of silver mist began to form around them, his magic combining with the humidity of the Louisiana night.

"Are you sure that's a good idea, William?" Horatio asked.

Out here on the bayou, there was no reason for the ghost not to manifest completely. Most people could not see him, even when he seemed so nearly solid to William. And those who might—children and madmen and artists, and of course sensitives like Antoinette—well, who would believe their claims?

Nelson "sat" at the front of the boat.

"What is he saying?" Antoinette asked.

"You can't hear him?"

Horatio frowned. "I'm a bit surprised she can't, actually. She saw me easily enough this afternoon."

The woman perched at the rear of the boat, just a couple of feet from William. Even in the midst of the bayou, he could smell the cinnamon scent of her. Something from her incense, or a perfume in her clothes, or just the aroma of her magic. He did not know, but he fancied it.

She shrugged. "The loa are always speaking to me. It's difficult sometimes to hear other spirits."

"He doesn't think it's a good idea for me to use magic to get out to your father's house."

"He may be right," Antoinette said, almond eyes shining with lamplight. "If old Philippe senses it, he might think you're an enemy. He collects things. You know that. All kinds of things that other magicians might want. And he guards them jealously. If the loa hadn't whispered to me about you, told me about your father even before you told me yourself, I might not have believed you. Sure wouldn't have helped you."

William smiled. "You have no idea how grateful I am."

Antoinette reached out and laid her hand over his. Her touch was warm and soft and William's breath caught in his throat. He wanted desperately to think of Sophia, but in that moment could not summon the image of her face to his mind. Later, he was certain, he would remember that failure and be ashamed.

"You are a good man, Mr. Swift. I feel it. The spirits know it, as well. Knowing it's in my power to help you, I could not turn you away. That is not the way I live."

"You're a remarkable woman, Miss Morton," William said. Reluctantly, he drew his hand away, glad that it was dark so that she would not see the way his face flushed.

"William, I don't mean to intrude," Horatio said, his single, spectral hand reaching out through the night as though to pluck William away. "But might I suggest that we concentrate on the purpose of this journey?"

With a glance back at the ghost, William nodded, feeling more than a bit foolish. He moved away from Antoinette and picked up the oars.

"That won't be necessary," she said. "Might be dangerous for you to use magic out there, but the Teche is part of my world. The loa of my ancestors will carry us to my father's house, and Yemanja, spirit of the waters, will lend her strength as well."

Antoinette laid her hands across her chest and closed her eyes, a sublime smile touching the corners of her mouth. She laughed softly, as if someone had just whispered a joke to her.

"That's right, my friends, that's right," she said.

The boat rocked once, and the water rippled around them, and then they were in motion. The wind swept across the bayou, but it wasn't only wind that propelled them. The water itself carried them.

For nearly half an hour the three traveled in relative silence. The foreboding darkness of the bayou at night had laid a shroud of uneasiness over the scene, and there was a sense of the power and majesty of the Teche. There were dozens, perhaps hundreds of small islands and promontories that jutted into the water. Things moved in the trees and along the shore, fish jumped in the water, and night birds called in the sky.

The breeze across the water was cool, but the air still held much of the day's heat, and the humidity made even the most open spaces feel closed and dank.

In time they came in sight of a small island upon which there stood a house that seemed entirely out of place. It stood three stories high, a fine old plantation-style structure with lights burning in two of the second-story windows.

"It's lovely," William said, not bothering to mask his surprise.

"Isn't it?" Antoinette responded happily. "But the crazy old man lives out here all alone. Had a wife once, or so my mother said. This house was built for her when they lived in New Orleans. She died before it was completed, but he settled out here anyway, with the ghosts of a family he was never going to have. I'm his only child, at least that I know of, and he barely even speaks to me."

William could not tear his gaze from the incongruous dwelling.

"Well," he said, "let's just hope he's pleased to see you."

Something splashed in the water not far from the boat. William glanced down, expecting to see nothing but ripples on the water where a fish had broken the surface for a moment.

Instead, in the lamplight, he saw the desiccated face of a corpse staring back at him.

Its hands reached up and grabbed the side of the boat, and as it began to pull, it opened its mouth and released a burbling, watery hiss that carried the stench of the grave and the swamp.

Ten

The wind had picked up as the sun began its graceful descent. It was not a harsh wind, though its breath was as cool as the icy waters of a mountain stream. Each gust toyed with the loose strands of Millie's hair like the playful fingers of a small child, gently lifting them.

Millie's sister, Constance, had pulled Millie's long hair into a loose knot at the nape of her neck, letting the shorter pieces fall forward, giving a soft frame to her thin, angular face. The wreath of tiny dried roses and baby's breath still clung to her head, though it had threatened to come loose more than once during the afternoon. She brushed the errant hairs away from her eyes, still marveling at the day.

She, Millicent Turner, was now Mrs. Stuart Wilkie. She could hardly believe it, even as she turned her head and saw her husband sitting in the open carriage beside her. Their tasteful, but not ex-travagant, wedding was just the beginning of their new life to-gether. Stuart had an income of two thousand pounds a year, and a family estate only two miles from the town of Camelford, where her father was the magistrate.

In the cool of the late afternoon, the long ivory satin dress she'd put on that morning, for only the third time since the initial fitting, felt delicious against her cool skin, the heavy fabric whispering against itself as she moved. As Constance had helped Millie dress, she marveled at how elegant and mature the high-necked lace col-lar made Millie look, and at how the satin fabric, cinched so tightly around her waist, gave her thin body the shape of an hourglass.

As the carriage hit a bump in the dirt road, Millie reached out and took Stuart's hand in her own. He turned and smiled at her. She returned the gesture, giving her husband a subtle looking-over in the process.

He was a handsome enough man, she thought to herself, even if he was twenty-two years her senior. He still had a full head of hair and the majority of his teeth, for which she counted her blessings. She only hoped that she'd be able to bear him the heir he so wished for, unlike his first wife, who'd died in childbirth ten years before.

She hadn't given much thought to what that really meant until her mother had taken her aside at the reception, and, through clenched teeth, explained what her wifely duties would entail. If she hadn't known her mother to be without a sense of humor, Mil-lie would've thought she was joking. She could hardly believe the *things* that had come out of her mother's mouth. Millie was posi-tive that she was not going to enjoy her first night at Wilkie Manor.

Not one little bit.

A queer, high-pitched scream came from somewhere in the sky

above them, jarring her from her thoughts. Millie looked up, but saw nothing.

"Possibly an injured hawk," Stuart reassured his young wife, though there was a slight edge to his smooth baritone.

Just as she began to relax, that horrid scream came again and she shivered, hugging herself tightly. Millie craned her neck to peer up into the night sky and her mouth opened in silent astonishment. Black wraiths darted across the night, moving in a strange, circular pattern until they nearly blotted out the moonlight above the carriage.

Stuart stood up in the open carriage, first staring up in horror and then—holding on to the seat ahead—shouting to the driver.

"Get us to the trees!" he yelled, but his voice was almost lost amid the shrieking of the fluttering wraiths above.

The driver cracked the reins and the horse began to gallop. Its eyes gleamed white in the darkness, wide and mad. Flecks of froth came from its lips and it neighed loudly, as though it also was terrified of those dreadful figures swirling in the sky.

As they trundled toward the cover of the trees, one of the wraiths shot down from the sky. Stuart shouted in alarm, a curse and a prayer to God, and he reached for her.

Too late.

The wraith grabbed her beneath her arms with long talons that gripped painfully, and lifted her from the carriage as though she weighed no more than a rag doll. Millie screamed her throat ragged as the thing looked down at her from beneath its black hood and she saw its hideously twisted features. The chill wind whipped around her as they darted skyward.

A hand clutched her ankle, solid and heavy. Another twisted in the fabric of her dress.

Millie looked down to see Stuart staring up at her, eyes desperate with fear and love and dread. The thing tugged her upward, talons digging into her flesh, drawing blood that would stain her wedding dress.

Stuart climbed onto the seat of the carriage and grabbed her around the waist. With a huge effort, he wrapped his arms around her, using himself as anchor, and then pulled.

She screamed again as the talons sliced her shoulders and the soft flesh under her arms, but the thing lost its grip. Millie and Stuart fell back down into the open carriage together. He threw Millie to the floor of the carriage and stood above her, valiantly shielding her from the wraith with his own body. The carriage came to a bumping halt, and the horse neighed pitifully before ceasing its cries altogether.

Millie heard the passage of one of the wraiths in the night wind, then a strange tearing sound. As she lay on her stomach with Stuart above her, she felt something hot spatter the back of her neck and arms, and then that same liquid poured down on her. She began to shake, almost rigid with shock.

Stuart's weight slumped full upon her for a moment, and she was pinned to the carriage floor. She stayed where she was, even as the warm stickiness covered the back of her bodice and stuck to her hair. Her gorge rose.

The air was rent with another chorus of shrieks from the wraiths, and then Millie felt Stuart's weight lifted from her. The sticky liquid that soaked through her clothes caught the chill of the wind, making Millie shiver. She sat up on her hands and knees to find she was alone in the carriage. As she crawled onto the seat, she froze in horror, all the air rushing from her lungs.

Stuart lay across the driver's seat of the carriage, his head simply gone. Weak spurts of blood pumped from the ragged stump. Bits of vertebrae and sinew jutted out.

Millie turned and vomited over the side of the carriage. She retched for only a moment before she felt something flutter above her, and then a sharp pain radiated from her back. With the taste of her own bile still strong in her throat, she felt her body lifted up into the air.

Below her, she saw the remains of the driver lying in the scrub grass on the side of the road, his torso flayed open from groin to gullet, viscera spilling out. His bowels lay like giant worms, steaming and hissing in the cool air.

Millie could not breathe. Her heart thundered in her chest and then she began to hyperventilate. Black pools of darkness spread across her vision and fresh pain radiated along her right arm and in her breasts.

She had always been a sickly child, unable to do more than sit and watch her peers through the parlor window as they played outside. Even as a young lady, she could do nothing more taxing than embroider.

When she let her head loll back and looked up into the twisted, hideous features of the wraith that carried her into the night sky, a terror rushed through her veins like nothing she had ever conceived of. Something inside of her heart burst. The pain was sharp and blinding, and then done.

The creature that was carrying Millie heard her final, shuddering breath, and then felt the life depart from the girl's flesh. It held on to its prize for a few moments longer, as though unwilling to believe the girl was dead, and now useless.

The wraith relaxed its grip, letting Millie's corpse drop. The dead girl plummeted like a lead weight into the rushing waters of the Camel River.

Swept away.

~

Swift's of London had been empty for nearly six hours when a man strode across Threadneedle Street under cover of darkness and turned down a side alley. He walked briskly, keeping an even pace, his hands thrust far down into his coat pockets. He kept watch, but the alley was empty this time of night. Only the wind blew through these byways after the city had gone to sleep.

He glanced around surreptitiously before using a large iron key he pulled from his inside coat pocket to open the side door, and then he slipped through.

The lights were off, but the man had no difficulty navigating the bank in the darkness. He moved with feline grace through the grid of small wooden tellers' desks, his body never brushing anything but air.

At the metal half-gate that separated the tellers from the entrance to the vaults, he paused and reached for the lock. Opening it was simple. At the vaults he used another key to open the solid metal door that was the first line of defense in protecting the valuables Swift's of London housed for its clientele.

He slid the key into the lock, and waited for the click. When he heard it, he pushed the door open. Once inside the long dark hallway that housed the three largest vaults, the man lit a wall sconce and the flame flickered up, illuminating the corridor and filling it with dancing shadows.

At the first vault he ran his hands along the smooth door. He let his gloved fingers find their way to the combination dial, caressing the indentations before closing his hand over it. The dial spun quickly, making a small whirring noise as it turned. He waited until he heard an answering click and then stopped and spun the dial in the opposite direction. Once again, he waited for the click before spinning it again.

In but a few moments, he had the vault open.

He stepped inside and walked to the first cabinet, immediately locating the drawer that was his target. Within the drawer, he found two objects, each wrapped in its own silk bag. Removing them from their nests, he weighed them both with his hands, then slipped one of the objects back into its bag and returned it to the drawer. The other he placed in his coat pocket, the weight of the thing pulling his jacket down on one side.

He slid the drawer closed and departed.

In the foyer, a beam of moonlight fell through the open door, a path of light through the darkness of the empty bank. The man glanced back the way he'd come, feeling triumph at a job well done. He had breached the security of the bank almost seven times since his work had begun. Each time he had become more adept at his job, taking less time to complete his theft.

Back out in the alley, he strode quickly along the cobblestones as the door closed behind him. When he reached Threadneedle Street he turned right, disappearing into the night.

Unseen.

CHRISTINE LINDSAY LIVED WITH her grandfather, Bertram, above the tobacconist's shop he owned, two blocks from the Mason's Arms along the main street of Camelford. The smell of tobacco was in everything, the curtains and bedspread, the sheets, even her clothes. Her grandfather had lost the ability to detect the smell before she was born, but Christine was not so fortunate. It seemed to her that she would never get it out of her nose.

She had never known her mother, and her father had been trampled by horses when she was twelve years old. Her grandmother had passed only a month later, her poor heart unable to take the strain of losing her only son. It was just Christine and Grandad Bert, now, and though he was a wizened, crotchety old sod, she loved him to distraction.

They slept only a little in the Lindsay home. The pains of age kept Grandad awake. More often than not he dozed in a chair half the night and woke in the wee hours of the morning, long before the sun would rise. He was always careful to be as quiet as an old man could be, though invariably the smoke from his pipe would fill the house with its pungent, acrid smell, and Christine would come half awake and lie there for a time until exhaustion overtook her again.

She had been up late last night. Frankie Turner, the farrier's son, had taken a fancy to her from the moment she began working as a barmaid at the inn, and the boy had been pressing his attentions upon her ever since. At first she had been put off by his ardor, but in the ensuing months he had matured nicely and developed a self-deprecating humor that she found charming. If he had also grown more handsome and his body more manly in that time, well, all the better.

So last night, behind the stables, she had at last allowed him to reach beneath her skirts and touch her in the most intimate of ways. The mere memory of it had made sleep difficult, and she had woken from delicious dreams more than once to find her own hand pressed between her legs.

Christine buried her face in her pillow, drifting between sleep and wakefulness, only vaguely aware of the darkened bedroom around her and the sheet that had become tangled about her. A night breeze cooled her skin, a sweet respite from the summer heat that the morning would soon bring. All told, she had managed only a couple of hours' sleep thus far, but she didn't have to work until nearly noontime, and her grandfather would indulge her if she decided to sleep in.

Exhaustion embraced her again and she began to drift off, there in the darkness on the soft bed that had once been her father's.

Her eyelids fluttered, and then her forehead creased in a frown.

The rich, earthy smell of the smoke from Grandad Bert's pipe filled the air. Either he was up even earlier than usual, or it was later than Christine thought. Could it be after four already?

Reluctantly, she forced herself to turn and look out the window. The trees behind the house were silhouettes against the night. The sky had indeed begun to lighten, just slightly. It was still dark, but tinged with an indigo blue that hinted at the coming of morning. Another night she would have been reassured, but with so little sleep, Christine groaned at the sight.

The branches of the trees were blacker than black, just shadows against the indigo sky. A cascade of stars gleamed far, far above, but some of their brilliance was muted now that sunrise was only a short time away.

Christine took a deep breath, relished the coolness of the breeze, and resettled herself upon the mattress, her cheek against her pillow as though it were her lover's chest. Again she thought of young Frankie Turner and the dexterity of his fingers.

A smile stole across her lips and she sighed to herself with satisfaction, and anticipation as to what the coming days would bring. With the smoke from her grandfather's pipe swirling through the house on the night breeze, she began to drift off once again.

The tiniest of noises disturbed her.

Christine frowned but did not open her eyes. Not yet. It was too early for the songs of morning birds, and this was no sound so sweet as that, in any case. Rather, it had been a kind of rasp.

It came again, and this time she lifted her head and turned once more toward the window. Nothing had changed. The wind must have caused the window to slip in its frame somehow. That had been it—a squeak, not a rasp. Outside, the tree branches moved in the breeze, some of them full and green, but several others bare, shaking like spindly, skeletal fingers.

One of them swayed and touched the glass, scraping against it as if it were some haunt, trying to get in.

In her bed, Christine shivered in spite of herself. The coolness of the night was no longer delicious. She reached down for her bedspread and pulled it up to cover her, turning away from the window. Foolish, she knew. It was only the wind, and the branches, and she wasn't a child, to be frightened of such things.

But it had been far too long since anyone had been there to comfort her in the night, and sometimes it was frightening—the dark, and the unknown things that lurked out there in the gloom. She shuddered, and then laughed softly into her pillow.

"Silly cow," she whispered. "Now you're only scaring yourself."

Again there came the scrape of the branch against the glass, and this time she started, twitching beneath the spread. Her eyes were wide open and her heart pounded. There would be no more sleep this night. As ridiculous as she felt, she was pleased that morning was not far off. She tried to lose herself in the familiar, safe aroma of her grandfather's pipe.

A thump against the wall, and she turned.

Nothing had changed. Still those spindly branches wavered in the wind.

Christine frowned. She had been half asleep before, but . . . it was midsummer. None of the branches should have been so bare.

Even as the thought struck her, the skeletal fingers reached out and rapped the glass again, and cracks spiderwebbed through it. Another branch—a dark, spindly hand, black as night—grabbed hold of the windowsill, and then the wraithlike figure rose up as though flying, and began to slip inside.

The branches rustled again, and a second wraith appeared, then a third.

Christine went rigid, muscles taut with fear, eyes wide as she tried to see the faces of the things, to see beyond the veil of night that seemed to shroud them. She thought she would vomit, but when she opened her mouth what came out was a scream of utter terror, a shriek that scraped her throat raw and resounded throughout the house.

Then they were upon her, cold fingers wrapping around her arms and legs, covering her mouth, muffling her wail but not her terror. They dragged her from the bed and her head struck the floor with a crack and she slid toward the window. The chill from their fingers went to the bone. She had never felt so cold.

She tried to scream again but no sound escaped her. The breath she drew was ragged and painful, and a tear slid down her cheek as she struggled to give voice to the frantic horror within her, the knowledge that the darkness had taken form and that death seemed only seconds away.

They lifted her and swept her out the window, and in the final moment before they shot across the sky with her in their clutches, sliding across treetops and into the indigo hour before dawn, Christine looked back at her bedroom window and saw her grandfather standing just within, staring after her. Summoned by her scream, he could only watch as the spindly darkness carried her off. He gripped his pipe in one hand and laid the other across his heart, his mouth open in silent anguish.

Her last glimpse allowed her to see him stagger against the cracked glass and begin to slide toward the floor, still clutching his chest, his old man's heart.

Then the air seemed stolen from her lips and she was swept up and up and up into the darkness, and unconsciousness stole over her and dragged her down into perfect, starless night.

∿

Tamara came awake abruptly, without the pleasant preamble of feline stretching and growing awareness that normally accompanied her each morning. Her eyes simply opened and she found that her senses were alert, as though awaiting some stimulus that her conscious mind had yet to recognize.

It took her a moment to recall that she was in Camelford, that this room was at the Mason's Arms, and the familiarity of Ludlow House was far, far off in distant London.

A heavy knock sounded upon the door, three solid thumps. She frowned and sat up. Clearly this had been what had roused her. Whoever had disturbed her, this was not their first attempt.

"Who is it?" she called.

"Farris, Miss Tamara," came the answer.

From the slant of light through the window, it was still quite early. She rose and pulled her robe around her and went to the door, where she drew back the bolt and opened the door so that Farris could enter.

His expression was troubled.

"What is it? What's happened?"

Farris glanced at the door, but did not speak until she had closed it and thrown the bolt again.

"News, miss, and of the unpleasant variety, I'm sorry to say. There's two gents downstairs I gather are what amounts to the local constabulary. Peelers they ain't, that's plain from the look of 'em. Don't suppose Sir Robert's influence has reached this far as yet. But there's a jail in town, and that means there's them what decides what crimes earn a man time within its walls."

Tamara stared at him a moment, then shook her head. "Farris, please, I've just woken and all I hear are riddles. If trouble has brought the police to the inn, I presume you've discovered the purpose of their visit."

The grim-faced man nodded. "That I have. I'm afraid another girl's been taken, miss. Only hours ago. And it appears there've been others murdered as well, a couple on the night of their own wedding. The magistrate's daughter, she was. Her and her new groom and their driver."

The words were a dagger to Tamara's heart. The days were passing too quickly. The clock was ticking toward the solstice—only five days remaining now—and she was no closer to discovering who had abducted the missing girls. All she had were rumors and legends, nothing more. Yet here another girl was gone, and three people dead, and what had she to show for her efforts? Nothing at all. She could only hope that Richard Kirk's mystic rapport with his sister was real, and not something that only existed in the young man's head. That the missing girls truly were still alive, and would be kept alive until the solstice.

Even so, she was the Protector of Albion. The idea that another girl had been stolen away by night in Camelford and three people murdered under her very nose did not sit well with her at all.

"The missing girl," she said, already turning toward the dressing table in her room. "Did you overhear her name?"

"I'm afraid so."

Farris's tone gave her pause. She turned to him again.

"What is it?"

"We know her, miss. It was the barmaid, Christine, the one you told me you spoke to at tea yesterday afternoon."

Tamara's stomach tightened and she thought she might be sick. She had a clear picture of the girl's face in her mind, the red hair, the spray of freckles across the bridge of her nose. Christine had been kind to her, and now she was in the hands of some dark power that meant to take her life.

"Oh, no," she whispered. "I won't allow it.

"Go back downstairs," she continued. "See what else you can learn from the constables. I shall dress and be down momentarily."

After Farris had departed, Tamara attended to her toilette as quickly as she could manage. Though she disliked relying upon magic for such simple things—believing that the power of the Protector of Albion was best reserved for more weighty tasks—she sped herself along by using an enchantment on her hair. It would have taken forever to pin it up so that it would be presentable, and she had no time to spare.

Less than twenty minutes after Farris had left her room, Tamara smoothed her skirt and descended the front steps of the Mason's Arms. There was no sign of Farris, the innkeeper, or the constables. Several guests were clustered together near the entrance to the bar, but that room was dark at this time of the morning. They whispered together, and Tamara was certain they were gossiping about the arrival of the policemen, and the troubles afflicting Camelford.

With these new murders, she wondered how many of the inn's guests would still be in town come evening, and wagered with herself that the number would be few. There seemed half as many travelers at the Mason's Arms yesterday as there had been the day before that, and it seemed likely others would now hasten their departure.

Tamara saw one of the whispering guests glance past her, toward a narrow corridor. She went that direction and came upon a door that hung open several inches. Male voices issued from within. She paused to listen, and then heard instead a low, sharp hiss from her left.

Farris had made the noise to get her attention. He beckoned to her from just inside a small room across the hall. She joined him quickly and stepped inside, glancing toward the other room only once before secreting herself with Farris in what seemed to be a small library.

"I presume the voices in that room must be those of the two constables and our innkeeper," she said in a hushed voice.

Farris nodded. "The very gentlemen, miss. I'm afraid I haven't learned much I hadn't already heard, save an additional bit of tragedy. A local boy's just brought word that Miss Lindsay—the barmaid, that is—her grandfather's passed on, and it seems he was her only kin."

Her heart sank. Even if she was able to save Christine now, the girl would be coming back to a different life, one without any family at all. When her own grandfather had been killed, and her father had been afflicted by the demon Oblis, Tamara at least had William to comfort her.

Suddenly she missed her brother terribly. But she could not let the ache of her own desire distract her from the horrors at hand here in Camelford, and in the forest around the town.

"Nothing more?"

Farris gestured into the hall. "Well, as you were coming along, I heard one of them mention . . . well, something about witches."

Tamara frowned, a fragment of memory skittering spiderlike up her spine. Christine had said something about witches at Slaughterbridge. It had been her intention to visit the site this very day. There were a hundred other creatures who could be responsible for these crimes, but the coincidence seemed worth noting, particularly given the local lore about witchcraft and Slaughterbridge.

"Go and ready the carriage," she instructed Farris, moving to peer out into the corridor, at the partially opened door across the hall. She could not make out many of the words from here, as though the men had purposely lowered their voices.

She turned to him again. "Is Serena still spying on the fairies?"

"I believe so, miss."

"Good. I'll be along shortly, and we shall see if we don't have better luck locating Richard Kirk today. Then it's out to Slaughterbridge."

Farris nodded and went to fulfill her instructions, moving with surprising grace.

She waited several moments and then slipped into the hallway. A glimpse as she passed the partially open door revealed the two constables and the innkeeper, Roger Price, gathered in an elegant sitting room, though all of the men were standing. Tamara pretended to be occupied examining a portrait upon the wall. She began to contort her fingers, whispering the first phrases of a German spell that would temporarily improve her hearing, but then the voices in that other room rose in volume, and no magic was necessary.

"The man is dead, gentlemen!" Price said. "I'll thank you not to treat his memory so shabbily within these walls, particularly as you haven't a single clue as to the whereabouts of his granddaughter."

"It'll be easy enough for you to find another barmaid, I should think," one of the constables, a man with a ragged voice, said curtly. It was clear he was unused to being upbraided by anyone.

Tamara flinched at his callousness.

"Ah, well, it's good that you're on the job, then, since you're so set upon locating her and the other girls that've gone missing," Price sneered. "I'm well aware that the two of you are more used to manhandling drunken brawlers than solving murders and mysteries, but you're wasting your time here."

"See here, sir," the other constable protested. "The dead girl in Market Square the other day, Betsy Harper, we figured she'd thrown herself from the clock tower. The whole village thought so. But after last night—"

"After last night, what, precisely? What do you gentlemen think you're going to learn here?"

"Well, sir, two of the girls did work for you."

Price cursed loudly. "You imbeciles. You think I've got them stashed in the basement or the stables? By all means, have a look around. And now I think that's quite enough of my time you've taken.

"I've had two girls who worked for me go missing in a handful of days, and I fear for them, gentlemen. These are fine girls, and I'm fond of both of them. Now you've four missing, and four people dead, and what are you doing with your time? Asking insulting and ridiculous questions. Now that you've inquired, shouldn't you be out actually searching for the girls?"

"There are dozens of men out in the forest already—" began the ragged-voiced constable.

"Yes, but the girls are still missing, aren't they? Which means the job isn't done yet. I've spent some time out there already myself, but now I've got my farrier and his son searching in my stead.

Someone's got to look after the inn. What excuse have the two of you got, then, for hanging about here and ridiculing a dead man?"

"That will do, Mr. Price," snapped the other policeman. "The old man rambled on about witches. Said he'd seen 'em as a boy, so he knew what they were when they come for the girl. Claimed they stole her out the window, carried her off into the sky. What are we supposed to make of that?"

"I couldn't say, constable, but you could bloody well show some respect for the dead. Witches! For God's sake. The only mystery the two of you are fit to solve is what's at the bottom of a glass of ale. Now if you're through, why not get on with your work, and let me get on with mine?"

Tamara turned toward the window in the corridor and set about examining her reflection there, fussing over the pins in her hair. The innkeeper emerged from the room first, grumbling in frustration as he headed into the tavern proper. The constables came out of the room after him, one of them clutching his hat in his hand, the other holding a pipe as though he meant to throw it at the retreating back of Mr. Price.

They hesitated a moment as they emerged and saw her in the hall, but then they made to depart.

"Excuse me, gentlemen," Tamara said softly.

The loutish pair turned and studied her appreciatively. Tamara acted the coquette, resisting the urge to scowl at them.

"Yes, miss, what can we do for you?" asked the man with the pipe.

She glanced shyly down a moment and then lifted her gaze, feigning anxiety and a delicacy that had never been hers.

"I couldn't help overhearing part of your conversation. I hope you'll forgive me for that. But there is so much talk in the village about these missing girls, and now . . . murder. A young lady cannot help feeling a bit afraid."

The other constable, a brutish man with a bent nose, grinned at her, revealing a few brown teeth and many gaps between.

"Ah, well, miss, you've got nothing to fear with us around. We'll keep an eye out for you."

Yes, Tamara thought, *I'm sure you will.*

"You're too kind," she told them. "It's a comfort, truly. Particularly as the girls who've gone missing, as I understand it, have all been quite young, and I feel I might bear a resemblance in that sense to the others who've fallen prey to whatever evil lurks in Camelford. What of the couple who met their untimely ends last night? Do you think the culprit is the same?"

"No reason to think so, miss," said the bent-nosed brute.

The constable with the pipe looked at his comrade. "No reason to think otherwise, you mean."

They looked at each other in consternation, and Tamara was grateful to the pipe-smoking gent when he turned to her, dropping all pretense.

"The bride was a young lady no older than yourself, miss. Truth is, we think they came for her and her new husband tried to stop them, ended up getting both of them killed."

Tamara stared at him. These men might be loutish pub creatures, but they were not as inept as she had first believed.

"You said *them.* Have you any idea who *they* are?"

The constables both dissembled a moment and then the brutish one slipped on his hat. "Only theories at this point, miss. All we can tell you is that it's best that you don't go out after dark on your own."

"After dark?" Tamara asked.

The pipe smoker shrugged. "It's all happened after dark, at least so far."

"Thank you, gentlemen," she said, noting how their initial response to her had been sobered by the topic at hand. "I'm grateful for your concern."

She was tempted to explain to them what Christine had said to her the previous afternoon about witches, but she knew it was a foolish impulse. Given their dismissal of the tale told by a dying man who'd witnessed the actual events as they unfolded, they were hardly likely to credit the opinion of an outsider, never mind a girl.

When they had said their goodbyes and departed, she hurried back toward the front of the inn, already casting her mind forward to the impending search for Richard Kirk. Hopefully, Farris would have the carriage nearly ready now.

The days were passing too quickly. Four human girls had been spirited away, and four people murdered. She had no idea how many fairies had been abducted or killed.

If Richard Kirk was correct, and the vanished girls had merely been abducted, they had only days to live. Tamara refused to give up on them. Every moment that went by was another bringing them nearer to their deaths, and the weight of that knowledge was heavy upon her conscience.

∾

STREAMERS OF SUNLIGHT fell through the branches of the trees high above, but those golden rays never seemed to reach the forest floor. It was as though the shadows swallowed the day and night never quite surrendered in the depths of the wood.

Rhosynn of Stronghold knew that her perception might well be colored by the grief in her heart, by her fear for her missing sister, but every tree seemed to hide an enemy now. She felt the forest closing around her as she moved among the trees, twitching and birdlike, watching every branch and leaf for signs of trouble.

The bow was light in her hands, an extension of herself, and the arrow felt right and murderous where her fingers touched it. The string of the weapon hummed with her need for vengeance.

"Rhosynn," Fyg said at her side.

She frowned and looked at her cousin, even as the other fairy girl slipped between two thin birches, a dark metal dagger clutched in her hand.

"What is it?" Rhosynn demanded. "Why would you speak, Fyg, and risk alerting the killers?"

Fyg flinched and pushed a lock of shimmering golden hair away from her green eyes. "Don't say that word, Rhos. Mellyn is dead, but Lorelle and the others are alive still, I know it."

Rhosynn sighed. The air was claustrophobic around her. The magic of the wood still danced upon her skin, but she felt strangely anchored to the earth, as though she would not have been able to take flight even if she wanted to.

"All right. Even so, I told you that you could come along only if you kept quiet. If the dark ones are here in the wood, it would be nice to catch them unaware."

Fyg nodded earnestly. Rhosynn appreciated that she did not mention the fact that no one was allowed to leave Stronghold alone now, and this little search party would not have been given permission to depart if there had not been at least three of them.

Rhosynn frowned. Three. She glanced around.

"Looking for me?" a voice whispered above her.

Swift as a fox, Rhosynn raised her bow and drew the string. Had she not seen the familiar magenta sparkle of Ghillie's eyes, she might have shot her cousin through the heart.

"Fool," she whispered harshly. "Come down here. And try to keep up from now on."

"Keep up?" Ghillie replied, fluttering down to the ground, into the deep shadow amid the trees. "It was you who lagged behind, cousin."

"That's what I was trying to tell you," Fyg confirmed. "That Ghillie had passed us by, and I'd lost track of her."

Rhosynn frowned. "It was a foolish thing to do, Ghil. They could be upon you in an instant. We'd not hear a sound, and you'd be gone. Stay within sight."

All humor drained from the group as Rhosynn recalled the details of Lorelle's disappearance. She had been quite close by, and still hadn't been aware of any danger.

"You're right. I'm sorry. I'll be more careful."

Fyg sheathed her dagger and crossed her arms sternly. She was the littlest of them, but the grimmest as well.

"She's not the only careless one. Rhosynn, you didn't even know that Ghillie'd gone ahead. If I hadn't hurried after you, and called your name, you'd have left me behind. With Ebrel now vanished, we've five of our people missing. If you don't have a care, one of us is sure to be number six. Ghillie and I want to end this as much as you do, but we must be smart about it."

Rhosynn smiled. "You're right, Fyg. My apologies. I was being a fool." She arched an eyebrow. "Though I don't think Ghil's got anything to worry about, does she? Wouldn't be her they'd take. Only the pure among us suit their appetites. And after her night with that French boy on the riverbank, she's hardly that."

Ghillie kicked her in the shin. Rhosynn let out a small yelp of pain, and then the fairies were laughing together again. It felt wonderful to share a moment of lightness, yet Rhosynn felt guilt, as well, as though it was wrong to allow herself even to smile while

Lorelle and the others were still missing, and their abductors remained unpunished.

"All right, hush now." Rhosynn adjusted her grip upon her bow, and nodded to her cousins.

Fyg and Ghillie started through the forest again, the shadows of the wood clinging to them as though they could smother the magic in them. More and more Rhosynn wished she and Lorelle had just fled this place the moment things had begun to get dangerous. But there was nothing to be done for it now. She would not leave until she had her sister back, or justice, if the worst happened.

The Council of Stronghold had only just begun to allow search parties—hunting parties, Rhosynn thought them—to venture out into the wood. The humans were all through the forest, but the magic of the outpost would keep them away from the enchanted part of the wood, which left it for the fairies to explore—

Rhosynn froze.

Out of the corner of her eye, she'd seen something move.

She glanced to her right and something glittered in the shadows. It was there only for a moment, and then gone, but she had seen it.

She swung the bow, drew the string, and took aim. "Sprite. Show yourself."

Nothing happened. Fyg and Ghillie stared at her, then glanced into the wood in the direction she aimed, then looked back toward her again.

"*Now*," Rhosynn said.

Serena darted around from behind the tree. She flew to within a dozen feet of the fairies and then hung in the air, tiny wings fluttering furiously, arms crossed just as sternly as Fyg's had been moments before.

"You does what now, Rhos? Hmm? Going to shoots us?" Serena demanded in her tiny, piping voice.

"I'm considering it," Rhosynn replied.

"Serena!" Fyg snapped. "Aren't you in enough trouble, little one? Now you're spying on us. Why, there are those at Stronghold who would accuse you of spying for our enemies, if they were to hear."

"We *isn't* a spy, grumpy Fyg, and how *dares* you to say it!" Serena shrieked. Tears sprang to her eyes, and her face flushed lavender. "You breaks our heart. Not a soul at Stronghold loves Aine like we does, and not a one wants her back more! *Shame* on you!"

Fyg had such a guilty expression on her face that Rhosynn would have laughed, had it not been that she herself felt a measure of shame. The council's treatment of Serena was inexcusable. Yet that did not give the sprite leave to spy on them.

"It isn't the enemy she's spying for," Rhosynn said. "It's the Protector of Albion."

Serena only harrumphed and looked away, not behaving at all like a captive.

"And how do we know the two aren't one and the same?" Ghillie asked.

The sprite's eyes went wide with fury, and she darted like a hornet through the air. With her tiny hand, she slapped Ghillie's face. It could not have hurt badly, but Ghil cried out as though stung, and backed away.

"Oh, you foolish little thing. I'll kill you for—" she began.

"No," Rhosynn said, holding up a hand. "She defends the honor of her friend. You cannot fault her for that."

Serena hovered once more in the air. She jabbed an accusatory finger toward Rhosynn.

"You pretends to be our friend, Rhosynn, but we doesn't have any friends left at Stronghold. Not with Aine gone. And now she'll die, and your sister, too, and the others, all 'cause the council doesn't think they needs the Protector's help. If they lives, it'll be Tamara Swift's doing, and none of Stronghold's."

"Fools," the sprite sniffed.

Then she darted off into the trees with a musical trill and a cascade of lavender light. Rhosynn didn't attempt to shoot her with the bow, nor did Fyg or Ghillie make any move to stop her.

Serena had spoken true, and it cut them deeply.

～

FARRIS NEEDN'T HAVE BOTHERED with the carriage. Tamara ought to have realized straightaway that Richard would be out in the forest once again today, searching for his sister. By late morning, she had joined the search party, though she had little hope that the ordinary men combing the woods would meet with success. She and Farris were searching, instead, for Richard Kirk.

They had joined a party led by Camelford's two inept constables, who obviously thought themselves responsible for the leadership and organization of the entire effort. No one argued with them. They might be poor constables, but they were strong men with keen eyes and seemed as desperate as any other man to find the missing girls. The men were welcomed among the searchers.

On the other hand, the group seemed troubled by the presence of a woman. Even the constables, who had made their appreciation obvious earlier in the day, observed many times that she'd be safer back at the inn. She had to remind them that it was they themselves who'd told her nothing bad had happened during the day—as yet.

Tamara ignored their hesitations, and they were forced to accept her help. They spread out through the trees, all staying within hailing distance of one another, and moved through the forest looking in the dense brush for any sign of the missing girls. Farris was off to Tamara's left, and a carpenter named Hayes to her right.

They wandered the woods for hours. Sometime after one o'clock, a group gathered in a clearing to share water, bread, and cheese. Tamara hadn't expected to find any clue as to the whereabouts of the girls, but she had begun to despair of ever setting eyes on Richard Kirk again.

When he walked into the clearing with his father, just ahead of Peter David and his hounds, Tamara let out a small gasp of surprise that caused several men to look at her. As she was the only woman in the group, Richard could not fail to notice her, and as soon as he had somberly greeted some of the others he waved away the food they offered and strode over to where she and Farris stood.

"Miss Swift, isn't it?"

"That's right."

"Thank you for your efforts. I admit, I'm surprised to see you out here."

"Because I'm a woman?"

Richard frowned. "Because you're a stranger. An outsider. Most of those traveling through Camelford these past few days have moved along more quickly than usual, but you seem to have no other destination."

"At the moment, I do not," she replied.

Tamara did not elaborate, and to his credit, Richard did not pursue the subject.

"Well, I'm grateful," he said, then nodded toward Farris. "To both of you."

"Least we can do," Farris replied. "Least any decent person could do."

The young man's gaze grew distant. His mind seemed already

to be turning back to the quest for his missing sister and the other girls, and Tamara could not blame him. She glanced around to be sure they would not be overheard.

"Richard," she began, watching his eyes closely, both to gauge his response, and to communicate to him her own sincerity, "you told me of the . . . special rapport you have with Sally. That you can feel her, even get a sense of her surroundings, and that you sometimes know things that she knows."

He blinked as though she had spat at him, and took a step backward, then took a look around to confirm for himself that no one was near enough to have heard her words.

"I was distraught that day, Miss Swift."

Tamara narrowed her eyes. "Are you now telling me that it isn't true?"

He averted his gaze, staring at the ground. "Not at all." With a thin, tired, uncertain smile he raised his eyes once more. "It's just not the sort of thing I'm used to discussing with strangers. Or with anyone else, for that matter. When I have spoken about it, well, you can imagine the sorts of things people have said about me."

"I can, in fact," she said.

Richard cocked his head to one side and looked at her as though for the very first time. There was a profound sadness in his eyes that did not mask the basic decency and warmth that also lived there.

"Yes," he said quietly. "Yes, I see that you can."

Farris cleared his throat to draw her attention, and Tamara followed his gaze to discover that the elder Mr. Kirk and the hounds master, David, were peering at her and Richard. She shifted her position to keep the young man between her and their observers, for his own privacy.

"Have you sensed anything more through that connection, anything else Sally is feeling that might help us locate her?"

Richard hesitated a moment. "There are . . . others there," he said, and once again his gaze seemed distant, though now in an entirely different way. It was as though he was seeing into some other world, a realm beyond the ordinary human senses, through which he could connect with Sally.

"This will sound peculiar," he added, then glanced at her, "though perhaps not to you, now that I think of it. Some of the girls that are around her have a sort of . . . light . . . to them. I'm not sure they're entirely human."

"Go on."

"The fear comes off all of them like something alive. It's enough near to buckle my knees when I feel it. And the trees—"

Tamara glanced past him, checking to be sure no one was coming closer. Farris busied himself by taking off his coat and picking brambles from the fabric.

"What of the trees?" she asked.

"It's as though the trees themselves are holding them. Pricking Sally's skin. Like claws." He said this last in a rasp, and in his voice she could hear some of the fear he had absorbed through his sister. Richard breathed evenly, but Tamara could see it was an effort.

His eyes closed. "It hurts," he said softly.

When he opened them, he blinked as though awakening. "There's one other thing. There are shadows, dark figures, tall and thin, all angles and glittering eyes. I have no idea what they are, but—"

"Witches," Tamara interrupted.

Richard stared at her. "What?"

"Christine's grandfather said they were witches."

For a long moment Richard said nothing. Then he shifted, as though released from some trance, and glanced around at the other men in the clearing, and at his father and the hounds master. When he turned back to Tamara, he nodded slowly.

"Well, maybe they are at that. Would explain a lot, wouldn't it? If you believe in that sort of thing."

The words were heavy with irony and frustration.

"Yes, if you believe," she said, lifting her chin. "I would be grateful if you'd let me know of any further developments, either in the search or through the rapport you share with Sally."

"I'll do that. Though I still am forced to wonder why you care so much. Whatever has happened to my sister and the other girls, it isn't as though there's anything you can do to help them."

Tamara raised her eyebrows. "So it might seem, Richard. But if something unnatural is at work here, I may be the only one in Camelford who *can* help them.

"That is, of course, if you believe in that sort of thing."

She stepped back and gave the smallest of bows. "You'll forgive me, I hope. There's business I must attend to elsewhere. But trust me when I say that I have not given up my dedication to this task."

"Of course," Richard said, inclining his head.

As she turned to go, and Farris fell in beside her, the young man watched them curiously.

Only when they were well away from the clearing did she speak her thoughts aloud.

"Witches," she said.

"So it would seem," Farris replied.

"But every reference we've come across in Grandfather's library suggests that they're extinct."

"Apparently not."

Tamara smiled and glanced at him. "All right. Let's see if Serena has returned to seek you at the inn, and I'll summon Bodicea."

"You sound as though you've got a plan brewing, miss," Farris said, as they found the path through the wood that would take them back to where they had left the carriage.

"I do," Tamara confessed. "Though I daresay you're not going to like it."

Eleven

With the stench from the corpse and the sickly sweet smell of the bayou threatening to overwhelm him, William slumped back into the boat and felt the blood drain from his cheeks as the dead thing released its hold and slipped back into the water. Antoinette watched him, her cat's eyes full of interest.

"You afraid of the dead, Mr. Swift?" she asked, her voice like honey.

He shook his head, not wanting to look weak.

"It's the movement of the boat. I sometimes get ill when I'm on the water."

She licked her lips and smiled. The woman knew he was lying but her expression said that was perfectly all right. He looked away from the elegant perfection of her beauty, his gaze drawn back to the water. It would be easy to lose himself in her loveliness, even in the midst of the horrors of this place.

Best to be careful . . .

A pale ivory hand thrust up from the water then, and snagged William by the shirtsleeve. Below the wrist, the arm was nothing but bone, yet it had such strength. William fought, beating at the dead hand, trying to get some grip on the boat, but it dragged him over the side as though he weighed nothing at all.

He gasped sharply as the cool, murky water engulfed him, filling his throat and weighing his body down as though an anchor was tied to his legs. He sank, choking, and welcomed the embrace of panic. He kicked out with both legs, struggling upward. Despite the weight, he pulled toward air.

Just a little farther.

When his face was only inches from the oily surface, he felt a vise clamp around his ankles, and then something tugged him down again, dragged him farther into the muck and the thick water of the bayou. His lungs burned and his eyes bulged, his body starving for air.

The corpse that had dragged him into the water still had hold of his shirtsleeve. He thrashed with the last of his strength, freeing his legs, and tore open his shirt. Freed, chest convulsing for air, he thrust himself upward. Just as he was about to break the surface he risked one glance down into the murk and saw the dead thing slipping into the depths with his shirt still clutched tightly in its hand.

Lungs on fire, he broke the surface at last and sucked down great gulps of air. After a few moments, he looked around for the skiff, which bobbed in the water eight or ten yards away.

"Horatio!" William called, his throat raw. But there was no reply from his ghostly comrade.

Fearful of whatever else might be lurking in the bayou, William swam as fast as he could toward the boat. He threw his arms over the side, and tried to pull himself up. The boat rocked and he nearly slipped back down into the water before he was finally able to heave himself inside.

He looked up and saw that the skiff was empty.

"Horatio? Antoinette?!" he called, but got no answer. He looked wildly around, but all he saw was the long shadow of Philippe Mandeville's plantation home.

Unsure of what else to do, he picked up an oar, and began to paddle toward shore.

Soon enough he stood at the front door, his thin undershirt soaked through, and grasped the long silver bellpull. He gave it a tug, but could hear nothing of its call inside. He waited, his teeth beginning to chatter, occasionally looking back at the boat to determine whether Horatio and Antoinette had returned.

After what seemed an eternity, the lock clicked, and the door began to slowly swing open. William stood there, waiting for someone, a butler or maid, to show him in, but there was no one.

"Hello . . . ?" he said. His voice did not echo. It was as if it were being sucked into the void, rather than a hallway.

Feeling foolish just standing there in the doorway, he stepped inside, and immediately the door slammed at his back. He jumped, turning to see if someone had shut it, but the foyer was empty, and entirely dark.

"This is ridiculous."

He put his hands together.

"*Inlucesco!*"

Immediately, a ball of green light appeared above his head, lighting his way. William began to walk slowly through the home of Philippe Mandeville and his eyes widened with further amazement at every step.

Horatio had said Mandeville was a collector, but that had been an understatement. This was more than just a home; this was a cabinet of infinite curiosities. There were odd things locked inside glass cases—deformed fetuses, pieces of bone—that lined the hallway and the shelves that packed each room he passed.

William shuddered as he glimpsed a jar of eyeballs, the colored corneas a murky gray with age. The optic nerves and their attending veins trailed behind the eyes in the milky liquid. William didn't want to think about who the previous owners had been—probably other intrepid explorers who'd tried to enter Mandeville's home uninvited.

As he passed by the doorways that led into other rooms, he saw even stranger things. One chamber in particular caught his attention. It was filled with small daguerreotypes of men and women, images so numerous that they covered the walls like vines; some hung from nails and others were arranged on myriad shelves. Yet otherwise it was remarkable only in that it was the most ordinary of any of the rooms he had encountered.

William stepped inside, noting the pale ocher walls and the thick crown moldings that had been painted a benign eggshell color many years before. The floors were heavy oak, stained a rich, dark brown. He picked up one of the framed daguerreotypes from a shelf on the wall.

He blinked and stared closer, turning the picture this way and that in his hands. For just a moment it had seemed to him that the beautiful, dark-haired woman in the portrait had moved, ever so slightly. A trick of the light, perhaps.

"Do you like my little portrait gallery?"

The voice was smooth, like creamed silk. It saturated the air, seeming to slip like smoke along the walls.

He turned to find a tall man with blond hair gone white at the temples standing behind him in the doorway. His skin was the palest William had ever seen on a human being. Once he had met an albino man with such papery skin, but this was no albino. His eyes were a watery cornflower blue.

Mandeville smiled. The cool white of his crisp summer suit set off the chalky bone hue of his skin, and reflected the low light.

"Are you the artist, Mr. Mandeville?" William asked, attempting to present himself as perfectly unruffled.

Philippe Mandeville smiled, his pale lips revealing unnaturally long, yellow-stained teeth. Both eyeteeth seemed to be missing from his mouth.

"Of course. There is both skill and art to the work. It fascinates me. And it helps me in the lonely hours." His voice was mellifluous, more compelling even than his daughter's dulcet tones. As he spoke he seemed to be weaving a spell with his voice.

There was nothing natural about this man.

Wary of taking his eyes off Mandeville, even for a moment, William attempted to return the framed photograph to its place by memory. Instead he bumped the frame against the shelf.

The sheer panic that lit Mandeville's eyes in that moment was more than alarm. William only caught a glimpse of it as he spun around and stopped another framed image from falling off the shelf. He snatched it up, feeling like a bumbling fool.

Carefully he placed both photographs back onto their shelf. Even as he did, he wondered about Mandeville's reaction. Were the daguerreotypes so valuable that the idea of dropping one, perhaps damaging it, would cause the man such a fright?

A fresh ripple of dread ran up William's spine. Cursing himself for turning his back on Mandeville he spun, certain that the man had used the distraction to steal nearer to him, perhaps armed with some enchanted dagger.

But Mandeville had not moved an inch, and the panic that had lit his face was gone. In its place was a curious, ironic smile, enough to make William wonder if he'd imagined seeing such alarm in those features.

"Daguerreotypes, aren't they?" William asked, keeping his voice even. "I had heard the process had been perfected recently."

The man gave a dismissive wave of his hand. "Nonsense. Have you not noticed the age of some of these images? I was using polished silver and iodine to create such portraits before that fool Daguerre was even born."

"Perhaps they ought to have named the process after you, then?" William suggested, trying to gauge his host's intentions.

"I labor for love, not notoriety."

William had no reply for that. He glanced around, anxious to be out of this room but knowing he could not leave without his prize.

"You're alone here?" he asked.

Mandeville laughed, and the sound was warm and rich, in direct contradiction to his demeanor.

"Now, I wouldn't say that exactly."

Mandeville took a few steps toward William, who backed up involuntarily, resulting in another laugh.

"I see that you think I wish you harm, Mr. Swift. Where would the fun be in that?"

For the first time, William detected a slight French inflection beneath Mandeville's smooth Southern accent. The man had assimilated well into the New Orleans culture, adopting the drawl of the landed gentry.

"Your daughter, Antoinette, brought me here. I've come to beg your indulgence. You possess a book I need badly."

Mandeville held up his hand. "I know what you seek, and I will give it to you gladly—"

William blinked, then stared at him in relief. "Thank you so much, Mr. Mandeville—"

The man shook his head, interrupting William.

"You did not let me finish, Mr. Swift. I was going to say that I will give to you gladly what you seek, but first you must do something for me."

William nodded.

"You must," Mandeville continued, "answer a riddle."

Dubious, William arched an eyebrow. "And if I cannot answer?"

Mandeville smiled again, but this time there was no trace of humor in it. "Why then, you and your friend will join my permanent collection."

Mandeville snapped his fingers, and one of the daguerreotypes flew off a shelf toward William, stopping only when it floated before his eyes. William gasped and raised his hands, a defensive shield of magic summoned instantly and pulsing at his fingertips.

But he faltered when he saw the picture, and then he shuddered with fear. The face in the daguerreotype was unmistakably familiar.

Horatio.

The ghost had been frozen in an image, his features contorted with anger and a ferocity that was only intensified by the sepia tone of the print. Abruptly the picture sailed back to its place on the shelf, landing with a loud clatter.

"What did you do to him?" William demanded.

Mandeville gave a gentle wave. "He's in no pain. The process is entirely reversible, *if* you answer my riddle correctly. Otherwise, your photograph will be next."

William wanted to strangle the man, to pull out every magical weapon he had in his arsenal, but something inside told him he would lose that battle if he chose to start it. He had learned a great deal, but even with the power of Albion at his disposal, he was still a novice . . . and he was a long way from home.

"Well?" Mandeville said, his seductive voice drawing William back to the question at hand.

William sighed, knowing his hands were tied.

"Tell me your riddle. But I swear to you that you will not add me to your collection without a fight, regardless of my answer."

"Oh, I would expect nothing less from one of the *great* Protectors," Mandeville sneered.

"Go on then."

Mandeville snapped his fingers, and two chairs appeared instantly in front of him.

"Please take a seat, Mr. Swift."

"I'll stand, thank you."

The sorcerer shrugged, and sat down in one of the thin white birch chairs, the seat crackling under his weight.

"As you wish. Now tell me," Mandeville purred, "what is the weight of your soul, and what is the weight of mine?"

∼

THE CARRIAGE RATTLED OVER THE RUTTED, uneven ground as Farris drove the horses toward Slaughterbridge. Bodicea did not like to be confined in such a small space. Even without flesh or bone, the queen preferred the fields and woods, the mountains, or, as her ghostly condition allowed, the sky. Even the streets of London town were more pleasing if she could wander them without restriction.

But the moment demanded her presence. Tamara had summoned her from her journeying across the moors and woods and shores of Cornwall, pulling her away from conversations with specters, in order to have her here, and so she would endure the cramped confines of the carriage for the benefit of Albion.

The ghostly queen hovered just above a seat, maintaining the appearance of solidity in spite of her translucent, shimmering form. Such pretense was a comfort both to her living companions, and to herself.

Tamara sat beside her, hands folded over her lap in a fashion that would have seemed demure if not for the way one clutched the other, tight enough to cause pain. Her every muscle was taut, and to Bodicea she seemed ready to scream.

Yet the Protector kept quiet, instead watching and listening to the sprite Serena, who was pacing back and forth upon the seat across from them, gesticulating wildly. Once Bodicea would only have been amused by the sight of the tiny creature's fury, but she had come to respect Serena's loyalty and ferocity in battle.

"... and then, Rhosynn and Fyg *dare* to call us a spy, so they do!" the sprite cried, full of righteous scorn.

The ghost scrutinized Serena. "Which was nothing but the truth, little friend. Why does it enrage you so?"

" 'Cause we wouldn't has to spy if they'd come to their senses, majesty," the sprite replied archly, crossing her arms and glaring at the queen.

"There is that," Bodicea allowed.

Tamara touched two fingers to her temple, as though to stave off a headache.

"Enough. Shall we attempt to focus? Tragic are the deaths we have been unable to avert, but I refuse to allow another life to be lost to this horror. There are four human girls still missing, and from the sound of it, five fairy girls have been taken from Stronghold. I shall hold myself responsible if I do not find them before the solstice.

"If they should die . . ."

She let the words hang.

Bodicea reached out a spectral hand, shimmering and transparent, and marshalling her concentration she managed to touch Tamara's wrist.

"We will not fail them," the ghost declared.

The girl looked up, grateful for the comfort.

"No. We won't. On my life, we *won't.*" Tamara glanced at the sprite, whose wings fluttered almost unconsciously. "Serena, did you get a sense that Rhosynn and her friends knew any more than we do about this?"

The sprite sighed heavily. "Not a bit, lady. Not a bit." Then she brightened. "Though we has the idea there's them at Stronghold as think the council's a bit rash, we does. That maybe there's some thinks a mistake's made, not talking to you."

Tamara nodded. "Well, perhaps they'll come around, given time. But we cannot wait for that. For now, we're on our own."

"Indeed," Bodicea said, narrowing her eyes. Her fists clenched with grim anticipation. "And the local ghosts will be little help, or none at all, I fear."

"So you said when I called you back to the inn," Tamara replied darkly. "I'm sorry to have put off your news, but I thought it important for us to get under way. And Serena was brimming with anger over her encounter with the fairies. Please, Bodicea, tell me what you've learned."

The ghost paused a moment, and as she thought of her journeys in the spectral world, of the fear that coursed through the wandering souls of Cornwall, she faded just a bit, so her manifestation was only a silhouette upon the darkness within the carriage.

"The dead are frightened," Bodicea said.

Serena swore and threw up her hands. "Frightened? What is

they scared of, majesty? We doesn't know of anything that can hurt one who's already dead."

"You're wrong there, sprite. There are many things that can harm the dead. Necromancy is a twisted sorcery. Though it is uncommon, all spirits fear such power.

"Once, all souls, living or dead, feared witches," she continued. "Those magicians, half-human and half-demon, may be rare now, but the ghosts of Cornwall know that they are not entirely gone. And where there is a witch, even the most confused of lost souls will know to avoid that place."

"But what about the specters you've seen? The knights in armor?" Tamara asked.

Bodicea nodded. "Old ghosts, they are. I believe they are watching us, wondering if we will succeed against our foes. Brave and noble knights they may have been in life, but as ghosts even they fear the witches. They refuse to actively aid us, because they know the wrath of the dark ones would be terrible."

"Witches, witches, *witches!*" Serena said, zipping into the air and flying back and forth between Tamara and Bodicea, wings like harp strings, purple-hued dust falling from them as she darted about. "Is ye saying ye know for sure they're here? That they's real? We's never seen a one, majesty, never a one. And at Stronghold, 'tis said the witches are dead, the bells rung, all the wicked, gone."

"Perhaps not," Tamara said, meeting Bodicea's gaze. "We keep hearing about witches, from Christine and her grandfather, and now from the ghosts of Cornwall. Perhaps they were gone for a time—I know not where, though the possibilities are limitless—and have only now returned. They're half-demon. Perhaps they have been in some dark realm, or frozen in time, awaiting some trigger for their awakening. What's important is that, even if we're not dealing with witches, whatever we *are* facing is just as powerful, and equally dangerous.

"What I'd like to know, however, is why the knights—of all the wandering souls of this area—have presented themselves in this way. If you're right, Bodicea, why is it only the knights who pay such close attention to our efforts?"

Outside, the sky had darkened, and the breeze that blew into the carriage was unusually cold. Several of the trees they passed along the road were dead and bare of branches, reaching for the sky with dark fingers. Bodicea could hear the river rushing nearby, and thought they must be nearing their goal.

"The last girl to disappear, the barmaid, told you the tale of Slaughterbridge," she said.

Tamara frowned. "About Arthur, you mean? The legend indicates that he was killed around here."

Serena flew in a wild spiral around the carriage, casting off purple dust in a shower that sparkled in the air.

"Arthur? Does you mean the Pendragon?"

"The Pendragon, yes," Bodicea said. "It's said that his son Mordred killed him at Slaughterbridge, and father slew son, as well. But Mordred died on the spot, while Arthur survived long enough to stagger off a ways.

"The few ghosts I could force to speak to me stayed off across the moors, and seemed not as afraid of the witches as those nearer by. They said the witches tormented the dead around Slaughterbridge, always searching for—"

"Arthur's burial place," Tamara finished. "Or the very spot where he died, and bled into the earth. Yes, I've heard both."

Bodicea gripped her spear, its edge only a phantom wisp.

"I believe the knights are watching because they have an interest the other ghosts of Camelford do not. I have seen them acting out a massacre, on a spectral battlefield, as though they had no choice but to relive that horror, again and again, day after day. It may be that they are the knights of the king you call Arthur, those who died for him here. So there may be something they dread more than the fury of the witches, something they wish us to prevent."

"And what might that be?" Tamara asked.

The ghostly queen shook her head. "That, I do not know. But I have thought a great deal about what I have seen and heard of the wandering phantoms of Cornwall, and I feel sure I am right, or nearly so."

"I trust your instincts, Bodicea," Tamara said, smoothing her dress anxiously and gazing into a corner of the carriage as though she might find answers in the shadows. "But there are still too many questions that remain unanswered. If the ghosts of these knights will not aid us, then the course I have chosen truly seems the only one we have left. All of the whispers speak of the witches' interest in Slaughterbridge. If we will find them anywhere, it will be there."

Bodicea felt doubtful, and if they had only a handful of days before solstice, they had no time to waste. "And if they do not come, what then?"

"They will come, one way or another," Tamara replied, eyes hard. "I have a spell that will draw them, even if it is against their will. It's not powerful enough to hold them, but if I perform it correctly, they will be unable to resist the summoning."

A shiver of dread went through the ghostly queen.

"I do not like the sound of that, Tamara. What will you do with them once you have them?"

The girl only looked back at her, and though Tamara was a Protector of Albion, and as strong-willed and clever as anyone Bodicea had ever known, in that moment she seemed so very young. The ghost feared for her.

"Lady Tamara!" Serena piped up in her tiny voice. "Majesty! The knights be here, now! In the wood!"

Bodicea spun, one arm passing entirely through the carriage door. Through the window she could see that the sprite spoke true. Three knights on horseback rode alongside them, spectral figures that the moonlight passed through, leaving them alight with an unearthly glow. They made no sound as they rode,

The leader had his sword drawn. Horse and rider followed a straight course; the branches and trunks of trees offered no obstacle as the ghosts went right through them.

"Go, Bodicea," Tamara said. "Tell them that knights should not shirk from battle, that I'm tired of having them do nothing but watch, and demand they perform their duty to Albion."

Bodicea hesitated. "The witches—"

"I'll wait for their answer, before I cast the spell."

"Hurry, majesty!" Serena squeaked, darting around the carriage, then out the window as though to drag Bodicea along behind her.

"You stay," the spectral queen told the sprite.

Then she moved out of the carriage, her ghostly shape flowing through the air. She held her spear in front of her and rushed away from the carriage toward the wood and the hesitant knights.

The ghosts turned their phantom steeds away, and moved deeper into the wood.

Bodicea passed through the trees in pursuit. "Damn you for cowards, each and every one!" she cried as she followed them. "The Protector of Albion demands your loyalty. The spirit of England itself—to which you are sworn servants—commands you!"

The ghosts rode on.

Bodicea saw flashes of spectral essence ahead, the shapes of horses made up from the substance of their souls, just as their armor and weapons were. For long moments she gave chase. Several times she thought she had lost them, only to catch a glimpse. But she would not be denied.

"Cowards! Halt!" she shouted, her voice that of the warrior queen who had ruled these lands once upon a time. It echoed now, just as it had then.

In a clearing that was bathed in moonlight, she came upon the knights. They had stopped in the midst of a grotesque phantom battlefield, with silhouettes and wisps of an ancient war strewn on the ground. A ghostly theater of the damned, they played out their mortal end with horrifying exactness. Some of the ghosts were nearly insubstantial, but others had manifested with such vigor that she could see the anguish and agony that had been etched upon their faces at the moment of their deaths.

As profoundly familiar as she was with the horrors of war, this gave even Bodicea pause.

The three knights on horseback watched her, forlorn, their eyes as lost as their souls.

"Albion needs you now," she said, her voice so low it was almost a whisper.

The ghosts hung their heads. Then the leader, whose sword was still unsheathed, began to lift it. Before he could complete the motion, before Bodicea could learn his intentions, a scream filled the air.

"No," she said, twisting around to stare back through the dense woods toward the river. Toward Slaughterbridge.

"Tamara."

⁓

Tamara swift watched out the window of the carriage as Bodicea disappeared into the forest.

Her fingers were curled into tight fists where they rested in her lap. There were too many mysteries here, too many variables. When this had all begun she'd thought it a simple case of murder or mischief, likely some demon dragging off unsuspecting innocents. Now there were ghostly knights and ancient witches and the legends of King Arthur and his bastard son, Mordred.

It all began to seem too large for her to contend with, even with Bodicea along. Perhaps it was time to summon William to Cornwall. Yet every moment that passed moved the abducted girls closer to death, and she had come out to Slaughterbridge in an attempt to confront the witches, to destroy them if she could.

The carriage began to slow. She heard Farris call to the horses.

"Ah, our handsome Farris," Serena said, clutching her hands to her breast as she flitted around within the carriage. "Loyal and strong, he is."

Tamara smiled. "Yes. He is."

The carriage stopped and shifted as Farris climbed down. Tamara did not wait for him, but flung open the door and dropped to the ground in particularly unladylike fashion. There was witchery afoot, and she could not be bothered with propriety.

The forest loomed ominously against the night sky and she was pleased that their path had not taken them into those dark woods. She was hardly dressed for another such trek. Yet even here on the clear, broad expanse of grass and beaten path between trees and riverbank, the dark woods seemed to encroach upon them, as though they bent toward them with malicious intent.

Tamara shivered. She had relished the chance to get out of London, but now she missed her home.

"Here we are, miss," Farris said, gesturing toward the bank, where the ancient arch of Slaughterbridge spanned the river.

As she surveyed the stone bridge, covered in moss and vines, the river running swiftly at this narrow point, Tamara put her doubts behind her. She was here now. The thought of another girl being snatched away, just because she hesitated, was too much for her to bear. She could not return to Camelford without attempting to draw the witches to her.

With the musical trill of her wings soft in the air, Serena flew toward Farris, making circles above his head.

"Ye best be careful now, brave Farris. Our heart is shattered if anything happens to ye," the sprite said.

"Not to worry, little one," the stout man said.

He reached up to the seat of the carriage and drew down a large pouch. From within, he produced two large revolvers that Tamara had seen him wield before. "Allen's pepperbox" they were called. A gift from his brother.

From his father, Farris had received the elder's regimental saber, and now he reached up once more, lifting it down.

Farris was ready for a fight. That pleased her. He was courageous, but not versed in magic, and certainly he had none of the power that was the Protectors' legacy. For her own part, she only needed the tools and ingredients necessary for the summoning spell she would use to draw the witches.

Tamara smiled. "I'd best get my own materials."

Tamara reached into the carriage to retrieve them, her mind traveling forward as she went over the spell step by step. Farris and Serena were speaking behind her, but she wasn't paying attention to their conversation.

A shriek from the night sky above shattered her thoughts.

"Miss—" Farris began.

"Witches!" Serena cried, cutting him off, and she darted toward Tamara.

As she spun, Tamara raised her fists, and a rich golden light crackled like metallic fire around her hands—magic summoned up from the soul of Albion and channeled through her own body, enabling her to protect herself.

Two figures hovered in the darkness above, black garments whipping in the wind like banners unfurling at the front of death's army. They were long and thin, bodies skeletal beneath those ragged robes, and darker than the night, like dreadful holes torn in the fabric of the sky, the deepest black Tamara had ever seen. Her heart fluttered at the sight of them and she felt ice travel through her every muscle, a cold unlike any she had known.

She looked at the witches, their gray, hideously contorted faces staring down at her, and she understood the touch of evil better than she ever had before. Tamara had fought one of the Lords of Hell, had faced him down without flinching, but the witches were worse. They were all that was good in humanity, twisted and bent to demonic purpose.

The witches descended, cutting through the darkness in utter silence.

Tamara screamed out her terror even as she raised her hands and sketched her fingers in the air. *To hell with defense.* She went on the attack.

"*Malleus lux!*" she shouted.

Golden light erupted from her hands and shot upward, illuminating the whole of the riverbank and the bridge. But this was no mere light. Nearly solid, the blast struck the witches. One of them took the brunt and it threw the witch out over the water, where the creature was lost in the darkness as the light diminished. The other was only glanced by the attack and fell, spinning, onto the carriage, landing with a splinter of breaking wood.

The horses neighed in terror, reared, and started to run.

Farris shouted for them to stop. He might have gone after them, but Serena screamed, drawing his attention.

The witch who'd taken the worst of the attack came streaking back across the night even as the other rose into a crouch on the back of the careening carriage. With only a gesture, she struck the horses dead.

The animals fell in a heap with the crack of breaking bone, and the carriage jittered to a stop, driving them into the dirt.

Serena flew into the air, darting directly at the eyes of the witch that dove for Tamara. It raised its twisted, taloned hands to shield its face.

Farris raised the twin pepperbox revolvers and pulled the triggers. The gunshots echoed across the nearby woods and the river. The witch that Serena was harrying only twitched as one of the bullets found its mark, punching a hole in the thing's darkness that the moonlight streamed through.

The darkness flowed, closing the wound.

Tamara saw this all in a moment, even as she turned toward the other witch. The wraith perched on the edge of the carriage, and was about to launch itself toward her. Or so she thought.

"The girls," Tamara said gravely. "I want them."

She lifted her fists again, preparing to attack once more, with an enchantment that would imprison the witch—at least long enough for her to deal with the other one. Spells ran through her mind, magic she could use to destroy them.

The witch thrust its hands out, spindly claws pointed at the ground. The blackness of its garments stretched out, a living darkness, and touched the earth.

"Stupid girl," it said, its voice like breaking glass. "You think you can best the daughters of Morgan le Fey?"

It laughed, then—*not it, she*—and Tamara had never heard a sound more terrible.

The soil shifted. Stone and root cracked. Fingers emerged from the earth and then the ground itself bucked and tore apart. Three figures rose up, formed of dirt and rock and clay, and reached for her. Homunculi, enslaved by the witches.

One of the creatures grabbed Tamara from behind, arm encircling her throat, choking her.

She cast a silent spell upon the nearest one and it exploded, showering dirt and stones all around. From within she saw emerge the ghost of a knight in armor, a pitiful creature whose eyes were full of terror. It had been the core of the homunculus. Now, set free, it fled into the night, dissipating in the air, crossing into the spirit realm, perhaps never to return.

Now I know what it is they fear, Tamara thought.

By then, the other homunculus had her in its arms and they crushed her between them, pinning her hands to her body, driving her down beneath their inexorable weight. Dirt spilled upon her and for a moment it was like being buried alive.

Then a ribbon of the darkness from the witch's robe slid over her, wrapped around her head, and covered her mouth far more effectively than a simple gag. Tamara could not scream, could not speak enchantments, could not use her hands. Still, there was raw power in her and she struck out with instinctual magic, the primal strength of the Protector.

The witch was unfazed.

The homunculus released her and Tamara's feet left the ground and suddenly she was flying, careening through the night in the grip of the witch's robe, its spidery talons grabbing hold of her.

"It is your good fortune that you are pure, sorceress. Your virginity saves you. Now you are the tenth, and we have only three more to gather."

She caught a glimpse of the trees far below, heard a gunshot as Farris shot at the other witch. Her last sight was of that creature batting Serena out of the sky, sending the sprite tumbling down, trailing dimming glitter, and Farris reaching up to catch her.

Then the witch left them, following her sister.

Tamara had a moment to feel relief that her friends would live. Then darkness spread over her eyes, and she could see nothing more.

Twelve

Nigel Townsend stood in the parlor at Ludlow House, pouring himself a glass of whiskey from an antique crystal decanter that was nearly as old as he was.

Though he bickered constantly with Nelson's ghost, and though the man had once had him clapped in irons on board the *Agamemnon,* he found he was worried. It was no simple matter to harm a ghost, but it could be done.

Of course, he was concerned for William as well, but Nigel's relationship with the young master Swift was even more contentious. They treated each other as allies, but William never had fully trusted him, and likely never would. In truth, Nigel felt the same. William had been improving both his store of sorcerous knowledge and his skill at spellcasting, but he had neither the natural facility nor the inclinations that were evident in his sister. Whether it be business or romance that distracted him, William seemed always to have some other priority that competed with his duties as Protector of Albion.

"One day," Nigel said aloud, raising his glass and studying the facets of color in crystal and whiskey, rotating the drink in his hand, "it will be the death of you, I'm afraid."

Someone passed by in the corridor and he turned, but saw only the swaying hem of a skirt before she was out of sight. One of the maids, certainly. Though if it was Sophia, that would be interesting. The girl was William's intended, and loved him, to be sure. But Nigel knew she was fascinated by him, and by what he was. Despite William's suspicions to the contrary, Nigel would not betray him by pursuing the girl . . . as long as he could help himself.

He did his best not to be caught in close proximity to her.

To her credit, Sophia's fascination seemed not to have corrupted her devotion to William. For all her faults, the girl was loyal.

Yet it wasn't entirely his own loyalty to the Swifts that prevented him from attempting to bed her, or to taste of her blood. Once upon a time there had been a young girl he had truly adored, a girl in the care of Ludlow Swift. One day his love for her, and her fascination with his curse—which she saw as a gift—had been the end of her, and that had spelled the death of his own heart.

It had laid ruin to his relationship with Ludlow, as well. They had renewed their friendship in time, but nothing was ever the same after that.

Nigel sniffed, and took a sip of the whiskey. Such ruminations were unhealthy, he decided. He put them all from his mind.

He sniffed again, and arched an eyebrow, mischief growing in his heart. There was a scent—one he recognized. Neither Martha, the aging maid who ran the household, nor Sophia had been the one who just passed. No, it had been Melanie, a young maid who had only been in the service of the Swifts for half a year or so. A pretty thing he had his eye on.

Nigel drained the last of his whiskey and set the glass down, then went out into the corridor in quiet pursuit of the girl. He never took blood from the unwilling, but there was nothing more exciting than finding a girl who was eager to give him all that he wanted of her, both her body and her blood. He wondered if Melanie would be the playful sort.

Breathing in her scent, he followed the maid. She had gone off toward the observatory. Nigel stole after her, keeping to the shadows where the lamplight did not reach.

From ahead of him, a scream echoed through the corridor.

He enjoyed playing at the role of predator, but now Nigel gave up the game and ran. The door to the observatory was open, and he rushed into the room to find Melanie standing with her hands covering her face in fright.

The view from the window revealed the grounds of Ludlow House cast in moonlight, and the scene was beautiful.

But the moonlight revealed something else, as well. The ghost of Queen Bodicea knelt in the center of the room, as if weary from battle, spear held before her as though it was the only thing that kept her from falling over.

"Mr. Townsend . . . ," Melanie said breathlessly. "I'm sorry. I shouldn't have screamed. But the—I'm . . . I'm not used to such haunts, and she just *appeared* there in front of me. I don't—"

"Hush, girl," Nigel said grimly. "It's all right. Go about your business."

With a grateful look, the maid rushed from the room.

"Bodicea, what's happened?" Nigel asked, moving to her side. He reached out and, though he himself was a supernatural and ought to have been able to make contact with her, his fingers passed through her as if through mist.

The queen looked up at him, and her mouth twisted in a snarl. "William. I must speak with him immediately."

She stood, ever regal despite her nudity. Even though she was a ghost, the war paint she had smeared upon her naked flesh seemed primitive and imposing.

"He's gone, on an errand," Nigel replied. "William and Nelson both. Only Byron and I are here."

Bodicea inhaled deeply, swelling her bosom. Nigel could not help but admire her, though the fierceness of her gaze was daunting.

"Calamity has befallen our endeavor in Cornwall," the specter admitted. Normally she was imperious, but at this news she lowered her gaze. "I left her side for but a moment, and at her instruction, but I am afraid that Tamara has been taken from us."

Nigel narrowed his eyes and shook his head, as if denying the words. He bared his fangs in anger.

"Speak sense, woman. Tamara cannot be dead or William would have felt it and returned. She cannot . . ."

His temples thrummed with an imaginary pulse. Nigel's heart had not beaten in centuries, but this night he felt as if it must. He thought he had given up on love, but what he felt now proved otherwise. He might not wish to court Tamara, but still he cherished her.

"I did not say that she was dead," Bodicea snapped. "She has been abducted, Mr. Townsend, by the very same witches that have taken so many other victims in that region, human and fairy alike."

"Witches? There hasn't been a witch in England in—"

"Enough!" Bodicea shouted, and she shook her spear at him. "You waste precious moments. Farris and his smitten sprite are safe, but I must see them back to the inn. The very instant William returns, you shall inform him, and instruct him to translocate to the Mason's Arms in Camelford, where he will find Farris awaiting him.

"I will be in search of Tamara, and the damnable creatures who have taken her."

Nigel would have bristled at her commanding tone, but before he could say a word, Bodicea vanished.

Alone in the observatory, he shook his head and gazed out at the moonlit lawns and gardens of Ludlow House.

"Perhaps it isn't William I ought to have been worrying about."

∾

PETER DAVID, the master of the hounds, was weary. He had a gentle heart, and with each young lady of Camelford who had vanished into the darkness, more and more of his genial demeanor had departed from him.

Peter was a quiet man who prided himself on his reputation, and on the fact that he had at the very least a friendly acquaintance with most of the people who lived in Camelford. That wasn't to say that the girls who had gone missing were like his own daughters, but certainly he was fond of them.

Like the other men who were searching—brothers and fathers, uncles and friends—he imagined the worst, and it curdled his soul.

"Come on, my darlings," he said to the hounds. "If we don't get some rest tonight, we'll be of no use to anyone come morning."

The dogs were all leashed by ropes that were tied to a single loop, and Peter held fast to the loop. Most of them would not wander far, but here in the deep forest, tucked away in the hills, even the best-behaved of them could be tempted to dash into the underbrush in pursuit of a squirrel or hare. He hadn't the energy or patience to round them up tonight, and so he kept a firm grip upon the loop, alternately tugging them along and being tugged himself. They weren't following a scent now—only his gentle proddings urging them to return home for the night.

In the morning, they would start again. He only prayed that the night would pass without another poor girl gone missing.

For much of the afternoon and early evening, he had been with Richard Kirk and young Frankie Turner, both men he had seen grown from infancy. Their passion had helped to drive him on, keeping him out after dark. But even with the moonlight making a surreal landscape of the woods, silver light filtering through branches and making clearings the stuff of fairy tales, it was simply too dark to do any real good now.

Reluctantly, they had all agreed to surrender their hopes for another night.

He'd said goodbye to the boys a mile back, but Peter's own home was outside of Camelford; even in the darkened woods he knew the direction well enough. His stomach rumbled hungrily, and he knew the hounds must be starving, as well. It wasn't a kind master who kept his beasts running so long without food.

"Just a little farther, friends," he said, voice low.

There was no path here. This particular area of the forest was unfamiliar. But the stars were the stars, and the hills did not lie. He had struck out on the right course, and had no doubt that it would take him home.

Yet as he dragged the dogs along, he found himself peering more closely into the nighttime shadows where the moonlight did not reach. Something horrid crept along the back of his neck, but when he reached up to brush it away, thinking a spider had fallen upon him, there was nothing there.

The wind seemed to have died.

Halfway up a long, sloping hill dense with old forest, Peter paused, unsure now of his direction. That was what he told himself. In his heart, he knew differently. His path was true, but he hesitated to continue.

"You're a fool, Peter David," he said, too loudly, trying to dispel his fear with the sound of his own voice. It helped a bit, for it did make him feel foolish. Not since he was a boy had he been afraid of the dark, of the woods.

But now, for the first time, he had an opportunity to wonder what had truly become of the missing girls. His hope was waning. If the hounds could not locate a useful trace of any of them, then they simply could not be found. But if that was the case, then what had happened to them?

What else was out here in the woods tonight?

"Come," he said sharply. Fist tight, he pulled the loop, dragging the hounds together. One of the largest, Hercules, tripped over his own legs while turning round, and stumbled. A thin, ugly mutt he called Gruesome nipped at Hercules's hind legs to get him up and moving again, and then Peter found himself pulled uphill.

His pulse raced, but he tried to keep his eyes on the woods ahead, ignoring the shadows to either side. He kept as best he could to wide spaces and clearings so that the hounds would not wrap their leads around trees. They yipped and growled low, murmuring far more than they usually did. The collective panting and grunting of the dogs was a familiar comfort to him, but this night he sensed that his animals were as tentative and unsettled as he was.

At the top of the hill, he reached a clearing that was bathed in silver moonlight, and he breathed a sigh of relief, even chuckled at himself. Peter sighed and scratched at the back of his head as the hounds moved restlessly, tired of one another's company.

The master of hounds started off again, moving due west, across the clearing and between two ancient oaks whose branches hung low, heavy with age. He wasn't an old man, but tonight he felt much like the oaks.

The hounds would not move.

He tried to tug them along with him, but they resisted stubbornly, digging paws into the ground, clawing up dirt.

"Come on, then, darlings. That's enough of that."

But his voice didn't soothe them the way it had his own anxious heart. Hercules began to whine. The best of them was Achilles, a tall, proud beast with bright eyes and a strong back. A growl came up from deep in his belly, and it spread to the others. Gruesome threw his head back and howled.

"Enough of your damnable music, lads! Enough! Come along!" Peter shouted, hearing the fear in his own voice, and hating it.

He gripped the loop with both hands and bent into the work, trying to haul them away from the clearing, and back into the trees. Still they did not budge. Now all six hounds began to howl and bark and snap at one another. Zeus foamed at the mouth, yellow drool sliding over his fangs and black quivering lip, and spilling to the dirt.

"Lord, Jesus."

Peter froze, staring at them.

The wind carried a stench into the clearing, rustling the leaves and making him flinch. He turned his nose away and held his breath.

The dogs bolted.

A frenzy came over them. They barked and snarled and tore up dirt as they ran in the very same direction he had tried to drag them. One moment whatever lay in those trees had terrified them, and the next they seemed determined to tear it to pieces.

"Stop, damn you!" Peter roared.

The hounds ignored their master. They reached the end of their leashes and his grip on the loop was such that they yanked him forward. He was flung through the air and landed hard on the ground, the wind knocked out of him. His fist opened and the loop came free, dragging away across the ground behind his animals.

Madness had overtaken them. Like ravenous wild things they raced for the trees. Peter lay with his considerable belly upon the ground, blinking dirt from his eyes. Where the moonlight reached into the woods around the clearing, he saw a single obelisk, a standing stone that marked a place of worship that was hundreds of years old.

Beyond it stood the grim reaper.

No, not the reaper. Death, he thought.

The tall, black shrouded thing was thin as a praying mantis. The terrible, cruel features were those of a woman, and that made it somehow worse.

She pointed.

The dogs halted. They began to whine now, even worse than before. Achilles was the first to turn, and they all followed suit. Peter's darlings looked at him, large, damp eyes gleaming in the moonlight. Gruesome growled, and raced toward him.

Hercules followed, and then so did the rest.

A terrible sadness clutched at his heart. The master of the hounds had known everyone in town, but not well. Never well. The dogs had been his greatest love, his closest friends. It wasn't fear but *sorrow* that wrapped him in a frigid embrace, alone there in the moonlight. More alone than ever.

They fell silent as they reached him.

Achilles bit first, fangs tearing through his jacket, ripping flesh and muscle from his shoulder. Then the others darted in, jaws snapping, pulling him apart.

Peter screamed.

And he wept.

And he died.

~

John haversham stood in the dark, just inside the doors
of Swift's of London. All of the hand-painted lamps were unlit.
Chairs were set against desks in orderly fashion. Not a single piece
of paper was out of place. Of course, that was how the proper Mr.
Swift would run his business. Haversham was surprised that there
were flowers arranged in pots in several places around the main
room of the bank. A bit chaotic for William.

He smiled to himself. He was selling the man short, he knew
that. William wasn't quite as bad as all that. But there was a part of
John that wanted so very badly to get him into the ring where he
often engaged his pugilistic tendencies, and beat him bloody. No
magic, just his fists.

Of course, that was the only way he'd have a chance in hell
of winning against one of the Protectors of Albion. He knew
it well. Just as he knew that Lord Blackheath and the rest of the
board would have him flogged—or worse—if he did anything to
disrupt the nascent relationship they'd forged with the Swifts. They
were thrilled to count the Protectors among their membership, despite the indignity they had to endure of suffering a woman to sit
on the board of so exclusive a gentleman's club.

What was worse, John actually *liked* William—when the man
wasn't being a prig about his interest in Tamara. William did have
a tendency to be a suspicious prat.

Not that his suspicions were entirely without cause.

It had been ridiculously simple for Haversham to break into the
bank. A well-placed spell and his own natural stealth got him in

without being seen, without unlocking a door, without breaking a window or removing a bar. He had no innate magical power, but he knew enough spellcraft, and he was an excellent thief.

The air was warm and stiflingly close inside the bank, as though the anxiety of the thief filled every room. The place was all wood and glass, and the only dust was what had fallen since transactions had ended for the day. Yes, William Swift ran his father's business as a tight ship. Haversham could only imagine how much it must have gnawed at him to know that he was being robbed, that the sanctity of Swift's had been breached, and that there seemed nothing at all he could do about it.

Unless, of course, he had come down here himself and waited for the robber to strike again.

Ah, but William was otherwise engaged. His attentions were torn between his impending wedding to Haversham's petulant cousin Sophia, and William's own duties as Protector.

Now John stood in the silence and gazed past the tellers' windows at the heavy iron door of the vault.

Which hung open.

Excellent, Haversham thought. *It's time to teach William Swift a lesson.*

Quietly, the soles of his shoes making only the softest scuff, he crossed the floor, moved between desks, and went around the last of the tellers' windows. From there he could see the doors that led to rear offices and the stairs that went up to the management suite, where William no doubt maintained his own office. There was honor and dignity in such a life, but it seemed so strange to Haversham that one of the Protectors of Albion should be something so mundane as a banker.

From inside the vault there came a loud sneeze.

Haversham smiled. Either that was the one place William's

cleanliness had not reached, and there was dust, or whoever was inside had caught a summer cold. He heard a man's voice curse softly, then the hitching breath of someone trying hard not to sneeze again, before yet another explosion emitted from within.

Without a sound, Haversham slipped around the door and stepped into the vault.

A slender man with thin blond hair and delicate features stood by the table at the center of the vault. He had pulled out several metal safe-deposit boxes, had opened one of them, and was examining its contents. In his right hand he held a gold necklace strung with rubies, and he played it over his fingers almost sensually. The man hadn't noticed John's entrance, and now Haversham put his hands into his pockets and leaned against the metal frame of the vault door.

"Why do I get the idea that doesn't belong to you?"

The man spun, necklace clutched in his hands as though it were a weapon. His eyes were frantic, and he shook his head.

"Who the *hell* are you?"

Haversham smiled. "A concerned citizen." He nodded, still casual. "Now, are you going to put that back and come along like a good boy, or is there going to be rough stuff?"

The man was young—perhaps William's age or even younger—and he had a cherubic quality. When he narrowed his eyes and his lips turned up into a sneer, though, that appeal disappeared.

"You're no peeler," the fellow said accusingly. He slipped the ruby necklace into his pocket. "Which means you're a trespasser. While I, sir, am assistant to the manager of this bank. My name is Harold Ramsey, and from where I stand, it looks as though I have found the thief who has been plaguing this fine institution."

Haversham tightened his hands into fists in his pockets. He smiled humorlessly, and gritted his teeth as he shook his head.

"Oh, you're a clever little bastard, aren't you," he said. "William already believes I'm the thief. You'd likely have no trouble convincing him. And here I was doing him a service. See, I care a great deal for his sister. So I decided to do her brother a favor. I thought if I watched the bank at night, captured the thief, he'd see he's misjudged me."

Ramsey started to laugh. "Well, you're well and truly fucked then, aren't you?"

"You'd think," Haversham said, not moving. "You'll pin the crimes on me. No one will question you. After all, I haven't a shred of proof that it was you and not me who was trespassing here tonight. No evidence at all.

"Except, of course, for your confession," John added.

"What are you on about? You haven't any confession from me."

Haversham grinned. It was a dark and ugly expression, and it unsettled his opponents. He knew, because he'd seen its effect on other men.

"No. I haven't." He took his fists out of his pockets and started walking toward Harold Ramsey. John Haversham knew a bit of magic, but he wouldn't need it for this. "But I will have one, and very soon."

Fear blossomed in Ramsey's eyes. That was good. He had already lost.

Thirteen

Caught off guard by Philippe Mandeville's challenge, William spent long moments staring at the sorcerer. He had never been very good at riddles. That had always been Tamara's forte. His sister would have solved the puzzle immediately, he felt certain. Had he the freedom to translocate to Cornwall and pose the question to her, he might return with the answer. Then he could lay hands on this mysterious book of Mandeville's, and go home to exorcise Oblis from his father's withering body.

But if he dared depart, he knew he would never get the book, that seemed certain, and Horatio's life—or afterlife—would be forfeit.

Mandeville adjusted his weight in the delicate birch chair, watching William intently all the while, his pale eyes flickering with curiosity.

"Have you an answer then?" the sorcerer drawled, his vowels long and trilling. He tilted his head, and a wolfish grin slowly spread across his face.

He thinks he's got me, William thought angrily. *He bloody well thinks I'm too stupid to answer the riddle.*

William scowled, his brain working rapidly to find the correct answer. The architect in him began to examine the riddle from all angles. Riddles weren't simply questions, but constructions, after all. They were built to be analyzed, unlocked, deconstructed.

What is the weight of my own soul?

What sort of question was that? The soul couldn't be weighed, for it was intangible. No scale could measure its mass or substance.

Then again, there was more than one sort of scale. Perhaps the weight Mandeville referred to was the gravity of a soul, the seriousness of the spirit of a man.

Or, perhaps he referred to the moral weight, or the burden of a man's sins.

Damn it! There are too many permutations!

"Come now, Mr. Swift," Mandeville prodded, "surely you wouldn't prefer a contest of spellcraft to one of wordplay. How much more intellectually stimulating this is!"

"A few more moments, please. I'm close," William said quickly, his mind going completely blank. "I just about have a handle on it."

Wordplay.

Was there a clue there? He thought there must be.

Words. Riddles often were about deciphering the hidden meaning in the words themselves, rather than in the trick of the question. So what wordplay existed here? The weight of a soul.

Weight.

Weight? Or, perhaps, wait.

William smiled. "The wait of my soul, sir, or its duration, is eternity."

Mandeville clapped softly, almost mockingly. "Well done, young man. And now the rest? The weight of *my* soul?"

He'd been so pleased with his solution that William had forgotten all about the second half of the riddle. Clearly it indicated that Mandeville judged his soul of a different weight—or wait—from William's. If Mandeville's soul did not have eternity, then what was its duration? How long would it linger? Even if the man had damned himself with his dark magics, his soul would still last for eternity . . . in Hell.

William frowned.

"Well?"

All right, get a hold of yourself, Will. No time like the present to figure this thing out!

His mind raced, blotting out all lines of thought but this one. Yet no solution presented itself.

Panic set in. If he could not answer, he might well win a sorcerous battle with Mandeville, but Horatio's spirit might be destroyed, or remain trapped for eternity.

William glanced at Horatio's portrait, his heart heavy.

If he *didn't* get this right he was damning not just Horatio but himself, as well, to imprisonment for eternity. The wait of his soul.

His gaze flicked over the faces in Mandeville's daguerreotypes; wide, terrified eyes scattered among angry, defiant ones. They all shared one thing, though . . . suffering. To be trapped in their purgatory—the very thought made William's blood run cold.

Then something caught William's eye, startling him. The image of Horatio had been frozen before, but now the tiny figure of the admiral's ghost moved! He waved his arm wildly. William's astonishment lasted a mere instant, as he recalled the motion he had seen in the portrait he had studied when first entering the room. At the time he'd thought it an illusion or trick of the light. Now he knew it was nothing of the sort. Instead, it was the darkest of magics.

William started to step toward the rows of pictures, but Horatio immediately waved him away.

From the corner of his eye, William saw Mandeville rising from his birch chair, and moving toward him. A terrible finality fell upon William. The riddle seemed opaque. He would not solve it.

This could end only one way.

Startling even himself, he flung out his right hand, muttering a hex he had mastered only recently. A flash of blue light sparked at the tips of his fingers and shot out at his host.

"Desino!"

The power of the spell burned the air around William as it arced across the ether, enveloping Mandeville, trapping him inside its mass. William wasted not a moment. He grabbed Horatio's portrait off the wall, and a tiny voice issued from the image of the ghost.

"Drop the frame!"

As though it had burned his fingers, he let the portrait fall. The picture crashed to the floor, smashing the frame into pieces. From within the enchanted sphere where William had trapped him, Mandeville roared his fury and struggled against the magic of Albion. In a moment he would be free.

From the shattered portrait rose a cloudy gray figure, coalescing into the ghost of Admiral Nelson. Horatio churned across the room, not taking a moment before he began to pick up several more of the ensorcelled images, shattering them in order to release the souls that were imprisoned within.

"The portraits, William!" Horatio said, his voice high and tight.

Behind them, Mandeville let out a howl of rage as he tore at his magical bindings.

William wasted not a moment. He tore one shelf of framed images from the wall and crushed them underfoot even as he swept his arm across another shelf. All of the pressure and frustration he kept within him came out in a rampage of destruction. With a cry of rage he shattered a daguerreotype with his fist and then began to strip more from the walls. His father, imprisoned within his own flesh by the demon Oblis. The bank, preyed upon by some mysterious, malicious thief. Sophia, so desperate to have every piece of him, never understanding that it was his dearest wish as well, but one he could never grant.

Chest heaving with exertion and fury, William stepped back to observe the wreckage of Mandeville's collection of captive souls. One corner still contained several shelves that he had not yet touched.

Mandeville shouted at him, cursing his soul to Hell, cursing his mother and his mother's mother, all the way back to Eve.

William summoned into his right hand a churning sphere of pure, primal magical force, and he hurled it into that corner. The room shook with thunder and that section of wall collapsed, shelves and frames broken into splinters and shards.

Many of the imprisoned, upon being released, simply faded away. Others lingered longer, and William wondered if the speed of their recovery from Mandeville's spell depended upon the length of time they had been bound by it. Whatever the case, their souls were finally free to pass into the spirit world, and beyond.

One daguerreotype remained, hanging on the wall.

William's hand closed around the last portrait. He hurled it to the floor and it cracked into several pieces. A strange buzz filled the air, so shrill that William covered his ears with his hands.

"Mandeville!" Horatio called, his voice nearly drowned out by the horrible buzz. William followed Horatio's gaze . . . but Mandeville was no longer there.

Abruptly the buzz ceased, and William was able to hear normally again. He and Horatio stared at the place where Mandeville had been, his body bound up in William's spell, but now there was nothing there, not even the chair.

"Where did he go?" William asked, his voice forlorn, almost hollow.

After this, there was no way he was ever going to procure that book. He had been a fool to think he could just waltz into Philippe Mandeville's home and secure the grimoire without greater preparation. But he'd been so intent and so desperate that he had not taken the time to formulate a real plan. He couldn't even figure out a damned riddle, one upon which his father's fate ultimately hinged.

William slumped against a shelf laden with books, his pulse racing and his temples throbbing. He couldn't bear to look at Horatio, he was so disappointed.

The light touch of a hand upon his shoulder startled him. He raised an arm to defend himself, thinking Mandeville had returned to destroy him. Instead he found Antoinette beside him. She gently caressed his arm, a gleam in her eye that hadn't been there before.

"Antoinette?" William began slowly. "But I . . . I thought you were . . ."

Her coquettish smile roused something in him. He felt his cheeks flush as she continued to stroke his arm, and he forced himself to glance away.

"I saw your portrait," Horatio said to Antoinette.

She nodded, but did not immediately speak. Then the ghost

moved nearer, studying her suspiciously. "When did he capture your soul?"

"I have been his prisoner for as long as I can remember," she said softly, at last letting her hand drop away. William felt both relief and disappointment as she stepped back and scowled at the shattered frames on the floor. "When we were attacked in the bayou . . . I abandoned you. I was his to command, so long as he had my soul. He compelled me to come here, to hide and await his pleasure."

Kindness soothed her features again as she glanced at William. "But when you freed me—"

"Your own father," Horatio said, looking down at the object in Antoinette's hand.

It was a daguerreotype. And William could guess the subject of the portrait.

Antoinette smiled at him. "He had to keep me in his thrall. I'm a Mandeville, after all. There's power in our family. You had him off balance and I—well, I had surprise on my side, didn't I? Once you freed me . . ."

She lifted the daguerreotype so William and Horatio could see the image of the man who was trapped there.

"He's an evil thing, but he won't be doin' much harm to anyone from now on." There was a note of defiance that grew in her tone as she spoke. Her dark eyes were almost black in the half-light, rage held in check by reality. "I'll keep him locked up till he's ready to come out again and play nice."

By the look on her face, William did not think Philippe Mandeville would ever taste freedom again. He stared at Antoinette as he began to understand how long she must have been planning the events that had unfolded here.

"This was . . . you wanted this to happen," he said.

Antoinette stared hard at him. "Are you suggestin' I drew you here all the way from England?"

His thoughts whirled. That would be too much to believe, but was it possible she had let whispers grow and rumors spread about the power of her father's grimoire, waiting for the day when a sorcerer would attempt to steal it, one with enough power to defeat him and release her from his influence? Oh, yes. More than possible.

How long had Antoinette been her father's prisoner, planning her moment to usurp him, studying his methods, his magic? William thought about how powerful she must be, and the idea unsettled him deeply.

"And the book? Does it even exist, or was it only bait all along?" he asked.

Antoinette smiled. Then she turned and placed the portrait inside a niche in the wall. William blinked, and the portrait and niche disappeared, the plaster becoming smooth and unblemished.

"I don't understand," William said. "The others—your father trapped their souls, but you've taken him physically. He's trapped in there completely?"

A dark look crossed her face. "Sometimes he wanted more than to just capture souls. I guess that just wasn't hell enough for the people he decided to punish, like my mother. She'll rest easier now."

Antoinette stepped out of the room a moment and when she returned to them she carried a large leather pouch, which she placed in William's hands with an arched eyebrow and a playful grin.

"This is what you came for."

Inside the pouch, William found a book.

The book.

"I don't know how to thank you—" he began, but she put a honey-colored finger to his lips.

"Shush now, or I'll change my mind."

William nodded. Antoinette leaned forward, her mouth brushing softly against the stubble on his cheek.

"Better get on now, William Swift, or I might be tempted to keep you here myself," she whispered, her breath hot against his ear.

"Thank you," William stammered, taking a step back from her. He too understood that his attraction to her could be as destructive as untamed fire. And that if she really wanted to keep him here, she might well be able to do it.

"Shall we return to Ludlow House then, Horatio?"

The ghost nodded, his translucent form already starting to fade.

"Antoinette," William said, as he began the translocation spell. "The rest of the riddle. What was the answer?"

She smiled up at him, her gaze unreadable.

"Philippe Mandeville made a deal with the devil himself a long time past," she replied. "The old monster's soul had no weight, nor wait, 'cause he didn't carry it anymore. He'd given it up, bartered for it. My father no longer had a soul."

～

For several long heartbeats, William hurtled through a gauzy gray nothing, a weird limbo space that tugged at him as though he was pushing through a viscous membrane. The sensation of motion fled, and his stomach lurched. He nearly stumbled as it ceased, and then he blinked, the world coming back into focus around him.

A changed world.

The dank, shadowy peril of the Louisiana bayou had vanished. Instead, he stood just inside the front door of Ludlow House.

"Thank the Lord," he whispered. "I do so love translocation."

The air shimmered beside him and Horatio's ghost appeared.

"Home at last," the specter said. "It does a heart good."

William took a deep breath, nodding. "Indeed it does, my friend. I'm grateful for your help, but if you'll excuse me, I feel as though I haven't bathed since birth."

Horatio appraised him grimly. "You do look a fright."

"I'm certain I don't smell any better than I look," William replied. Indeed, the stink of the swamp was still on him, and the smell of death, and there was a film of filth covering him that he was sure would take a vigorous scrub.

The ghost drifted along beside him as he headed for the stairs.

"Right, then, young master Swift. I shall be only a shout away, should you need me. But if I do say so, you ought to surrender to the siren song of sleep, and rest for as many hours as its embrace will hold you."

William paused at the bottom of the steps, grinning as he turned to Horatio. "A good fight always brings out the dramatic in you, Horatio."

The specter inclined his head in a strange sort of bow. His form wavered, becoming less substantial, so that he was little more than a whisper of an image on the air.

"As it has ever done," Horatio said. "Sleep well, William."

"Thank you, Horatio. For everything."

Then the ghost was gone, and the air in the house was still and quiet. William wondered if anyone else was awake.

He gripped the banister and started up. As his foot touched the third step, there came a rap at the front door.

He knitted his brows as he glanced back down. No voices came from outside, and the very stillness was unnerving.

What time is it? he wondered. The switch back from Louisiana had made him lose track entirely. *Seems awfully late for visitors.*

It was a safe bet that Martha and the other staff members who maintained their quarters in Ludlow House would be asleep by now. Nigel was likely prowling around somewhere, unless it was his turn to watch over Father. William grimaced in discomfort at the thought of answering the knock in his present condition, but curiosity overcame the embarrassment of his appearance and he went down to the door, unlocked it, and pulled it open.

Upon the doorstep stood Stephen Roberts, the rugged-faced peeler who had been investigating the thefts at Swift's of London, and with him was John Haversham. The latter wore an expression of amusement and self-satisfaction that immediately set William's teeth on edge.

"Good evening, Mr. Swift," Roberts began, obviously taking note of William's appearance but choosing not to comment. "Sorry to disturb you at this hour, sir, but I thought you might wish to know right away that your thief has had another go at the bank tonight, but he won't be trying it again. He's caught, sir, thanks to—"

"Excellent," William said. "Well done, Roberts. My thanks."

Then he turned his gaze upon Haversham, unable to stop the sneer that touched his features.

"And as for you, sir. I confess I had begun to believe I was wrong about you. No matter what my feelings might be about your intentions toward Tamara, I'd hoped that as a gentleman and a member of the Algernon Club, you could be trusted. But now I see that my instincts were correct after all."

A storm of anger swept across Haversham's face. He put his hands in his pockets, as if by doing so he could prevent himself from physically attacking William.

Only at that point did William notice that Haversham was entirely unfettered. A frown of confusion creased his brow.

Then he saw the way Roberts shifted in embarrassment.

The peeler stroked his gray mustache.

"Sorry, Mr. Swift. Bit of a misunderstanding, it seems. Mr. Haversham isn't the thief, sir. In fact, it's him what caught the scoundrel."

William closed his eyes tightly and reached up to squeeze the bridge of his nose. He wondered how bad he actually smelled, felt the grime on his face, and then dropped his hand.

He opened his eyes.

"John, I'm sorry. My other duties have occupied me all of this very long day and night, and exhaustion has prompted me to behave unforgivably."

Haversham arched an eyebrow, nostrils flaring. "You won't get any argument from me."

Taking a deep breath, William turned to Roberts. "But you've got the thief in custody now? In chains, I hope."

"Yes, sir. And I'm sorry to say, you know him."

William froze. "Know him? Who is it, then?"

"Your own man, Mr. Swift. Harold Ramsey. Your assistant, if I understand it correctly."

William gaped, mouth open. He sputtered for a moment before he could speak.

"That's . . . Not Harold! We were at university together. He's been my friend and confidant for *years*."

The peeler nodded. "Yes, sir. But he's confessed to the crime. Mr. Haversham thought to keep an eye on the place—I gather to exonerate himself after you expressed certain suspicions—and he caught Ramsey at it. And the man himself hasn't bothered to argue the facts. Not after Mr. Haversham administered certain pressures—"

"I beat the daylights out of him." Haversham grinned proudly.

"Even so," Roberts went on, "Mr. Ramsey has an intimate knowledge of the items stolen, from whom they were taken, and how. As your trusted employee, his betrayal solves the mystery of how the thief was able to get into Swift's and inside the vault without difficulty."

"But . . . why?"

"According to Ramsey, he's always felt that he ought to have been given a position of management at Swift's. When your father was incapacitated and Ramsey remained a member of the staff and wasn't called upon to take a greater role at the bank, he believed it was proof that he would never receive such a promotion. He stole from you for the money, sir, but also out of some sense of vengeance."

William's heart sank. "My God. Harold." He shook his head, gazing at the men who stood on his doorstep. "He never spoke up. Never even asked. We could have discussed it."

"Men of weak will grow easily spiteful, Mr. Swift."

"And what will happen to him now?" William asked, a terrible regret pressing upon his heart. He felt betrayed, certainly, but in some way he also felt the betrayer. Shouldn't he have noticed Harold's discontent? When he had turned away Harold's inquiries after Tamara—the man had hoped to court her—did Harold believe William thought him somehow beneath the Swifts' station in life?

Haversham stared at him. "What do you *suppose* will happen, Willy? He'll go to prison. Where he belongs. He's a thief, isn't he? If I'd been the culprit, you'd have been screaming for my head."

William nodded slowly. "Yes. Prison. What other choice is there?" He stepped back and opened the door wider. "Once again, John, you have my apologies. Would you gentlemen like to come in?"

"No, sir, it's awfully late," Roberts said. "The missus will be furious as it is. Thank you, though."

"Not at all, Roberts. Thank you for all you've done." William looked at Haversham. "And thank you, sir."

Haversham nodded but said nothing. As he and the peeler turned and started away, toward a carriage that waited in front of Ludlow House, William wondered if the tensions between himself and his sister's suitor would ever cease. If they did not, he had only himself to blame.

He closed the door and leaned his back against it, exhaustion and sorrow overcoming him.

~

SOPHIA'S HEART LEAPED. She had lain awake, unable to sleep a wink until she could hold William again, until she could look into his eyes and be reassured that this journey would be his last until the wedding. She had to speak with him, to reveal to him all the pain in her heart, and this time she would not allow their conversation to degenerate into spite and bitterness. She loved him, and knew he felt the same. It was time they behaved like lovers and not squabbling children. She had to let him know how much his attention to the details of their wedding meant to her.

Surely, he would see that he had been remiss.

Now her sleeplessness was rewarded.

A carriage had come up the drive, the hoofbeats of the horses carrying clearly on the night air. Rushing to the window, she'd heard the knock upon the door, and the low rumble of men's voices.

Quickly, she had pulled her robe on and left her room, moving along the corridor to the stairs. The voices were clearer there, and one in particular was familiar. William had come home!

As she went down the stairs, she heard the distant sound of other voices, coming from within the house, though she could not make out the words.

A smile blossomed on her lips and she descended more quickly.

She heard the front door close, and one set of footsteps sounded within the house. The men who had come up in the carriage must be departing. All the better, she would have William to herself.

But as she came to the landing on the second floor, lost in the shadows there, she saw a dark figure move across the foyer. Its shape was familiar to her. Not William, but Nigel.

Her heart sank. All her excitement had been for nothing. William had left again.

But when next she heard a voice, it wasn't the vampire's.

"Good evening, Nigel. I knew I'd find you awake," William said.

Relief swept over Sophia again. She put her hand on the banister and took a step down. There in the shadows, she was unnoticed by the two men.

"I'm afraid it is not a good evening at all, William. I have been awaiting your return, and I have troubling news," Nigel said, his dark purr of a voice sounding even graver than usual.

Sophia froze.

"What is it?" William demanded. "What's happened? Is Sophia all right?"

"As right as ever," Nigel said evenly. "No, I'm afraid the news concerns Tamara. Earlier this evening one of the maids had a frightful encounter with Bodicea. Our ghostly majesty had journeyed from Cornwall with a message. She asks that you come at once, with all the means at your disposal. Your sister has run afoul of a coven of witches, it seems."

"Witches?" William cried.

"And they have taken Tamara. It's almost certain that they mean to kill her tomorrow night, on the solstice, so we haven't any time to spare."

There was a dreadful silence in the foyer. Sophia stood, unmoving, upon the stairs, uncertain whether to reveal herself, afraid that even her breathing might be heard.

At last, William spoke. "It's my fault. I never should have let her go without me."

Tears slipped down Sophia's cheeks. She closed her eyes and shook her head.

"If I'm to show up in Camelford and expect the people to take me seriously, I must wash and change clothes," William said to Nigel, down there in the darkened foyer, with only the moonlight from outside allowing any illumination. "Give me fifteen minutes, and then I'll want to speak to you and Byron before I depart. You'll have charge of the household, Nigel."

The vampire snarled. "Are you mad? I'm coming with you."

"And how will you manage that?" William asked, not unkindly. "I cannot translocate us both. I know you care for Tamara, and I wish that you could accompany me. But time is of the essence. And there is my father to consider."

"Of course," the vampire said. "Much as it pains me. If Tamara is in peril, my every instinct is to go to her aid."

"I'm entrusting Ludlow House to you. Your presence here will ease my mind so that I can focus on Tamara's safety. You aid her by safeguarding our home and family."

William came to the bottom of the steps. It was the first time Sophia had gotten a glimpse of him since his return and even in the darkness, where he was barely more than a silhouette, she could tell he was a mess. His hair was unkempt, his jacket was torn, and a damp stench wafted up from him.

He took the steps two at a time, his head down, and only looked up when he was about to reach the top. There her beloved nearly collided with her.

"Oh, Sophia, darling, you startled me!" William said as he looked up.

In the gloom, the sadness of his expression spoke volumes.

"Don't go," she whispered, voice tight. "You must not go, William, not again."

William stared at her, eyes wide. "You heard. But . . . if you heard, you'll know that I have no choice. Tamara's disappeared. My sister needs me."

"But *I* need you, William!" she cried, voice shrill and hysterical. "Damn you, don't you see that *I* need you? I know you fear for your sister, but with all her power, she can protect herself! You rush off to here and there with never a thought for the woman you claim to love, the woman you claim to desire, the woman you say you wish to marry!"

"You're speaking madness, Sophia! My sister is caught in the hands of witches. Her *life* hangs in the balance. I do love you, but only a lunatic would fail to see that I must go to her."

Sophia began to shake. Her hands trembled as she lifted them to cover her mouth, to keep from screaming at him.

"A lunatic, am I? Perhaps . . . perhaps I am. But if you have the bank, and your father, and your duties, and the horrors of this world to contend with, and all of them are more important to you than I am, then when will you have time for me?"

William stared at her a moment. There was anguish in his eyes, but he shook his head.

"I am sorry, darling. You don't know how wrong you are. But I cannot take the time to argue the demands of my life, yet again. Not now. With regret, I must go."

Sophia held a hand over her mouth. Her eyes stung with tears. "You don't understand, William. Without you, I am alone. My mother . . . my father . . . every time you leave me, I fear you will not return. I can barely contain the screams that come up from my soul. If anything were to happen to you, I fear madness would claim me at last."

He stared at her, eyes full of regret and mouth open. Then he pulled her into his arms and held her tightly, kissing her on the head and whispering lovely assurances into her hair.

Sophia felt cold and hollow. The words did not penetrate.

"I will come back to you. I promise."

Sophia stepped back, glaring at him, and then struck him in the chest. "You can't know that."

William hung his head. "I love you, Sophia. But Tamara is my sister. I must go."

He tried to step around her.

Stunned, shaking her head vigorously, Sophia grabbed his arm. "If you leave now, then there will be no wedding. I shall not be waiting for you when you return."

William stared for a moment, then pushed past her without so much as an answer. He ran up the stairs, stripping off his filthy jacket as he went.

Sophia peered into the darkness above until she could no longer see him. Then, slowly, she sank down to sit upon the steps, hugging herself, nightgown soft around her, tears burning her eyes.

Fourteen

The pain in her head was blinding. It felt as if there were a tiny man inside her brain case, hammering away at her cerebrum, pulping her gray matter into mush.

Tamara opened her eyes only to find herself in utter darkness. She tried to sit up, but though she could feel her limbs, they would not obey her commands. Alone and paralyzed, she despised the feeling of utter helplessness that overcame her, and quickly it was eclipsed by rage.

Fury flowed through her like liquid fire, igniting something inside that at once terrified and fascinated her. The anger grew like some strange parasite, ready to tear apart its host and breathe air for the first time.

Tamara opened her mouth not by any conscious thought but with a primal surge. A scream clawed its way from her throat, full of such pain and rage that it sounded as though no human voice could have produced it.

There was magic in her howl, too, the power of a kingdom's soul. It curled around her mind, sifting the pain from her head and replacing it, instead, with *words*.

Her mouth began to move of its own volition, her lips forming the syllables that rose up in her.

"Ab aeterno a posse ad esse iure divino resurgam!"

A blinding flash of white light enveloped her, pain searing every inch of her flesh, from soles to scalp. Yet the spell continued to issue from her lips. Her words seemed to gain a life of their own as they burst forth and spread their tendrils out into the ether.

A sizzling filled Tamara's ears, and then her nostrils filled with the acrid stink of burning human tallow, the stench of which caused her to gag. There was a scream—one that was not her own—and then she was free.

At first she thought herself still enwrapped in darkness. Then she blinked away the effects of that bright flash and realized it was night, and the moonlight cast a warm, buttery glow. She looked around and found that she was sitting at the foot of a huge, ancient rowan tree, its massive trunk shattered as though gouged open from within. The moonlight illuminated the raw and jagged edges of the wound. Her mind made the connections instantly. She had been the cause of the tree's death. She had been trapped within it, and her magic had eviscerated the venerable rowan in order to escape.

No. The fault lay not with her. The witches who had imprisoned her were the true killers. Still it saddened her to have had a part in the destruction of a thing of such power and majesty.

A terrible gurgling sound caught Tamara's attention. She turned to see a dark shape rising from the ground. In the moonlight she saw that it was a witch, its face half-melted in a ruin of bone and gristle.

The witch hissed at her and Tamara summoned a defensive spell. Magic burst from her fingers and enveloped her. Weak as she was, she had instinctively summoned the Shield of Armor, a simple yet powerful protection that she and William had learned in the first days after inheriting the mantle of Protector.

The grotesque, wounded witch flinched from the brightness of the magic.

"All right, pretty," the hideous thing snarled at her. "You're free for the moment. But there'll be no other human girl for us now. You're the sixth. The magic in your bones will make the ritual all the more effective. We'll see each other very soon."

Tamara shivered under the glare of that ruined face.

The witch turned, staggering away. Neither one of them was in any condition to fight. Tamara was grateful. She doubted she would have survived. But the creature had made clear that this was only a respite . . . now that they knew the magic that was in her, that she was Protector of Albion, they were determined that she be their thirteenth sacrifice.

Worried that the injured witch might return with others, Tamara knew she had to depart quickly. But she spared one last glance at the rowan she had destroyed and saw in the moonlight a black splotch on the ground.

Warily, she reached for it, and realized it was the still-intact cloak that the wounded witch had left behind.

She reached to pick up the cloak, but paused, wondering what kind of dreadful enchantments might lie in that garment. Tamara might share the mantle of Protector, but in so many ways she and William were still novices. She wished that Bodicea were here. The warrior queen would not hesitate.

Forcing herself to be decisive, she bent and picked up the cloak. Tamara folded the garment tightly and tucked it under her arm, before standing and scanning the grove for an exit.

The cloak stank of death and smoke, but she ignored the stench. If there was power in it, she wasn't about to leave the hideous thing for the witches to reclaim and use against her. She wasn't some English rose who fainted at the first sign of unpleasantness.

Tamara started toward the edge of the grove, her thoughts awhirl. It seemed clear that the witch had been left to keep watch over her. *Little did she know what the task would cost her,* Tamara mused as she picked her way through the tangle of tree roots that grabbed at her feet.

A frown creased her forehead as she glanced down.

That's odd.

She had never seen such massive roots before. Turning back, she saw that the tree from which she had escaped was part of a strangely uniform circle around a central clearing. The trees in the circle were all rowans, roughly the same age and height, and all with those enormous roots.

As though they were planted this way by design, she thought.

She glanced about, searching the moonlit woods for any sign of other witches, then hurried back into the circle. She approached the nearest intact tree and studied it more closely. As she walked round it, she saw something jutting from the bark and stepped back as a cry caught in her throat.

A human arm protruded from the trunk of the rowan.

Tamara took a tentative step forward and reached out, breathlessly inching her hand toward the cold, pale fingers. She touched the hand . . .

It felt cold and lifeless.

A moment later, as if woken by her touch, it *twitched*, then grasped for her. Tamara stepped back, heartsick, for now she knew exactly where the witches were keeping their victims.

Becoming wild with fear and horror, she turned to race back into the forest.

Then she let out a scream at the figure that confronted her, appearing as a spill of darkness in the moonlight.

The witch stood so close that Tamara was certain it could have breathed her in. Its eyes were ink-black pits rimmed with a fringe of barely visible gray lashes. Tamara felt herself falling into the witch's eyes, and willed herself to back away, to tear herself from the hypnotic lure of those half-human, half-demon orbs.

She closed her own eyes and took in a shaking breath. When she opened them again, the hold was lessened, and Tamara found that she could think again.

Why hasn't it attacked? It had me unaware, so why am I still alive?

"What do you want?" Tamara spat at the newcomer.

The witch laughed, making a sound that felt like insects burrowing under her skin.

"Hello, Tamara Swift . . ." it began.

Tamara flinched at the sound of her own name.

"Of course we know who and what you are. We are not animals. Though you treat us as such," the creature whispered. "I am Viviane, witch queen, and you have scarred my sister Morveren. If we didn't have other plans for you, you'd be made to suffer for that."

Her voice weakened Tamara's resolve, sucking the life from her limbs like fast-acting poison.

"My," the witch continued, "you are a pretty one. Soft and lush. If only you would listen to reason, you and I might enjoy each other's company, but those of your type are ever too righteous. I fear it's back into the rowan tree for you."

The witch raised a hand, twisted fingers working in the air. Her cloak swirled around her as though it moved of its own accord. Her grotesque face split into what Tamara thought was a smile, but might have been a leer, as she began to intone something under her breath.

Tamara recognized several words in that guttural tongue, but more than that, she *felt* the intent of the spell as it began to work upon her. A spell of forgetfulness.

"No!" she cried, and she quickly cast two spells of her own, simultaneously throwing up the most powerful magical protection she knew and muttering the beginning words of the incantation for translocation. She felt the translocation spell take hold of her, and for a moment she thought she had escaped unharmed, as the witch and the grove receded from her view.

That was lucky, she thought to herself.

Yet even as she was in the midst of translocating, she realized she hadn't a clue what she meant.

What *was lucky?* she thought.

∿

"UNDER THE SAME SKY, under the same moon, like an autumn leaf, let the spirit winds carry me to my destination."

The words swept around William and caught him up, shifting him out of the world of flesh and blood. He closed his eyes and did not open them again until he felt solid ground beneath his feet and the breeze caressing his face. Until he was surrounded by the scents and sounds of a cool summer night in Cornwall.

William took a deep breath to dispel the sense of dislocation, and glanced around. He stood on the ragged grass beside a fast-running brook. There came a quick popping sound, then a discordant trill like the stroke of a badly tuned harp, and the ghost of Admiral Nelson manifested in the air beside him.

"Hello, William," the ghost said quietly, as though fearful he might be overheard. "Are you well?"

"Well enough, Horatio. Got to get my bearings here, though. See if you can locate Bodicea while I go to the inn to ask after Tamara. Perhaps there's something to be learned there. Find me at the inn when you've retrieved her majesty, and our search will begin in earnest."

The ghost gave William a quick, worried nod, then disappeared back into the ether.

After Horatio had gone, William studied his moonlit surroundings more carefully. He had calculated his arrival point to the best of his ability, and if he'd gauged correctly he wasn't far from the inn that his sister had been using as her base.

Back in bloody Cornwall again, he thought miserably, as he followed the brook upstream toward Camelford.

But it wasn't merely the locale that troubled him. His mind still echoed with Sophia's admonishments.

Would she truly leave him? How could she be so selfish, asking him not to come to Tamara's aid? What could she have been thinking, to imagine even for a moment that he would *consider* leaving his sister's fate to chance? William loved Sophia to distraction, and it seemed clear that she was deeply troubled and needed his attention.

When he returned, if she would accept him, he would give her that attention and sort out the pains of her heart. But he would never sacrifice his sister for that love.

When he returned to London he would make it up to Sophia,

even if it meant looking through a hundred place settings and cut-lery patterns.

For now, however, his duty was to Tamara.

His translocation had put him farther from the inn than he had planned, and much farther than he would have liked. The walk seemed endless, but finally William found himself approaching the Mason's Arms inn.

It's rather small, he thought to himself, wondering if they would even have a room for him, since he had arrived there so unexpect-edly. The place was really more tavern than inn. Travelers might rest here, but now that he thought of it, there likely weren't many who passed the night in Camelford.

He entered the tavern. The place seemed a bit larger on the in-side, but that wasn't saying very much. The few tables he found were placed haphazardly around the room, with a large stone fire-place taking up the bulk of the back wall. There was a barkeeper behind the counter.

Immediately he spotted Farris, sitting at a table in the farthest corner. The man's face was ashen, and his hands were tightly cupped around a large pint. His hair was mussed, and his shoul-ders were rounded unhappily.

"Farris . . ." William said as he strode through the tavern.

The butler looked in the direction of his voice, his worried eyes perking up at the sound of William's voice, as though he'd just awakened.

"Master William!" he said eagerly, standing and crossing to meet his employer with a hopeful expression. He clasped William's hand and pumped it with great vigor.

"Mistress Tamara," Farris muttered, his voice indicating that he was dangerously close to tears. "She's . . . she's . . ."

"Let's go outside, my good man, and you can tell me what's

transpired," William said quickly, hoping to avoid any more curious stares from the barkeeper, who was watching them intently, hoping perhaps to get a good bit of gossip to pass around town. William ignored him and took Farris's arm, leading him back to the entrance.

Once they were outside and under cover of darkness, William let Farris pour out his story. It seemed that when Bodicea had returned to Camelford after traveling to London with the awful news, the ghostly queen had begun the search for his sister without him. At that very moment, she and Serena were combing the woods, looking for any trace. Farris had wanted to accompany them, but they had made him promise to stay at the inn to wait for William's arrival.

"It's my fault, Master William," Farris said. He hung his head, his large frame strangely made smaller by this confession. In the darkness, he cut a sad figure.

"What do you mean?" William asked.

"If only I'd been stronger, if only I'd held on longer, and not let the witches carry 'er away . . ."

William shook his head. "Impossible. You're only one man, and creatures like that possess superhuman strength. You can't control the fates of those around you."

"It's only . . . she's just a young girl. Anything could happen—"

Damping down his own fears, William put a comforting hand upon Farris's shoulder. "She'd have your guts for garters if she heard you talk like that."

Farris nodded, chagrined. "If only she's still alive . . ."

"How many girls have been taken thus far, Farris?" William asked, trying to find some clue to the witches' plans in the details.

"Including . . . including Mistress Tamara, there've been six, Master William. Not counting the two murdered, that is." Farris blanched a bit as he said this last. "Holly Newcomb, Christine Lindsay, Sally Kirk, Mary Raynham, Miss Tamara, and the sixth, I've only just heard—"

William frowned. "What, you mean it happened tonight?"

Farris nodded. "Just after we encountered the witches, if I understand it correctly. Katherine Monroe is her name. Poor thing."

"Poor things all," William echoed. "But we'll have them back, Farris. Every last one."

"Yes, sir. I'm not certain how many fairy girls has been snatched. P'raps Serena will know better."

"I shall ask her," William replied.

They fell silent then, the two men lost in their own thoughts. The night birds sang and the trees across the river rippled with a passing breeze. The stone bridge that arched across the water echoed back the sound of the river's voice.

Yet another sound intruded upon the gentle night, a familiar low trill that sent a shiver through William. Farris glanced up with a start, and William spun to see the night air shimmer.

The ghost of Queen Bodicea appeared, fierce and regal as ever, and neither man could gaze directly upon her. Both were instinctively flustered by her blatant nudity.

"William!" the queen said. "Come quickly. We've found her!"

"Tamara?"

"Don't be a fool. Who else? Come away *now*."

Pulse racing, relief flooding through him, William glanced at Farris.

"Go on then, sir," the stalwart footman said, face alight with his own elation. "See to her. I'll await your return."

"Good show, Farris. Make certain her rooms are ready for her. A bath, as well." William turned to Bodicea. "My sister's well, then?"

The phantom's expression was grim. "She will be. But the night has not been kind."

William grimaced. "All right. Let's be off, then."

"There is a cottage, a mile southeast of here. I shall lead you."

He nodded and reached out. For just a moment Bodicea focused so that her ghostly fingers could touch his flesh and they grasped hands. Then William intoned the spell of translocation, while he could feel her guidance and follow it.

A moment later he found himself in a small clearing, just outside the door of a rough-hewn cottage. Bodicea manifested beside him, but he rushed to the door without waiting for her. He swung it open with such force that it banged against the wall, shattering the silence within.

A ghost hovered at the end of the bed, a pale, shuddery thing. So insubstantial did it seem that for a moment William did not realize it was Nelson. When he did realize it, he saw the worry on the admiral's face, and understood that it was his fear for Tamara that diminished him so.

Tamara.

It was larger inside the cottage than William would have believed, roomy enough for a small table and chairs, a tiny larder, and a bed. Tamara lay on the bed under layers of blankets, shivering as though stricken with fever. Aside from Horatio's ghost, she was attended by Serena—the sprite sat on the headboard looking down at her, wings fluttering worriedly—and a stranger who sat on the edge of the bed, holding Tamara's hand.

Barely more substantial than Horatio, Queen Bodicea passed through the door as though it weren't there, marching over to stand by her fellow ghost. The two of them were like a thin veil of mist, transparent and drifting.

William went quickly to his sister, ignoring the stranger completely even as he stood up to make room for the newcomer.

"Tamara?" William whispered.

He touched her face, then felt her forehead. She had no fever,
and the moment he laid his hand upon her the shivering ceased, as
though she drew strength from him. And perhaps there was truth
to that. They were not just siblings—they shared the magic of Albion. It coursed through them both, and they restored each other.

Her skin felt cold to him, but there was color in her cheeks. She
lived. Even so, seeing her so vulnerable thrust a dagger into his
heart and made him catch his breath. If anything had happened
to her—

"She'll be all right, I think. Just had a bit of a rough night," the
young man said, his voice low and calming.

William turned and looked up at him. Some innate goodness—
even innocence—radiated from within this fellow, clear as the candle that burned in the lantern that hung just inside the door.
William immediately felt at ease in his company.

"Your help is greatly appreciated, sir. I don't believe I've had the
pleasure . . ."

The man thrust out a hand in greeting. "Richard Kirk, Mister
Swift. My sister is among the missing, and Miss Swift was very kind
to me. I would be remiss if I did not return the favor. However, I
must say that it was your friends who discovered her."

William followed Richard's gaze to where Horatio and Bodicea
floated worriedly.

"Excuse me," William said, "but to whom do you refer when
you say that *my friends* are responsible for finding Tamara?"

Richard frowned in confusion, and glanced at Horatio and
Bodicea. "They *are* your friends, are they not? I was in the woods
searching for my sister and came upon them. They said—"

"You can see them? The *ghosts*?" William asked, knowing that he sounded incredulous.

The young man smiled.

"I supposed that was what they were," he said quietly. "Yes, I can see them perfectly well. And the sprite, too. Though I've seen her sort before, darting about the forest at night. Pretty things, sprites, but dangerous."

"Aye, boy, more than ye knows," Serena said, shooting Richard a sharp look.

The sprite took flight then, shooting across the room with a blur of purplish light. She went to a chair across which had been thrown some sort of heavy dark garment. Thrusting her hands into it, she gathered it up and dragged it from the chair, flying back toward the bed with the heavy burden. The weight of the thing almost dragged the little creature to the ground.

"Have it, we does, William Swift," she cooed, dropping the dirty thing at William's feet before flying back to her perch on the headboard.

William bent and picked up the dark cloth.

"Foul . . . !" he gasped, so horrified at its stench that he dropped it again, kicking it into a corner of the room. "What in the world is that *thing*?" he said, wiping his hand on the leg of his trousers.

Richard also seemed to be repulsed by the smell, backing away from the bed.

"It's a witch's cloak."

William jumped at the sound of the thin, weak voice, and spun to see that Tamara had awoken. She sat up, perching on one elbow, her long pale hair in a tangle around her shoulders and back. Her face was smudged with dirt, but her eyes still held the spark and warmth and intelligence that he always looked for in his sister.

"Tam, are you all right?"

She nodded weakly. "I think so. A bit of brandy might be in order, and something to eat."

Even as she spoke, Richard poured her a small glass of brandy. They all waited as he brought it to her, and once she had sipped from it, William stared at her expectantly.

"I've got some bread and cheese. Little more, I'm afraid."

"That would be wonderful," Tamara replied.

Richard busied himself at the larder. Tamara looked up at her brother, a bit less pale.

"I don't remember much, Will. But I do remember holding this cloth in my hands, and understanding its nature." She paused to catch a breath and moisten her parched lips with another sip of brandy. "I remember combating the witches, then being dragged up into the sky. The one that carried me, she said something . . . I'll share with you a bit later. And I recall a terrible smell . . ."

She paused.

"But that's all."

She eased herself back onto the bed, shuddering.

"I know I should remember, that it's important, but I just can't," she said, sighing miserably.

Richard brought her a plate with a block of cheese and a small knife, as well as several raggedly cut slices of bread. Tamara accepted them gratefully, cut herself a wedge of the cheese, and devoured it.

Bodicea glanced at Horatio, and the two ghosts were so close they seemed about to drift together, pass through each other. The admiral nodded, and Bodicea turned to hold William's gaze.

"Long, long ago I did battle with witches. I know their strength all too well. You are the Protectors of Albion, but you are still only two, and you have not yet reached the full potential of the power you have inherited. You will require help, if you are to destroy these creatures. Without the fairies, we have little chance of defeating them."

"But they want nothing to do with us—" Tamara began.

"I should say," William squeaked, "that it's quite the opposite. *We* want nothing to do with *them*. Allying ourselves with the fairies, Bodicea? Have you lost your senses?"

Nelson made a sound as if he cleared his throat.

"You forget yourself, William. You speak to her majesty, Queen Bodicea. Her skill in battle is unmatched by any woman in the history of Albion—"

"By any *woman*, Horatio? By anyone, you mean," the queen replied angrily.

Horatio shifted awkwardly. "Perhaps, majesty, perhaps. The point, William, is that if Bodicea declares that the witches are more than our match, you cannot doubt her."

Tamara looked over at her brother.

"So be it," she whispered.

∼

THE CLOAK LAY BETWEEN THEM like a gauntlet.

Sibille stared at it, shock registering on her ethereal features. Unable to take her eyes away from the horrible thing, this most respected of fairies, most powerful among the members of the Council of Stronghold, spoke without looking up.

"Witches . . ."

There was a muttering from the assembled crowd of fairies.

They had come to see vengeance meted out to the little sprite and her human and ghostly friends, but now fear echoed through the throng, changing the mood of the assemblage.

Tamara looked over at her brother. She could feel the tension that gripped William's body, causing a slight tic in the jaw muscle on the right side of his face. Bodicea and Horatio stood at her other side, manifested so powerfully that they seemed almost alive as they glared at the fairy council. She didn't need to turn her head to know that Richard and Farris stood protectively behind her, guarding her back. Serena would be perched on Farris's shoulder, wings aflutter, defiant as ever.

Giselle Ravenswood stood beside Sibille. She gazed grimly at Tamara. "Since your last visit to Stronghold, two more have vanished. The witches have murdered one of us, and hold six others captive."

Tamara nodded. "Six fairy girls and at least five human. They need thirteen all told. On the solstice, the witches will kill them all. We mean to stop it, but we need your help."

Giselle nodded.

Sibille looked up at Tamara, fear reflected in her pale, cold eyes. "It is yours."

～

I WILL PACK MY THINGS *and be gone before he returns,* Sophia thought angrily as she grabbed another valise and swung it onto the bed.

Normally she would never have packed her own suitcases, but she was so angry, so hurt that she didn't even give the action a thought.

She yanked open one of the dresser drawers, exposing her frilly cream underskirts. Taking her anger out on the defenseless pieces of cloth, she stuffed them roughly into the large case. She realized then that she hadn't a clue how to pack the valise properly, but she really didn't care. She slammed the lid down, ignoring the bit of lacy frill that poked out from under it.

Looking at her clothes, Sophia wondered again how Elvira always had managed to put so many items into so few cases. She had already filled three trunks, and there were still so many things left unpacked.

Shaking, she reached for the latch on the front of the valise, trying to force it to turn. She hadn't the key to properly lock it, but she wasn't about to go to Elvira and ask for it. The old maid would have experienced heart failure if she had seen the state of Sophia's room.

The place was well and truly a mess. Clothing that had been thrown this way and that took up every available space, drawers were pulled from their berths, and even the curtains were askew.

Sophia ignored the mess and continued her packing. She half-expected William to return and beg her not to go, to sink down on one knee and ask forgiveness for his follies. Still, she was so startled when a rap sounded against her door that she dropped the silk handkerchief she was holding. It fluttered to the floor, but Sophia didn't reach for it. Instead, she ran for the door, a hysterical sob burbling in her throat.

"Oh, William, I knew you would see—" she said, as she threw open the door.

Nigel Townsend stood on the threshold. Sophia hissed and drew back as though he were a serpent about to strike. Anger flooded her, and she glared at him.

"You're not William," she said flatly.

"And I thank my maker every day for that kindness," Nigel replied.

He smiled, revealing the opalescent teeth that glistened in his mouth. She usually marveled at how long and sharp those teeth looked, but today she only glanced at them warily.

Nigel gave a slight bow.

"No, I am not William Swift, milady, but I do come bearing

news. Nelson appeared briefly in my chambers to inform me that William and Tamara have been unavoidably detained. They must stay in Cornwall for a few more days, at the very least."

He purred his words, and, again, Sophia wondered if there was any cat in the man. She knew he was a vampire; that he wanted to sample her blood so desperately that she could feel his need rolling off him in languid waves.

Then her heart skipped in her chest as his words sank in. Once more, William had forsaken her. She turned her back on Nigel, and began her work again, in earnest.

"Sophia, are you . . . going somewhere?" he asked, amusement in his voice.

Sophia turned on him, glaring, trying to find the words that would express her hatred and her sorrow and her fury. None would come. In the end she simply threw herself onto the bed and began to sob.

Nigel tried to speak to her, and to her surprise his tone was soft and kind, as though he were truly a man—a gentle man—and not a monster. But even had he been the kindest man in the world, Sophia would have spurned his placating words.

Salty tears slid down her cheeks, most dampening her pillow but several reaching the corners of her mouth. She licked them away, savoring the salt, nurturing her anguish.

For several moments longer, Nigel tried to assuage her sadness, but Sophia ignored him entirely. At last he left the room, assuring her that she had only to ask if she wished to speak of her troubles.

She sank into the soft down of the pillow, her breath still coming in shallow, ragged starts as he closed the door firmly behind him.

Sophia rolled over and stared at the ceiling. She tried to catch her breath and after several minutes the flow of tears stemmed a little. She had not felt right these past few days. Her chest ached, and her skin burned. She wondered if she had a fever.

She wanted her mother, someone who loved and cared for her, and *only* her. With William being so callous to her, she needed a loving hand to touch her brow, take away the pain she felt inside and out. She knew of only one such person who lived here at Ludlow House.

She would go to him, and he would ease her weary mind. He would know the words she needed to hear.

She sat up, and her head throbbed horribly, nausea churning her stomach. She felt so terrible that she almost lay back down, but the thought of that comforting voice and those gentle eyes gave her the strength to stand. Clutching the side table, she dragged herself to her feet, where she swayed once, but finally managed to stay upright.

And she went to him.

Fifteen

The moonlight offered William a clear view of the woods around him. He had spent the past few hours traipsing through the trees in the company of Horatio and Bodicea, looking for ghostly knights. The translucent forms of his companions were sometimes difficult to see as they passed through shafts of moonlight.

The dawn crested the eastern horizon, and they had nothing to show for all their effort.

His attention on the beauty of sunrise, William stumbled over an exposed root. He hissed a loud curse and sat down quickly, holding his foot, investigating to see if he'd done any real damage. The pain in his ankle faded almost immediately, so there was no sprain, but his toe throbbed and he wondered if he might have broken it.

For a moment he considered telling the ghosts to go on without him, but then he caught Bodicea's disdainful gaze as she floated nearby.

"I'm getting up, I'm getting up . . ." William sighed as he clambered back onto his feet and hobbled over to where the ghosts were waiting.

"This way." Bodicea pointed with a long, muscular arm, tracing gossamer wisps in the early morning light. Her arm, like the rest of her, was bare save for the streaks of war paint.

William liked to tell himself that he had long since gotten used to her nudity, but that was far from the truth. He had become expert at ignoring it, most of the time, but that was hardly the same thing.

"We are close to the spot where the knights repeat their battle," the queen continued, floating forward so that Horatio and William had no option but to follow her.

They moved through the trees, William going at a much slower pace, since he had to avoid all of the overhanging tree branches that his allies did not.

Bodicea halted abruptly, holding up her spear to alert the others. The three of them watched through a gap in the trees as a spectral gray mist moved swiftly into the clearing that lay before them, seeping out of the forest and filling the space with unnatural speed and purpose.

"What in God's name—" William whispered, but Bodicea put a finger to her lips, silencing him.

He opened his mouth to add something else, but she shook her head, and glared in a way that spoke volumes. Bodicea pointed out to the field, and the sight that greeted William took his breath away.

The gray mist parted to reveal dozens of knights locked in bloody battle, silver armor against ebon black. William could hear the sound of metal clanging against metal, the grunts of effort as the knights lifted their heavy broadswords to hack and impale one another. Yet the sounds did not match the action of the phantom battle. Rather they seemed echoes of these events, unnatural sounds coming to the world of the living from some faraway time, drifting from the realm of spirits to the land of men. The smell of freshly spilled blood mingled in the air with the stink of sweat and the stench of human fear.

"Incredible," he whispered.

With a quick glance he saw that Horatio watched with equal fascination. He imagined the sight of such a battle raised powerful memories in the ghost. The man had been a legend in his own time; his missing arm and eye bore testament to his greatness. Even though he was but a shade of the man he had been, William wagered that Horatio's ghostly heart must race at the sight of such furious combat.

Sensing his companion's stare, Horatio pulled his gaze away from the battlefield to give a wicked smile. He turned to Bodicea, who nodded. She, too, knew the call of battle.

William had never been one to court death, but since he had taken on the mantle of the Protectorship, he found that death courted him. He hadn't thought he possessed the makings of a warrior—and he still didn't, really—but in this moment he could not deny the surge of aggression he was experiencing, and his own soul's cries for glory as he contemplated the fighting.

The ghostly knights clashed, swords resounding on shields, shouts of pain and exhortations to battle carrying through the woods. In the dawn's light they were often only suggestions of figures, and as the sun began to rise in earnest they faded with each passing moment. Yet the blood that streaked their armor and spattered their faces seemed to paint their silhouettes all the more firmly.

William studied the specters, trying not to lose sight of them as they turned in the sun, sometimes disappearing altogether. His gaze rested on one particular knight whose ferocity was unmatched. The ghost turned to attack a black-armored foe and William saw the coat of arms painted upon his shield.

Could it be?

"The Pendragon," he whispered.

He had to stifle a shout as he reached out to tug at Horatio's jacket, completely forgetting himself in that moment. His hand passed through the admiral's insubstantial form, but Horatio sensed his excitement.

"Yes, I see it, too," he rasped. Nelson's awe seemed to match his own.

As a boy, he had sat in his grandfather's chambers and listened to the old magician as he spun tales of the Knights of the Round Table. He had read the books over and over again. Yet now he bore witness to those very knights, in combat against some dark force, the gallant men in service to Arthur Pendragon, bloody on the field of battle.

Mesmerized, he started forward into the clearing. Bodicea hissed and darted for him, reaching out her spectral hands, but she could not stop him, and he paid her no heed.

He had to be closer, to *really* see them. Bodicea tried to block his path with her spear, but he passed right through it.

"William!" Bodicea whispered harshly. "We must not interfere until it is finished."

"But they'll all have disappeared by then," he protested. Even as he said this he could see the bodies of the defeated already starting to vanish from the field. He took a few more tentative steps forward, trying to determine exactly what was happening to the disappearing shades.

He cleared the trees and started through the tall grass.

"William!"

The voice made it clear that she brooked no argument, and it stopped William in his tracks. He turned to find Horatio floating toward him, his one good eye alight with righteous fury.

"Do *not* reveal yourself to them," Nelson said. "There is danger here."

Horatio started back toward the trees, gesturing for William to follow and giving him no opportunity to protest. William started to obey, but paused when he felt a cold breeze caress the back of his neck.

"What in . . ." he began, but then he saw the rictus of terror that etched upon the faces of Bodicea and Horatio.

He twisted around in alarm to find a huge knight in the armor of Pendragon's enemies, lumbering at him and wielding an enormous double-bladed war-ax. The knight's armor gleamed coal-black. Even the chain mail was a dark gray. The horned helmet he wore protected his face so well that William could not see his eyes.

The monstrous knight swung his war-ax. William hadn't time to think, never mind dodge. He screamed and closed his eyes, expecting instant death.

Then he blinked.

Foolish William, he thought.

The knight was a ghost. The ax had, of course, passed harmlessly through him. He opened his eyes, and saw the knight prepare to swing again. This time he was prepared. He jumped backward out of the way. He could feel the cold bite of the ax as it passed inches from his face. It might not cut flesh, but the phantom weapon cleaved the spirit world with a force that penetrated the veil, ever so slightly.

So that was the breeze on my neck—the bastard was trying to cut my head off from behind.

"Only a coward attacks while his enemy's back is turned!" William shouted. The giant only laughed, and gave forth a bellow like the crack of a tree felled by a storm.

Channeling the magic of Albion, William raised his hands. A verdant light crackled around his fingers, and he began to intone a spell in medieval French, a hex on the spirit that could not destroy the ghost, but would cause the lingering soul a great deal of pain.

Before he could cast the spell, the ghost took a step back, as if troubled by this new development. The black knight turned and fled back to the battlefield.

"That's right, run away!" William called after him, surprised and a bit giddy at the fear he'd inspired.

But he faltered a moment later when he realized that the knight had not fled in fear, but in wisdom. The towering man in his black armor, bleached gray now as the morning sun began to rise more fully, ran toward his fellows and shouted for their assistance.

A cadre of black-armored knights turned away from the battle and joined the giant. Together, they marched toward William, Bodicea, and Horatio, brandishing their weapons with a homicidal glee.

"Bloody hell . . ." William whispered, and a ripple of fear went through him. These knights would be harmless to most living beings, but he was a creature of magic. If they focused enough, they could hurt him. And what of Bodicea and Horatio? What might the ghostly knights do to them?

He lifted his hand to begin another spell, but was interrupted by Bodicea's loud, inhuman battle cry. She darted past him, having transformed the spirit-substance of her spear into a sword. She swung the spectral blade above her as she charged. The knights were startled for a moment by the appearance of this screaming, naked madwoman, and Bodicea used that moment of confusion to her advantage. The queen floated and danced among them, hacking them apart.

"For England! For Victoria! For Albion!" Horatio shouted as he joined the fray.

"For Arthur!" he added with a triumphant laugh.

The admiral used his longer, thinner sword to stab through the gaps in his opponents' armor, disabling them quickly. Horatio always surprised William with his skill as a swordsman.

One of the knights roared and charged at William, who completed the spell he'd begun earlier. The greenish light sprang from his fingers like darts and a swarm of them flew at his attacker. They struck the ghost, tearing holes in his phantom armor, in his very spiritual essence, and the knight shouted in pain and fell to the ground, dissipating like mist burned away by the rising sun.

After a few minutes of heavy battle the three of them had decimated their opponents. Bodicea hacked away at one of the knights even as he vanished into nothingness. The cries from the battlefield faded, but there were still a few knights left standing.

Pendragon's knights.

They moved closer so they could watch Bodicea as she whooped and howled over her victories. Now that the last of her foes was vanquished, one of Pendragon's knights stepped forward, removing his blood-spattered helmet. He was a handsome man with long dark hair, piercing blue eyes, and an aquiline nose.

He lowered his head in deference to Bodicea. She nodded in return as she held her sword down at her side.

"I am Sir Yvain," the knight began. "These good knights and I serve Arthur, King of Britain, called the Pendragon, and owe you our thanks for your aid against Mordred's horde."

William cleared his throat. "It was our great pleasure and duty, Sir Yvain. I am William Swift, Protector of Albion. It is my honor to introduce Lord Admiral Horatio Nelson and her majesty, Queen Bodicea of the Iceni."

The knights bowed as one.

"We fight this battle for eternity. For this moment you have given us a reprieve from the tedium of its sameness," Sir Yvain said, as he and the other knights began to fade into the ether. "We thank you for your help, Lord Protector William, Admiral Nelson, your majesty . . ."

"Wait!" William called, before they had completely disappeared. Sir Yvain and the others manifested again, though the sun streamed through them as if they were the merest suggestions of men.

"How may we help you, Lord William?" Sir Yvain said graciously.

"Tell me," William asked, "the witches that haunt this place: what is it exactly they are looking for?"

The dead knight's blue eyes sharpened at the mere mention of the word *witch*. He hung his head.

"They seek to raise the dead, my lord," the knight said softly. He looked up. "To bring back to wretched life the murderer of the Pendragon, the regicide and patricide . . ."

He paused as if his own words pained him.

"You don't mean . . . ?" William whispered.

Sir Yvain nodded.

"Mordred, my lord. Arthur's bastard son. Morgan le Fey always intended her child to be king of Britain, to use him to give the witches reign over us all. Even as he himself died, Arthur slew the boy, forestalling such darkness from befalling the land. We knights, we few, drove the witches from Britain and many thought their line extinguished. But such was not to be. For long centuries the daughters of Morgan le Fey, these witches, have waited for the perfect night to raise Mordred from the dead. Now they have come. Whatever signs and portents they watch, be they in the stars or in the earth, they believe the time is nigh."

Horatio's ghost drifted forward, eyes intense, staring at Yvain. "Then help us, good knight. Aid us in our battle and together we will prevent this terrible resurrection, and destroy the witches."

A murmur ran through the knights. None of them wanted to look at the newcomers. At last Sir Yvain shook his head.

"We cannot, Admiral. To our endless shame, we cannot. There is nothing in life or the afterlife that my men and I would like better than to aid you in your quest, but were we to even attempt it, you would only be placed in greater peril."

William shook his head. "What do you mean? What peril? I don't understand."

The knights began to fade once again, dissipating in the morning light until only Sir Yvain remained.

And then even the last visible trace of that noble ghost vanished.

"There are curses on the living," a disembodied voice said, "and there are curses on the dead. The battle is ended, for now, but you have stopped nothing. Tomorrow, it will begin again."

Then they were gone.

A breeze blew across the field.

William could hear Bodicea and Horatio talking quietly, but the words were lost on him. He could not tear his gaze from the place where the knights had been, this phantom battlefield. Nothing remained to indicate that combat had taken place, yet the fight went on.

Forever.

⟶

TAMARA DID NOT TRUST THE FAIRIES. Even though they had pledged their help to the Protectors of Albion, she still felt certain that they had only their own best interests at heart. She worried that they would not hold up their end of the bargain—not unless their hands were forced.

She tried to focus on the positives of the alliance. In the spirit of their agreement, the Council of Stronghold had appointed a fairy girl called Edrell to assist the Protectors in their research, and to act as liaison between the Swifts and Stronghold. A slight, ethereal thing with sharp, intelligent features, Edrell had proven quite knowledgeable.

For hours she had worked with Tamara and Serena, helping them as they paged through dozens of arcane volumes and magical histories in search of any spell or passage that might provide some edge in combat with the witches, which were notoriously difficult to kill.

Tamara had translocated back to Ludlow House and retrieved every book of arcane lore she thought might contain some reference or spell that could help them. William had asked her to go quietly and be careful not to let Sophia know that she had been there. Tamara inquired about this strange request, but his response had been only a sad, troubled expression, and so she decided to wait until this crisis had been averted to ask him again.

As quietly as possible, she had retrieved those texts. They were piled about her room at the inn and, thus far, had proven useless.

As it spirited her away across the sky, the witch that had abducted her had told her the only reason they had not killed her was
because she was a virgin, that she would be the tenth and that three
more had to be gathered. Tamara had escaped, but the witches had
been quite busy. Six fairies had been abducted, and with the vanishing of Katherine Monroe, a total of five human girls. That made
eleven virgins.

Tamara had no doubt that the witches would find two more by
the appointed time.

It had been quite awkward to explain to William, but the detail of the girls' virginity was too important to be ignored. Serena
had confirmed that Aine was a virgin, and Edrell knew Tamsyn
well enough to make the same assertion of her. The truth was
inescapable. Brother and sister agreed that the virgin girls, both
human and fairy, were being gathered for some sort of ritual sacrifice to be conducted on the night of the solstice.

Their research had turned up nothing that might hint at the
purpose of that ritual. Now Tamara, Edrell, and Serena focused on
attempting to find any information that might help them destroy
the witches.

Some of the books were too heavy for the sprite to lift and Serena had grown snappish and cold. Tamara did not like the way
sprite and fairy glared at each other when they thought she wasn't
looking, but it couldn't be helped. The only way to repair the damage to the relationship between Serena and the fairies of Stronghold was to get the missing fairy girls back, safe and sound, Aine in
particular.

The work here was all that mattered.

They pored over the books until dawn, but with each passing
hour Tamara became more agitated. She did not want to think

about the outcome if they could find nothing that would help them against the witches. The creatures were so powerful that she could conceive of no plan that did not involve terrible casualties on her side.

Her research had not taught her much, however.

The ordinary world had many tales of witchcraft that confused the creatures with more mundane practitioners of sorcery. As a result, there was sparse information about true witches. What bits she found helped her little. True witches were unsociable creatures that did not take kindly to outsiders who invaded their territory, and they sought only to destroy what they did not know or understand. Half-human and half-demon, they combined their innate demonic power with skilled spellcraft.

Most of what she found regarding true witches consisted of the mythology of their creation, and a few tales of their supposed end. It seemed that a group of true witches had attempted to conquer Albion centuries before, and had been stopped only through an alliance of all of the supernatural races in Britannia. One of the tomes Tamara had read referred to this conflict as the Second War of Smythe.

She had never heard of the *first* war of Smythe, nor of Smythe himself, for that matter.

Dawn came and went, the morning was two hours old, and Tamara began to fear for herself and her friends, and even more for the fairy and human girls who had been abducted by the witches. When darkness fell again, the solstice would be only hours away. The girls were doomed if she could not find something.

Frustrated, she closed her book and put her head down on the table. She shut her eyes and felt the morning light beginning to filter through the windows of the room. In the stillness, she heard a soft, unmistakable whistling sound. She lifted her head to see that Serena had fallen asleep inside one of her dresser drawers. The sound was the drone of the sleeping sprite's breathing.

Tamara pulled a chemise from the back of the drawer and covered the little sprite with it to keep her warm.

She took a deep breath and blinked, forcing herself to stay awake. Edrell did not look at all tired. She bent over the thick, leather-bound volume she was presently reading, thoroughly engrossed. She was roughly Tamara's height, and her alabaster skin and golden eyes shone brightly in the morning light. Her long, swanlike neck was craned forward as she studied the pages while she turned them. Her long red hair was tied securely in a knot, to keep it out of her eyes.

As if sensing Tamara's gaze, Edrell looked up and smiled. She had a more amiable demeanor than the other fairies Tamara had met. If she would only be kinder to Serena, Tamara thought, she might even come to like her.

"Anything?" Tamara asked, though she knew the answer.

Edrell shook her head, putting down her book. "Nothing, Protector."

She insisted on calling Tamara "Protector," even though Tamara had specifically asked her not to do so. It was meant as a sign of respect, but somehow it just made her feel old.

Tamara stood and stretched, wincing with pain from the bruises she had sustained in her brief captivity, and still quite drained from the ordeal. She wished she had taken Farris up on his offer to help. She could at least have had him fetching coffee for them as they worked. Instead, he and Richard Kirk were out looking for the master of the hounds. The man and his dogs had gone missing the night before, while out looking for Richard's sister. Richard had insisted on joining the search to help find him.

Tamara thought that the smartest thing to do was to keep Farris by the young man's side. If they stayed together and were careful, she thought they would stand a chance of remaining safe . . . and alive. She just hoped none of the human search party came across the witches. It would surely be the end of any who did.

Though she had not wanted to say so, she imagined that was precisely what had happened to Peter David.

A knock came upon the door, startling her.

Tamara shot a warning glance at Edrell, who nodded in understanding. She then intoned a hasty cloaking spell, and the fairy and the sprite vanished from view, no longer visible to human eyes.

Tamara went to unlock the door and swung it inward. Of all the visitors she might have expected . . . John Haversham would never have even made her list.

She let go of the door and it began to creak slowly forward, until it was about to close in his face. Remembering herself, she caught it again.

"John? Whatever are you doing here?"

Haversham smiled, causing Tamara's heart to skip.

"You don't look happy to see me, Tamara," he said softly, reaching out to move a tendril of loose hair that had fallen across her cheek.

Tamara sucked in her breath. His nearness always seemed to make her a bit woozy. She hoped it didn't show.

"We were—I mean, I was in the middle of doing some research."

John laughed. The sound was rich and mellow, somehow quelling her nervousness a bit.

"May I come in?" he asked, stepping over the threshold as she nodded. He looked around the room, and one eyebrow raised.

"So many books, Tamara," he said as he made his way to the

table. He picked one up, flipping through the pages, then turned, his eyes searching hers. "I've come to help. You don't need to hide anything or . . . *anyone* from me."

"Oh," she said, a bit flustered. "Of course." She lifted the cloaking spell, revealing Edrell and Serena, who was just waking, and cast a wary glance at the new arrival.

Edrell studied John curiously, but there was no hostility in her gaze.

"John, you know Serena, and this is Edrell. The Council of Stronghold has agreed to an alliance so that we can find the missing girls, and stop the—"

"Witches?" he finished for her.

Her mouth fell open in surprise. "How did you know? Every arcane scholar believes them extinct. How could—"

"The Algernon Club has its eyes everywhere. They learned of your predicament and have sent me to offer whatever assistance I can." John executed an elegant bow. "I am at your service, Miss Swift."

Edrell giggled, obviously taken with John's charm. Tamara felt a small stab of jealousy, but quickly pushed it away. She was here to find the missing girls, not to attract John Haversham's attention.

"Wonderful. You can be of great service by burying your nose in these texts," she said as she saddled him with two of the heaviest volumes from the table.

John took them effortlessly, winking at her when their fingers accidentally brushed in the exchange. Tamara felt her face growing hot but fought the blush, trying to hold onto a bit of her composure. What was he up to, she wondered, after the way he had parried all of her romantic interest thus far?

She returned to the table, focusing on the books that lay in front of her. John settled on the edge of her bed, and she tried to blot out the tantalizing images that rushed across her mind.

Stop it, she chided herself. *What are you? Some sort of rutting animal?*

Tamara returned her attention to the last book she had been reading. Just as she had managed to reimmerse herself in the text, she heard John adjust his position on the mattress. Its creak seemed to call to her.

She gritted her teeth.

Before she could berate herself again, she heard a slight stirring in the air around her. There was an almost imperceptible tearing noise, and then William and the ghosts appeared within what was fast becoming a very crowded room.

Her brother began even before the ghosts had completely manifested.

"Tam, you won't believe it, but we've discovered the witches' plan. Do you realize who the ghost knights are? They're the Pendragon's men! We met Sir Yvain's ghost and—"

William stopped dead, and clamped his mouth shut the moment he saw John Haversham sitting on his sister's bed.

"Hello, Willy boy," John said, standing up, a sly grin spreading across his face. "Fancy meeting you here."

～

JOHN HAD TO APOLOGIZE TWICE to get William to open his mouth again. If things hadn't been so tense, and time had been on their side, Tamara would have just left William mute. But things were precarious and they had no time for pettiness.

"It is a ritual, Tamara, just as we suspected," William said.

"A ritual requiring the blood of thirteen virgin girls, some fairy and some human," Edrell interrupted.

"Yes, according to that witch," Tamara agreed, then looked at William, attempting not to blush at the way John Haversham scrutinized her after this revelation. "Though we haven't found anything to tell us how many of each."

William had the gleam of amazement in his eyes. Tamara looked at the ghosts of Bodicea and Horatio, then stared at her brother again.

"Well? What is the ritual for?"

"They intend to use the virgins' blood to resurrect Mordred, the bastard son of Arthur Pendragon. That's why the stories of the witches say they haunt the woods around Slaughterbridge. They were seeking Mordred's grave."

"That's . . . Are you sure?" Tamara asked.

"We have it from the ghosts of Arthur's knights themselves," Bodicea declared.

"Though they won't lend a hand, the lily-livered cowards," Horatio sneered.

"Not cowards," Tamara said. "During our battle at Slaughterbridge, I saw what happened to those homunculi when we destroyed them. There were ghosts of knights trapped within. That's why they fear going near the witches, because their spirits would be captured and used against us."

Edrell stood perfectly still, lithe and ethereal, almost like a ghost herself. "Where does that leave us?" she asked.

"We fights, is where it leaves us!" Serena cried in her tiny, piping voice, wings blurring as she darted around above their heads.

"We must fight, of course," Tamara said, slowly. "But I'm afraid we haven't found a single spell or enchantment or reference to a weapon that would help us kill the witches. Had we another dozen Protectors or equally powerful sorcerers, perhaps . . ."

They all stood together in Tamara's room—fairy, human, ghost, and sprite—and stared at one another in silence.

"If we cannot find anything to aid us against the witches, some advantage, the outlook is very bleak," Edrell said. "I have no doubt, great Protectors, that with your power and the valiant efforts of your ghostly comrades, combined with the might of the warriors of Stronghold, we will be able to kill *some* of the witches. But unless we destroy them all, we shall not prevail. We must have an advantage."

William stroked his chin, glancing at each of the figures in the room in turn. At last he turned his attention on Bodicea.

"You've fought them before, you said. This description of them as half-human and half-demon, is that accurate?"

The ghostly queen nodded gravely. "As far as I know."

Edrell stood not far from William. She fluttered her wings as she spoke and would not meet his gaze.

"Oh, it's true, Protector," the fairy girl said. "All the tales of conflict between witches and fairies speak of them this way."

"True, true it is!" Serena piped up.

"All right," William said with a nod. "Perhaps we ought to consider focusing on one element of their nature. What might we do to the human or the demon part of them, to overcome their witchery?"

Tamara stared at him, nodding. "Yes, of course. Damn me for a fool, how could I not have considered it? But we haven't time, now. The solstice is this evening. If I'd thought of it before, we could have focused our research on—"

"Wait a moment!" William cried, turning from her toward the

ghosts. "Horatio, do you remember coming across that bit on demonic possession in *The Lesser Key of Solomon,* when we were
researching ways to drive Oblis from my father?"

Horatio nodded, his brow furrowed.

"Yes . . ."

Smiling, William began to pace, engaging in his best professo-
rial discourse. "It was useless in driving the demon from Father's
body but it may be precisely what we need."

Tamara saw Edrell and Serena exchange a brief glance, no
doubt thinking that William had lost his grip on sanity.

Horatio had his remaining hand behind his back, as though he
was standing at attention even as he drifted toward William. "My
young friend, I'm afraid you misremember. The spell was useless to
us because it was the reverse of our goal. It provided the magical
process for purging a human soul from the body of a demon."

Tamara let out a little cry, and everyone turned to look at her.

"Oh, William, that's just mad enough to work," Tamara whispered, turning to her brother even as the beginnings of a plan
began to germinate in her mind.

The rest of those gathered in the room still looked mystified.

"You'll pardon us if we're all just a bit further behind in your
deductive process," John Haversham said, looking from William to
Tamara and back. "What are the two of you raving about?"

"You don't see it?" William asked him, and he sounded almost
gleeful. "The witches are half human and half demon. So what
happens if we remove the human element from them, Haversham?
What then?"

Bodicea whooped in triumph.

"Excellent, my friends! Without their human souls, what are
witches, but demon scourge? And we know very well how to deal
with the likes of those!"

"I will translocate to Ludlow House, get Grandfather's copy of *The Lesser Key of Solomon*, and return here as fast as I can," William declared.

"Go on, then, Will," Tamara said. "The rest of us will prepare so that we can begin searching for Mordred's grave immediately upon your return. Most likely the abducted girls will be kept near there. We haven't a moment to lose."

William smiled warmly and took Tamara's hands in his. They had hope now. He stepped back, and began the incantation of the spell of translocation.

"Under the same sky . . ."

He'd barely gotten the words out when the air shimmered around him and he disappeared.

"All right," Tamara said, turning to the others. "William will only be a few minutes. Let's be ready. Edrell, you and Serena must go and inform the Council at Stronghold, and enlist them in the search.

"The rest of us will split up. Horatio, you and William should take the southwest of Slaughterbridge, while John and I will scour the area northwest. With William and myself separated, if either of us finds anything we can cast a spell that will signal our location. If Bodicea discovers the grave she can find us easily enough. And I imagine the fairies will be able to track us in their own forest.

"Bodicea, go to Farris and Richard. They're out in the woods looking for the master of the hounds and the missing girls, along with the rest of the village. Enlist them to your search. Perhaps if you can find the knights they can tell us where Mordred's grave is. Otherwise, search the area to the east of Slaughterbridge."

Tamara took a deep breath before adding her final thought.

"We may have a chance after all, my friends. But we must find the grave and stop the witches before midnight. If we fail, many will die."

~

WILLIAM DID NOT WANT TAMARA to go off into the woods alone with Haversham. He had tried to talk her into taking Bodicea with them, but Tamara pointed out that someone had to find Farris, and brief him on the plan. He had then offered Horatio's services, but she simply shook her head.

"I am not a child, William," she said. "I can take care of myself."

"It isn't that I don't trust you, Tamara. It's that rogue Haversham who gives me pause. You simply don't understand what a threat he is to your virtue."

"Farewell, brother. Godspeed."

William hesitated only a moment, and then, resigned, he called to Horatio and they departed to begin the search for Mordred's grave.

~

LATER IN THE DAY, doubts began to creep into Tamara's thoughts. She would never admit it to William, but she could not dismiss the fear that he might be right.

All through the afternoon, as she and John searched the woods, she felt slightly uncomfortable. It wasn't anything he *did,* exactly; it was the way he was *looking* at her, as though he was . . . well . . . *hungry.*

As night fell, and the shadows in the forest grew deeper, Tamara began to lose hope.

"Do you suppose they've hidden the grave with their witchery?" Tamara asked her companion. "Perhaps that's why we can't find it." She had been thinking this for some time, but hadn't wanted to admit it. If it were so, then it would be nearly impossible to find the place without research they simply didn't have time for.

John shrugged. "I don't know, Tam. Maybe so."

Tamara glanced curiously at him. Had she heard correctly? John had referred to her by her pet name. No one called her Tam, except for William and—once upon a time—her grandfather, Ludlow. She was surprised, but pleasantly so.

They continued on, their search taking them deeper into the woods, where they were surrounded by ancient oaks, sweet chestnuts, and beech trees. The gathering night was cool and dark, the sun quickly becoming a memory, the moon partially obscured by clouds.

Tamara paused. A shudder went through her, and she actually swooned a bit—she had never fully recovered from the encounter with the witches. John reached to prop her up, but she pulled away from him as the moment passed. Now she glanced around, and discovered that she was seeing the forest with different eyes.

"What is it?" John asked, a worried note in his voice.

She nodded, largely to herself. "I remember. Not a lot, but some."

"Anything about the witches? Did they say anything to you?"

As he spoke, he had the oddest smile.

"I don't remember. I can't . . . Wait. Yes. Something about my magic, as Protector, making their ritual more powerful."

John raised an eyebrow. "You mean to say that they're set upon having you?"

Tamara nodded slowly. "I can hear her voice. Viviane, she said her name was. Witch queen. She said they'd have no other, now that they knew I was—"

She stopped herself from saying *a virgin*. Surely, John knew as much.

"That means they're expecting you to come," he said.

"Perhaps," Tamara replied, glancing around, trying to get her bearings. "So let's not disappoint them. I don't remember much more. There was a clearing, atop a hill. When I escaped I translocated, but only made it as far as the bottom of the hill, then just staggered from there, finding my way. When at last I couldn't stand any longer, I called for the ghosts, and they found me."

"And this hill?"

Tamara nodded. "It's somewhere nearby. I recognize this path." She pointed to the old, nearly invisible trail that led through the trees, and raised her hand, tracing the night sky.

In the darkness ahead, outlined by the murky dusk, they could see a hill rising up from the forest, hidden in the trees.

"It's here. Very close," Tamara said.

A curious look swam in his eyes as he regarded her. It seemed almost like regret.

"What is it?" she asked.

John shook his head with a forced smile. "Nothing. It's nothing."

Now was not the time to press the issue, but she was troubled. She would remember this, and ask him about it later.

Tamara raised a hand and whispered a spell. A line of golden light shot into the sky, floating and burning there as a beacon to her brother. They had chosen the spell because it could be tailored so that only those who were named in the incantation could see the beacon. Only the Protectors and their allies. The witches still would not know they were coming.

John moved quickly then, hopping over exposed roots and sidestepping hanging branches. His agility was remarkable, making it seem as if he were following some unseen map. Tamara tried to keep up, but found her skirts unsuitable to the task. Had they not been so rushed earlier, she would have put on her brother's boots and trousers again, much more suitable garb.

"John, please, wait," she said, out of breath. She kept her breath as low as she could, to avoid warning their enemies. "We must wait for William and Horatio, and gather the others. We can't simply gallop into the midst of battle with the witches. They'll destroy us."

Her hair was disheveled, her face covered in dirt and sweat. She stopped near a fallen, weathered tree and sat down. She needed to rest, even if he didn't.

John returned to where she was sitting. He watched as she lifted her skirt only the tiniest bit, enough to unlace her shoe, then remove it. She turned the boot, causing a few pebbles to fall out on to the ground.

"We must wait," she insisted. "Keep watch, of course, but we must be cautious."

John nodded absently, but his gaze was riveted to her foot and ankle, bare but for her stockings. She almost lowered her skirt, but hesitated as he moved toward her, gracefully lowering himself onto one knee. He took her foot in his strong hands and brought her slender leg up, to touch the soft, pale flesh of her ankle with his lips.

Tamara sucked in her breath, unable to speak. Her heart thundered almost painfully in her chest, constricting her ability to breathe—even think. It was similar to what she felt when Martha laced her corset too tight. Black spots floated in front of her eyes, so she closed them, losing herself in the sensation of John's lips on her ankle.

Her disorientation grew, and she felt as though she was falling under a spell.

And wasn't she? *The spell of John Haversham,* she mused absently. Yet if there was enchantment here, if he influenced her in some way to feel the rush of passion and hunger that filled her, Tamara embraced it.

How long she had wanted him.

She felt a melting sensation in her stomach and a tightening in her cunt. She waited, wondering if this was as far as it would go, or if John planned to thrill her body more.

What are you doing? This isn't the time or the place for such things.

Tamara wanted to listen to the voice in her head. She knew that it spoke the truth. Lives hung in the balance.

Yet even as her conscience cried out for her to push him away, John moved his kisses farther up her leg until he was at her knee. She opened her eyes to find him staring at her, his gaze dark with desire.

Her every sensation seemed exaggerated. The world spun. The trees rustled with whispers of love and of passion, and she burned for him. Tamara felt her body swaying weakly, surrendering to him completely. Wet heat emanated from the core of her. It was magic of one kind or another, and she didn't care.

Didn't care at all.

He reached for her, grunting as he pulled her to him, then gently laid her on the ground beside the fallen tree. John ran his hand up the inside of her thigh, his long graceful fingers burning her wherever they touched. She moaned, and it was a low guttural sound that started somewhere in her belly, then traveled up and up until it broke, unfettered, from her twitching lips.

I can't. Not now, she thought.

Not now . . .

But there was nothing she could do. It was as though she was trapped inside the shell of her own body, unable to react save to accept the pleasure John offered her. She bit her lip as his fingers slipped through the slit in her drawers, his fingers finding her body wet and ready for him. Tamara moaned as he slowly slipped two fingers inside of her. She cried out, and he plunged his fingers deeper. It hurt, yet it felt so wonderfully *delicious* at the same time.

John pulled his hand away, leaving her cold and empty. She opened her eyes and saw him undoing the front of his pants. Part of her was terrified at the thought that at long last she was about to surrender her maidenhead to John Haversham, but despite her fear, her yearning would not be denied.

He knelt beside her and brushed her lips with his own, then kissed her deeply. When he drew back she saw that his cock was exposed to the cool air. Tamara gasped. She had never seen a grown man thus unclothed, and in all her fevered imaginings she had not pictured it quite so large. John kissed her neck, working his way up her throat until he found her mouth again. He caught her lips with his, slipping his tongue into her mouth. Hungrily, she devoured him in return.

He pushed her legs apart, ripping at her drawers until they were sliding off her, and then she was naked from the waist down. Her cunt ached. She wanted him so badly it was like a bruise throbbing uncontrollably inside of her.

"Is this your desire?" he asked, his voice a growl in her ear.

She found herself nodding, almost against her will.

"Then say it, Tam. Say you want me inside of you."

She whimpered as he slipped his fingers in her again, and she was even wetter than before. He pushed farther in, rubbing at the nub of her clitoris with his thumb as he moved his fingers in and out of her.

Tamara moaned with every thrust, all rational thought departing, taken over by primal urgency. She could not breathe, could not think. Nothing she had experienced in her life had prepared her for this.

"Say you want me, Tamara."

She groaned as he increased the speed, thrusting his fingers deeper and deeper inside her.

"I want you . . . I want you inside of me," she moaned. "Please, please . . . make love to me."

He crawled on top of her, his cock pressing against her leg, and then he found her, and groaned. She felt the smoothness of him brush against her wetness.

"Please, John, please . . ." She nearly screamed with her urgency. *NO!*

Something inside of her cracked. Confusion swirled in her mind.

Scrambling, she twisted herself out from beneath his body, pushing him off her. She propped herself up, and crawled as far away from him as she could, naked and vulnerable in the shade of the old trees. Leaves, sticks, and dirt attached themselves to her knees. She grabbed for her drawers, which lay sadly in the dirt, and clumsily slipped them back on.

"I can't," she said. "Perhaps I want to, but I *can't*. Not here. Not now. I'm sorry, John."

He nodded, but remained strangely silent. He stared at her oddly, a mix of confusion and consternation in his expression.

"You have to believe me. Under different circumstances, but not now. Not while we're needed. I could never forgive myself if my own selfish needs caused those girls to die."

John nodded again, and his breathing was beginning to return to normal.

"I understand," he said, his eyes devouring her with a feline hunger that almost made Tamara reconsider. "But know that we will do this again."

He stood, offering her his hand.

"That is a promise," he added.

Tamara tried to stand, but then waved him away, too disoriented to rise. She blinked, feeling as though she had drunk too much brandy.

"What—" she began.

What have you done to me? she would have asked.

But in that moment she heard a familiar musical tinkling, and looked up to see Serena darting through the trees toward them. Her wings were a colorful blur, gossamer where she passed through shafts of moonlight.

The heat lingered within Tamara but now, even in her strangely muddled state, it was crowded out by embarrassment.

Sixteen

In the dark of the woods at the base of the hill, the night breeze caressed Tamara and she trembled. Her heart raced and she took long, shuddery breaths, trying to hide the lust that still clutched at her.

Serena flitted around above her, a trail of sparkling purple drifting in her wake. Tamara blinked and stared at her, for a moment tempted to reach out and touch the magical dust that eddied in the breeze.

"We wonders, milady, we wonders," the sprite said in that high voice. "Ye've been drinking, have ye?"

Tamara shot Serena a stern look. "Certainly not!"

But her disapproving expression only mirrored the little sprite's own.

Serena had arrived accompanied by delicate Edrell with her silken gown and ethereal presence, and now from the trees all around came other fairies. Tamara recognized Rhosynn, whose sister was among the missing, as well as her friends Fyg and Ghillie, whom she had met at the last convocation. There were others. Many others. Some of them drifted down from the trees in a gentle sway, like feathers floating to the ground.

All of them watched her curiously.

Tamara could not stand their scrutiny. Her face flushed with heat and she glanced over at John. His eyes glittered with what appeared to be genuine regret, and perhaps even fear for her. He stared longingly, and her legs felt weak again.

She shook her head, denying the yearning. This was wrong, and not only in a moral sense. Serena's question had offended her, and yet she *did* feel drunk. A fog of disorientation surrounded her, and Tamara took a step toward John. She shivered and her skin prickled with gooseflesh, and for a moment she swayed on her feet.

"Tam, are you all right?" John asked.

In her high-pitched voice, Serena muttered something that was accompanied by a derisive snort, but Tamara could not hear the words.

"Fine," she said. Mustering her strength, she stood straighter and shook herself, clearing her mind.

"I'll be fine. Just a bit out of sorts. Perhaps my encounter with the witches earlier has befuddled me more than I realized. Their enchantments are powerful."

That's it, she thought. *Surely, it must be. Otherwise I never would have allowed passion to interfere with our purpose.*

"Oh, yes," Serena piped up. "The witches."

Edrell of Stronghold moved through the air as though dancing upon it. She gestured with one hand toward the sprite. "That will do, little one."

But Serena only crossed her arms and hovered in the air, wings fluttering at her back.

Tamara glanced away, then turned to John again. She still felt more than a bit dizzy, and wanted nothing more than to fall into his arms and let him catch her, let him wrap himself around her again.

A terrible certainty came to her. *Enchanted. It's no joke, girl. Perhaps you really* have *been enchanted.*

Anger blossomed in her heart. She was in love with John, but the idea that he might have magically influenced her was more than she could bear. Yet her suspicion was blunted—perhaps by that very magic. She became even more certain that she had been ensorcelled.

Her emotions were not her own.

"John, there are some things that must be said," she began.

But the fairies had continued to arrive. Dozens of them now filled the woods around Tamara and John, archers and warriors and ordinary court fairies alike. All had come to fight the witches, to stop the solstice ritual before their sisters could be sacrificed. With Serena and the fairies now so close at hand, Tamara hesitated.

"The moment our task is complete," she added.

"Of course," John replied, and he looked both troubled and entirely innocent.

Yet Tamara knew she could not trust his voice or his face. She wished that she could, but William's suspicions had niggled at her brain so long, and John's own behavior had done little to erase them.

Shaking off the passion that confused her, Tamara fixed her entire concentration upon their task. Taking deep breaths, she steadied herself and peered through the trees that grew on the hill.

Somewhere up there, the abducted girls and fairies were imprisoned, and waited in terror for the ritual to commence.

Tamara knelt and thrust her fingers into the loose soil where she and John had been rutting like animals, only moments before. A wave of revulsion rolled through her, and she felt violated and unclean.

Focus, she told herself.

Breathing evenly, she allowed herself to feel the magic of Albion in the soil. The Protector was always connected to the soul of Albion, able to channel that power whenever necessary. Now, though, by concentrating on her rapport with the mystical spirit of England, she could feel the way that the dark sorcery of the witches pushed natural magic away. The hill ahead had been entirely tainted by witchcraft. It pulsed with the dark power of the witches.

The purity of that contact with Albion's soul helped to clear Tamara's head. She stood and glared at John for a moment. His face twisted into a cheerless grimace and he shrugged, as if trying to communicate that he did not know what had upset her so. Tamara could not allow herself to believe him.

She looked up through the branches, and beyond them to the stars.

"Time is wasting. If they don't arrive soon—"

"No need for such drastic pronouncements, sister. We *have* arrived," William said as he emerged from the woods, moving up to stand beside Edrell.

The fairy girl smiled shyly at him, and he stood a bit taller. William seemed to fairly crackle with magic in anticipation of the fight. Blue light—pure magical force—danced around his fingertips. For the first time in her life, Tamara looked at her brother and thought him heroic.

She moved over and embraced him. William stiffened, startled by this show of affection, but then he patted her back as he'd done when she was very small. Tamara laid her cheek against his chest for a moment, and then pulled away from the embrace.

"You've memorized the spell?"

"Of course," he replied.

Tamara had studied it with him before they embarked upon the search, but now it was muddled in her mind.

"Refresh my memory, please," she said.

"Are you all right?" William asked with a frown. "Normally I'm the one whose memory—"

"I'm fine," Tamara snapped, a bit too harshly. "Just exhausted. Now, please, William."

He nodded, but studied her with worry in his eyes. Quietly, he spoke the words to her. They repeated them together several times until Tamara was sure she would remember.

It was simple, really. An invocation, and repetition. If they could capture the nuance of the invoking, they would gain an advantage against the witches. If not, they would die.

Simple.

William glanced back into the darkness of the woods, beyond the fairies. Several figures moved among the warriors of Stronghold. Tamara saw Bodicea and Horatio first because they glimmered with that silver, spectral light peculiar to ghosts. Then the other two were near enough that she could see their faces.

Farris wore a belt into which he'd thrust his pepperbox revolvers, and he carried his father's sword. Richard Kirk had come to fight for his sister's life with a hunting rifle in one hand and a thin sword in a long scabbard strapped across his back.

Tamara closed her eyes, lips moving as she repeated the words of the spell from *The Lesser Key of Solomon* again and again. Even as she did, a smile played at the edges of her lips and a spark of excitement ignited within her. She spun toward her brother.

"Will, this spell . . ."

"Yes, I think it will work, don't you?"

"I do. But if we survive this night, it may help us in other ways as well," Tamara said. "When you first told me about the spell, I was too horrified at the prospect of Father's soul being driven from his body, giving the demon dominion. But now . . . Oblis has such a powerful grip upon Father's flesh and soul that there were spells we did not dare try for fear we could kill Father in the process. But if we can use this invocation to draw the humanity out, to exorcise the human soul—"

William gaped at her. "We could remove Father's spirit, *temporarily*—"

Tamara smiled. "And send Oblis back to Hell."

"Do you really think it would work?"

"We'll look more closely at it when all this is over, but I think it could, Will. I really do."

Serena flew down toward them and hovered between their heads, wings beating like a hummingbird's. She crossed her arms again and glared at them expectantly.

Rhosynn of Stronghold bowed her head courteously.

"Protectors, with all due respect, each moment brings our sisters nearer to death. Edrell claims you have a plan. We would know it, now, if you please."

"Of course," Tamara said. She glanced once at John, who stood now on the outskirts of their gathering, as though uncomfortable being any nearer to her. "Straight to it, then. For the ritual to work, the witches need one last human virgin as sacrifice. Thus far they have taken only five girls from the area. I believe they await me, that they fully expect me to come to them in an effort to thwart their plan. My memory of my brief captivity with them is blurred, but I recall the witch queen's voice. She told me that my magic would make their ritual far more powerful, would ensure their success. Of course they could perform the ritual without me, but they haven't taken a sixth human girl because they have already chosen me. So I will go to them."

"Now, wait a moment!" Haversham protested from the shadows. "It's foolish to simply give yourself over to them. Why, we ought to take the hill this very moment, all of us together, and bring the attack to them."

Tamara arched an eyebrow. "And what of the girls, John? As far as we know, the witches are not aware of William's arrival, or of your own. They don't know that the fairies of Stronghold have put aside their differences with me.

"If we simply march into their midst, we lose what little surprise we have. No, my mind is made up. I'll go ahead. The rest of you move with stealth and surround the hilltop clearing. My arrival will doubtless distract them for a few moments."

"But—" John began again.

She quieted him with a dark look. "We require every advantage."

He stared back. As abruptly as if she stood on a sailing ship caught by a wave, Tamara listed to one side, unsteady upon her feet. All of her earlier disorientation came rushing back. Her legs went weak and her vision blurred.

"Milady!" Serena squeaked, flying toward her. "Are you attacked?"

Thinking her ensorcelled and the battle about to begin, the fairies all brought their weapons to bear, some drawing bowstrings, others raising swords, and the most powerful among them only sketching in the darkness with long, slender fingers alight with sparkling magic.

"No, no," Tamara said quietly. "It's not the witches."

She turned upon John with a withering glare. "Whatever it is that you are doing, stop it. *Now.*" Her voice was low and menacing.

The disorientation passed.

Haversham lowered his gaze, regret writ upon him. Tamara shook her head in frustration. She was grateful for his concern, but disdainful of his methods.

"Enough. Time runs out," Tamara said, glancing around. "We go."

William came to stand beside her, laying a hand upon her shoulder for a moment. A silent communication passed between them, bearing all of the love and regret and cherished memories that brother and sister shared. Tamara smiled thinly, and then turned from her gathered allies, facing the hill once again.

With silent trepidation, and the weight of the unknown upon her heart, she started up through the trees toward the clearing at the top.

~

WILLIAM WATCHED HIS SISTER until she had disappeared into the forest and the night. He took a deep breath to steady himself. Much as he knew Tamara's logic was sound, it was all he could do to let her go up there on her own. He had yet to encounter these monstrous witches himself, but from the way Farris had described them, the daughters of Morgan le Fey were terrible creatures indeed.

The ghosts of Bodicea and Horatio shimmered in the dark, appearing nearly solid. If not for the moonlight passing through their spectral forms and the way he could see the trees right through them, they might have seemed alive.

Bodicea strode nearer, the illusion of walking complete, save that her feet did not touch the ground. The phantom queen clutched her spear in one hand and regarded him closely.

"William?"

"Her strategy is perhaps our only hope," Horatio said. The ghost of Admiral Nelson abandoned all pretense of flesh, and floated after Bodicea, the two of them watching William carefully. "But we ought not allow her to get too far ahead. The witches will move swiftly toward completing their plans, once they have her."

William took one last look up the hill, but had no hope of seeing Tamara in the night-dark wood.

"Right, let's move quickly now," he whispered, turning to the others who had gathered around him. "We must work together, fairy, ghost, and human alike."

Farris and Richard Kirk stood close by, grim purpose etched upon their features. Serena flitted through the air above Farris's head and then settled upon his shoulder. Her tiny wings fluttered so quickly that he imagined her as a brutal wasp, ready to attack. The savage expression on her face did nothing to dispel the impression.

Rhosynn, Fyg, and Ghillie stood nearby, so close to one another that they appeared to grow from the same root. The fairies watched William for a moment, then turned and gestured to the others in the woods. As one, the sisters of Stronghold began to move into the trees, spreading out across the hill without so much as the snap of a twig or the rustle of branches. The only sound was the whisper of the wind through the leaves.

"Bodicea. Horatio. Quickly now, the other side of the hill. Watch for me to move, and then attack. For the lives of these unfortunate girls. And for Albion. Should Mordred live again, none of us shall be safe. The kingdom itself will be in peril."

"For Albion," Horatio said, chin raised. He dared not raise his voice, and so it was not a proper battle cry, but the dignity engraved upon his spectral features communicated the gravity of his intent.

The ghosts departed, splitting up, with Bodicea taking the westward route around the base of the hill and Horatio the east.

William nodded in approval and gestured for Farris and Richard to spread out as well, to either side. The sprite took flight, but kept close to the man who had become far more than a butler to the Swifts.

In the center, William started up the hill. He narrowed his eyes and peered into the darkness, wary of witches or the strange homunculi they had created from the earth, using the trapped ghosts of Pendragon's knights. He passed beneath branches that creaked in the wind, and he flinched, staring upward, expecting dark figures to leap down upon him from the trees.

But there was nothing. Only darkness and the wind.

Whatever evil unfolded here tonight, it centered upon the clearing at the top of the hill. Tamara had surmised that the ritual would require the witches' entire focus, and it appeared that she was correct.

Then something shifted in the trees behind him. William turned, tensed to defend himself, but again saw nothing. He paused there on the hill, heart pounding and throat dry with fright, and then he saw that his allies had all spread out to circle the cliff and advance to its top.

And in the darkness, back the way he had come, several new figures now appeared. At first he felt a wave of fear, that these were enemies. Then he recognized the wavering specters of men in armor, grim knights whose immortal souls could not rest until they were certain that Mordred could not rise again.

William wished for their aid, but he could not compel them. And he understood that it wasn't cowardice which held them back. If the witches were to gain control of them, pervert them into homunculi and enslave them, the knights would become a danger to the Protectors and their allies, rather than a help.

For a moment he gazed at them, though. A grizzled, bearded knight held his helmet beneath his arm. He was but a trace upon the darkness, an outline in the air, yet he offered a small bow.

William returned the gesture, then turned to continue up the hill.

Only then, alone in the darkness, maneuvering through the trees with what stealth he could manage, did he realize that there was one among his allies who was unaccounted for.

John Haversham had disappeared.

A shiver went through William. He knew he ought to be able to trust the man by now, but he simply could not.

THE WIND DIED as Tamara stepped out of the trees and into the clearing at the top of the hill. The music of grief surrounded her, the high, mournful moaning of the six abducted fairies and the desperate, fearful, whispered prayers of the human girls who'd been snatched from Camelford.

Their captivity was grotesque. The sacrifices were bound to the rowan trees that surrounded the clearing, not by rope or chain, but by magic. Their flesh had been subsumed by the wood and bark of the trees themselves; hands and faces and in some cases pale legs thrust from the wood, but their bodies were trapped within the very trunks of the trees.

It was obscene. Unnatural.

The clearing was alive with shifting shadows. The moon burned brightly above, yet dark shapes drifted across the sky, eclipsing it moment after moment. One by one the witches descended, alighting upon the ground around her.

Tamara tried to focus on the nearest rowan tree and the familiar face there, the pale, freckled features of Christine Lindsay, cheeks streaked with tears and eyes wide with numb terror.

"Protector," whispered an insidious voice that crept beneath her skin. "We are honored."

One of the witches stepped nearer. Her hood obscured her face but what little of that long, twisted face Tamara could see was terrible enough. The wraithlike creature stalked toward her, impossibly thin beneath her robe, as though she was only skeleton and cloth.

"You knew I would come," Tamara said firmly.

The witch bowed her head in acknowledgment. The others began to shift in a macabre dance around her, drifting toward one another, the cloth of their robes creating a horrid *shush*ing, a rasp in the darkness. Their voices were the night itself, muttering and moaning, the wind in the eaves of a decrepit house.

"It is your duty to come," said the witch before her. "We had only to wait. The Protector could not turn away."

The demon-woman raised her head and now Tamara saw the eyes in that long, distended visage, each with a corona of gleaming yellow encircling a blackness darker than the devil's heart.

For a moment Tamara felt very small, like a little girl again, and she wished for nothing more than to be able to go back to the bedroom of her childhood and curl up beneath the lovely, thick blankets to watch the sun rise on the gardens of Ludlow House. She would always be that little girl. She had no business being here, throwing herself upon the mercy of these things, defying the powers of the darkness. It would swallow her, just as she had feared in those childhood days when shadowed dreams had woken her at night.

Witches, she thought. *Oh, what have I done?*

"Will you fight us now, Tamara?" whispered the witch.

The others continued their dance and the susurrus of their voices began to drown out the cries and moans of their captives. Soft, cruel laughter came from everywhere and nowhere.

"You cannot defeat us," the monster said. "You must know that."

Tamara nodded. "I know." She stared into those bottomless black eyes and held the witch's gaze, becoming resigned. Then she stepped to one side and went around the witch, walking slowly. The whispering shadows of the daughters of Morgan le Fey parted to let her by. A sea of darkness, they shifted with her as she walked.

"The grave is here, then? In this clearing? Mordred's grave?"

The witches began to laugh again, but there came no answer.

They swept across the clearing and Tamara steeled herself, tried to clear her mind. She glanced around at the rowan trees. Some of the captive girls, fairy and human alike, stared at her from out of the wood with only vacant madness in their eyes. Tamara shivered and would not look at them.

"The solstice approaches," whispered the darkness. "Midnight is almost here."

The wraiths flowed to the center of the clearing and she understood then that they had never touched the ground. They were in flight, always, moving just above the earth like ghosts. The witches raised their hands in unison, extending long, gnarled talons. For the first time she could get a sense of how many there were, and thought perhaps thirty or forty at least.

Thirty-nine would be three times thirteen, and that seemed right. Magical covens were purported to consist of thirteen.

Could she and William destroy thirty-nine? Tamara bit her lower lip, and a terrible sadness washed over her, for she thought not.

At the center of the clearing, the spot around which the witches gathered was slightly raised. The grave of Mordred. Tamara held her breath and stared at it, for until this moment she had been unsure that it was real. Even with the spectral knights they had encountered, this bern, beneath which lay ancient bones, was the first solid proof she had seen. All of the stories, all of the legends, were real.

The blood of myth had soaked into the soil of Cornwall centuries ago. A dream had come to life, and the soul of Albion had gleamed brightly before the darkness had snuffed out its light.

The darkness was called Mordred, and this night, the breeze came alive again, and it whispered his name.

The witches opened their mouths grotesquely wide and then began to wail. Hands held high, they summoned ancient magic and the ground in which Mordred had been buried burst into flame. Fire erupted there, flames licking the sky. The blaze raged at the center of the clearing, casting a sickly orange light upon the black folds of the witches' robes and reaching into the darkness of the forest around them.

The faces of the captive girls, human and fairy, stretched into masks of terror, creating a horrible tableau.

Witches surrounded Tamara. She saw the half-melted face of Morveren, the witch that had guarded her the first time she had been brought here. Then two others grasped her arms. On instinct Tamara reached down into herself, then farther down into the soul of the land, and summoned the magical power that was hers to command. Her muscles tensed, her hands clenched into fists, and the magic began to spill out.

"Too late for that," one of the wraiths whispered into her ear, her breath cold on her skin, and stinking of rot.

A terrible lethargy swept over her then. All of the strength left her, and the cold of the thing's breath penetrated her flesh, straight to the bone. It moved through her like poison. Dread filled her, and sorrow, as the touch of the witches drew up from within her every moment of grief and doubt and anguish she had ever experienced or imagined.

Darkness.

Mordred, the shadows said in her mind.

Brother.

The witches considered themselves daughters of Morgan le Fey, and Mordred was her son. Their brother. A part-man with the blood of Albion on his hands.

And Tamara's death would help to restore him to life.

The witches darted across the clearing, hurrying now. The fire blazed higher, roaring with infernal power. The wraiths went to each of the rowan trees and thrust their hideous fingers into the wood as though it were water, drawing out the girls, one by one. Six fairies. Five human girls.

Tamara made six.

"That's twelve," she said. "Not thirteen?"

The witches drew them all toward the fire. They dragged Tamara now, since her legs were too weak to hold her, and her feet dug furrows in the ground. Her vision blurred, leaving nothing but flame and faces, the girls, the fairies, the witches' endless black eyes.

"You are a clever girl, Tamara," said a voice, sweet and familiar.

She blinked and raised her head, then managed to stand. The

heat from the fire seared her cheeks and dried her eyes. The stink of sulphur filled her nostrils and she breathed through her mouth.

At the edge of the blaze stood a single witch, a figure with a strangely regal bearing. The others kept back ten feet or more from the fire, but this creature came close and faced Tamara. The witch laughed softly, an odd melancholy in the sound, and drew back her hood.

A shushing went through the others and they shuddered. Tamara wondered if it was the beauty of this bright-eyed, blond-haired figure that troubled them, and she knew it must be a glamour.

"We have met before, Protector of Albion. I am Viviane, witch queen."

Viviane, Tamara thought. *But before, she was hideous. What—*

"You are wise not to fight, girl. You may touch the soul of Albion, but we are the black poison in its heart. We have slain Protectors in the past. You could not hope to stand against us."

Viviane smiled, the firelight raging behind her, casting her in shadow and silhouette. She moved ever closer. The other witches began to chant softly so that the sound crept across Tamara's skin.

The fire leaped and crackled in rhythm with their voices. The wraiths gripped the fairies and the village girls tightly, but they all seemed as disoriented as Tamara herself, so that they were just hanging in the grasp of their captors.

"You are clever, though," the witch queen said. "And correct. The ritual requires six human girls, six fairy girls, and a thirteenth. A virgin *witch.*"

Tamara blinked, mustering what lucidity she could. "You? You're going to just . . . give yourself . . . to burn?"

Seventeen

The chanting grew louder. The hellish blaze roared; the entire clearing became a scene from the inferno.

The witches began to drag the innocents toward the flames.

Viviane stepped in close to Tamara. The witches gripping her arms tensed at the sudden nearness of their queen, but Viviane's wide blue eyes were locked upon Tamara's.

Tamara breathed in and inhaled the sickly sweet breath of the witch queen, and she shivered with the intimacy of it.

"Tamara," Viviane whispered, her voice somehow very close, so soft despite the chanting and the crackling blaze.

"Tam."

Blinking, Tamara tried to focus on the beautiful monster in front of her. As she did, Viviane's face *changed*. For just a glimmer of a moment, Tamara was looking at John Haversham.

She gasped.

John gazed at her with sad eyes.

"You ought not to have fought the enchantment I put on you, girl. So beautiful and clever and brave. I wanted to touch and taste you, to feel the softness of your skin."

Flesh and bone shifted, the glamour wavered, and again she was Viviane, the witch queen. Her smile had become a snarl.

"But most of all, I wanted to live.

"I told my sisters that I would bring you to them, that in the guise of your heart's desire I would lead you here. I insisted that we have you, and only you. Foolish girl, if you had only let me take your maidenhood, then neither of us would have to die tonight, don't you see? I don't want to burn."

Masked in her glamour of beauty, Viviane slid her fingers behind Tamara's head and bent to her. The witch queen brushed her lips against Tamara's, and the kiss was electric. Tamara gasped, and an erotic wave swept over her.

A cry of protest rose up in her mind, but she could not escape the truth. She had been enchanted into seduction before, but not by John Haversham. John had never come to Cornwall. It had been Viviane all along, who had inflamed her, entranced her.

Touched her. The idea repulsed her, but the thrill of that kiss upon her lips was undeniable.

"It was so perfect," Viviane whispered. "Wait until the very last moment and then seduce you. The enchantment released you from your inhibitions, or it should have, but even under my spell you fought against your passion. I nearly tried to force you, but then the damned fairies arrived, and the moment had passed."

Once more, softly, Viviane kissed her. Tamara did not try to turn away.

"And now we die," the witch queen said.

The witches holding Tamara hissed and began to drag her back, away from the fire, away from Viviane. The witch queen smiled at Tamara, and then her face changed again, the glamour gone, her flesh now gray and twisted, face long and cruel.

She turned away, gesturing to her sisters to begin bringing the girls toward the flames.

Tamara gritted her teeth. Viviane had ensorcelled her before, and now once again the witches had disoriented her with a beguiling spell. But they had underestimated her. These girls were about to burn. She herself would die. Viviane might be willing to sacrifice herself rather than admit to her sisters that she did not want to die, but the fairies and human girls did not have a choice.

Viviane had attempted to use her, and her cheeks burned with the blush of embarrassment. But that was nothing next to the fear and fury in her at the thought of the people the witches had already murdered, and these other girls about to die. And what of Albion? What would happen to the soul of England if they succeeded, and Mordred rose again?

"No," she whispered, under her breath.

The witches holding her stiffened and turned to study her closely. Their arrogance would be their undoing. Once before she had shattered the control of Viviane's witchery.

She was the Protector of Albion.

Tamara bared her teeth in fury. The ground here was steeped in the black magic of witchcraft, but the land was still Albion. Closing her eyes, Tamara reached down into the earth with her very soul and a peaceful calm filled her, along with magic that raced through her veins and made her feel as though her entire body glowed with power.

Her eyes snapped open. She turned to look at the witch on her right, twisted her wrist in the creature's grip, and opened her hand.

A spear of brilliant golden light erupted from her palm and impaled the witch. The creature howled as she was thrown back to the ground.

Tamara glanced at the other, uttered a spell, and branches burst from the ground and punched upward through the witch's flesh, pushing out from her throat and eyes, from her belly and legs, tearing her flesh and wrapping around her, huge, razor thorns glistening with black blood.

Yet still she was not dead. She screamed and writhed. The one Tamara had first attacked was climbing to her knees.

The chanting stopped. The virgin captives collapsed to the ground as the wraithlike witches abandoned them. Screaming in fury, they rushed toward her.

Viviane spun and glared at her, but then a look of madness spread across her face and she grinned.

The witch queen bent and grabbed one of the human girls by a fistful of her hair, then turned and hurled her into the fire. Shrieking in agony, the girl tried to pull herself from the flames, blackening, skin splitting, burning too quickly in the heat of that arcane blaze.

"No!" Tamara screamed in anguish.

Viviane glanced at her, a sad sort of merriment in her eyes. Then her expression flickered and Tamara thought she saw surrender there. Not to her, but to fate.

"The time has come!" Viviane cried. "There is no turning back!"

"William, on your life, come to me now, or all is lost!" Tamara screamed.

The witches circled around her and she clapped her hands to her ears to keep them from bursting, so horrible was their screeching. Several of the black wraiths flowed across the clearing and surrounded Viviane, their queen. At her command, they began to lift the bewitched girls from the ground and turn toward the flames.

Staring in horror, Tamara could barely draw a breath as she raised her hands, chanting a spell. Serpents of silver light darted across the night and coiled around one of the witches. A blond girl fell from her arms, near the fire, and began to crawl weakly away. From the cast of her features, Tamara knew it must be Sally Kirk, Richard's sister.

One of the fairy girls was next into the fire. Even as the witch hurled her onto the conflagration, she tried to break the bewitchment upon her. Beautiful, gossamer wings appeared on her back, but their purple hue burned black in an instant and they crinkled to ash.

Tamara wept, even as the witches surrounding her moved in closer, blocking her view of the fire. She turned, furious, and lashed out with another spell, an arrow of golden light spearing the nearest of those wraithlike creatures.

The spell. She could not kill them without that spell from *The Lesser Key of Solomon*. In the madness and horror of the moment, she struggled to find the words.

Then William cried her name and she turned to see her brother rushing into the clearing, with the fairies at his side. In their shimmering gowns and with translucent wings painting the darkness in soft colors, they ought to have been beautiful and elegant, but there was something in their aspect that was just as terrible as the witches.

A man shouted and raced in from her left, and she saw that it was Farris, with Serena flitting about his head and Rhosynn and a cadre of other fairies flying just above the ground, rushing at the witches. From her right she saw Richard Kirk enter the clearing with still more of Stronghold's daughters.

"Sally!" Richard called, his voice desperate as he rushed toward the nearest of the fallen girls, searching for his sister. "Sally!"

The sound of his voice cut through the shrieks of the witches and first one, then another and another of them turned away from Tamara.

One of the wraiths separated from the others, and in the firelight Tamara had a glimpse of the half-melted face of Morveren.

The witch started toward her. "Still pure, you are," she said. "Midnight hasn't come yet, and we've already performed the first sacrifice. It's not too late."

Tamara shook with rage and revulsion. Past Morveren, she saw William running toward her. No, not toward her, but toward Viviane and the other witches who even now were carrying fairies and human girls to the fire.

The fairies rushed to aid their kin.

When Viviane saw the attacking force, she turned and gestured for the witches to put the girls down. For the moment, the ritual was interrupted. The witch queen glanced across the clearing at her, and Tamara was sure it was a knowing grin upon Viviane's features.

She had been well aware of the forces massing against her and her sisters, and yet she had not warned the other witches. Girls were burning, fairies screaming, witches were wounded, ruined, and Viviane had not bothered to try to stop it.

Tamara flinched with understanding. Viviane had not been willing to openly defy her sisters, the daughters of Morgan le Fey, but they had consigned her to death by fire, chosen her for their sacrifice. She would not stand against them, but she was not going to help them end her life, either.

Betrayal. Vengeance.

Witchery.

Farris stalked toward the witches around Tamara, both pepper-box revolvers drawn.

"Get them out of here!" Tamara shouted. "Take the girls to safety!"

Fingers contorted, twisted like the talons of a witch, she shouted the spell from *The Lesser Key of Solomon*. The magic was summoned up inside her in an instant, and she felt it rush from her, blowing her hair back. Crimson light, red as blood in the gleam of moon, erupted from her hands and coiled around Morveren as the scarred witch lunged at her.

The creature screamed, threw back her head, and once again opened her hideous mouth grotesquely wide. Something raced up out of her mouth, a swift, twisting thing, withered and thin but still bright as starlight.

It was all of her that was human, and Tamara had just torn it out of her, so that only demon remained.

Morveren bent over, face even more hideous now. The demon opened her maw and flames licked the back of her throat. Those black eyes were sunken more deeply and the skin at her temples split as small horns burst through.

"Foolish girl, do you know what you've done?"

Tamara smiled. "Oh, yes. I know *precisely* what I've done. I've made you stronger, uglier, and more terrible . . . and you're not a witch, anymore. No magic, darling."

The demon raised her gnarled hands and stared at them. She snarled, opened her mouth, and thrust her head forward. Flame roared from her gullet, but Tamara threw up a protective ward that dispelled it easily.

Howling in fury, the thing lunged at her, flying through the air. Demons had hellish power of their own, but when they appeared in the flesh that power was limited, and Morveren was only a newly formed demon.

Tamara raised her hands, spheres of golden light forming around them.

A pair of shimmering ghosts darted through the air above the clearing.

"A curse upon your souls!" screamed the specter of Queen Bodicea, and she descended from the night sky and brought her sword sweeping around to slash into the nearest witch.

The ghost of Admiral Nelson appeared at Tamara's side and slid past her, his translucent form nevertheless formidable.

"Allow me, my dear!" Horatio cried, and he impaled the demon-Morveren upon his blade.

The creature screamed, unused to such agony. Horatio thrust deeper and twisted the blade. The demon began to claw at his spectral flesh, slashing through it, but Horatio drove Morveren to the ground and withdrew the blade. The ghost raised it high and as the demon tried to rise, he hacked off her head.

Morveren struck the ground with a thump that seemed to shake the very hill itself.

Bodicea struggled with one of the witches. Black ribbons of hatred, of poisonous sorcery, wrapped themselves around her, but the spectral queen fought on. The other witches rose into the air, shrieking horribly, faces distorted, and started to rush at the fairies and their human allies who were trying to drag the confused and terrified girls from the clearing.

Tamara glanced at the moon, wondering how long it was until midnight.

This wasn't over yet.

The fire still burned over Mordred's grave.

～

RHOSYNN OF STRONGHOLD DASHED through the air, all else forgotten. Lorelle lay on the earth, so fragile, so small.

The witches were screaming, rising up. The Protectors were fighting. Their ghostly allies had arrived. The stench of foul blood filled the clearing, mixing with the sulphur of their hellish blaze.

The fairy warriors attacked the witches. They spread out, as archers drew back their bowstrings and let fly arrows enchanted with all of the magic of Faerie, of the homeland. As Rhosynn ran to Lorelle's side she heard a cry as of the anguished damned above her, and looked up to see a witch flailing in the air, gripping a fairy arrow that jutted from her heart. The thing plunged into the fire over Mordred's grave and her hands beat at the flames for a moment before she was engulfed entirely. She writhed in the fire, still alive.

A crimson band of magic snaked into the fire after her and a black spirit erupted from the burning witch's mouth and eyes, the human soul driven from inside her.

In the flames, the thing was changed now, a demon only. It crisped quickly to nothing but charred bones. The Protectors of Albion had found their edge.

"Rhos?"

She looked down. Lorelle gazed up at her, moving weakly, speaking with great effort. Rhosynn dropped to her side and slid one hand beneath her head, helping her up. "Oberon's hand! Are you well?" she said.

Lorelle smiled wanly. She pushed herself up and from nothing, gossamer wings appeared upon her back. Their color was dim, but she could move them, and she rose farther, feet coming off the ground.

"I am, Rhos. I am."

Rhosynn felt her face twist into a mask of hatred. "Excellent. Then let us kill the witches."

"Oh, yes. Let's."

∾

THE SHOTS FROM HIS PISTOLS echoed throughout the clearing, cutting through even the shrieking of the witches. At Farris's feet lay Christine Lindsay, the barmaid who had been so kind to them at the Mason's Arms. He would not allow harm to come to her. Another girl, one unfamiliar to him, crawled weakly toward Christine and they clutched at each other for safety.

"Make for the trees! Get out of the clearing! I will cover your retreat!" he shouted to them.

The girls obeyed. Rising to a shaky crouch they began to hurry for the edge of the woods. Dark silhouettes, black against the black night, diverted toward them, shrieking as they rushed through the night toward the girls.

Farris fired at them again and again, the impact of each bullet traveling up his arms, making his bones and muscles ache. He shouted at the damned creatures as they whipped around the night air. The bullets struck them, jarring them, but not deterring them. Farris kept reloading. One of the witches darted away from the fire, out into the trees, and disappeared a moment.

Then she returned.

Her eyes were black pits rimmed with sickly yellow light and her distended features were like unto the dead, the damned, screaming in eternal torment. She flew right at Farris.

"Not my Farris, ye ugly cow!" cried the little sprite who flew around his head. No larger than a hummingbird, she streaked away. His heart skipped a beat as she darted straight at the witch.

"Serena, *no!*"

She did not heed him. Serena flew straight at the witch's face, thrust out her tiny hands, and struck the creature's left eye like a bullet. With a sickening noise the sprite punctured the witch's eye. Greenish ichor spilled out and the thing screamed with agony, tumbling to the ground, clawing at her face, digging furrows there with her talons. She cursed in some ancient tongue Farris could not understand.

Then the witch's right eye popped wetly and Serena burst from the socket.

"Not my Farris!" the sprite cried, savage and triumphant.

The witch rose and began to stagger around, blinded.

But there would be no pause. The night was filled with the screams of innocents. Farris turned and saw witches grabbing at Christine Lindsay and the other girl who was with her, carrying the squirming girls toward the fire.

A pair of fairies locked in combat with a witch drove her, and themselves, into the fire, all of them wailing as they burned.

Twenty feet away, in the shadows and light that danced across the clearing from the flickering blaze, he saw Richard Kirk helping a girl who must have been his sister, Sally, rise to her feet. Farris felt a moment of hope, a single spark of it, at the sight of this reunion.

A witch darted down from the sky, coming at Richard from behind. She thrust out her hand and his skin erupted with angry red pustules that burst almost instantly, as though his flesh were boiling. He screamed and writhed, and just as he would have fallen, the witch flew nearer, grasped his head, and tore it from his shoulders.

Richard Kirk's body fell to the ground with a wet thump while the witch flew off, cackling madly, his head in her hands, a bit of spine dangling below it.

Farris had never felt such pure hatred before.

The pistols were empty, but it mattered not. Bullets were not harming them. Not yet. He thrust the guns into his belt, and drew his father's sword from its scabbard. He'd reload when the Swifts' magic took hold. Then the witches would pay for the darkness they'd wrought.

"Damn you all."

∼

WILLIAM SAW RICHARD KIRK DIE. There was nothing he could do, and though he had wished many times that his grandfather had never chosen him to share this horrid legacy, this was the first moment in which he actually *hated* Ludlow for it.

A scream tore through the night off to his right, and he glanced over to see two witches dragging a fairy archer to the ground. Her wings manifested behind her as she tried to fly to safety, and the witches tore them off, laughing all the while. In that pitiful moment, the fairies had never looked more beautiful to William, nor had the witches looked uglier.

The air was a blur of darkness, of fluttering cloaks and horrible talons. He struggled to think with the screeching of the witches digging at his ears. He and Tamara had to put a stop to this.

A witch dropped down in front of him, leering, and her abyss-deep eyes froze him for just an instant. Terror clasped at his heart.

William bit his lip, raised his hands, and said the words. Crimson magic leaped from his fingers, wrapped around the witch, and tore the humanity from her. The monstrous thing screamed, the pure thread of her human soul erupting from her maw, flying off into the ether.

She died easily enough after that.

He leaped over her remains and at last saw Tamara ahead of him. She was perhaps fifteen feet from the fire. The ghosts of Bodicea and Horatio flanked her and the witches dove down at them again and again. Several were low to the ground, moving like predators, preparing to lunge.

Bodicea twisted and saw the witches coming, and the spectral sword in her hand shimmered and elongated, becoming a spear. As a witch leaped at her, she brought the point up and impaled the shrieking creature. Her opponent thrashed for a moment, then grabbed hold of the spear and dragged herself forward. She raked her talons across Bodicea's face, dragging furrows through the warrior queen's ectoplasmic features.

The ghost cried out and fell back. Her shimmering form wavered, became less solid, until she was barely a suggestion of a figure in the night.

"Abominations!" Horatio shouted. The witches darted away from him, a wave of them descending upon Bodicea. In that moment, she was vulnerable, and they swept in to finish her off.

"Face me!" he demanded.

But the horrors were set upon their task. They would be back for Horatio when Bodicea was destroyed.

Somewhere nearby William heard Farris roar in fury, but he did not even turn. That good man would have to see to his own survival for several moments longer.

"Tamara!" William cried.

She risked a glance at him, one hand up, a shield of magic bursting from her palm even as with the other she cast the spell that tore the humanity from yet another witch. William didn't know how many of them were dead now, four or five perhaps, but it wasn't happening quickly enough. Richard Kirk was dead and fairies were dying all around them.

Horatio attacked the witches surrounding Bodicea, his spectral sword hacking and slashing at them, but they would not die.

William ran to Tamara's side. A witch descended upon him from behind, long talons grabbing his hair in a gnarled fist. He shouted in pain and tore himself away. Blood trickled down the back of his head and into the collar of his shirt as he spun to see the fiend with a hank of his hair in her fist. On instinct alone, he reached down into the soul of Albion and lashed out with a blast of pure magic that impaled the creature, driving her back into the fire. The witch screamed and lurched from the blaze, staggering, then flew off into the night sky, bathed in crackling eldritch flames.

Tamara grabbed his hand. William turned to look at her.

"It's got to be together, Will," she said.

"Yes. It ends now."

The melee went on around them, but they tightened their grip. William felt the connection to the soul of Albion, to the spirit of ancient England that had mystically chosen them to protect the land, at all times. But this was different. When he and Tamara were together it was as though a circuit was complete, from Albion and running through the two of them.

Together, they intoned the spell, their voices increasing in volume until they were shouting the words. They drew the sigils in the air. Tamara cried out. William arched his back, the power flooding him, and he shook with it, as though struck by lightning.

Crimson light flashed out from the Protectors of Albion, erupting from their hands and chests and backs and mouths. The witches were snared by the spell and it coiled around them, shot through them, and pinned them to the ground. As one they shrieked, heads thrown back, and William saw the beauty of their vestigial human essence as it was driven from their hideous forms.

All that remained were demons.

Without their magic, the demons were no match for the fairies. Rhosynn and her kin began to slaughter the witches in earnest. William heard the boom of Farris's revolvers, effective now.

Tamara ran at the monsters that were attacking Bodicea, but a bright light gleamed from among them and the night was filled with a familiar battle cry, the savage, primal scream of the warrior queen.

Bodicea burst from the throng, spear swinging, and plunged that spectral weapon through the skull of a demon.

From the woods came the mournful sound of a horn, and then a loud battle cry, a single voice at first but then joined by a chorus of shouts. Hoofbeats echoed off of the night sky as the ghosts of the Pendragon's knights rode into the clearing.

"For Arthur!" cried a ghostly knight.

"For Albion!" shouted another.

Now that the witches had no magic, the knights could fight them at last. As they attacked the offspring of their ancient enemy, their souls became so focused that their weapons gleamed as though solid.

The knights and the fairies joined together in attacking the demon-things. Unable to withstand the onslaught, the remaining creatures fled from the clearing, down the hill and off into the forest.

"After them!" Rhosynn cried, wings lifting her into the air with the music of magic. "Leave not one alive!"

The fairies and ghostly knights gave chase, then, darting and riding off into the trees after their prey. In moments, William and Tamara stood in the clearing on that hilltop with Bodicea and Horatio, Farris and Serena, and the three remaining human girls from the village of Camelford, most glancing around, disoriented and confused.

Sally Kirk cradled her brother's headless corpse in her lap and wept, shuddering in silent grief.

∼

THE FIRE ON MORDRED'S GRAVE burned low, quickly dying, so that in moments there was only a small flame there, the ground itself aflame as though the ancient remains of Arthur's bastard burned underground.

The moon provided enough illumination, however, and Tamara left her brother's side and walked across the clearing. One of the girls from the village whimpered at the approach of strangers, scrambling across dirt and grass in fear.

Farris knelt with Christine, the barmaid from the Mason's Arms. Tamara was pleased that she was alive, though her survival would be tainted when she learned of her grandfather's death.

Tragedy. All around them.

In the chaos of battle she had moved halfway round the clearing to the other side of Mordred's grave. Now she walked toward it and stepped right over the flickering remnants of that blaze.

A frown creased her forehead and she paused, turned, and kicked dirt onto the struggling flames, smothering them. Only a thin trail of smoke came up from the ground . . .

The remains of the witches were almost unrecognizable. Cloth and bone and pulp and fragments of a brittle gray substance like the carapace of some crustacean. Tamara shivered as she gazed down upon a hideous mess that had once been a witch . . . a demon.

She had not seen the witch queen fall, had not seen her destroyed. None of the others knew Viviane on sight, and so could not say for sure that she had died.

Tamara stood at the edge of the clearing atop that hill, in the ancient rowan circle, and stared at the treetops that spread out below. Was the witch queen fleeing through the woods even now, or flying across the midnight sky? Bitter and sorrowful, had she abandoned her sisters at the last to save her own life, or was she one of the heaps of charred bones that lay now around Mordred's grave?

Did she watch, even now, from the darkness of the forest? And if she did, what emotions roiled in her black heart?

If Viviane had escaped, it might well have been before William and Tamara had performed the spell that would have stripped her of her humanity, and her magic. She might be a horrid demon, damned for eternity to wear a hideous countenance, never again to be beautiful.

Or she might be the last of the Daughters of Morgan le Fey.

Tamara shook herself. If she ever saw the witch queen again, Viviane might be just as inclined to thank her as to kill her. There was simply no way to know.

She could only wonder.

Her lips still tingled with the soft brush of Viviane's lips. Her cheeks flushed with embarrassment at the thought and at the memory of the things she had let Viviane do while she was magically disguised as John Haversham. What lingered with her, though, was that last kiss, which had revolted and excited her. It had only been a glamour, a beautiful mask to hide her ugliness, and Viviane had enthralled her with magic, affected her judgment.

Was her mind still clouded, then?

So many questions gathered in her mind, but Tamara knew she would find no answers this night.

"Tam," William said.

She flinched and turned to face him. Lost in thought, she'd failed to notice his approach.

"We should depart," her brother said. "Take the . . . the survivors back to the village."

Tamara nodded, grief-stricken at the knowledge that Holly Newcomb and Mary Raynham had not survived. Their victory felt hollow to her. Sally Kirk lived, but had to return to her mother, Ellie, and tell her that Richard had been killed. Serena once again had her best friend, Aine, in her life, but two of the fairy girls had also been sacrificed in the aborted ritual, and fully half a dozen other fairies of Stronghold had died in the battle.

A hollow victory, at best.

Yet she knew that for those who lived, it was far more than that. They had survived. They could go from the rowan circle atop that old hill and live, and love, and find laughter. Tamara knew that she and William would do the same.

But not tonight.

"You go," she said. "I'll be along."

William watched her a moment, then left her there in the moonlight, and went to join Farris and the girls. Tamara glanced at them, saw the tiny, bright form of Serena flying in small circles above Aine's head, the reunited friends unwilling to be parted even for an instant.

"So happy my Aine is safe," Serena sang giddily, zipping about. "So glads you is with us again!" She alighted upon Aine's shoulder just long enough to kiss her cheek, and then darted away again.

"I missed you so much," Aine replied. "I was afraid for both of us. But I swear, Serena, I'll never listen to one of your dares again."

Tamara spared a final glance at the remains at her feet, and then out across the treetops below the hill. Unbidden, one hand came up to touch her lips. Then she turned and followed William and the others where they had left the clearing. With a heavy heart, she passed a small pool of Richard Kirk's blood on the way.

She slipped into the trees and started down the hill, leaving behind her the grave of Mordred, and the ghosts of the last witches of Albion.

EPILOGUE

In the days after their return to London and to Ludlow House, Tamara was unusually solitary. Highgate was gifted with a string of pretty summer days, warm sun and gentle breezes. In the mornings, Tamara walked the grounds of her family estate, meandering among the gardens. In the afternoons she took tea either alone or with Sophia, and in the evenings she sat at the desk that had once belonged to her grandfather and she wrote the most hideously lurid, blood-drenched tale of evil and betrayal that she could imagine.

And she could imagine a great deal. *The Inquisitor* would be the most dreadful of penny dreadfuls.

William gave over several days to mollifying his intended bride. Tamara was pleased to see him choosing love over responsibility, at least for a little while. Swift's of London could survive without him for a while longer. When he did return to business, nearly a week after the events in Cornwall had come to a close, he made certain to speak with Sophia each day and to pay close attention to the details of their impending nuptials . . . or, at least, the details to which she directed his attention.

The most curious thing had transpired in their absence. Tamara would never know what, precisely, had engineered such a change within her, but she could not find it within her heart to despise her future sister-in-law any longer. Sophia's frantic, exasperated antics upon their return only amused her.

And when the woman saw that her bridegroom meant to concentrate upon his obligations to her, and that Tamara had returned from Cornwall in a state of wistful melancholy, then Sophia, too, was changed. Gone was the sardonic edge in her voice and expression, and gone was the sense of competition between the girls.

From time to time, however, when they were discussing such wedding particulars as the menu or floral arrangements, Sophia would glance at Tamara to see if she was being patronized. As the days passed, however, the two relaxed into a warm sense of comfort in each other's presence.

In her heart, Tamara still wished that Sophia weren't quite so needy, but she allowed herself to accept the fact that this trait did not make the girl a villain.

Sophia was to be her brother's wife—and very soon, since the preparations were now nearly complete. They might never be great friends, or sisters, but they would be family, and Tamara made a conscious decision to cherish that.

John Haversham called upon Ludlow House on the very afternoon they arrived home, but Tamara had instructed both Farris and Martha to turn him away. Kindly, but firmly. John returned each day and was met with the same response. At last, on the fifth day after their return, she took his hand and brought him along on her wander through the gardens, and told him the tale of the witches of Cornwall.

The first words from his lips were an apology for not having gone with her to Cornwall. He began to explain that he had responsibilities, not least of which was to the Algernon Club, and that he had also been quite aware of how inappropriate it would have been for him to accompany her.

Tamara shushed him. Observing William and Sophia, she had acquired a refined understanding of responsibility in recent weeks. His response and behavior, she assured him, had been precisely what they ought to have been.

John remarked that she was much changed, that her quietude seemed both sad and peaceful, and Tamara did not argue with him. He confessed that he had put his duties to the Algernon Club before his own heart. He had wished to court her, but held his feelings in check so that he did not compromise his obligations to the club. Her absence, and his fear for her, so far away, had made him realize what a fool he'd been. Tamara smiled softly and shook her head, glancing away in a manner that was entirely too demure for her.

"We are a tragic pair, John. My brother does not trust you. And though we often argue, I have come to rely upon William's perception. We are grateful for your efforts in uncovering the thief who plagued the bank, but now it is I who hold *you* at arm's length. Improper as it is for me to say, I welcome your courtship. But despite the fact that we travel in the same circles—both magical and societal—I must insist that we proceed with caution."

She gazed into his eyes, searching for truth, and was not sure what she found.

"I do care for you, and I find you nearly irresistible," she continued. "That is my confession, and I hope you shall not use it against me. Perhaps that will be the great test for both of us."

"As you wish," John said, inclining his head. He caressed her arm gently and bent as if to kiss the top of her head.

Tamara caught her breath, trembling slightly.

But John only took her hand in his once more, and they continued their garden stroll. The breeze swirled the delicious scents of the flowers all around them. Tamara told him the wedding would be the following Wednesday, and asked if he would be her escort on that most wondrous of days.

John kissed her hand and they kept walking.

∼

Later, after he had gone, Tamara found Sophia taking tea in the observatory, enjoying a quiet respite from the final wedding plans.

"Has he gone?" Sophia asked.

"Yes."

"But he will be back?"

Tamara smiled. "For the wedding, and almost certainly before. You do realize that your cousin isn't quite the rogue you painted him?"

Sophia sipped her tea for a moment. When she set the cup down, she gave Tamara a knowing look. "I'm beginning to realize that. But not to worry. I won't say a word. I would so hate to ruin his reputation."

The two young ladies shared a quiet laugh and then set to talking, as they had so often of late. When one of the maids came in with another tea setting for Tamara, and then departed, Sophia traced the rim of her own cup and a worried expression crossed her face.

"So it's to be tonight, is it?"

Tamara looked up, frowning. "What is—"

And then she stopped. How could she have forgotten? Her breath caught and her heart raced.

"Tonight," she agreed, nodding her head. "The wedding is only five days off. Neither of us wants to wait any longer."

"Do you think it will work?"

Tamara stared at her.

"I'm sorry," Sophia said quickly. "I don't mean to cast doubt—"

"No, no. I was only thinking," Tamara said with a gentle smile. She sat back in her chair, cup in hand, and glanced out at the gardens behind Ludlow House. "William went through a great deal of trouble to retrieve that spell from New Orleans. It ought to work. Truly. But if it does not, our time in Cornwall introduced to us another possibility."

"A different spell?" Sophia asked.

Tamara nodded. "It's a far greater risk than the other. But we cannot go on like this. If the ritual does not work, we'll try this spell. It may be the end . . . the end of Father. We have heard tales of an exorcist in Istanbul who might be able to help us, but we have pursued false hopes before. No, we must exhaust all options."

Sophia reached out and put a comforting hand over Tamara's own.

"You will succeed. I know it. I can feel it. You and William . . . together, there is nothing you cannot do."

~

THE EVENING MEAL WAS DELAYED that night. William had sent word from Threadneedle Street that he intended to go to the jail, to speak with Harold Ramsey, the young man who had gone from his trusted assistant and loyal friend to cunning thief without anyone being the wiser.

Sophia knew that William would never have suspected Ramsey if the man had not been caught in the act, and that he was crushed by the betrayal. She thought her fiancé was entirely too kind-hearted where the thief was concerned. William was trying to make sense of the actions of a loathsome criminal. To Sophia, there were no mitigating circumstances. Ramsey had thieved from his friend and employer. As far as she was concerned, he ought to be flogged in front of the Tower.

But Sophia did not dwell on the fate of Harold Ramsey. Her heart and mind this evening were filled with much happier anticipation. Whatever sadness and regret William carried over his thieving friend, certainly it would be erased this very night, when at last his father would be free of the demonic force that possessed him.

In recent days Sophia had agonized over her own future, wondering if William could ever truly dedicate himself to her. He had assuaged her fears upon his return from Camelford, and been ever so attentive to her and to their wedding plans.

But in those days she also had found comfort in the kindness of his father. Henry Swift was afflicted—the demon within him made him say and do horrid things. But the demon was not always ascendant, and in those times when the weakened man had his wits about him, he had been a friend and confidant to Sophia, assuring her that William truly loved her and that his sincere attention to his duties only revealed how attentive he would also be to his duties as a husband.

Of course, Henry had been correct. But in the days that William had been away, she had only the elder Swift's assurances to soothe her fears. With her own parents deceased, Henry had become precious to her. And now came the news that he was soon to be freed of the influence of the demon. She couldn't have been happier had he been her own father.

In the usual course of things William, Tamara, or Nigel would bring Henry his meals after they had eaten. But with the household awaiting William's return before dinner could be served, she had asked the kitchen to prepare a plate for Henry.

Now she hurried up the stairs to the third floor, her excitement only barely contained.

The dish was warm in her hands as she went down the hall to the room at the back of the house. Once, she knew, it had been a nursery. Now it was a prison, swaddled in wards and enchantments to keep Henry from escaping with the demon inside of him.

As she approached the door, the air shimmered beside it. A musical trill filled the hall and Lord Byron appeared.

"Good evening, darling Sophia," Byron said, a familiar lusty twinkle in his eye. Not fully materialized, the ghost had only wisps where his legs ought to be. Even so, he offered a deep, gentlemanly bow. Though Byron was hardly a gentleman.

Sophia blushed a smile. "Good evening, Byron."

"May I say that you are ravishingly beautiful, as always, my dear. The anticipation of your wedding day brings a fetching flush to your cheeks."

She arched an eyebrow. "Why, Byron, that seemed like a genuine compliment, without a hint of inappropriate suggestion. I'm not sure whether to be flattered or insulted."

The poet's ghost posed as though leaning against the wall. His grin was full of mischief now. "Not to worry, Sophia. It's a momentary fever, but it shall pass. I will continue to admire you . . . particularly in the bath, even after you've become Mrs. Swift. You have a deft touch with soap."

Sophia ought to be have been outraged. Instead she only rolled her eyes. "Well, *that's* better. You had me worried a moment."

Byron gave another courtly bow and drifted aside. "The demon's been awfully quiet. I don't like when he gets this way. Seems to me as if he's listening to the goings-on in the house."

"When he's quiet, it often means that the demon has retreated," Sophia replied.

The ghost gazed at her warily, floating nearer. "Don't be taken in, Sophia. Oblis is clever, and will stop at nothing to torment us all."

She held the plate in one hand and opened the door with the other, casting a withering glance at Byron. "I am no fool, sir."

"It was never my intention to imply otherwise," the ghost replied.

Sophia did not favor him with any further comment. She entered the nursery and closed the door softly behind her. Once inside, she took a breath to calm herself and steadied the dinner plate in both hands. The news was too wonderful to allow Byron to spoil it.

"Good evening," she said.

Henry Swift sat in the chair, chains crisscrossing his body, trapping him there. He turned toward her, and she braced herself for the venomous glare of the demon.

Instead, she was greeted with the soft, kindly, sorrowful gaze of a man who had turned old before his time.

"Sophia? Oh, my dear, it's always so nice to see you," Henry Swift said.

With a sigh of relief, she approached. "I've brought you dinner, Henry."

"Soon it shall be 'Father,' " he said.

She beamed at him, full of joy. "That will be so wonderful."

Sophia sat in a second chair, facing him, and set the plate on her lap. It seemed demeaning to feed the man, but there was no other way. And she really did not mind. When she lifted the fork to give him a bite, she found Henry looking at her quizzically.

"What is it, Sophia, dear? You are positively abuzz. You've had some good news, I take it."

Her excitement bubbled up into a small laugh. "Oh, excellent news, Henry. Truly."

"Well, do share."

Her mouth opened, but for a moment no words came. She hesitated, studying him closely. Then Sophia waved away any doubt. Byron's warnings were insulting; she *wasn't* a fool.

This man had been so kind to her.

"It's to be tonight, Henry. I don't know if there's really a demon within you. I've never been sure of that. But if there is, and all goes well, tonight you will be rid of that demon forever. And if not, well, then, your children will finally recognize that. Either way, you will be free of your chains."

The man was speechless. Joy lit his eyes and he shook his head, taking a deep, shuddering breath.

"Do you really think so?" he said at last.

"Tamara seems confident."

Henry smiled cautiously. "Oh, Sophia. I don't dare hope."

Sophia patted his hand. "I shall do all of the hoping for both of us. Now here, have a bite to eat."

She brought the fork to his mouth and he chewed a small bit of veal. After he had swallowed, he took another deep breath.

"Thank you, my dear," Henry said. "You've no idea how grateful I am for your company."

~

$\mathbf{T}$HE NIGHT WAS COOL but the air in the carriage felt warm and stifling. William had the curtain pulled back and he gazed out of the window at the trees and fields in Highgate as Farris guided them homeward. The clop of the horses' hooves was a rhythmic comfort to him, lulling him into a kind of trance.

William scowled and let the curtain fall back into place.

Enough, he thought. *Let the past be past.*

Ramsey had remained silent under the questioning of the authorities. Only when William had at last gone to see him in jail did he reveal the motive for his crimes. There was bitterness and jealousy, of course. He envied the life William led.

If only Ramsey had known the truth, William was sure the man would not have envied him at all. But he felt as if his lot in life was somehow diminished, and that William did not appreciate his friendship or his service. It was the furthest thing from the truth, but there was no arguing with the man's perceptions.

William had felt certain all along there was more to it than that. And sure enough, face to face with William, Harold had crumbled into tears and confessed that his sister was an opium addict, and that she and her new baby required medical care, and he had been too ashamed of their circumstances to come directly to William and ask for help. Bitterness and desperation had corrupted his heart.

William had thus decided that he would not press charges against the man. It was likely he would be set free, if Swift's did not pursue the case, and he had no intention of doing so.

Ramsey had been grateful, but William had made it clear that the man was never to cross his path nor seek him out. Not ever.

Let the past be past.

Outside, Farris called gently to the horses and the carriage slowed. William felt them turn and glanced out the window again. They were on Peacock Lane, heading up toward home. In the distance, at the top of the hill, he could see lights burning in the house.

His heart lightened. Sophia would be waiting for him. Tamara would be there as well. All of the preparations for the exorcism had been made. After dinner, they would proceed. He tried to suppress the hope that rose in him, and was only partly successful.

Soon Farris called to the horses again, and the *clip-clop* of their hooves slowed. The carriage came to a halt.

William did not wait for Farris to open his door. He popped it open and dropped to the ground before the man had even begun to climb down from the high seat. Whip in hand, Farris glanced down at him.

"The dinner bell's ringing, I suspect," Farris said pleasantly.

"Indeed. Thank you, my friend."

Farris nodded once. He was stout of build and equally stout of heart. William did not know what they would do without him. The little sprite Serena sat on his shoulder and whispered something into his ear. Something naughty, given the expression on Farris's face. For a creature of magic, wings humming and glittering at her back, Serena was a wanton little strumpet.

She had celebrated with Aine that first night, blissfully happy to have her best friend back, safe and sound. But, still stung by the way the fairy council of Stronghold had treated her, Serena had decided to return to London with Farris and the Protectors, though she promised Aine she would visit soon . . . and invited Aine to come to see her at Ludlow House at her leisure.

William had not had the heart to protest.

"Good evening, then, Master William."

"And to you, Farris. I'll see you inside, shall I?"

"As soon as I've seen to the horses, sir."

"Very good," William replied.

As the carriage moved away, William went to the front door.

The lights inside were warm and welcoming. A breeze stirred and he thought he could smell the flowers from the garden all the way from the back of the house. How colorful the wedding was going to be.

He turned the knob and pushed open the door, smiling for the first time that day.

A terrible scream filled the house. It was a man's voice, raw and terrified.

"What the devil?" William shouted.

Down the corridor to the right of the stairs he saw the young maid, Melinda, clap her hands over her ears and rush into the parlor as if to escape the sound. Behind her came Martha and Klaus, a chef only recently hired.

Another scream tore the air, and now William realized it was coming from above. He started for the stairs and then stopped, staring up, jaw hanging open, as his father stumbled down from the second-story landing.

"Leave me alone, do you hear?" the man shrieked. "My head, don't you understand? It's splitting open, my poor head. Feels like my brain's going to spill out!"

With an elegant leap, almost like flying, Nigel came down the stairs behind him. The vampire alighted upon the second story landing in a predator's crouch and turned with a snarl to stare at his prey: Henry Swift.

"Close your mouth, demon!" Nigel snarled. "Do you take us for fools?"

"Leave me be!" Henry wailed pitifully.

William felt his heart go cold. He stared at his father as the man held the banister, hurrying down the stairs as best he could.

"Oblis!" he cried, his voice echoing through the foyer. "I don't know how you've gotten free, but—"

"William!"

Tamara pushed past Martha and Klaus and shouted his name. William glanced at her as she rushed into the foyer, and then his sister froze, much as he had done. She stared at their father, or the demon who wore his form, and an expression of anguish distorted her features. Then it passed, and all that was left was hatred for the creature who had toyed with their hearts for so long.

"Nigel!" Tamara snapped. "How did this happen?"

They had the demon surrounded on three sides. Nigel came down the stairs slowly in pursuit of him.

"I don't know," the vampire said. "I heard his cries and came out after him, same as you."

Henry reached the bottom of the steps. He moved weakly, stiffly, and when he glanced up his face was pale and drawn. There were dark circles beneath his damp eyes and he looked at William with such befuddlement that he could almost believe it was truly his father there, and not the demon Oblis.

"William," Henry said. Then he glanced over at his daughter. "Oh, Tamara. What has become of me? Of this house?"

Tamara took a tentative step toward him. "Father?"

Holding his breath, heart racing, William stared at the man. "Can it be?" he whispered. "Truly?"

Henry touched one hand lightly to his forehead, thin hair unruly and dampened with sweat. "Oh, my children. I have one of my headaches. I feel as though I've had a terrible fever." Mystified, he looked from son to daughter. "Have I been ill?"

"Father," William said slowly, taking a step toward him. Tamara did the same. "You were in the nursery."

"Careful, now!" Nigel warned as he reached the bottom of the stairs. "We've all been taken in before."

"Father, is it you?" Tamara asked.

But Henry could only stare at William. "Yes. The nursery. What was I doing there, William? Someone has much to answer for. There were . . . chains . . ."

"How did you get out?" Tamara demanded.

For a moment he seemed to search his memory. Then he smiled gently. "There was a girl. A pretty girl. Sophia, I believe she said. She set me free."

William froze, staring at his father.

"Sophia . . ."

"The girl," Nigel muttered.

"Oh, no," Tamara said softly. "If this truly is Father, and the demon has left him, then where—"

A voice came down from the landing above them. The voice of the demon.

"Not to worry, Tamara. I haven't gone far."

William stared at the ethereally beautiful figure of his fiancée where she stood along the balustrade of the second floor landing, gazing down at the foyer . . . at him. Her lips moved, but it wasn't Sophia's voice that issued from her mouth.

It was a voice from Hell. The voice of Oblis.

"No," Tamara whispered.

Nigel snarled as he turned and started up the stairs.

"Wait!" William shouted.

The vampire froze on the steps, glancing back at him. William and Tamara moved across the foyer and in a moment were side by side, staring up at Sophia, whose features were twisted into a mask of hatred.

"Why?" William asked. "All this time we've tried to draw you out of Father. Why now?"

"What is it?" Henry Swift muttered behind them. "What's happened to the girl? What are you all *talking* about?"

William and Tamara ignored the frightened, demanding voice of their father.

"Ah, well, you have pretty little Sophia to thank for that," Oblis said, sneering the words with her mouth. "She was so happy, you see, when she discovered that the sweet old man, her future father-in-law, who had been her only source of succor these past days, was to be freed at last from the grasp of the demon."

Oblis laughed, his own voice mingling with Sophia's, and the sound made William retch. He put a hand to his lips to keep back the bile that rose in his throat. The magical bonds that had held Oblis in place had been created to hold him physically, not to prevent the vapor demon from leaving the flesh of Henry Swift. So focused had they been on exorcising the demon, they'd never imagined he might depart of his own free will.

How simple it had been for Oblis to slip from one innocent and into another. Once out of Father's body, he had freed Henry from his chains, orchestrating this hideous tableau.

William shook his head, hating himself for his foolishness. Not his Sophia. Wasn't his father's torment *enough*?

"She was so pleased to share the news," Oblis continued. "And, well, I couldn't very well sit and wait for you to drive me out, could

I? That would be defeat. If, indeed, you have found a way to pry me away from the souls of your loved ones, then I must at last depart your company. But on my own terms. I *won't* have it said that you bested me."

That was the moment when William finally understood. Nothing they could do would reach Oblis in time. Tamara must have understood as well, because she uttered a small sound, a little breath of horror expelled from her lips.

"I depart in triumph," the demon said, and his grin split the edges of Sophia's mouth so that blood ran down her chin.

"No!" William cried. "Sophia, *no!*"

Nigel lunged, bounding up the steps.

William and Tamara raised their hands simultaneously and began to shout the words to a spell that would confine the demon, at least for a moment.

But they did not have a moment.

Sophia, driven by the demon within, threw herself over the balustrade, faster than the Protectors could act. The house was filled with screams as she plummeted to the floor of the foyer. In dreams, later, William would be unable to escape the image of Oblis, smiling at him with his beloved's lips and eyes, as Sophia fell.

At the last moment, the demon twisted her head so that she would strike at the perfect angle.

Her neck broke with a crack like a whip.

～

WILLIAM RACED TO SOPHIA'S SIDE and fell to his knees, drawing her lifeless form into his lap. His tears dappled her face.

The demon rose from her body like mist on the moors, taking form as a vapor. Its bodiless mouth opened in eternal laughter, its eyes burned red in the air, and it floated up through the ceiling and was gone. The laughter seemed to echo through the house long after it had departed.

William thought the sound would linger there forever.

In 1838, siblings William and Tamara Swift inherited a terrible legacy from their grandfather and became Protectors of Albion, the magical defenders of the soul of England. . . . In 2003, the BBC's cult website debuted *Legacy,* an animated serial drama by actress/writer/director Amber Benson—best known from her role as Tara on *Buffy the Vampire Slayer*—and novelist Christopher Golden—author of *Strangewood, Wildwood Road, Of Saints and Shadows,* and *The Boys Are Back in Town.* For seven weeks the first Ghosts of Albion story unfolded, and the serial averaged more than 100,000 hits per week and won a special commendation at the 2003 Prix Europa. *Legacy* detailed the return of the demon lord Balberith, the murder of Albion's protector, Ludlow Swift, and the efforts of his heirs—William and Tamara—to deal with the power and responsibility that had been left to them. Their allies, both ghosts and the vampire Nigel Townsend, rallied around them. Balberith was defeated.

Soon after, *Legacy* was followed by an original novella, *Astray,* and then a second hour of animation, *Embers,* which introduced new characters, including Sophia Winchell.

For more information about Ghosts of Albion and to experience these early adventures of Tamara and William Swift, please visit www.ghostsofalbion.net.

AMBER BENSON is best known for her portrayal of Tara on *Buffy the Vampire Slayer*. An actress/writer/director, her most recent work includes the independent films *Chance* and *Lovers, Liars, and Lunatics*, both of which she also wrote, produced, and directed. Other films include *The Crush, King of the Hill,* and *Simple Things*. She stars in the upcoming Sci-Fi Channel movie *Attack of the Gryphon*. Benson is also the creator of a comic book series with Ben Templesmith called *Shadowplay: Demon Father John's Pinwheel Blues* for IDW and has just completed work on a brand-new original dark fantasy novella with Christopher Golden entitled *The Seven Whistlers*. She lives in Los Angeles, California.

CHRISTOPHER GOLDEN is the award-winning, bestselling author of such novels as *The Myth Hunters, Wildwood Road, The Boys Are Back in Town, The Ferryman, Strangewood, Of Saints and Shadows,* and the Body of Evidence series of teen thrillers. With Thomas E. Sniegoski, he is the co-author of the dark fantasy series The Menagerie, as well as the young readers fantasy series OutCast, which was recently acquired by Universal Pictures. Golden was born and raised in Massachusetts, where he still lives with his family. He graduated from Tufts University. His latest novel is *The Borderkind,* part two of a dark fantasy trilogy from Bantam

Books entitled The Veil. At present, he is writing a lavishly illustrated gothic novel entitled *Baltimore, or, The Steadfast Tin Soldier and the Vampire,* a collaboration with Hellboy creator Mike Mignola. There are more than eight million copies of his books in print. Please visit him at www.christophergolden.com.

ABOUT THE TYPE

This book was set in Minion, a 1990 Adobe Originals typeface by Robert Slimbach. Minion is inspired by classical, old style typefaces of the late Renaissance, a period of elegant, beautiful, and highly readable type designs. Created primarily for text setting, Minion combines the aesthetic and functional qualities that make text type highly readable with the versatility of digital technology.